SHAKEN SPIRITS

ALSO BY ALICE DUNCAN

The Mercy Allcutt Mystery Series

SHAKEN SPIRITS

A DAISY GUMM MAJESTY MYSTERY
BOOK 14

ALICE DUNCAN

ePublishingWorks!
love what you read.

April 2019
Paperback ISBN: 978-1-64457-073-9
Hardcover ISBN: 978-1-64457-074-6

ePublishing Works!
644 Shrewsbury Commons Ave
Ste 249
Shrewsbury PA 17361
United States of America

www.epublishingworks.com
Phone: 866-846-5123

First and foremost, my (almost) infinite thanks go to Peter Brandvold, who gave me his own character, Lou Prophet, to play with. In his salad days, Lou was a hard-drinking, womanizing, well-armed and dangerous bounty hunter. By the time Lou shows up in Daisy's world, he's old, tired, worn-down, one-legged and cranky, but Daisy, Sam and I had a whole lot of fun with old Lou, and expect to continue doing so, unless Mean Pete makes me give Lou back to him.Many thanks also to my wonderful beta readers, Lynne Welch, Sue Krekeler, David Bedini, Karen Rhoads, Iris Irene and Gina Gilmore. I really appreciate your help. I need all the help I can get, and I needed every one of you.And thanks to P.J. Graves, who told me about Gay's Lion Farm!

READER INVITATION

Now you can experience the smells and flavors of Aunt Vi's kitchen, just like Daisy! Once again, we were fortunate enough to convince Aunt Vi to share one of her mouth-watering recipes. When you finish the story, page ahead for *Aunt Vi's Hungarian Goulash*, which is not to be missed. Enjoy!

ePublishing Works!

ONE

When I woke up at home, aching to beat the band, I couldn't remember what had happened. The final thing I recalled was sighing when the last band and the last float in the 1925 Tournament of Roses Parade passed us by, and we got ready to walk home, chatting happily amongst ourselves.

My fiancé, Detective Sam Rotondo, who worked for the Pasadena Police Department, had joined us for the special event. Even though we weren't married yet, Sam was part of the family.

It being the first day of January and mid-winter and all, the weather was brisk, although you can hardly tell one season from another in Southern California. However, winter is colder than summer, even in Pasadena.

Therefore, I worried a bit about Sam's left leg, which had sustained a bullet wound a few months prior to that day. It seemed to hurt him more when the weather turned chilly. "Are you sure you can walk all the way to Colorado?" I asked him before we left home, being the solicitous fiancée I was. Oh, and Colorado is a street in this case; not the state.

"Of course, I'm sure," said Sam grumpily. He didn't like to have his weaknesses pointed out, even if they weren't his fault.

"Just asking," said I, miffed, although I'm not sure why. I knew Sam well enough by then to know he'd be a touchy old grouch if anyone mentioned his leg. "Have you taken any aspirin this morning?"

He heaved an exasperated sigh. "You know I have. You're the one who gave them to me along with the glass of water."

"Yes, yes, I know. I just worry about you, is all."

Sam rolled his eyes ceiling-wards. He was always doing that.

"Well, I *do*! It's because I love you."

"Are you going to be a nagging wife?"

"Yes."

"Good. Just checking."

He grinned, and I felt like smacking him. He enjoyed getting me all riled up for no reason, the fiend.

"Anyhow," Sam continued, "I have this lovely new cane to use if my leg bothers me." He brandished same, and I felt my face flush. I'd given him that new cane, a Malacca number with a swell horse's head handle, as one of his Christmas presents. He'd needed it because I'd broken his old cane over the head of a vicious murderer. But I didn't like to think about that.

After we'd settled the cane-and-leg issue, Ma, Pa, Aunt Vi, Sam, and I all began the walk up to Colorado Boulevard, where we aimed to find a place from which to watch the big parade. We were joined in this endeavor by the Wilsons, our next-door neighbors to the north. Pudge Wilson, the young scion of the family, had celebrated his thirteenth birthday not long back and had graduated to full Boy Scout status. He wore his uniform proudly and always attempted to do at least one good deed every day, preferably early so he didn't have to think about it again.

It became apparent shortly after the Wilsons joined our party that Pudge's good deed on this New Year's Day was to assist Sam Rotondo, who didn't appreciate Pudge's efforts on his behalf. I kind of wanted to take Pudge aside and tell him to lay off that particular good deed, but I didn't get the opportunity. We walked in a clump and got to Colorado Street together. Pudge then made himself useful by clearing a spot on the curb from which we could watch the parade. I worried about Sam having to stand for so long, but I didn't press the issue. Anyhow, Pudge had thought to bring his camp stool, which folded up when not in use.

"If anyone gets tired of standing, just sit here," said he, giving Sam a meaningful glance.

"Thank you, Pudge," I said, since Sam didn't seem inclined to acknowledge the boy's thoughtfulness.

Pudge, who had been sweet on me for quite a while by then, blushed up a storm. He was so cute. I have no idea why his nickname was Pudge, because he was approximately as big around as a broom straw. I'd asked Mrs. Wilson once, and she'd merely shrugged and said she didn't know either.

The Rose Parade was beautiful, as usual. The Tournament of Roses Queen that year was Miss Margaret Scoville, a pretty young woman whom I didn't know personally. Criminy, that made me feel old—and I'd only just turned twenty-five in November! But there you go. All my school friends were married or working or having babies or whatever, and a whole new crop of lovelies had sprung up while I wasn't looking. Time flies, even when you're not having fun.

After the parade ended, we started the short walk home.

And that was all I remember.

When I woke up, Dr. Benjamin, our wonderful family doctor, stood at the head of my bed. Spike, my late husband's beloved black-and-tan dachshund—everyone else in the family loved him, too—lay on the folded quilt at the foot of the bed, staring at me and looking worried. Sam, Ma, Pa, Aunt Vi, Mrs. Wilson, Mrs. Benjamin and Pudge had clumped together around my bed. Ma and Aunt Vi were crying into their hankies. Mrs. Wilson held Pudge's hand in hers, and it looked to me as though they were squeezing each other's hands hard.

I'm pretty sure I blinked at the assembled masses. "Wh-what happened?" I asked. Not original, but I really wanted to know.

"You were hit by a car," said Pa, his voice shaking slightly.

"I was?"

"Yes," said Ma. She sniffled and added, "Sam insisted on carrying you home."

"With your *leg*?" I said upon a gasp, my left arm having given a particularly sharp twinge just then.

"No," said Sam, his voice grim. "In my arms."

I'd lifted my head slightly to ask my stupid question, but let it fall

3

again, exhausted and annoyed. Besides, lifting my head hurt. "You know what I meant."

"Yeah. I know." Sam brought a chair from the kitchen into my bedroom—which was right off the kitchen and, therefore, easy to fetch —and fell onto it with something of a *plunk*. "You nearly scared the life out of us," he added.

"Oh, Daisy, we were so frightened," whispered Ma. Pa put his arm around her and gave her a hug. "You were bleeding *everywhere!*" She turned and wept onto Pa's shoulder.

"There was blood all over the place," Pudge contributed. He sounded a little more excited than troubled. What the heck. He was a boy, and I understand boys are like that.

"I-I still don't understand precisely what happened," I said. Looking to Dr. Benjamin, who was probably the most coherent member of the group gathered in my bedroom, I asked, "Do you know, Doc?"

"Only what your father told me. A car hit you and slammed you into a nearby pepper tree." For the record our street, Marengo Avenue, was lined with pepper trees. "Sam carried you home, and Vi telephoned my house."

"I'm sorry," said I, grieved to have been the one to spoil his holiday. "But thank you."

"I'm not sorry. I'm glad I was home," said he in his brisk way. "Dorothy and I were getting ready to listen to the football game. Well, I was, anyway." He grinned. His wife only looked sort of pained, and I got the impression Mrs. Benjamin—Dorothy—wasn't as fond of football as was the doctor.

"I hurt all over," I said then, taking a mental scan of my body's aches and pains. "Is anything broken?"

"Your left shoulder was dislocated," said Dr. Benjamin. "With the help of Sam and Joe"—Joe is my father—"We managed to jerk it back into place."

I grimaced at what sounded like an icky process. I noticed Sam grimacing, as well, so I suspect my assessment had been correct.

Dr. Benjamin grinned. "A dislocation is slightly better than a break. At least your bones are all intact, but I'm going to have to bind your left arm to your body, and you're not going to be able to use it for a week or two. You need to allow it to heal, and that requires rest. You're lucky the arm wasn't broken."

Lucky, was I? Somehow I couldn't find it within myself to be grateful. "But I need both of my arms!"

"Daisy, you need to heal," said Sam in what, for him, was a gentle voice. "It'll take time. That's what you're always telling me about my leg." As already mentioned, Sam had been shot in his left thigh by an evil woman some months prior to this current disaster. He wasn't a patient…patient, so I was irked at him for giving me the same advice I was always giving him.

"But…but what about my job? Have you ever tried to manipulate the Ouija board with only one arm to use? Or shuffle a deck of tarot cards? Or lift a crystal ball?"

In case that sounds like several odd questions, let me tell you why it wasn't. I earned my living, and that of my family, by practicing the art of spiritualism. I used my Ouija board and tarot cards all the time to talk to other people's dead relatives. Do I truly believe I can communicate with ghosts? Good heavens, no! I'm not an idiot; but I am a *really* good spiritualist-medium.

"No. I think you're the only one who has to worry about those things," said Sam tartly. Then he grinned. "But, hey, we're a matched set now. I have a bum left leg, and you have a bum left arm."

"Somehow, that doesn't make me feel better."

"You were all cut up, too," said Pudge, still excited unless I missed my guess. "Like Mrs. Gumm said, when it hit you, that car flung you really hard against that tree, and you got scraped all over."

"Oh." No wonder everything hurt.

"But I disinfected all your wounds and got you bandaged. You'll be fine in a couple of weeks. Except for your arm. That might take a little more time."

"Oh, no." I began to cry then and felt like a fool.

"It will be all right, sweetheart," said Pa, leaning over to give the top of my head a peck.

"And you'll regain full use of your arm," said Doc Benjamin, probably trying to cheer me up. "Although you'll have to be careful not to lift anything heavy or do any strenuous activities with that arm for a while.

It will take time to fully adjust to being back in its proper place, and the muscles in your arm and shoulder were all strained severely. Human joints aren't like Lincoln Logs, you know."

"What's a Lincoln Log?" I asked.

"Toy logs you can use for building stuff," said Pudge. "They're keen."

"Oh." To my knowledge, I'd never heard of a Lincoln Log, but I filed the name away in the back of my brain. My good friends, Johnny and Flossie Buckingham, had a little boy whom they'd named after my late, beloved husband, Billy. Maybe little boys liked building things with Lincoln Logs. Heck, maybe little girls did, too. I didn't know much about children at that point in my life.

"Who was driving the car that hit me?" I thought to ask.

"We don't know," said Sam.

"What do you mean, you don't know? You mean whoever it was got away? You didn't even copy down the number plate?"

"Didn't have one," said Sam.

Silence filled the room as I contemplated Sam's comment. "Isn't there some kind of law in California that says you have to get a number plate on your motorcar?" I asked. "And a driving license? I thought that was the law nowadays."

"Yes. California has required licensing of autos since 1914...maybe it was 1917. But the car that hit you didn't have a number plate. Don't know if the driver had a license, but if I ever find him, he'll never get another one." Sam sounded as if he meant it.

"Good," I said. Then I dripped a few more tears, feeling sore, pathetic, and stupid.

"Oh, Daisy, we were all so worried about you," said Vi. "But you just rest in bed for a few days." She turned to my mother. "Peggy, let's set the table. Dinner is ready. All I have to do is serve it up."

"Good idea," said my mother, the Peggy in question.

"Oh, dear," I said. "I feel like a loafer. I'm the one who should be setting the table and laying out the foodstuffs." I did those two things because they were the only two things I *could* do when it came to cooking. Nobody in my family would allow me to cook anything, because they knew I couldn't. And I'd tried, too. Melancholy reflection.

"Don't be silly, Daisy," said Ma, stiffening her shoulders, taking a quick swipe at her recently dripping eyes and nodding at Vi. "You just rest."

"But——" I said.

"You, young lady," Aunt Vi said sternly, "do as your mother says. And that means, don't do anything. Just rest."

"I'll bring a tray in for you and Sam," said Ma. Glancing at Sam, she said, "Unless you want to join us at the table, Sam."

"That's all right. I'll stay here with Daisy. She might need help cutting up her food."

"Good point," said Pa. He dropped the arm he'd had around my mother's shoulders and turned abruptly. Heading toward the kitchen, he asked Pudge and Mrs. Wilson, "Will you be joining us for dinner? There's plenty for everyone."

"Oh, Ma, can we?" asked Pudge, sounding as if he'd never heard such a great idea before. Well, he was only thirteen.

"We have our own meal cooking, Pudge," said Mrs. Wilson, smiling at her son. She knew why Pudge wanted to dine with us. It's 'cause Vi was a *much* better cook than anyone else in the known universe. Turning to me, she said, "Take care of yourself, Daisy. I'll send Pudge over to check on you from time to time."

"Thank you," I said weakly.

"You're welcome."

"Yeah," said Pudge, squaring his own shoulders and trying to look tall. "I'll check on you every day."

"Thank you," I said, still weakly.

"But the Benjamins will be joining us, won't you?" Vi asked the doctor and his wife.

But they, too, declined Vi's invitation.

"It's tempting," said Mrs. Benjamin. "But our meal, too, is cooked and ready for us to eat."

"I'm sorry for interrupting everyone's New Year's Day," I said, snuffling again. "I didn't mean to."

"Nonsense," said Doc Benjamin. "You need to rest more than you need to worry."

If he said so. But I did worry. I worried about my livelihood and

7

that of my family. As the primary bread-winner therein, I catered to people in Pasadena who had lots of money to waste. I appreciated them for wasting so much of their money on me.

But how could I practice my skills if I couldn't use my left arm?

And who had hit me with his or her car? Stacy Kincaid, my best client's daughter and the only person whom I knew for a fact would like to run me down and kill me, was in jail. The reason she hated me was because I'd been, in part, responsible for her getting arrested. But for Pete's sake, she'd assisted her lover-boy in committing a foul murder! Not to mention the fact that she'd participated in a child-trafficking scheme in which her cohorts kidnapped children and sold them to perverted men. She was evil, and she wanted me dead, but I figured that was only fair. I loathed her and wouldn't be at all cut up if someone were to do her in.

That sounds terrible, doesn't it?

I don't care. It's the truth.

"I'm going to sit with you for a while," said Sam, dragging my mind from the swamp of its distressing thoughts. "And then I'm going to do my best to find out who hit you and why."

I gazed at my darling fiancé with eyes swimming in tears.

"Th-thank you, Sam."

He took my right hand and gave it a little squeeze. I shrieked in pain, and he dropped my hand like a hot rock.

Good Lord, I really did hurt everywhere.

TWO

Fortunately for all of us, my aunt, Viola Gumm, had her wits about her even in times of crisis. As she'd proposed, she and my mother set the table for the wonderful meal she'd had cooking while we'd been gawking at the Rose Parade. She'd prepared a New England boiled dinner, which consisted of a ham simmered with a bunch of vegetables. She'd put all the ingredients in a huge pot and set it on the stovetop to cook as we watched the parade. Smart woman, my aunt. She was also acknowledged, by people who knew about such things, to be the best cook in Pasadena, California. Not only did she cook for us, but she also worked as a cook for my best client, Mrs. Pinkerton.

Unfortunately for all of us, Mrs. Pinkerton was the mother of Stacy Kincaid, the one person I could think of who might want to see me dead in a ditch. Mrs. Pinkerton was also an extremely wealthy woman, and one with little common sense or self-control. It had become clear to me at that point in my life that very rich people didn't *need* common sense or self-control, because they could purchase the services of others who thought and did things for them.

Luckily or unluckily, Mrs. Pinkerton depended on me a lot. I appreciated her for it, although I didn't understand precisely. However, I'd been spiritualist-mediuming since my tenth year, and Mrs. Pinkerton believed the folderol I spewed. Or rather, she believed the folderol Rolly, my made-up spirit control, spewed via the Ouija board, tarot cards and crystal ball.

Speaking of that stupid crystal ball, it would evidently be a long time before I'd be able to lift *that* heavy piece of nonsense again.

Oh, Lord.

"You'll be all right, Daisy," said Sam, reading the worry and frustration in my expression. He didn't try to take my hand again, which I guess was a good thing, although I could have used some physical comfort at the time.

Thank God for dogs. Spike, sensing my need for consolation, crept up the bed from the quilt at its bottom and nuzzled my hand. I dared lift it—which hurt—and laid it on his head. Spike sighed, smiled, and went back to sleep. I've often wished I could emulate Spike's philosophy which was, basically, if you can't eat it or play with it, pee on it and leave it be. Well, I wouldn't pee on anything, but I'm sure you know what I mean.

"Thanks, Sam." I turned my head to look at him, since my neck was about the only part of my body that didn't screech in agony every time it moved. "Can you think of anyone who might have hit me with the car?"

"Not offhand."

He was lying. I could tell.

"You're lying, Sam."

He heaved a sigh. "Not lying exactly, but you do have one or two enemies, you know."

"But...But...But the only person I know who *really* wants me dead is Stacy Kincaid!"

"There are remnants of the Petrie family still extant in Pasadena, sweetheart," said Sam softly. He too reached out and gave Spike a stroke or two behind his ears. Spike sighed again. He loved his humans.

"The Petries? But...I thought all the bad guys in that family were dead or locked up, too. Do you know any who aren't?"

"Not specifically."

I gazed at my beloved. "You're not being awfully helpful, Sam."

"I know, I know. But I've got to do some investigating before I can focus on anyone in particular."

"Do you know what kind of automobile it was that hit me?"

"Cole Sportster Sedan. Looked like a 'twenty-three to me."

"A Cole Sportster? I don't think I've ever heard of a Cole Sportster."

"Cole Motor Company in Indianapolis, Indiana. Not a lot of them around, which is moderately encouraging, since it should be easy to track the owners of Coles."

"Huh," I said, borrowing one of Sam's favorite words.

"Might have been stolen, which will make finding the driver who hit you harder to do."

"Can you think of anyone besides Stacy who might want to see me rubbed out?" I'd just read that expression in a book and kind of liked it.

"Sure. Tons of them."

"*Tons?* What do you mean, tons?"

"Well, you've run up against the Ku Klux Klan, don't forget."

"But they were trying to kill Mrs. Pinkerton's gatekeeper!" Mrs. Pinkerton's gatekeeper was a Negro gentleman named Jackson. He was a nice fellow, and those terrible KKK people actually *shot* him. His mother, a real, live Voodoo Mambo from New Orleans, Louisiana, had given me a Voodoo juju, which, she said, would bring me luck. I wore it on a ribbon around my neck all the time. If I hadn't ached so much, I might have grasped same and scolded it for not bringing me luck that first day of January in 1925.

"Heck, I can think of ten or twelve more people who might hold a grudge against you."

"Oh, Lord."

"You definitely should watch your step until we figure out who hit you with that car. And don't forget," said Sam, interrupting my melancholy contemplation, "There might be friends of that student who might hold a grudge."

"That student killed a *librarian*. I think there should be a special place in hell for people who kill librarians."

"What about that doctor at the institute? What was his name?"

"Dr. Melton. Yes, he was a slimy fellow."

"Slimy, was he?" Sam chuckled.

"Yes! He tried to put his hands all over me when I met him. I know he's smart, or he wouldn't be a professor at the California Institute of Technology, but he's still slimy. I don't like him any better than Davidson, although I guess Davidson had a legitimate grudge against that horrid professor—providing he was telling the truth. Melton used Davidson's research and claimed it as his own in a book he wrote."

"A book nobody will ever read."

"Good point."

"Melton's wife was something, too," said Sam with a reminiscent smile. I'd like to have smacked him for remembering the gorgeous and slinky Mrs. Melton, but I couldn't for reasons already mentioned.

"Sam." I tried to sound stern.

"Don't worry. I'm not out looking for female companionship."

"You'd better not be."

"Trust me, you're plenty enough for me to handle."

I don't think that was meant as a compliment.

Sam went on in a meditative voice, "Although I believe she's available now. She divorced Dr. Melton, thanks in part to you."

"That wasn't my fault! Anyhow, from everything Gladys told me, she was just as bad a philanderer as he was." Gladys Fellowes was the extremely pregnant wife of one of the Caltech professors who'd been involved in the project in question. Dr. Fellowes, however, wasn't a cad or a philanderer. Both he and Gladys were upright and respectable citizens of our fair city.

Gladys Fellowes, in case you're interested, was an old high-school friend of mine, although we'd never been awfully close. That's because Gladys, whose last name was Pennywhistle until she married Dr. Homer Fellowes, is a brain and I'm not. She even liked *algebra*! The mere notion of algebra makes me want to hide in a closet. Geometry, on the other hand, was kind of fun as long as we were drawing pictures and/or proving theorems. Then algebra trod upon geometry's toes, and I got confused again.

"Anybody else?" I asked, feeling grumpy. But, really, can you blame me?

"Yeah," Sam said, scratching his chin as he thought.

"Who?" This was getting downright frightening.

"I'll have to think about it. Maybe I'll make a list. I'm sure it'll contain some Petries."

"Poor Miss Petrie at the library is *so* ashamed of the bad branch of her family." Miss Regina Petrie, who would soon become Mrs. Robert Browning thanks, in part, to me, was my favorite librarian at the Pasadena Public Library.

"She shouldn't feel that way. There are lots of crooks with last names shared by good people."

"I know that, but she's sensitive."

Sam rolled his eyes again.

"And I'm supposed to make her wedding gown!" I cried, thinking of one more thing I couldn't do without the use of my left arm. "How can I make her wedding gown and the bridesmaids' dresses if I can't use the sewing machine?" I had to blink away tears.

"When's the wedding."

"J-June," I said, sniveling.

"Plenty of time. It's the first of January. You'll be fit as a flea come February."

His turn of phrase dried my tears. "Fit as a flea? What does that mean?"

"Beats me. One of the guys at the department says it a lot."

"Oh."

Sam and I sat in silence for a moment or two. For some reason, I tried to figure out why a flea might or might not be fit, and why anyone would come up with a saying like that. I personally detested fleas. So did Spike.

After a few seconds spent pondering that useless train of thought, I said, "What about your idiot nephew?" Sam's nephew, Frank Pagano, had run away from his home in New York City and landed on Sam's doorstep with an unwelcome thump a few months prior to that day.

"As far as I know, Frank's still with my poor sister in New York," said Sam. "I haven't heard any different. Anyway, I don't think he's murdered anyone. Yet. Although there's always time. The kid's young."

"Hmm. Well, I know he doesn't like me much, but I can't imagine why he'd want to kill me."

"I can't either, but he's stupid. Stupid people can often be dangerous, especially if they allow themselves be led by smarter people."

"I guess so," I said, feeling downtrodden, abused and oppressed. "But who might be smarter than he and want to kill me."

"I don't know. I'll put a trunk call through to Renata as soon as I can, and maybe I'll find an answer for you."

"Thanks, Sam. I think. I mean, I do thank you. I appreciate you helping me so much."

"Good." Sam grinned and patted my hand. Very gently.

"Anyone else?" I asked, not sure I wanted to know.

"Probably. I'll need some time to think about it."

After no more than a split-second's thought—about as much thought as I ever gave to anything, I fear—I blurted out, "What about you?"

"What do you mean, what about me? *I* don't want you dead. At least not at the moment. Maybe after we've been married for a few—"

"I didn't mean it that way! Still, you've locked up far more crooks and bimbos than I have. You were a policeman in New York City before you came to Pasadena, after all."

"Bushwa."

"Don't you 'bushwa' me, Sam Rotondo. What if some horrible thug in New York City hired a torpedo to take you out?"

Sam squinted at me for a second or two. "I beg your pardon?"

Aggravated, I said, "You know slang as well as I, Sam Rotondo. It's possible, isn't it?"

A frown beetled Sam's brows, and his bushy eyebrows drew together. In a suspiciously snooty voice, he said, "Highly unlikely."

"Nertz."

"Dinner's ready!" came the chirpy voice of my darling aunt from the door of my bedroom.

Dropping his frown, Sam obediently got to his feet and met Vi at the door. She held a tray upon which two plates piled high with foodstuffs rested, along with dinnerware and napkins.

"You should have called me in to fix that tray, Vi," said Sam.

"Nonsense. Daisy needs you more than I do. I have several able-bodied family members to help in the kitchen."

"Thank you, Vi," I said from my bed.

"You're welcome, dear. Just you rest. Sam can bring the dishes back to the kitchen when you're through eating."

Technically, it was New Year's Day, and it was a bit past noon. But, as we did on Sundays, we ate our dinner at lunchtime on New Year's Day. Which reminded me of something else.

As Sam settled the tray on my night stand, after carefully removing the lamp and books therefrom, I said, "I wonder if I'll be able to go to choir practice next Thursday."

Without glancing up from his chore, Sam said, "I doubt it, but if you do go, I'll drive you."

"I can—" I began. Then I shut up.

Peering at me, Sam grinned. "You can what?"

Heaving a soft sigh, mainly because a big one would have ached too much, I said, "I was going to say I can drive myself, but I guess I can't, can I?"

"Not until you get the okay from Dr. Benjamin, you can't. Even then, I don't think you should go out alone."

"Out of curiosity, how did the accident happen? Evidently someone hit me with a car, but where were you guys? I mean, was I standing alone in the middle of the street or something?"

"Not originally." Sam sat back down on the chair beside my bed and glanced from the tray of food to me. "How are we going to do this?"

"I'm not sure," said I. "Maybe I can sit up?"

"Do you think you should?"

"Well, I can't eat lying down. At least I don't think I can."

"Let me help you sit up. It's going to hurt, so brace yourself."

"Oh, Lord."

"Yeah."

Sam was right. It hurt. A lot.

THREE

"That's why Doc Benjamin left you that bottle of morphine syrup, Daisy," Sam said when I'd almost stopped sobbing.

Spike, by the way, startled by my cries and moans, had fled to the dining room where there were…well, diners. He lived in hope that someone would drop something. And someone always did, most often on purpose.

"But I don't *want* to take morphine syrup! My Billy killed himself with that stuff!"

Sam thoughtfully handed me a clean hanky, which he'd fetched from my top dresser drawer. I have no idea how he knew that's where I kept them. Maybe he'd used his well-developed detectival skills. Or maybe Ma or Aunt Vi had whispered the secret when I'd been unconscious. I didn't bother asking, mainly because I was busy mopping up tears and feeling sorry for myself.

"Daisy," said my beloved, staring down at me from his considerable height. Well, he was about six feet tall. As I was only around five feet, four inches—and that's when I was upright—it seemed considerable to me.

"What?" I sounded sullen even to my own ears.

"Billy had been shot during a war and had a body chock-full of shrapnel. His lungs were eaten away by mustard gas. You got hit by a car and will be sore for a week or two. There's a world of difference between your condition and Billy's."

That sounded reasonable. Because I was so sore and cranky, I didn't want to say so. However, as I was a trifle sorer than I was cranky, I grumbled, "You're probably right."

"You know I'm right."

"Maybe. But I don't want to admit it."

With a chuckle, Sam said, "At least you're honest." He picked up the bottle Doc Benjamin had left for me. After pulling his reading glasses from his coat pocket, he peered at the instructions the doctor had written on the label. "Says here you should take a teaspoonful when your pain gets out of hand." He eyed me critically for a second or two. "I'd say the pain is out of hand. If you want to eat your dinner, you'd better take a spoonful of this stuff first."

"I'm not really hungry," I told him, "but I don't want Vi to be upset with me for not eating."

"Morphine syrup is strong stuff," said Sam. "It might make you sick to your stomach if you don't take it with food. So drink the syrup and then eat your dinner."

"Yes, sir." I'd have saluted, but it would have hurt too much. "Anyway, I wouldn't want to alarm Aunt Vi. She worries when I don't eat because…Well, you know."

"Yes," said Sam. "I know."

After Billy's death, I couldn't eat. Just couldn't. As a result, I got so skinny I nearly disappeared. As of January 1, 1925, I still hadn't regained all the weight I'd lost during those terrible months.

"So you'll take a spoonful of this stuff," Sam commanded.

"I guess I'd better." I sighed heavily.

"I'll cut up your ham for you. Want butter on your potatoes, carrots, cabbage and rutabagas? Vi left a bowlful of butter on the tray."

"Speaking of trays…" I squinted for about a third of a second before I decided squinting was too painful an expression with which to deal, so I stopped. "If you'll go to the closet, you'll find on the top shelf the tray we used for you when you were confined to bed. It's got those little fold-up legs, so it'll be easier to eat from than if I try to balance a tray on my lap."

"What lap?"

"You know what I mean."

"Yes, I do."

Almost as obedient as Spike, Sam went to the closet and fetched the tray. Sam would never be *as* obedient to my orders as Spike, because I'd taken Spike to the Pasanita Dog Obedience Club's doggy-training classes two years prior, and he'd placed first in his class. Spike always did what I told him to do. Sam, not so much.

Oh, and I had that leggy tray in my bedroom closet because that's where I stored it after I finished nursing Sam when he'd been released from the Castleton Hospital where he was taken after he was shot. It had been touch and go for a while, and we were all worried, but he survived. Thank God. He'd been about the most appalling patient any person who's ever nursed anyone could have wished for. Not that a nurse would ever wish for that kind of patient, but…Oh, never mind.

Sam carefully poured out a spoonful of morphine syrup. I eyed it malevolently. I wasn't joking when I said my darling Billy had killed himself with the stuff. He had. But what Sam had said was also true: Billy's problems and mine were totally dissimilar, except that we were both in great pain. According to the doctor, my pain would go away soon. Billy's never would have left him, and he'd finally ended his life after he'd endured what he'd decided was enough pain and misery. The year after his death was probably the worst of my life, but I don't like to think about it.

"Here," said Sam, guiding the spoon to my lips. "Be careful. Don't want a spill."

I opened my mouth, shut my eyes, and Sam shoved the spoon into my mouth. I swallowed. The stuff was *vile*!

After I'd gulped down the morphine syrup and grabbed the glass of water Sam had thoughtfully provided for me—I guess he'd tasted morphine syrup himself a time or two—I drank deeply. I was so greedy to get the sweet-bitter taste out of my mouth, I dribbled.

"Careful," said Sam, using one of the napkins Vi had provided to mop up my chin and the bed covers. Then he opened the tray's legs and set the tray over my blanketed limbs. It really was a clever little thing, that tray.

"S-sorry," I gurgled. "I don't know how Billy could stand that stuff."

"Wait and see if it doesn't help you feel better."

"Guess I'll have to, won't I?" I said testily.

"Guess so." Sam grinned at me. "As I asked before, would you like butter on your vegetables? And your dinner roll?"

"Oh, yum. I love Vi's dinner rolls."

"Indeed. Your aunt makes the world's best dinner rolls. I'll butter one of them for you, too. I'll cut your ham, but you'll probably be able to handle the soft vegetables and the roll—as long as I split it and butter it—by yourself."

"Yes, please. Thank you, Sam. You're being very nice to me."

"Yeah. I know."

I stuck my tongue out at him. Childish, I know, but he only laughed. Really, though, this being-waited-on nonsense was for the birds. Sometimes I'd have fantasies about being wildly wealthy, like some of my clients, but I honestly don't think I'd enjoy having servants following me around all the time. I'd make a stinky queen, wouldn't I?

"Want a little mustard on your ham?"

"If you'll put a dab on my plate, I'll swipe my bites of ham through it."

"If you say so."

"I don't like lots of mustard, but I like a little bit."

Sam nodded as if he were actually pleased to be taking orders from me. Ha. That'd be the day.

"And after you butter my rutabagas and dinner roll, will you please tell me how I happened to get hit by that car? It seems to me that if someone was driving poorly, he or she would have hit more than a single person, especially in that huge crowd milling around after the parade was over."

Frowning as he cut ham, Sam said, "That's another reason I find the accident—if that's what it was—troubling. We were all standing in a group, waiting for Pudge to fold up his camp stool so we could walk home, when you suddenly went reeling into the street."

"I did what?"

"You went reeling into the street," Sam repeated, carefully setting my plate of food on the tray he'd erected over my legs.

"Why did I do that?" I glanced from my plate of food, which looked delicious, although I honestly wasn't very hungry, to Sam's concerned face.

"I don't know, but I suspect, given the suddenness of your departure from our group and the fact that you were instantly hit by a car, someone pushed you."

"Oh." My gaze remained fixed upon Sam, and I suspect I looked as befuddled as I felt. "I don't remember being shoved."

"You don't remember being hit by the car, either," he reminded me.

"True." I forked a piece of ham, dipped an end into the little squirt of mustard Sam had plopped on my plate, and stuck it in my mouth. I started with the ham because it had the strongest flavor, and I hoped it would help drown out the evil taste of the morphine syrup. "I wonder if I'll ever remember."

With a shrug, Sam, too, ate a piece of ham. After he swallowed, he said with a deep, satisfied sigh, "Delicious."

"That's the only reason you want to marry me, isn't it? Because then you can continue to eat Vi's meals."

With a grin, Sam said, "That's not the only reason, although it's a mighty good one. I also like you pretty well."

"I like you pretty well, too, Sam. Except when you're mean to me."

"I'm never mean to you."

"Yes you are."

"Nertz."

The telephone rang. On New Year's Day. Talk about nertz!

Sam and I exchanged frowns. Sam rose from his chair and carefully set his plate of food on my night stand, although I'm not sure why. I don't think he aimed to answer the 'phone, but he stood there, on guard, looking as if he aimed to protect me from whoever was on the other end of the wire.

It is true that telephone calls in our house were almost always for me, due to the nature of my business, and they generally came from women wanting me to conduct séances and so forth. However, even *I* hadn't expected a telephone call that day. Maybe it was my brother or sister, both of whom lived somewhere other than Pasadena. If one of them were calling, he or she probably only wanted to wish everyone a happy new year.

Wrong.

Pa appeared in my doorway. "It's Doctor Greenlaw. He saw the accident and wants to know if you're all right. Want me to tell him you're recovering?"

"If he saw the accident, why the devil didn't he come over and help?" demanded Sam, who didn't care for Dr. Fred Greenlaw. There's a reason for his dislike—a very poor one, if you ask me—but I won't go in to that now.

"He said he tried to get to us, but the crowd was massive, as you know, and people kept blocking him. By the time he got to where he thought we'd been, we were gone."

Before Sam could say anything else of a corrosive nature, I said to Pa, "Please thank him for telephoning. You can tell him about my left arm being dislocated. It's very nice of him to call."

"I'll let him know," said Pa, and he vanished. I heard him speaking into the telephone receiver. The telephone itself hung on the kitchen wall to the right of my bedroom, which led directly off the kitchen.

"That was nice of Fred," I said to Sam.

"Yeah," said Sam.

"You're a crosspatch and an old grouch, Sam Rotondo."

"Huh."

Then I heard a knock on the front door. And the telephone rang *again*. Good heavens.

The person at the front door turned out to be Mrs. Killebrew, who lived across the street from us. She didn't stay, but she told my parents Pudge Wilson had advertised my accident up and down the street on both sides, and she just wanted to inquire as to the state of my health and to bring the family a fruitcake. She made fruitcakes every Christmas, although she'd complained in recent years that they weren't as good as they used to be because she couldn't get dark rum in which to soak the cakes. I'd never have told Mrs. Killebrew this, but I didn't like fruitcakes, rum or no rum. Vi made the occasional fruitcake for Mrs. Pinkerton, but she didn't force the family to eat them.

Don't get me wrong. I adored Mrs. Killebrew, who was a very nice lady, and for whom I felt sorry because she'd lost her elderly husband a month or so earlier. So I could sympathize with her on that account, but at least her husband had been old and not young, like my Billy. Not that it matters.

I also love fruit. If I were given an orange to eat, I'd devour it. In fact, I devoured at least one orange almost every day, since we had two orange trees in our yard: a navel and a Valencia. They produced fruit pretty much all year long. But I think retaining the skin of an orange, lemon and/or grapefruit and candying it—or whatever the process is called—is a lousy idea. I love dehydrated apricots, peaches, apples and stuff like that. And prunes. But fruitcakes? Not to my taste.

Not that it wasn't sweet of Mrs. Killebrew to bring us a fruitcake, even if nobody in the household would eat it.

Oh, never mind.

As for the telephone call, the caller turned out to be Harold Kincaid, probably my best friend. Harold was another person Sam didn't care for very much. The reason he disliked Harold was the same reason he disliked Dr. Fred Greenlaw, even though both men are lovely individuals. The one little thing—Sam claims it's not a little thing, but I think it is—that annoys Sam is that they both prefer men to women when it comes to romance. When I first learned about this particular... What would you call it? This peculiarity? I guess that's as good a word as any, I was surprised, but I didn't care much.

For some reason, men seemed to care a *whole* lot about stuff like that. I don't understand it. I mean, who cares whom anyone else loves? It's nobody else's business as far as I'm concerned.

Anyway, that's not the point. The point was that Harold called. Pa said Harold said Dr. Greenlaw had called *him*, and he (Harold) wanted to offer his best wishes and find out how I was doing. So Pa told him. He (Pa) also told him (Harold) I'd be laid up for at least a couple of weeks and that I couldn't get out of bed at the moment. The English language is pronominally deficient, if you ask me. Not that you did.

At any rate, Harold said that was all he wanted to know, and I should expect to get a gift from his mother, who had become hysterical when Harold told her about my accident—which, apparently, wasn't an accident. Mrs. Pinkerton's hysteria was nothing out of the ordinary, so I didn't fret much about her condition.

"So you can expect something, probably large and expensive, from Mrs. Pinkerton," said Pa.

"Oh," I said, looking at my father, who grinned at me from my bedroom door. "Isn't that nice?"

"I'm sure it will be," said Pa. He turned and went back to the dining room, when the stupid 'phone rang *again*. So—although I didn't see him do it, I know he did—Pa detoured to the telephone on the kitchen wall and answered it for the third—or was it the fourth? I can't even remember—time that day. My poor father was going to have to eat a cold dinner if he kept answering the blasted telephone.

As soon as I heard the *click* as he hung up, I hollered, "Just leave the receiver off the hook, Pa!"

"That would be rude, Daisy," came my mother's voice from the dining room.

"But Pa's dinner's getting cold!" I retorted.

"I don't mind, sweetie," said Pa.

"I'll answer the telephone, Joe," Sam offered. That was nice of him. Of course, he'd already eaten more of his own dinner by then than my poor father had been able to get down, thanks to the 'phone and the door.

"Thanks, Sam," said Pa. "I'll take you up on that offer."

Our doorbell scritched. We have one of those old bells that twist. People like Harold and his mother have chimes. La-di-dah.

"What the heck?" I said. "Is the entire world going to come calling or telephone? Darn Pudge Wilson anyway!"

"The kid was scared to death for you, Daisy. I think he's sweet on you," said Sam.

I sighed again. "Yes, I know he is." Something then occurred to me kind of slowly, like maybe a centipede that had lost a few legs. Only that sounds disgusting. "You know what, Sam?"

"Probably not. What?"

23

"I think that syrup is working. I'm about to drop my fork because I'm suddenly so exhausted."

"Whoops!" Sam rushed over, took my fork from me, removed my tray, and I sank down onto the bed pillows, which he'd thoughtfully fluffed for me. For so grumpy and grouchy a man, Sam could be a sweetheart when he wanted to be.

FOUR

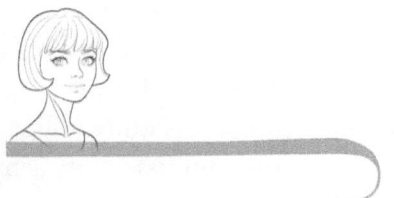

And that's all I remember of New Year's Day, 1925.

As reported by Sam, who remained with my family (according to all reports) for the rest of the day and into the evening, the telephone continued to ring and folks continued knocking on the door.

When I woke up the next morning, my bladder was screaming. When I tried to get out of bed in order to walk to the bathroom, the rest of my body joined in. Poor Spike, startled by my loud cry of agony, walked up from the foot of the bed and licked my face.

"Thanks, Spike," I moaned to my faithful hound. "I hurt everywhere."

Spike was all sympathy. His eyes told me so.

I don't know how long it took me to get out of bed that morning, but during every second of it, my entire body throbbed to beat the band. I hobbled to the bathroom and more or less fell onto the toilet. You probably didn't need to know that part, did you? I'm sorry. But really, it was the most painful day of my life. Physically, I mean.

As I sat on the pot, I cursed my idiocy for not taking a swig of morphine syrup before I attempted this journey to the bathroom. Then I remembered my Billy and how horrified I'd been whenever I saw him drinking the stuff, and I burst into tears.

In other words, I was a complete mess. The fact that I couldn't use my left arm in the attempt to balance myself didn't help matters any. As tears streamed down my face, a knock came at the bathroom door.

"Daisy?" My father said. "Sweetheart, are you all right? You should have hollered. I'd have helped you."

Feeling miserable and extremely sorry for myself, I said in piteous accents, "Thanks, Pa. I'm all right."

As awful as it sounds, I'm accustomed to lying. Heck, I lied for a living. But I seldom told whoppers like the one I'd just told my father.

"You are not," he said, sounding faintly critical. "You were hit by a car yesterday, your body is torn up, your left arm is useless, and you shouldn't try to do things by yourself when you have a family to help you."

His words made me feel worse, although I hadn't thought such a thing was possible until it happened. Miserable, I sniffled and said, "Th-thanks, Pa. I didn't know it would hurt this much."

"Nonsense. I could have helped you get out of bed."

"I'm sorry." Being scolded on top of being in hideous pain only made me feel more injured, but I didn't tell my wonderful father that. He worried about me, and that was sweet of him.

He was also right. I'd been an idiot not to realize that, even if Ma and Aunt Vi had already left for work, Pa would be there in the house and would have assisted me in any way he could. I guess my brain, along with the rest of me, had become rattled when that cursed car hit me.

I hobbled to the bathroom door, opened it, and Pa instantly put an arm around my right shoulder. I shrieked, "Ow!"

Grimacing, Pa said, "Sorry, sweetheart. There's not a single inch of you that isn't wounded, is there?"

Snuffling like a blubbering baby, I said, "No. *Everything* hurts. All my muscles ache, all my scratches and scrapes sting, and my left arm and the left side of my body are howling in agony."

"Better take a spoonful of that medicine Doc Benjamin left for you."

And *that* comment, of course, reminded me not merely of how stupid I'd been not to have thought of it myself, but also of my dead Billy, and I cried some more. As Pa gently walked me down the hall and into the kitchen, I stopped dead in my tracks, momentarily diverted from my suffering. The kitchen was full of flowers! And cakes. And cookies. And unopened packages. And a whole lot of other stuff. Blinking, thinking my eyes had deceived me, I just stood there, staring.

Pa understood. "You have no idea."

"I don't?"

"Nope. The whole house is full of flowers and candy and cookies and cakes, and just about everything else you can think of. Mrs. Pinkerton sent you a huge box. We've been waiting for you to wake up so you can open it and see what's inside."

"Oh." I wasn't sure what to do. The notion of looking at everything and writing thank-you notes to people daunted me even more than the things themselves pleased me, which tells you what kind of shape I was in.

"And Harold's bringing you lunch."

Turning my head slightly—even doing that hurt—I stared at Pa. "He's what?"

"He's bringing you lunch. From the Castleton. He said you like their Lobster Newburg."

"Lunch? Castleton? Lobster? But...but what about Vi?"

Pa chuckled. The vibration shot through my battered body and made it twang like a banjo string.

My head hurt. My brain hurt. My entire body hurt. And the house was full of stuff people had given us. What was going on?

"Um...Maybe I ought to take a teaspoonful of that hateful syrup. I can't quite seem to figure out what's been happening here while I was asleep."

"You did sleep for a long time. That's good, because you needed it. Here." Pa pulled out a chair. "Why don't you sit at the kitchen table, and I'll bring you the bottle and the spoon? Sam is really worried about you. You might want to telephone him. I'm sure he'll drop by as soon as he can."

"Sam?" I spoke the name as if I'd never said it before.

"Yes, sweetie. And Pudge Wilson has already stopped by to see if there was anything he could do for you."

It's nice to know people cared. I kind of...well...this is a hateful thing to say, but I actually *didn't* care at that particular moment. In fact, I'd as soon that car had done me in if life was aiming to be this excruciating for very darned long. Naturally I didn't say so to Pa, who would have been aghast.

Instead I said, "How nice."

Pa came back with the bottle and the spoon, set them on the table while he pulled out a chair for himself. Then I slowly and painfully removed the cork from the bottle and tried not to spill when I lifted the bottle—

"Let me do that," said Pa, grabbing the bottle from my shaking hand. "Daisy, you *must* let people do things for you until you're better. For pity's sake, you need help. We're here to help."

To prove it, he poured out a spoonful of the vile syrup and held it—in his completely steady hand—in front of my mouth. I obediently opened same and swallowed the syrup. Then I shuddered because it tasted so bad. Then I yipped in agony. That shudder had been extremely painful.

Was I in bad shape, or was I not in bad shape?

"I'm sorry, sweetheart. Here, I poured you some coffee. Maybe that will drown the taste of the syrup."

"Thanks, Pa," I said in a disgraceful whimper.

Without even asking, Pa added sugar and milk to my coffee and lifted the cup to my lips. I managed to swallow a bit of coffee without dribbling. Again I said, "Thanks, Pa."

"You're more than welcome. And Mrs. Jackson came by last night with a plate of her famous beignets."

"M-Mrs. Jackson? How'd she find out about my accident so soon?"

"Probably from Harold or Mrs. Pinkerton. Or from her son. Mrs. Jackson's son, I mean."

"Ah, yes. Of course." Mrs. Jackson was the mother of Mr. Joseph Jackson, Mrs. Pinkerton's gatekeeper. Mrs. Jackson not only made Voodoo jujus for people she liked, but she also made the most incredible pastries I'd ever eaten in my life, and that includes Vi's. Mrs. Jackson's beignets were…I don't know. Magic or something.

Pa placed a plate with a pastry on it in front of me. I gazed down at the beignet and, for the first time in a long time, didn't want to eat it. It's true I'd nearly starved myself to death after Billy died, but I hadn't had trouble eating since then. Until that day. Actually, truth to tell, I didn't want to move my right arm or bend a finger for fear of the jolts of agony that would follow the movement. Pitiful.

"Eat it, Daisy," said Pa, sounding stern.

"May I wait until I stop hurting so much? Even moving my right arm hurts." And, since my left arm was strapped to my body, I couldn't use that one at all. I didn't point out this salient fact to my darling father.

"Of course you may. Didn't mean to bully you," said Pa.

"You're not bullying me," I said upon a shallowish sigh. I couldn't even *sigh* deeply that day! And I'm an expert sigh-er. "You care, and I love you for it."

Pa cut a piece of my beignet, forked it, and lifted it to my mouth. I obediently opened same and took the bite. Delicious. I closed my eyes and savored the flakiness of the pastry and the exquisite sweetness of it as I chewed.

Then somebody knocked at the front door, and I darned near fell out of my chair. Fortunately, Pa was there to steady me. Because of the volume of the knock and the way Spike took up his "Oh, goody, a friend has come to call" clamor, I suspected Sam.

I was right.

Using the handsome new cane I'd given him for Christmas, and after greeting my father and Spike, Sam walked into the kitchen, pulled out another chair, and sat on it with a thud. "They found the car," were the first words out of his mouth.

I stared at him, feeling blank, although my various aches and pains were becoming less distinct. Then it was I realized that, not only was morphine syrup incredibly pain-relieving in and of itself, but it kind of blurred the edges of reality. No wonder people got addicted to the stuff.

"Did you hear me?" Sam demanded.

"Yes."

Sitting himself in his own chair, Pa said, "Where'd they find it?"

"Angeles Crest."

"That's a long way away," said Pa.

"Yeah," said Sam. He squinted at me. "You okay, Daisy? You don't look so good."

What a charmer. "Thank you, Sam. Your assessment is correct. I don't feel so good, either."

"Figures," said Sam, nodding. "You're going to be in pretty bad pain for another week or more."

"Goody gumdrops."

"But get back to the car," Pa said. "Who found it on the Angeles Crest?"

"A ranger who works at Mount Wilson. The machine had been abandoned near the observatory up there."

"Do you know if it was a stolen car?" I asked. I still didn't quite dare pick up a fork or break off a piece of that powdery beignet for myself. Regrettably, it looked as if Pa had forgotten he was in charge of feeding me that morning.

"Yes. It was reported stolen on New Year's Day. A man named Randford called the police station to report that his 1923 Cole Sportster Sedan had been stolen from the driveway in front of his house. He lives in the San Rafael district."

"My goodness," said Pa. "That's a rich man's neighborhood."

"It is," I agreed, thinking of a woman named Mrs. Hastings for whom I'd conducted a séance a year or so prior, and who lived in the San Rafael area. That stupid séance had almost made me give up my work as a spiritualist-medium because a ghost actually *had* appeared, through me, at the séance. The poor guy had been murdered, so I didn't blame him for being peeved about his demise, but he didn't have to tell everybody about it through *me*, did he? Well…maybe he did, but his sudden vocal appearance had scared me almost to death.

"Yes, it is. Doan is the officer who took the report."

"Doan had to work on New Year's Day?" I said, feeling sorry for Doan, whom I'd known slightly for several years by that time.

"The police are on duty all the time, Daisy," said Sam. "I'm lucky I got the day off."

"I'm glad you did," said I. "Heaven knows how I'd have got home if you hadn't been there."

With a smile that did a good deal to soften his granite-like surface,

Sam said, "I suspect Pudge Wilson could have created a travois or a stretcher or something using his Boy Scout skills."

"Good point," I said with a little smile of my own. "That would have been two good deeds on one day, so he could have skipped today."

Pa chuckled and Sam grinned.

"Anyhow," Sam continued, "the car was found on the Angeles Crest, but it looks as if someone tried to wipe away any fingerprints. It's a shame for Mr. Randford that the bears and raccoons took such an interest in it."

"Oh, dear. What did they do? The bears and raccoons, I mean?" I asked.

"Tore up the seats and…well, let's just say they did some intimate business on the car seats."

"You mean they pooped on them?" I smiled, imagining a big brown grizzly bear sharpening his or her claws on a fancy new automobile's interior seats and then doing his or her duty on the resultant fluffy stuff.

"You might say that," Sam said in a voice as dry as mummy dust.

"Too bad," said Pa, who didn't seem as amused about the fun the bears and raccoons had enjoyed as I did.

But heck, anyone who can afford to live in the San Rafael hills and own a wildly expensive motorcar can probably afford to get seats to said motorcar replaced. Mind you, that might be an unjust assumption on my part. Maybe the fellow was poor and only lived in the hills and had that luxurious automobile because…Well, I couldn't think why a poor man would live in San Rafael or own a Cole Sportster. Not that it matters. I'm sure the guy was upset, and he had sufficient reason to be. If any old grizzly bear had ripped our Chevrolet to shreds, I'd have been irked, too.

"Has Mr. Randford reclaimed his automobile?" I asked.

"Not yet," said Sam. "We're still processing it."

"What does that mean?"

"It means we're searching for any fingerprints that might not have been wiped off or anything else that might help us find the culprit who stole the machine and ran you down with it."

"He didn't actually run me down," I said. "He ran me into a tree."

Sam gave me a "Stop being so literal" grimace. Then he noticed the beignet on my plate and his eyebrows soared. Kind of like flying caterpillars. He had bushy eyebrows. "That looks good."

"I'll get you one," said Pa, instantly rising from his chair and heading for the bread box.

"They are good," I said, although I hadn't yet touched mine and had only eaten the one bite Pa had sawed off for me. "Have it with some tea or coffee. These came straight from Mrs. Jackson, according to Pa. They're her world-famous beignets."

"World famous, are they?" Sam said as if he didn't believe me.

"Perhaps only locally famous," I admitted. "They're the best pastries I've ever eaten in my life. Well, maybe Vi's Scotch shortbread can match them, but I can't think of anything else that can. Anyhow, does Scotch shortbread count as a pastry?"

"I have no idea," said Sam.

"I think so," said Pa.

"Thanks, Joe," said Sam when Pa put a plate loaded with two beignets in front of him. Actually, "loaded" isn't the right word. Mrs. Jackson's beignets were so light, they'd probably float off the plate if they didn't have so much confectioner's sugar sprinkled on them.

Sam picked up his fork and dug into his beignet. Bravely daring, I also picked up my fork. That didn't hurt too much, so I stabbed my beignet with it and managed to bring it away with a bite of beignet on it. By the time I got the bite to my mouth, I was reconsidering eating the rest of the thing. Doggone it! I was in agony!

Darn whoever it was who nailed me with that stupid car!

FIVE

It's embarrassing to admit this, but Sam fed me the remains of my beignet. Then he carried me to the living room, where he settled me on the sofa, covered me with a lovely afghan my dear friend, Flossie Buckingham, had crocheted for me, set Spike on the sofa next to me, and said, "There. I'm going to bring in that bottle and spoon and, when you start hurting again, take some more of that syrup."

"I don't want to become—"

"You *won't* become addicted to it, Daisy! Your pain will last a couple of weeks. Dammit, even *you* must recognize the difference between your circumstances and Billy's."

I glared at him resentfully. "What do you mean, 'even *I*'? That was a nasty crack, Sam Rotondo."

Naturally, Sam rolled his eyes at me. "Listen, I'm not casting aspersions—"

"Like heck," I muttered.

Very well, so I was being almost as awful a patient as Sam had been. When I realized I was behaving badly, I tried to stop. Didn't entirely succeed, but I tried.

Somebody knocked on the door, and Spike leaped off the sofa and began barking deliriously. Sam and I exchanged a glance, and Spike made it to the door just a bit before Pa did. Because Spike obeyed his humans, even humans other than me, he sat and stayed when Pa told him to. I adore that dog! He's the only male being in my personal world who *always* does what he's told to do.

"Miss Petrie!" said Pa, sounding surprised.

"Regina?" I was surprised, too.

"Yes," said my favorite librarian in her soft, musical voice. "Robert and I heard what happened to Daisy, and I thought I should bring some books by, since she probably won't be able to get to the library any time soon."

"How very kind of you," said Pa, opening the door wider and admitting not merely Miss Petrie, but her fiancé, Robert Browning (not the poet), as well.

"Regina and Robert!" I cried, feeling soppily emotional. "How nice of you to think of me." Naturally their kindness brought tears to my eyes. I swear to heaven, I'm not generally as much of a wreck as I was those few first weeks in 1925.

"Daisy!" said Regina, hurrying over to the sofa. "And Detective Rotondo! How nice to see you here, too."

I could tell by Robert's dragging feet that he wasn't as elated to see Sam as was his beloved. That's because Sam had considered Robert a suspect in a murder case a couple of months prior to then.

"How do you do?" Sam said politely to Regina. "Good to see you, Browning," he said to Robert. I was the only person to whom he was impolite, darn the man. Not casting aspersions, my foot.

"Oh, Daisy! I'm so sorry. You look *awful!*" Regina stopped in her tracks, slapped a hand over her mouth, and said, "I'm so sorry. I didn't mean you look awful in that way. Only that you look as if somebody has beaten you to a pulp."

Sam held up his hands in a gesture meant to deflect suspicion. "Wasn't me," said he.

Sam, Pa, Regina and Robert laughed. I didn't. "It's all right," I told her. "I do look awful. I know I do, because I saw myself in the mirror this morning. With luck and a few weeks, all the scrapes and bruises will heal up and go away." Because I didn't want her to worry, I added, "And

I'll be well in plenty of time to make your wedding gown and the brides-maids' dresses."

"I hadn't even thought about that!" she cried as if shocked I had. "Daisy, don't even *think* about sewing or working or anything right now. You need to get better before you worry about other things."

"Absolutely," said Sam. And Pa. And Robert. They made a nice trio. Sam was the basso profundo, Robert the tenor, and Pa was kind of bari-tone-ish.

"I hope these books will help you while away your recuperation time," said Regina, sitting carefully on the sofa beside me. It was a long sofa, and I'm kind of short, so there was plenty of room for both of us. And Spike, who joined us on the sofa, sitting between Regina and me. He'd have liked to sit on my lap, but I warded him off. I don't think he understood the reason for this rejection, but he obeyed me, bless his little doggy heart.

"Thank you. I—" My voice choked off, and I had to swallow tears. Really and truly, I'm not usually so pathetic. "I don't think I can hold a book yet."

"Oh, my goodness, I'm so sorry," said Regina, genuinely compas-sionate. She loved to read, too, and understood how difficult it might be for a person not to be able to hold a book.

"Maybe there's something on the radio that can keep you amused," Robert suggested. I guess he and Sam had reached some kind of détente, because they sat next to each other on the piano bench. Pa drew up a chair, and he plunked himself into it so that we formed a kind of semi-circle.

"That's a thought," said Sam. "Do you know of any amusing radio programs?"

"I'd have to put on those ear things," I told the huddled masses. "I think they'd hurt, even if I could move both of my arms to lift them over my head." I'd purchased a radio-signal receiving set for my deceased husband approximately three years earlier, and Pa listened to it sometimes. I think he liked listening to baseball and football games. Neither of those things would amuse me, but I didn't say so.

"I'll bet the detective and I will be able to fix that for you," said

Robert, standing with a smile. "It's easy to rig up a radio receiving set so more than one person can listen to it."

"Really? I had no idea," I told him, wondering if there might actually be something on the radio that would help relieve my boredom. Not that I'd had time to get bored yet. I was still dealing with agonizing pain. Added to which, right then I only wanted to close my eyes and sleep for a hundred years or so. Eating that beignet had worn me out.

"Perhaps I can read to you for a little while," said Regina. She was *such* a kind woman.

"Why don't you do that while Detective Rotondo—"

"Call me Sam," said Sam, interrupting Robert. Impolite, I guess, but it was for a good cause.

"Very well. Why don't you do that while Sam and I fix the radio? Daisy might like some of those stories in my collection."

What collection was that? I didn't have the energy to ask.

"Let me help, too," said Pa. "I love stuff like that."

Truer words were never spoken. Well, not often anyway. Pa was an inveterate tinkerer. He adored working on automobiles and pretty much every other kind of mechanical device a person could think of.

So the men walked off, leaving Regina and me on the sofa, me wishing I were asleep. I don't know what Regina was thinking, but eventually she said, "I brought some books for you, Daisy. Since you can't hold a book yet, let me read a little bit of this one." She held up a book. I had to lift my head to see it, and that made me squeak a little in pain. Regina drew back. "Oh, Daisy! Don't try to move. Just stay there."

"Thank you," I said, snuffling. I know I've said it before, but I honestly can't *believe* how pitiful I was during those few days. Contemptible, even. Then I said something even more pitiful. "You know what I'd like to hear, if you really want to read to me?"

"What?"

"Rudyard Kipling's *Just So Stories*. I know that sounds stupid—"

With a sweet smile, Regina said, "It doesn't sound stupid at all. When I'm sick, I go back to the books I loved as a child." Her smile tilted upside down. "But I didn't bring a copy—"

"We have one," I said, interrupting her. How rude, huh? Evidently interrupting people was rampant that day. "On the book shelf in the inglenook." I'd have gestured toward the inglenook, but I didn't dare.

Regina promptly rose from the sofa. "I'll get it. Which story do you want first?"

"Let me think. Maybe *How the Elephant Got His Trunk*. Or…I know! *How the Rhinoceros Got His Skin*! I love the part where the Parsi says, 'Them that takes cakes which the Parsi man bakes, makes dreadful mistakes'. Although I do love the great green greasy Limpopo River, too."

"I'll be happy to read both of them to you," said Regina, rummaging around in the inglenook, searching. "Here it is!"

She brought our family's old, battered copy of Kipling's *Just So Stories* over to the sofa and sat in the chair Pa had vacated.

Before she began reading, she said musingly, "I wonder if you'd enjoy Robert's collection of dime novels. Some of them are quite cunning. Then again, some of them are downright ridiculous."

"Oh. Is that the collection he was talking about?"

"Yes. They're…Well, they're kind of fun. Pure fantasy, of course. I'm sure the old west wasn't really like that."

"Dime novels, eh? You know, I don't think I've ever even *seen* a dime novel, much less read one."

"That's because you grew up in Pasadena. I'm sure no one in Pasadena, except Robert, would allow a yellow-back novel into his house."

"Stuffy lot, aren't we Pasadenans?" I said, wishing she'd start reading. At last she did.

We were alone there in the living room, Regina Petrie and me, for several minutes, Regina reading, and I resting. I had very nearly drifted off to sleep when the men returned rather precipitately, jarring me out of my almost-slumber and making every muscle in my body screech and twang. I muttered a curse under my breath. Regina, startled, looked up at the gang of three who'd invaded our privacy.

"Good heavens, what's the matter?" she asked, standing and closing the book, but keeping a finger in it to hold her place.

"Sam just said the car that hit you is owned by Bernard Randford."

"Oh?" I swiveled my eyeballs and managed to see Robert Browning,

37

who'd made the comment. I didn't quite dare turn my head. "So what?" That wasn't very polite, was it?

"He's an executive at Underhill," said Robert. "I know him quite well." Robert Browning worked, also in an executive capacity, at the Underhill Chemical Company in Pasadena. Another of their big muck-ety-mucks had been a louse and a criminal, and had been murdered a year or so before. No great loss.

Wow, I was cranky as that grizzly bear who tore up Mr. Randford's car, wasn't I?

"Oh." Robert's information was kind of interesting, although I didn't think it was interesting enough for the men to have busted in on my nap. "I'm sorry his car was stolen. I'm even more sorry somebody used it to hit me."

"I am, too," said Robert, coming closer and with a worried frown on his face. "I'll give him a ring. I'm kind of surprised he hasn't telephoned me before this, since we work closely together."

"Maybe he didn't want to spread bad news in the new year," I suggested feebly.

"Maybe," said Robert. "But it looks as if you were trying to take a nap. I'm sorry, Daisy. But Sam, Joe and I got the radio to broadcast without a person having to wear the head phones. Here. I'll put it on the piano bench or a table and plug it into an electrical socket...Um..." He glanced around, evidently looking for an electrical socket. I decided to let Pa help him, since I was irked at having had my nap interrupted before it had even begun.

"I'd better be going, Daisy," said Sam, coming over to sit next to me where Regina had sat earlier. "I'll have to interview Mr. Randford. Maybe we can find out something if we look into his life."

"Sounds grim," I said. "I also don't like the Underhill connection. How come everyone who works there except Robert and the younger Mr. Underhill are louses?"

Robert laughed as he bent over to plug in the radio set. "There was only one louse working there, Daisy. Well, two, if you count that fellow, Kingston—or whatever his name was."

"Does Miss Betsy Powell still work in the stenographic pool there?" I asked. Miss Powell attended our church, the First Methodist-Episcopal Church on Marengo and Colorado. She screamed a lot.

Maybe that isn't a fair statement. Yes, she had screamed, but only when a couple of people had died during communion services at church. Perhaps watching people die is reason enough for a person to scream, although I'm personally not a screamer and would be embarrassed to death to produce the noises Miss Powell had produced during communion services those two times.

On the other hand, I guess people don't get murdered during communion services as a rule, so perhaps she should be forgiven.

Oh, dear. Maybe Sam had a point when he told me I was like the Typhoid Mary of murder in Pasadena. I didn't like to think so.

"Yes, she does. In fact, I do believe she and Bernard had been keeping company lately."

Aha! A connection, and one I didn't like. Suspicious, by golly. Very suspicious. "Oh. Is he the fellow who's come to church with her the past few weeks?"

"How would Browning know that?" asked Sam, sounding a trifle cross.

"Yes," said Robert, chuckling. "I don't know. Reggie and I go to First Presbyterian."

"Oh."

"You attend the Methodist Church, don't you?" asked Regina.

"Yes. Anyhow, the man who's been accompanying Miss Powell is sort of middle-sized with salt-and-pepper hair and one of those skinny little pencil moustaches that look really stupid," I told everyone.

"Daisy," said Pa. Usually it was Ma who reprimanded me for speaking ill of people, but Ma was at work, so I guess Pa was taking up the cudgels of propriety on her behalf.

"It's true," I said, whining slightly. I was also ashamed of myself.

"That sounds like him, all right," said Robert. "Would you like me to turn on the radio for you? I'm not sure what's broadcasting at the moment, but maybe I can find some music or something."

"No thanks, Robert. I do thank you for fixing the radio, though. That was kind of you. Now we can all listen to the radio of an evening."

Laughing again, Robert said, "Or something. But we'd best be off. Reggie has to be at the library at noon today, and I should get to the office. Good to see you, again, Daisy. I hope you recover quickly and completely."

"Yes," said Regina, rising and smiling sweetly at me. Everything she did was sweet. She was an exceptionally nice person. "Get better soon, Daisy. I'm going to miss seeing you at the library."

"I'm going to miss going," I said, feeling like crying again. For once I controlled myself.

"I'd better get going, too, love," said Sam, leaning over to give me a kiss on an undamaged part of my forehead. For the record, he had a hard time finding one. "I'll be back later, and I'll tell you if we discover anything interesting about the stolen car."

He'd called me *love*! Sam never called me love in front of other people. I darned near started crying *again*. "Thanks, Sam." I didn't want him to go. But there was no reason for him to stay, except that I was a puling, pathetic, sniveling human being. "Come to dinner."

"You bet," said he.

"I'll save any good books for you," said Regina. "And I'll bring them to you until you're on your feet again."

"Thanks, Regina."

"Spike and I will see everyone to the door," said Pa, probably figuring I needed rest more than I needed company. He was right.

"Please do look into Mr. Randford," I called to Sam as he strode off. "I don't trust anyone who works at that place. Well, except for Barrett Underhill and Robert."

Everybody laughed. Except me.

"Well, I don't," I said crabbily.

"Oh, Daisy!" cried Regina, giggling. "You're *such* a cut-up."

Whatever a cut-up was.

"Good God," said Sam.

"Daisy, Daisy, Daisy," said Pa, clearly unhappy with his second daughter for not saying anything nice about anyone. If you have nothing nice to say, you're not supposed to say anything at all. That's what my mother, father, aunt and other assorted relatives had always taught me. As you can tell, the lesson hadn't stuck.

"You're a caution, Daisy!" said Robert, laughing harder.

Whatever a caution was.

The rest of that day was mostly spent in slumber, if you were me. A few people came to the door, but Pa fended them off, except for Harold Kincaid, who made good on his promise to bring me lobster Newburg. He brought some for Pa, too. Pa had to help me eat it since I couldn't lift a fork. Then he helped me to the bathroom when I needed to go.

And then I took another spoonful of morphine syrup after the ordeal of visiting the bathroom, conked out shortly thereafter, and stayed conked until it was time for bed.

SIX

The following day was even worse than the day after New Year's Day. I hadn't believed my body could hurt any worse than it already did, but I was, unhappily, mistaken. I didn't attend church on Sunday, the fourth of January, but the rest of the family did. At the time they all left for church, I'd been parked on the living-room sofa again, the radio-signal receiving set within what would have been easy reach, if I could have moved an arm or two. Sam opted to stay with me.

I objected. "But you should go to church to see if Miss Betsy Powell brings Mr. Randford with her," I told him.

"We already know he's the man she's seeing. We did interview him, you know, because he owns the car that hit you."

"Oh," I said, having forgot that pertinent fact. "That's right, you did."

"May I bring you something to eat or drink, Daisy? Did you have breakfast?"

Sam sounded so solicitous, I wanted to hug him. But I couldn't. Even if my right arm didn't twinge every time I even thought about moving it, my left arm was still strapped to my body. It had only been going on three days since that villain, whoever he was, had struck me with that motorcar, and I was already so resentful, my temper threat-

42

ened to erupt. I'd have to wait until I felt better to release my fury, however, because Sam deserved better from me. Which made me even more resentful. I was sure in a terrible bind, wasn't I?

"Thank you, Sam," I said, sniffling only slightly. "Ma fed me a piece of French toast, and I had a cup of tea. Sort of. She cut it up for me. The toast, not the tea."

Sam shook his head. "I'm so sorry, sweetheart."

"Thanks, Sam." Then, because I couldn't seem to help myself, I blurted out, "But you're going to take a closer look at that Randford person, aren't you? I don't trust anyone who works at Underhill except the two men I mentioned before. Not only that, but Miss Betsy Powell has an abysmal track record when it comes to men, so I wouldn't trust any man she's seeing." I paused for breath, and added, "And she screams like a banshee every time anything happens to anyone."

With a grin, Sam said, "I think you need to stop worrying about Randford, love. The poor man's car was stolen, and he was outraged that anyone had used it to try to kill you."

His words sobered me. Not that I was riotously happy before he spoke them. "You really think someone was trying to kill me?"

Sam shrugged. "Looks that way, doesn't it? I mean, you were shoved out into the street, and then conveniently hit by a car. There was no other automobile traffic on the road at the time, because the area had been cleared for the parade."

"Oh, dear. Does this mean I need to hire a food-taster, like those old kings used to do?"

With a laugh, Sam said, "I don't think so. But I'll be sure to take any candy you receive to the lab for testing before you eat it."

"I have candy?"

"You haven't seen all the stuff people have sent to you yet?"

"Um…No. I mean, I've seen lots of vases of flowers and some of the packages stacked around the house, but I've been too miserable even to look at anything closely, much less eat any candy if anyone sent some."

"You're in for a treat when you're able to sit up and study your surroundings. It looks like a funeral parlor in here. Can't you smell all the flowers?"

I took a tentative sniff of the air and discovered Sam was right. "By golly!" I said, surprised. "It does smell like a funeral parlor!" I sobered instantly. "I guess that isn't funny, is it?"

He shrugged. "I think it is, but I imagine your perspective is warped at the moment."

"Warped?"

"Maybe warped isn't the correct word."

"If someone tried to kill me, I should say it isn't."

A knock came at the door, and Sam rose from the chair he'd pulled up to the sofa. "I'll see who it is."

"If whoever it is has a gun, bring him in and let him shoot me," I muttered.

"Not on your life," said Sam. "Maybe after we've been married for a couple of years."

I couldn't help myself. I laughed. That hurt, so I stopped.

"Kincaid," said Sam when he'd opened the door. Spike had already announced the visitor to be a friend, so I wasn't overly surprised.

"Good morning, Detective Rotondo," Harold said in a jolly voice. He knew why Sam didn't care for him, thought it was funny, and always behaved with humor and tolerance toward Sam.

That's more than I'd have done if I were Harold. He'd told me once that so-called "real" men didn't care for men like him because they feared men like him might seduce "manly" men. I'd told him he was full of beans, but Harold had only laughed. I hadn't yet asked Sam if Harold's assumption was correct.

"Come on in," said Sam, sounding friendlier than he usually did when Harold was around.

"Thanks. I see the flower garden continues to grow." I guess Harold had glanced around the house when he'd brought me the lobster Newburg.

"It does. And Daisy hasn't opened any of her presents yet, either. Maybe you can help her with them."

"I'll be happy to."

A questioning note in Harold's voice evidently pushed Sam to say, "I want to examine the packages to see if there might be anything... dangerous in them."

"Dangerous? Do you really think someone deliberately set out to hurt Daisy?"

"Yes," said Sam. His tone brooked no equivocation.

"Oh," said Harold.

"After Sam told me what happened to me, I think he's right, Harold."

Harold walked over to the sofa, upon which I lay. He frowned as he gazed down upon me. "You look absolutely terrible, Daisy."

"You're such a sweetheart, Harold. I had no idea I looked so bad."

His nose wrinkling, Harold switched his gaze from me to Sam. "She's kidding, right? I mean, she's seen herself in the mirror, hasn't she?"

Sam said, "Yeah."

"Yes, I have," I said tartly. "I expect I'll heal, but right now I hurt all over and don't appreciate people telling me how awful I look."

"Sorry, sweetie," said Harold, taking a seat in the chair Sam had vacated. Spike instantly jumped on his lap, so Harold had to placate the hound. I was beyond placating, but I'm sure you've figured that out by this time.

"Why don't I bring all the packages to the couch, Daisy," offered Sam. "Then you, Harold and I can go through them together."

Wow, he'd called Harold Harold! I couldn't remember another time he'd done that. Therefore, instead of scolding some more, I said, "Thanks, Sam," and felt better for it.

So Sam dragged up another chair and then went away. I don't know where all the packages were, and I couldn't sit up to look, but he came back with an enormous one first.

"Ah," said Harold. "I remember that. It's from my mother."

"It's huge," I said, gazing at it and wishing I didn't have to open it. Harold's mother, Mrs. Pinkerton, was a generous woman, but totally impractical. I couldn't imagine what she might have sent me that was so large. And I *really* hoped the big box didn't contain dozens of little boxes.

"Want me to untie the ribbon and open the box?" asked Harold. He carefully set Spike on the living room floor. Spike's feelings were hurt; I could tell. I managed to pat the sofa with my right hand, and

Spike jumped up to join me, soothing his rumpled feathers. Fur. Whatever.

"Yes, please," I said.

So he did, while Sam trotted off to collect more presents.

"Good God," said Harold as he peered into the box.

"What is it?"

"You won't believe it."

"If you show it to me, I might," I said brusquely.

"All right, all right. Don't get snippy."

"Sorry, Harold. It's just that I feel so ghastly."

"I know, sweetie." Harold sounded as if he felt sorry for me. As well he might. Heck, *I* felt sorry for me.

Sam had just walked up to the sofa carrying three or four more wrapped boxes—I couldn't turn to see precisely how many he held—when Harold reached into the box and pulled out its contents.

"Good God," said Sam, stopping in his tracks.

"Yeah," said Harold.

And he lifted out a porcelain figure of a dachshund. The thing was gigantic. About as big as Spike himself, actually. I mean, that's not as big as a great Dane or an Irish wolf hound, but it was big for a porcelain figurine. It was also painted with colorful flowers on a white background. No respectable dachshund would *ever* allow himself to be clad thus.

As Harold settled the porcelain hound on his lap, I stared at it. Then I looked at Spike, who had tilted his head as if he, too, were inspecting the fake dog. I think his upper lip curled.

I wasn't sure what to say.

Fortunately, Sam didn't suffer from my muteness. "What the hell is Daisy supposed to do with that?"

With a shrug, Harold said, "Beats me."

"Her heart's in the right place," I said weakly.

"She's a nitwit," said Mrs. Pinkerton's dutiful son.

"Maybe you can put it on the side porch," Sam suggested. "Among the flower pots."

"Best idea I've heard so far," said Harold.

"It's the *only* idea I've heard so far," I told the men.

"It's a good one," said Harold.

"I guess so," I agreed.

"Well," said Sam, "better set it aside so we can deal with the rest of this junk."

So Harold did, and we did, and the living room on that Sunday morning soon resembled a late Christmas morning, what with wrapping paper, ribbons and assorted gifts stacked hither and yon. A couple of the gifts were quite nice. Flossie Buckingham had crocheted a beautiful bed jacket for me, bless her. The Longneckers, who lived a couple of houses down from us on our side of Marengo, had delivered a pretty teapot and two pretty teacups in the same china pattern. I wasn't quite sure what to do with a tea service for two, but perhaps after Sam and I married, I could make tea for us. Someone else would have to make cookies to eat while we drank the tea, because I...can't. Vi would probably be happy to do it.

George and Marianne Grenville, along with Marianne's mother, Diane Chapman, had sent me a copy of P.C. Wren's book, *Beau Geste*, which had been published the prior year. "Aw," I said. "How nice of them. I'll never read that book again, though. It made me cry."

"It's still a lovely gift," said Harold. He flipped through the beginning pages of the book. "It's a first edition, and it's been signed by the author. This might be valuable one day, Daisy. I'd hold on to it if I were you."

"Of course I'll hold on to it!" I said, irked that he thought I might toss it out. "I'd never throw away a gift." I glanced at the porcelain dachshund at Harold's feet. "Even something as ridiculous at that stupid dog statue."

Both Sam and Harold laughed. I didn't.

Anyhow, I won't describe all the thoughtful presents people had been kind enough to give me. There were a ton of them, and the idea of writing thank-you notes for all of them made every single one of my aches and pains twang.

"I'd better clean up these papers and boxes and so forth," said Sam, being unusually helpful. "Harold, why don't you help Daisy open her cards? I don't want the place to be a mess when the family comes home from church."

"Sure thing," said Harold.

I wanted to lift my head and stare at Sam Rotondo but, of course, couldn't. How nice of him, though, to clean up because he didn't want the house to be messy when my folks got home. Almost made me cry again, but I managed to restrain myself.

"Want me to start on the envelopes?" asked Harold as Sam picked up discarded boxes, paper and ribbons.

"Yes, please." I was wearing out fast and wasn't sure how many of the cards and letters I'd have the energy to read—or listen to, since Harold aimed to do the reading—when a gasp from Harold made my eyes open wide. They'd been half-shut.

Harold turned his head and hollered, "Sam, you'd better see this!"

"What is it?" I asked, alarmed by the worry I saw on Harold's face and heard in his voice.

"What is it?" asked Sam, stomping into the living room and dusting his hands together.

"Listen to this," Harold ordered. "'Tell your lover-boy I will do a better job next time.'" He flapped a piece of paper in the air. "This sounds like a threat."

Snatching the paper from Harold, Sam glared at it, turning it over. "Damn it, we shouldn't have touched it. It might have had fingerprints on it."

"I didn't do anything with the envelope. Well, not much anyway," said Harold.

"Nobody knew what it would contain until it was opened," I pointed out in case Sam decided to get mad at Harold. At the moment, he was just irked in general. Actually, so was I.

"That *is* a threat, darn it," I said. "And I'm scared!"

"It's all right, Daisy," said Harold, patting one of my hands.

Sam squatted beside the sofa.

"Don't do that!" I scolded him. "You'll hurt your thigh."

"To hell with my thigh," said Sam. "Listen, Daisy, we'd better talk about this."

"You'd better hire a guard or two," said Harold.

"But what if they're after you and not me?" I asked Sam.

"So far, they—whoever *they* are—have injured and threatened you, not me."

"Maybe they want to hurt me to get back at you," I suggested, thinking my notion a sensible one.

"Why would anyone want to hurt me?" asked Sam.

"Why would anyone want to hurt *me*?" I asked in return.

"We came up with about thirty or forty people who fell into that category the day before yesterday, don't forget."

"How could I ever forget? But it wasn't thirty or forty."

"Close enough."

Grunting, Sam got to his feet. "You were right. I shouldn't have done that," he said.

"You two have the most interesting conversations when I'm not around," said Harold musingly. "You really talked about who might want you dead?"

"Yes," Sam and I said together.

Sam made a face indicative of pain, and I said, "Take some of my morphine syrup."

"I don't need any of your morphine syrup," said the exasperating man, limping to a chair and falling into it.

"Well, I do. Then I think I'll just go to sleep until you figure out who's trying to kill whom," I told him.

"Sensible idea," said Harold.

"Yes," said Sam. "It is, but she doesn't mean it. As soon as she's able, she'll be up and around and snooping."

"I will not!"

"Yes, you will," Sam and Harold said in a rather pleasant duet, Harold taking the tenor part this time.

"Bah."

My family arrived home from church at that moment, however, so I didn't have time to berate the men any more. But really! Did they *honestly* think I was idiotic enough to put myself in danger in order to find the culprit who had run me down with Mr. Randford's motorcar?

Actually, I'm sure they did. Curse all men.

Pa stared at the one note Sam had laid on the dining room table. "That's typewritten," he said.

"Yes, it is," said Sam.

"I don't like it." Pa.

"I don't, either." Sam.

Harold, Ma and Vi nodded their agreement.

Mind you, as I still lay on the sofa in the living room, I couldn't see them, but I could tell what was going on by the various noises.

"This is terrible!" cried Vi. "Who in the world would want to harm Daisy?"

"Or Sam!" I called from the sofa.

SEVEN

A nd that's enough about that. I was laid up for three weeks, and didn't feel great even then. I was, however, up and about, if not entirely pain-free. Most of my scrapes and scratches had healed over. The only real problem remaining from my experience was a bum left shoulder. I was also a trifle perturbed by the notion that someone evidently wanted me dead.

Very well, more than a trifle.

We hadn't received any more threats, and nobody had sent me any poisoned candy. I know the latter because Sam wouldn't allow me to eat anything until he'd had it tested by the police laboratory. And *I* still didn't quite believe someone actually wanted me dead. If anyone wanted anyone dead, I figured they'd want it to be Sam rather than me. He was responsible for putting more folks in jail than I was, after all. Not that I wanted anyone to hurt Sam, either.

Oh, fiddlesticks.

My being laid up was a trial for everyone, including my clients, most of whom called or dropped by to see me. After the first week or so of my confinement, I no longer wanted to smack anyone who dropped by. The first week was touch-and-go, and I nearly lost my temper two or three times, which would have been unkind, since all of my callers only wanted to wish me well. Unless maybe one of them wanted me dead.

Pudge Wilson and Dr. Benjamin visited me every day, Pudge in hopes he'd get to do a good deed close to home, and Doc to make sure I was healing properly. According to him, I was. According to me, the jury was out. When I could hold books again, I reread my favorites: *The Circular Staircase* and *The Case of Jenny Brice*, by Mrs. Mary Roberts Rinehart; and *The House Without a Key*, by Mr. Earl Derr Biggers. And then I read *The Circular Staircase* again, because I couldn't face anything more thought-provoking.

Fortunately for me, about that time Regina and Robert visited, bringing me several of Robert's collection of dime novels. I read a couple of them. They were hair-raising adventures of lawmen and bandits in the old west, and they were pretty darned entertaining, considering I generally enjoyed mystery novels.

Poor Mrs. Pinkerton had been forced to attend a preliminary hearing for her disgusting daughter without me being there to support her, a fact that grieved her greatly. Her son, Harold, attended the hearing with her, and I heard all about it from him. He told me his mother was "too upset" to visit me, but she sent me a bundle of money via Harold, I guess to keep me happy. I'd have to get happy before I could stay that way, but I didn't tell Harold's mother that. I did tell Harold, who wouldn't squeal on me.

I held the money, which I hadn't counted yet, in my hand and stared at Harold. "Harold, I don't deserve anything at all from your poor mother, much less this much money!"

"She's far from poor, and you do, too. Don't forget it was my darling sister who was responsible for Sam being shot, that woman being battered nearly to death, and you nearly getting killed. And she's probably behind whoever ran you down the other day, too."

"Do you really think so?"

"Wouldn't surprise me," he said with a shrug. "Anyhow, you know as well as I do that as soon as you can get around again, Mother will be after you every day and have you come over to read the tarot cards and jiggle the Ouija board for her."

"Jiggle?"

With a shrug, Harold said, "Whatever you do to make it work."

I sighed heavily. "Yes. I suppose you're right about that. I still feel...I don't know. Undeserving of so much money from her for doing nothing."

"You almost got killed. That's something. A pretty darned large something," said Harold. Nodding at the wad of bills in my hand, he added, "Since you don't seem inclined to count that stack, I'll tell you it's supposed to be five-hundred mazumas."

"Five hundred *dollars*!" I squealed.

"Yes. And don't tell me again you don't deserve it. I saw you the day after that car ran you into that tree. You deserve considerably more than five hundred aces."

"But not from your mother."

"Like hell. She owes you more than that."

"But..." I didn't know what to say.

"Anyhow, Stacy's probably going to turn states' evidence, so stop feeling bad about the blasted money."

"What?" My brain was still kind of scrambled, this conversation having been held during the first week of my misery. "What's turning states' evidence mean?"

"She'll rat out some of the other gang members in exchange for getting a light sentence. Instead of attempted murder and child exploitation, she'll probably be sent to some country-club-like prison somewhere, stay for six months, then be escorted out in one of Mother's Rolls Royces."

"I didn't know your mother had more than one Rolls Royce."

With a roll of his eyes that precisely imitated one of Sam's patented eye-rolls, Harold said, "Stop taking everything so literally!"

"Oh." I stared at Harold. "That doesn't seem right."

"What?"

"The...whatever you called it and the country club."

"Of course it doesn't seem right. That's because it's *not* right," said he. "However, it's merely one of the benefits of being rich. You can buy your way out of pretty nearly any ticklish situation if you've got the bucks."

"Hmm."

"You know that as well as I do, Daisy. So use that money for something frivolous. The good Lord knows Mother would."

"Yes, well, I'm not your mother."

"Thank God for that!"

We both laughed. Which hurt, so I stopped laughing and sighed instead.

Sam had to attend the same hearing I'd missed, and he was considerably crabbier than Harold about Harold's sister's probable plans.

"She deserves to be locked up forever," he said, grumpy as all get-out when he arrived at our house for dinner that evening. Dinner, by the way, was roasted chicken with mashed potatoes, gravy, green beans and carrots. It's one of Vi's best meals. Then again, pretty much all of Vi's dinners are the best.

"I think so, too, but I'm not a judge or a lawyer."

"If her mother didn't have so blasted much money, that brat would swing for the crimes she committed."

"My goodness," said Ma, who wasn't used to Sam sounding so bloodthirsty.

"It's true, Ma," I told her. "Her darling Percival Petrie's aunt—I think she was his aunt, anyway—darned near murdered Sam."

"Oh, dear. Oh, dear," said Ma, who didn't like to think about unpleasant things.

"Sam's right, Peggy," said Vi, gently setting the chicken on a platter. Then she placed the platter in the warming oven while she made gravy. Making gravy was a dark and mysterious art to me, although other people didn't seem to be afraid of it. I felt so utterly worthless sometimes. "That child has been a problem since the day she was born. It astonishes me that both she and Harold came from the same parents. Harold is a wonderful man."

"Yes, he is," I said, giving my fiancé a hideous scowl. He only grinned back at me, and I got the impression he didn't despise Harold as much as he liked to pretend.

"From everything I've heard about the girl," said Pa, entering the dining room from the hall, "I think she'd benefit from working on a chain gang for a while. Maybe in the hot sun in a state like Mississippi or Alabama. She could learn how the other half lives."

"We don't live like that!" cried Ma. Literal-minded; that was my mother.

"I know, Peggy," said Pa, coming over and giving her a peck on the cheek. "Just a little exaggeration. The girl needs discipline, is what I'm saying."

"Oh," said Ma, pleased to have the issue cleared up. "Yes, I agree about that."

"I think a chain gang is too good for her," I muttered, thinking black thoughts about Stacy Kincaid.

"Daisy," said Ma.

I then rolled my own eyes, but made sure she didn't see me do it, because if she did, she'd have scolded me some more. I still couldn't move around very well, this being the sixth day after that blasted car had hit me, but I was able to set the table, so I did. Sam, bless his heart, helped me.

That evening, after Sam and I had washed the dishes—Sam washed and dried, and I told him where everything went—we retired to the living room, where I more or less collapsed onto the sofa. Sam sat next to me, took my hand and patted it. Spike jumped up and managed to snuggle his way between two of us. Spike never liked being left out of things when couches and his humans were involved.

"You holding up all right?" he asked.

"Yes. I still hurt a lot, but I think I'm better. Well, I know I'm better."

"Did Doctor Benjamin say when he was going to unwrap your shoulder?"

"Probably the end of next week. That means another week without work, which means I won't be earning any money—" I remembered the $500 Mrs. Pinkerton had sent to me that very day and decided to stop whining.

"You don't have to worry about money," said Sam softly. "If you get into a bind, I'll help you. You know that."

Because I was an emotional wreck, I began sniveling. "Oh, Sam! Thank you. You're so kind to me, and I'm so mean to you."

"What brought this on?" he asked, sounding puzzled. "You never used to apologize for being mean to me."

"I'm sorry!" I blubbered.

It was probably a good thing someone scritched the doorbell at that moment. Spike went into his customary paroxysm of boundless happiness, and Pa got up from his chair to answer the door. He told Spike to sit and stay, which Spike did.

The door opened, and I heard Pa say, "Mrs. Killebrew! Come on in."

Mrs. Killebrew? What the heck was she doing, visiting us for the second time in a week? I mean, we'd been across-the-street neighbors for as long as we'd owned our lovely little bungalow, but normally we just waved to each other and exchanged Christmas cookies and stuff like that. And, of course, she'd brought us that fruitcake the day of my non-accident. The fruitcake was still wrapped up and sitting on a shelf in the kitchen. As Vi had said more than once, there's no way a fruitcake can ever go bad because it's bad to begin with. None of us told Mrs. Killebrew that, of course.

"Thank you, Mr. Gumm. I saw Detective Rotondo's Hudson outside and thought I might catch him here."

"You want to see Sam?" asked Pa, sounding puzzled.

Wiping my eyes with my handy hanky, which I'd been keeping in the pocket of my day dress since I'd been dripping uncontrollably for a week by that time, I glanced at Sam. He winked back. Big help. He did, however, abandon me on the sofa and walk to the door, where both Spike and Mrs. Killebrew greeted him enthusiastically.

"Good evening, Mrs. Killebrew," he said, taking the hand she held out and shaking it.

"Good evening, Mr. Rotondo. I hope you don't mind me calling on you here."

"Not at all. Come on in to the living room and see how Daisy's doing."

"How is the poor child? Recovering well?" Mrs. K sounded concerned on my behalf, which I thought was sweet.

"She's still in a good deal of pain, but she's getting better."

"I'm so glad." Mrs. Killebrew walked to the sofa, stopped dead in her tracks, stared at me, clapped a hand to her cheek, and cried, "Oh, Daisy, you poor thing!"

Naturally, that set me off again. I swear, I was like a dripping faucet that first week or two. "Th-thank you, Mrs. Killebrew. Please, have a seat." I'd have waved my arm to indicate various chairs scattered about, but I couldn't.

"Thank you, dear. I'm so very sorry this happened to you."

"Me, too," I said, still sounding sloppy.

"Good evening, Beatrice," said Ma, walking into the living room from the dining room. "How nice of you to call."

Mrs. Killebrew turned and smiled at my mother, who was holding out her hand to the newcomer. Mrs. K took Ma's hand and squeezed it in both of hers.

"Good evening, Peggy. I wanted to check to see how your Daisy is doing. And..." She hesitated for a minute, then said, "And I have something I'd like to discuss with Mr. Rotondo."

"Absolutely happy to discuss it with you," said Sam, walking up to the two ladies. "Will we need privacy?"

Privacy? What the heck?

"Perhaps that might be a good idea, Mr. Rotondo," said Mrs. K.

"Just call me Sam, please. Everyone does."

"And everyone calls me Beatrice," Mrs. K said with a girlish giggle.

Very well. So they were Sam and Beatrice. I was Daisy. Pa was Joe, Ma was Peggy, and my aunt was Vi. And I *still* didn't know what the heck Sam and Beatrice had to discuss—in private—with each other. Doggone it! I was Sam's fiancée! I *should* know when other women had dealings with my betrothed. Never mind that Mrs. Killebrew was considerably older than my parents and had several adult grandchildren. One of whom, an extremely pretty blonde named Linda, was approximately my own age.

I felt discarded. Abandoned.

Before he left our house to walk across the street to Mrs. Killebrew's pretty little bungalow—little being a comparative term in this case, her house being a lot larger than ours and even had a little one-bedroom cottage behind it. I think they call those little cottages mother-in-law houses or something like that. I hope I'd never have to find out. Not that I didn't like Sam's mother; heck, I'd never even met the woman, although I know she disapproved of her son, born a Roman Catholic, marrying a Methodist. Anyhow, neither ours nor Mrs. Killebrew's home was a mansion—Sam bent over and gave me a kiss on the forehead.

"What's going—?"

"Tell you when I get back," he said with what I could only consider a wicked grin.

And off the two went. Across the pepper-tree-lined street to Mrs. Killebrew's bungalow. My parents, Vi, and I stared at each other. I'm sure my expression of befuddlement was as great as or greater than those on the faces of my parents and aunt.

What in the world did Sam and Mrs. Killebrew have to talk to each other about? At night. In private, of all things?

I smelled a rat. Something rotten in the state of Denmark. Or, rather, the state of California, which was where we lived.

Then an awful thought occurred to me.

Was Sam going to leave me for Linda Killebrew?

The cad!

EIGHT

A tap came at the front door about fifteen minutes after Sam and Mrs. K left. I almost told Pa not to answer the door, but I think I was the only one in the family who was actually miffed by Sam's strange behavior. The rest of the family members were merely puzzled.

"Sam!" said a happy-sounding Pa.

I growled something under my breath. I think only Spike understood what I'd said. I didn't then and still don't, but Spike and I spoke the same language that night.

"Don't get huffy, sweetie," said Sam, strolling over to the sofa as if he hadn't a care in the world.

"I'm not huffy," I said huffily.

"We didn't know you had business with Mrs. Killebrew," said Pa. His voice was conciliatory. Pa was the peacemaker in the family. Ma was unimaginative, humorless and dogmatic—and probably the kindest and sweetest person in the universe. Vi knew how everyone was supposed to behave and made sure they did so. I was the only one liable to fly off the handle. Not that I could fly off anything just then.

"I didn't have business with her until recently," Sam said, answering my father and sitting next to me on the sofa. He patted a cushion for Spike, who took him up on his offer and bounded onto the couch next to me. I wished I could bound. I'd bound all over Sam Rotondo and beat him to a jelly.

"It's Linda, isn't it?" I said, trying not to cry.

As I dabbed at a leaky eye with my hanky, Sam gave me a look of incomprehension. "Who's Linda?"

"Linda Killebrew! You know very well who Linda is, Sam Rotondo! She's Mrs. Killebrew's granddaughter, she's beautiful, she's blonde, and she's been visiting her grandmother a whole lot lately!"

"I don't believe I've ever met the lady," said Sam, still sounding perplexed. The bounder (speaking of bounding)!

"I think I've seen her a time or two recently," said Pa musingly.

"See? It *is* Linda!"

Sam put a hand on my shoulder. I wrenched said shoulder, my left, from his grasp and screeched in pain. "*Damn* you, Sam Rotondo! You're leaving me for a blond hussy!"

"Daisy!" came Ma's definitely shocked voice from just outside the living room. Guess she'd been in the dining room. "Linda Killebrew is a lovely young lady, and I don't allow my children to swear."

I turned my face into a sofa cushion and sobbed as if my heart were breaking. Which it was, darn it.

"Daisy?" Sam's voice sounded tentative. I guess he didn't dare put a hand on me again. "Daisy?"

"I think you might be over-reacting a little bit, sweetheart," said Pa, his tone judicious.

Huh! Showed how much *he* knew!

"All Sam did was walk across the street with Mrs. Killebrew. Why don't we let him tell us about it before you jump to unlikely conclusions?"

"They *aren't* unlikely!" I wailed, reminding myself of Mrs. Pinkerton, which was a dismal thing to be reminded of. "I don't blame him. I'm all bashed up and ugly, and Linda is gorgeous. And she's *younger* than I am! I'm an old hag!"

"Daisy," said Sam, a little more forcefully. "Will you calm down for a second so I can tell you—"

"I don't want to hear about it!" I sobbed. Our poor sofa cushion was sure getting a work-out that evening.

"Daisy," said Sam, his voice now firm and commanding. "Stop over-reacting and listen to me."

"*No*! You're a two-timing *villain*!"

"I'm thinking about buying Mrs. Killebrew's house!" Sam all but shouted at me.

"You're what?" cried Pa, elated unless I missed my guess.

"Oh, Sam, how wonderful!" Ma rushed up to the sofa and handed me a clean hanky. I snatched it out of her hand and snuffled into it, beginning to feel like a dim-witted dunce.

"It was supposed to be a surprise for Daisy," said Sam. "Maybe I shouldn't have kept it a secret. But jeez, I've only just worked out the details with Mrs. Killebrew and her son. That's why I went over there just now. I don't want to do anything definite about buying it until Daisy has a chance to look the place over and decide if she wants to live there."

Slowly I sat up. My left shoulder ached like mad. My face was wet with tears.

I was, clearly and indisputably, an imbecile.

"Better now?" asked Sam almost as if he feared my answer.

I wanted to disappear into the sofa cushions and never come out again. I'd seldom in my life felt so ridiculous.

After another several snuffles and a few more tears, I blubbered, "I-I'm sorry, Sam."

"That's all right, love. It's nice to know you care." After a moment's hesitation, he added, as if he weren't quite sure, "I think."

Very well. I started crying again. "I-I feel s-s-so stupid!"

"You're in pain, Daisy. That makes people nuts sometimes. Remember how weird I was after I got shot?"

"I'm not weird!"

"Of course you're not," Sam said in a rush.

"Nope. Not at all," said Pa, likewise afflicted.

"Oh, Daisy, how can you be so silly?" asked Ma, who evidently didn't give a care if she hurt my feelings. I wouldn't have, either, in her position. I'd been not merely weird, but probably maniacal, as well.

"I-I don't know," I admitted. "I g-guess I feel and look so awful, I can't imagine anyone wanting me. Especially after that stupid scene."

Spike, knowing when his human needed canine care, licked my chin and gave me a tentative wag. I would have hugged him to my bosom, but I could only use one arm, and that one only slightly. I did, however, recommence sniveling.

Therefore, I felt even stupider than I had before.

As tenderly as he could, Sam said, "Tell you what, sweetheart. Tomorrow, we'll dust off Billy's old wheelchair, and I'll push you over to Mrs. Killebrew's house. We can go through it, and you can decide if you'd like to live there. Mr. Eric Killebrew—Mrs. Killebrew's oldest son —and I have worked out all the details. All we need is your approval. Or disapproval, if you don't like the idea."

"Oh, Sam!" I warbled, my emotions tumbling over each other in the chaotic havoc remaining of my innards. "I've always loved that house!"

"You have?" He sounded surprised and pleased. "That's...That makes me feel good. I wasn't sure you'd like living across the street from this house." I felt his neck snap as he lifted it to peer at my parents. "Not that we don't want to live near to you folks, especially since my job entails odd hours and so forth."

"We'd love it," said Ma.

I glanced up from my hanky, since her voice had sounded suspi-ciously watery. Sure enough, she had tears in her eyes. I held out her formerly pristine hanky, but she shook her head. "That's all right, dear. I'll get a clean one from my drawer."

I eyed the sopping mess I'd made of her hanky and didn't blame her.

Pa pulled up a chair and plunked himself down into it. "When did you get the idea to buy Mrs. Killebrew's place, Sam?"

"It was an accident, really. I was standing on line at the canteen at the station a while back, and Eric Killebrew—he's Judge Wilbur's clerk in the district court, courtroom four—asked me if I was the fellow he'd seen visiting your house so often. So we got to chatting, and he told me his mother wanted to sell the family home and come to live with him—Eric—and his family in Los Angeles. Since Mr. Killebrew passed on, she doesn't have any other family nearby, and I guess she's finding that house a little too much to take care of on her own."

"My goodness, that was a lucky accidental meeting," said Pa, smiling up a storm.

"What a wonderful idea!" said Ma, similarly animated. I suspect they were both attempting to make up for my disgraceful tantrum, which wasn't theirs to do, but mine.

"I'm so sorry, Sam," I said, feeling as though my heart—and what was left of my brain—were residing in the basement under the living room, probably smashed into tiny little pieces and having been kicked underneath the furnace. "I don't know what made me say such awful things to you."

"I don't either," said Sam, tentatively putting a hand on my left shoulder again. This time I didn't wrench it away from him. "And I'm sorry you were upset. I'm sure it's just the result of your injuries. Being in pain all the time can wreck a person's mood."

I don't know about anyone else in the house at that moment, but Sam's words instantly made me think of my late, beloved Billy. He'd been in pain all the time, and Sam was right. Billy's monumental pain and wrecked health had been responsible for his many foul moods and temper fits. And I'd tried so hard to understand and be patient—and had almost invariably failed. Naturally, that made me want to cry again. I resolutely sniffed back my tears.

"I'm going to try to walk over there with you. Is that all right, Sam? I don't want to get out Billy's wheelchair. It…it makes me feel bad."

"It made me feel better when I had to use it," said Sam with uncharacteristic candor. He wasn't generally so apt to admit he'd been a pain in the hind end when I'd nursed him.

"But my situation is different from Billy's. I only have minimal injuries that will get better in a couple of weeks."

Boy, it hurt to admit that! Both my Billy and my Sam had been much more grievously injured than I. Of course, they'd both had fits and tantrums, too, so maybe Sam was right. Fits and tantrums went with the recuperative territory.

He squeezed my shoulder—gently—and said, "It's all right, Daisy. We all understand. You're hurting. But I do hope you like the house."

"I'm sure I will." I'd almost stopped snuffling, although I now sounded as if I had a fierce cold in my head, and my nose would probably never become un-stuffed. And I didn't even want to think about my puffy red eyes. "What about that darling little court on South Los Robles where you live now?" I asked Sam.

After peering at me as if I were nuts for a second or two, Sam said, "I gave notice to my landlady."

"I'll bet she's sorry to lose you."

"Yes," said Sam with a little sigh. "She cried. I felt like a louse."

"Aw," I said, touched. "That's so sweet."

"Yes, well, she didn't think so. But I expect she'll get over it. I told her I'd visit from time to time."

"That's so nice of you." I took another swipe at my nose with my soggy hanky, my heart having gone all mushy and sentimental.

"And you can still dine with us!" said Ma, as if she'd just recalled this most significant fact.

Being able to eat Vi's cooking was about the first thing I'd thought of when Sam had plunked his plan in my lap. Which pretty much shows you where my brain resided most of the time—in my stomach. Then again, the notion of having to cook meals for Sam and myself had been worrying me a whole lot in recent months. As I've mentioned often already, I couldn't cook. Anything. Boiling water presented a challenge.

"That's probably the main reason Sam wants to buy the place," I said, trying to be funny.

"It is," said Sam, winning himself a soft smack from me—but he also got a giggle, so it was all right.

After they'd evidently decided I was over my fit of the dismals, Ma and Pa bade Sam and me a good-night, and wandered off to their bedroom. Vi had gone upstairs to her room not long after we'd finished dining.

We sat in silence for a few minutes. Then I asked Sam a question. I asked it tentatively, because I wasn't sure I should ask it at all—but I really wanted to know the answer.

"Um, Sam?"

"Yes, Daisy?"

"Um...I probably shouldn't ask this."

"You shouldn't ask what?"

"Well...Isn't Mrs. Killebrew's house kind of expensive?"

"Expensive?" He frowned at me. "No. Why?"

"Really? I'm glad to hear it. I don't want you to go broke housing us."

"Daisy, we don't have to worry about money."

"Well, I *don't* worry about money. Not normally. I mean…Um…I didn't think policemen could afford to buy homes in Pasadena. I read in the *Star News* that most of the officers in the PPD live outside the city limits, because Pasadena is…well, so snooty. And expensive. I mean, I make lots of money as a spiritualist-medium, but I didn't think—"

"Sweetheart, I don't have to live on my police salary."

I think my mouth fell open, although I couldn't find words in it anywhere. I clacked my teeth together and managed to say, "Oh?"

"Nope. I'm a wealthy man, believe it or not."

"Really?"

"Really."

"How'd that happen?"

"I own a chain of jewelry stores in New York City with my father. He's the mastermind and genius behind the design of the jewelry. I'm the money man. I've always been good with money, both the making of it and the keeping of it."

"Really?"

"Really."

For some reason, Sam's news bothered me. "You know, Sam, I understand Italians have formed a bunch of gangs in New York, Chicago and places like that and run illegal liquor. Are you sure you didn't get your money that way?"

With a glare that would have made me run away if I were able, Sam said, "Are you serious? Do you *honestly* think I have any association *at all* with a bunch of murdering bootleggers?"

"Well…Not really, but you know, you're Italian and…" My words trickled to a stop.

Sam continued to glower at me.

"Um…I'm sorry, Sam."

"I should hope to hell you *are* sorry! You have no idea how hard it is to get a good business established and keep it going. And did you really, for one minute, think I'd get involved with murdering crooks? I'm a *policeman*, dammit!"

"Um...I...guess not."

"You *guess* not?" Sam stood and stamped around the living room for a few seconds. Spike watched him, worried. So did I, and I worried too.

"I truly am sorry, Sam. It's just that I had no idea."

"But you jumped to the conclusion that, because I don't have to live on my policeman's salary, I'm a damned *bootlegger*?"

"No," I said in a voice that was as small as I could make it.

Pa entered the living room, his robe on, and gazed upon us with concern. "What's going on in here?" he asked.

"I told Daisy about the jewelry-store chain in New York, and she thinks I'm involved with bootleggers!" Sam told Pa.

"She *what*?" Pa, plainly shocked, looked from Sam to me. "Whatever gave you that idea, Daisy?"

"Well, nothing. I mean, I don't genuinely think Sam has anything to do with bootleggers, but I didn't know he had a lot of money either." As you can imagine, I was feeling stupider and stupider as the seconds ticked past.

"Good Lord, Daisy," said my father. "Sam showed me detailed reports of his financial status when he asked me if I'd give the two of you my blessing on your nuptials."

"He did?"

"He did."

"When? Why didn't I know about this?"

"Daisy," said Sam in his "patient" voice, which drove me nuts, "it's a time-honored tradition for a man to ask the father of his intended for his blessing."

"But it's 1925!"

"What's 1925 have to do with it?" asked Pa.

"Anyhow, this happened in 1923," said Sam, his voice more dry than patient.

"Nobody told me," I said, my voice having gone tiny again.

"Good Lord, Daisy." Glancing from me to my betrothed, Pa said, "We didn't raise her like that. Honestly, Sam. But she's always had quite an imagination."

"I guess so," said Sam, not noticeably appeased.

"I'm sorry!" I said, a little louder. "If anyone had bothered to *tell* me about your big bucks, I'd never even have thought about bootleggers!"

Both my father and Sam stared at me for several seconds. Then Sam heaved a gigantic sigh and sat next to me on the sofa again. Pa walked back up the hall, shaking his head.

"I'm sorry, Sam," I said for the I don't know how manyth time. "I just didn't know, was all."

After a few fraught seconds, Sam seemed to lose his anger. Rather, he grinned and said, "Didn't want you marrying me for my money."

"But you don't mind marrying me because of my aunt's cooking?"

"Well, sure. But that's a whole 'nother thing. I mean, money is nice to have, but food is essential," Sam said.

That put the final end to my bad mood. I laughed until I almost cried again.

NINE

The following day, Sam drove his big black Hudson up to the curb in front of our house at half past twelve. We'd agreed on this time as it was during his luncheon break. It was also late enough in the day so that, even in my ailing state, I should be up, if not about a whole lot.

In truth, I felt the least little bit better that morning than I had the day before. I think having Sam clear up my insane misunderstanding about his visit to the Killebrew house, not to mention his admission that he had lots of money, had helped heal my innards as well as my outards. I don't think that's a word, but who cares?

Oddly enough, even before Sam showed up at the door—in fact, quite a long time before—Spike had started scratching at it, as if he *really* wanted to go outside and see what was going on in the wide world of Pasadena.

When I peeked out the front window, I told him, "Gee, Spike, nothing's happening out there. Samson's not even there. At least I don't see him anywhere." Samson the cat belonged to the Wilsons, and he sometimes liked to lounge on our front porch in order to drive Spike nuts. "I know you like Sam, but hold your horses, all right? He'll be here pretty soon."

Spike made it abundantly plain that he didn't *want* to hold his horses. His behavior seemed peculiar to me, as he'd been the most obedient dog in the known universe ever since he'd graduated first in his class at the Pasanita Dog Obedience Club two years prior.

When I heard Pa greet Sam in the driveway to the side of the house —he'd been tending the little flower bed there so our neighbors would have a nicer view than that of a mere driveway—I even had to nudge Spike in order for him to stop paying attention to the front door and hie himself to the side door. Spike greeted Sam with his accustomed vivacity…and then returned to the front door.

"What's up with him?" asked Sam, staring after Spike with some bemusement.

"Don't know. He's been hovering around the front door all morning. I almost had to drag him away from it in order to get him to say hey to you."

With a small frown, Sam said, "I know I usually come through the front door, but isn't that unusual behavior for Spike? Heck, he generally leaps all over folks who come to call, no matter which door they use."

Pa chuckled.

I said with a certain snap to my voice, "He leaps until I tell him not to, and then he desists. He is a most obedient hound."

"Yes, I know. I wasn't casting aspersions," said Sam, grinning at me. Then he tilted his head and surveyed me from tip to toe. How embarrassing. However, he said then, "You look better today, sweetheart. How do you feel?"

Because I wasn't absolutely sure how to answer that question, I first took stock of my various bodily ouches. After ruminating and flexing here and there, I said, "I think I'm getting better! Gee, I didn't think I'd ever get better. Especially after that scene I made yesterday." Then I turned around, trying to twirl—and yes, I know, that was a stupid thing to do—squealed, "Ow!" and would have fallen over a dining room chair had not Sam caught me.

"Careful there, Irene Castle. You aren't ready to dance just yet," Sam said, laughing. "Did you hurt anything? Pull off any scabs or anything?"

"No," I said, my voice a piteous squeak.

"Don't go jumping around yet, Daisy," Pa advised. "It's only the second week in January, and you have a couple of weeks of rest and recuperation to endure before you attempt leaping over chairs or waltzing."

"You're both right," I acknowledged, still feeling like an idiot. "But I actually *had* felt better. Until I attempted my twirl."

"Ah. That was supposed to be a twirl, was it?"

"Darn you, Sam Rotondo! You don't have to make fun of me!"

"I'm not making fun of you, sweetheart. I just don't want you overdoing." He glanced at the floor.

So did I. I had expected to see Spike there. I presume Sam had, too. As a rule, when folks came over, he danced at our feet, frolicking and happy, joyful that several of his humans had gathered together. He probably thought we got together just for him.

Not that day.

He wasn't there.

"What the heck?" Sam and I said together.

"He's at the front door," Pa said, sounding as baffled as Sam and I.

"Golly, I can't imagine why he's so enamored of the front door today," I said. "But let me get my hat, and then I'll be ready to go with you to Mrs. Killebrew's place, Sam."

"Need any help?"

"No, thanks. I laid everything out last night."

"Efficient," said he.

"Efficiency is one of my trademarks," I said, not really meaning it; although, now that I think about it, it kind of is. I was always prepared for whatever I anticipated the day would bring. Because I'd anticipated this particular day would bring a walk across the street on a brisk January day, I'd laid out a brown wool jersey skirt with an over-blouse of a lighter-weight cream-colored jersey. To complement this simple day wear, I aimed to wear the perfectly *gorgeous* cardigan sweater Flossie Buckingham had knitted and given me at Christmas. She'd used yarns of different colors, mostly brown, cream and tan, in an irregularly striped pattern. It might sound odd, but it was a simply smashing sweater and, while it would be perfect for a casual occasion, it was also *tres* fashionable.

My old brown cloche hat would keep my head warm on the trip

across the street. And, because I was unbalanced (so to speak) thanks to my left arm still being strapped to my side and my various bruises and bumps making me limp, I'd already tugged on a pair of black cotton stockings and my old—but fashionable—low-heeled and comfortable black walking shoes.

Nobody could *ever* say Daisy Gumm Majesty, spiritualist-medium to the elite of Pasadena and Altadena, was not dressed impeccably. Well, except when I was cleaning the house and doing laundry, but I'd bet even Queen Victoria had never worn her crown when she did laundry. Not that she'd ever had to do laundry, but...Oh, never mind. Heck, even when I did housework, I wore a decent day dress.

"Look what I brought you," said Sam when I emerged from my bedroom, my hat pinned to my hair and my sweater buttoned over my blouse.

And darned if he didn't dangle a beautiful Malacca cane before me, complete with a...I peered at it more closely. Then I gasped in surprise and delight. "Sam!" I squealed. "It's a *dachshund*!"

"It is," he said proudly. "Now not only do we have matching injuries, but we now have matching canes, only yours has a dachshund-head handle and mine has a horse's head."

I took the cane from him and clutched it to my bosom. "Oh, my goodness, where did you get it? I've never seen anything like it!"

"That's because it's the only one there is. I had it made for you at Arnold's Jewelry Store. Well, not the cane itself, but they crafted the head for me."

"Wow, that's one superior cane," said my father, looking as if he almost wished he limped so he could get a cane of his own. "And it'll help you keep your balance, too." He grabbed Sam's hand and wrung it. "Thanks for taking care of my girl, Sam"

"She's my girl, too, Joe," said Sam. "I don't want anything else to happen to her. At least not until after we're hitched. If we ever are," he added glumly.

The truth was that our engagement seemed to be dragging on quite a bit. If Sam hadn't been shot and if I hadn't been run into by a car, we might have been hitched already. But you never know what life is going to hurl at you—or hurl you into—so we were coping as best we could.

71

Except when I flew off the handle. Or when Sam got grumpy. I wasn't the only impediment to our nuptials, in other words.

"Thank you, Sam." Naturally, I'd had to grab my hanky and mop up the few tears that had spilled from my eyes, Sam's gesture having touched me so deeply.

And shoot. If he had enough money to get Arnold's Jewelers to fashion a special-edition dachshund-head handle for a cane, he really *must* have plenty of the green stuff to keep us in comfort. Don't tell anyone, but his revelation that he didn't have to depend on his police-department salary had done my mood a world of good. I hate to be thought materialistic, but...well...I guess I am. At least as much as most folks, anyway.

Hmm. Now that I knew we wouldn't be hurting for money, I'd have to have a chat with Sam about making regular donations to the Salvation Army. After all, two of our dear friends—well, *my* dear friends—headed the Pasadena chapter (or whatever you call it) of the Salvation Army. Not only that, but both Johnny and Flossie Buckingham had been of great service to me more than once. They'd also assisted the Pasadena Police Department. They deserved donations from us.

But never mind that. We were on our way to look through Mrs. Killebrew's house. We were going to see what well might become *our* house! This was exciting. If I were up to a celebratory leap or two, I'd probably have leapt, but I wasn't, so I didn't, my aborted twirl earlier having squelched any desire to perform further antics of a like nature.

The cane did help me walk to the front door, as it kept me quite well-balanced in spite of having the use of only one arm. "This was a brilliant idea of yours, Sam."

"Thanks. I know my cane helps me when I need it."

"I hope neither of you will need your canes much longer," said Pa, who accompanied us to the door.

You'd have thought Spike wanted to slither through the crack under the door, he'd pressed his nose so close to it. I shook my head. "What the heck is the matter with you today, Spike?"

He didn't answer, but he did look up at me eagerly, his tail wagging deliriously. He wanted to go outside; that much was obvious.

"All right, all right. Let's go then. But sit and stay and wait for your command." Spike understood sentences like that, and he sat.

But darned if he didn't break his training as soon as Sam opened the front door and before I'd given him the "Okay" command that was supposed to release him from durance vile. He scooted through the doorway as if his tail were on fire.

"Spike!" I hollered.

I took a step, intending to get my dog back, but Sam put a hand on my arm. "Wait, Daisy. Something's wrong."

"What?"

"Look. There's something wrong with the porch steps."

I looked. Spike, wagging his tail as if he were filled with the greatest joy a dachshund could experience on a front porch, had begun licking the porch steps!

"Joe, you'd better check it out. Neither Daisy nor I are very good at bending right now."

"Yeah," said my father, hurrying to Spike. As soon as he knelt beside the dog, I saw his nose wrinkle. "I'll be hornswoggled," said he, surprise writ large on his features and amazement in his voice.

"What is it?" I asked.

"It looks—and smells—as if someone's painted the porch steps with some kind of grease!" He grabbed Spike's collar and dragged him, protesting, back a step or two. Then he took another couple of sniffs and said, "Bacon grease, unless I miss my guess."

"Someone smeared *bacon* grease on our front porch steps?" I cried, flabbergasted.

"Yes, and you aren't to go near them until I clean them up," said Pa, both is face and voice grim.

"But...Oh, dear."

"Yes," said Sam. "I'll help you, Joe. Daisy, you go on in the house and keep Spike with you. We'd better check the side porch steps, too, and the back ones."

"But you just used the side steps a few minutes ago," I pointed out as I herded my hound inside the house. Spike wanted to be on the porch where the bacon grease resided.

"True. But I'm going to look at them anyway, and I also want to check the back steps before you go anywhere near them."

"Let me get a bucket of soapy water and some rags." Pa hurried off to the kitchen.

Spike still wanted to go outside.

"You mean...You think this was another attempt to hurt me?" I asked in a small voice.

"Yes," said Sam. No equivocation there. Just a plain old "Yes."

"That's...um...distressing," I said.

"Very," said Sam.

"Yes," said Pa. "It's very distressing, and it means whoever hit you with that car isn't through with you yet."

And if that wasn't a dismal thought, I didn't know what was.

However, when we finally made it to Mrs. Killebrew's house, she greeted us with tea, cookies and her son Eric, who seemed like a nice fellow. I do believe he'd already grown up and moved away by the time Billy, my folks, and I bought our bungalow across the street.

Then we were given a tour of the house and grounds. What a lovely home! Even the front porch was charming, with a low, white stucco fence enclosing it. It could be made inescapable (by Spike) if we closed the little wrought-iron gate. I could picture Sam, Spike and me sitting on the porch during warm summer evenings, watching the world go by. Not that a whole lot of the world walked down Marengo Avenue during the summer months. Or any other months, for that matter. Still, I loved the porch.

I don't know how long Mr. and Mrs. Killebrew had been married, but evidently Mr. Killebrew had built the house for his missus, and they'd lived in it all their married lives. The love they'd put into it showed in every carved newel post and mantelpiece. The little back house was just as charming, and a good deal smaller. Perfect for... well...a mother-in-law or someone like that. Although—please don't tell Sam I said this—I wouldn't really want his mother living there. She disapproved of me, which thought always made me sad.

I managed to walk upstairs on my own, holding tightly to the banister. The upstairs was every bit as charming as the downstairs.

"Peter loved carpentry," said Mrs. K, sniffling a little. "He was so good to us all."

"He was indeed," agreed Eric. "I miss Pa."

"Are you sure you want to sell the house?" I asked. "It's...it's so beautiful. And there's so much of you and your family...I don't know. Built into it, I guess I mean to say. I don't know how you can bear to part with it."

After heaving a sigh as big as Pasadena itself, Mrs. Killebrew said, "I'm sure. I'll always adore this home, but it has served its purpose, and now it's time for me to let it go. Eric and his family are well established in Los Angeles, Peter Junior is in Arcadia, and Gabriel is a Presbyterian minister in San Luis Obispo. Linda, Eric's eldest, is getting married soon—in June, in fact—and I do want to be present for that. She and John—John Culbertson, her intended—have built a gorgeous home in the city of Glendale. So I'm selling this one because the family no longer needs it. I hope it will serve another family as beautifully as it served us for all these years."

"And then Ma will come and live with us," said Eric with a loving look for his mother. "She doesn't need this big place to take care of."

"That's true," said Mrs. Killebrew with another sigh. "I'll miss it, but I won't miss cleaning and dusting it all the time. And the yard work is just too much for me these days. But I have the name of a wonderful gardener if you'd like it. He comes once a week to cut the grass and prune the bushes and does other things like that." She gave me a sympathetic look. "If you can afford to have a girl come in a couple of times a week, I think you should do it. This place has four bedrooms, a front parlor, a back parlor, a dining room, a kitchen, and two bathrooms. And then there's that little back cottage. Altogether, it's just too much for me."

It sounded as if it would be too much for me, too, but I wasn't about to admit it. I adored the place!

"We can get domestic help if we need it," said Sam as if that sounded like a good idea to him, too. "First we have to get Daisy healed."

"And you," I said.

"Ah, yes. Mother told me about your accident, Mrs. Majesty. And I understand your wound was sustained in the line of duty, wasn't it, Mr. Rotondo?"

"Yes. To both of those things," I said. "Only evidently, my accident wasn't an accident."

Eric's eyebrows lifted. "I beg your pardon?"

I glanced at Sam to see if he'd object to me telling the Killebrews our theory of the Daisy incident. He nodded his assent.

So I told mother and son someone had singled me out on purpose to smack me into that pepper tree on New Year's Day and then told them about the bacon-grease episode.

"Good Lord," said Eric.

Mrs. Killebrew's hand flew to her mouth. "My goodness! That's terrible!"

"Yes. Clearly I've offended someone really badly."

"That's no reason to…to…to…do that sort of thing!"

"No," said Sam. "It isn't. If you should notice any strangers in the neighborhood, please let one of us know."

"I certainly will," said Mrs. K.

"I'm going home again this afternoon," said Eric, "but I'll keep a watch out when I'm here."

"Thank you," said Sam.

"Yes," I said. "Thank you very much."

Mrs. Killebrew's brow wrinkled. "You know, Daisy, I did see something a little odd this morning."

I was all ears. "You did?"

"I didn't think much about it at the time, but it strikes me as strange now. I saw a young man carrying a paint bucket and a brush up the street, headed toward Colorado."

"What did he look like?" Sam wanted to know. He retrieved a pocket notebook and pencil from his pocket and poised the latter over the former.

"I didn't see him well. He wore a cloth cap and overalls, and he was carrying what looked like a paint bucket and a paint brush. He was on your side of the street, and you know how all those pepper trees hide people from view."

"Yes," I said.

"Did you notice the color of his hair or clothing or anything like that?" asked Sam.

"I...I think he had dark hair, and I think...Well, I'm not sure. He wore overalls, and I took him for a workman. A house painter or someone like that." She shook her head. "I wish I'd paid more attention, but you know, one doesn't stare at every passing stranger, even if they do appear...well, somewhat out of place, you know?"

"Will you give me a call if you see this fellow again?" I asked.

"Most certainly. I'll be happy to. I do hope you catch whoever's doing these awful things before anything worse happens to you, Daisy dear."

"Thank you, Mrs. Killebrew. And thank you for inviting us to see your wonderful home. I just love it, and I think Sam and I would be very happy here."

Sam nodded. "I do, too."

"That makes three of us," said Eric, smiling and rubbing his hands together. He really was pleasant fellow.

Sam said, "Let me get Daisy safely tucked in across the street, and then I'll come back over and sign the papers. Is that all right with you?"

"I'm so happy you and Daisy want the house, Mr. Rotondo!" said Mrs. Killebrew. "I always imagined Daisy living here with her husband, only I didn't imagine her husband would be you!"

As soon as she spoke her sentence, she blushed to the roots of her beautiful white hair and lifted her hand to her mouth, as if to stuff the words back into it.

We didn't mind. Both Sam and I laughed. After a shocked second or two, Eric joined us.

And we'd still get to eat Aunt Vi's meals! I tell you, life was good.

For the most part. There was still the teensy matter of someone wanting me dead.

TEN

Thus it was that a home for Sam and Daisy Rotondo, should the two ever marry and share a last name, was secured during the second week in January, 1925. I felt kind of like floating, but I could still barely walk.

By the time Thursday during my second week of captivity came around, I decided I might as well attend choir practice. My left arm remained strapped to my body, but I could probably get Lucille Zollinger to carry my hymnal and choir book for me. Or, heck, I could just sit with Sam in the sanctuary and listen to what the choir was going to sing for the next couple of weeks, although that seemed kind of like cheating.

You know, this is petty, but the main reason I wanted to go to choir practices was so I could show off my dandy new cane. I know, I know. But we all have our little—and sometimes not so little —vanities.

Vi fixed a wonderful meal for us, as usual, on Thursday evening. Because I was still unable to use my left arm, I attempted to help Ma with the dishes, but she did most of the work. Sam put all the pots and pans in their proper places—I directed this operation, since he didn't have first-hand knowledge of where our pots and pans resided.

After everything had been cleared up and we were in the living room, Pa said, "Want to play cards, Sam?"

Pa, Sam and Billy had loved playing gin rummy together. I felt ratty squelching my father's fun plans for the evening, but I did it anyway.

"Pa, would you mind if Sam took me to choir practice tonight? I haven't been since the New Year's Eve service, and that's been more than two weeks."

Sam and Pa glanced at each other. Sam lifted an eyebrow at my father.

"I mean, if you don't mind, Sam," I said in a rush, belatedly realizing he might have thoughts on the matter.

"It's all right with me, Daisy," said Pa. "As long as Sam doesn't mind. After all, you're making him work on an evening off." He said it with a grin, but his words made me feel guilty.

Turning to Sam, I said, "I'm sorry, Sam. I didn't even think about asking you before I offered your services for my pleasure. I'm not very nice sometimes, huh?"

"Oh, you're all right," said Sam, grinning in his turn. "I'd enjoy listening to the music, although I don't know how you're going to participate."

After taking short survey of my bodily parts, I said, "Yeah. I don't know, either. But I can...Well, I guess I can't very well hold my hymnal in one hand, huh?" Feeling defeated, I said, "Never mind. Next week will be fine, and I'll probably be able to use both arms by then."

"Nonsense. I'll take you," said Sam, rising from the sofa where he'd been sitting and holding my hand—which I thought was sweet of him. Holding my hand, I mean. Sam didn't generally relish overt displays of affection. He'd been displaying more of them since New Year's Day, however. "I like listening to the music. We can sit together and just enjoy it."

"Mr. Hostetter will probably try to persuade you to join the choir, you know," I reminded him. Sam possessed a truly spectacular bass voice, which he'd used to great effect when our church hosted a production of Gilbert and Sullivan's *The Mikado*. Sam had played Go-To, a noble lord of Titipu, the fictitious Japanese town in which the play takes place. I'd reluctantly agreed to play the role of Katisha, a horrible woman who was mean as a snake. Not that snakes are commonly mean. From everything I've ever read about them, snakes were docile unless provoked. Kind of like me (that's supposed to be a joke). Anyway, I discovered I *loved* playing nasty old Katisha. In my daily life and in my spiritualist-medium career, I'm always nice to people. It was fun being mean to people and not getting scolded for it.

"Yeah, I know," said Sam with a small smile. "I might just surprise the both of you one of these days and actually join the choir."

"Sam!" I cried, overjoyed. "Will you? Really?"

"Don't celebrate yet. My working hours are always iffy, and I'm not ready to join the choir yet, but I actually do like to sing."

"And you have *such* a splendid voice!" I trilled, ecstatic, although I'm not sure why. "Mr. Hostetter would absolutely *love* it if you'd join the choir. You'd be the star of the bass section!" Mr. Floy Hostetter had been the choir director of the First Methodist-Episcopal Church, which we Gumms and this Majesty attended, for ever since I could remember.

"Don't tell the other basses that," Sam advised wryly. "But yeah, I'll be happy to go to choir practice with you, sweetie."

"You'd probably better drink a spoonful of that morphine syrup before you go," said Pa.

That took the wind out of my sails. Not that they'd been flying very high to begin with. "Oh." I took a brief inventory of my injuries and sighed. "Yes, I suppose I'd better."

"I'll get it for you," said Pa.

He was a good as his word, and he came back into the living room with not only the medicine bottle and a spoon, but with a peppermint drop for me to suck after I'd swallowed the nasty stuff. "Thought you might need this, too," he said, grinning.

"You're so thoughtful, Pa."

"Yes, you are, Joe."

"Gotta take care of my girl," said Pa, and he administered the evil-tasting concoction. Then he stuck the peppermint drop in my mouth, and I commenced sucking on it.

After sucking for a second or two, I said, "Let me get my coat and hat, Sam, and I'll be with you…" I had been going to say "in a sec," but that would have been a lie. "I'll be with you as soon as I can be."

Both Sam and Pa laughed. Ma, who had been reading *A Passage to India*, by a British gent named Mr. E.M. Forster, glanced up and looked as if she were confused. "What's going on?" she asked.

"Sam's taking me to choir practice," I told her.

"Oh. How nice," said she, and went back to reading.

I'd read *A Passage to India* a month or so before getting hit by that wretched car, and I'd kind of liked it. It wasn't a detective novel, which is my preferred reading material, but it had been interesting as it was set in India and all that. What I mainly learned from reading the book was that the class system in India is more clearly defined and openly accepted than the class system in the United States of America, which isn't supposed to have one. But we do. Not that I'm saying a class system is necessarily a bad thing; I'm just saying it might be worthwhile to be realistic about life in the good old US of A once in a while. Oh, never mind.

So I got my hat and coat and Sam helped me on with same. He buttoned the top button of my coat over my left arm, since my left arm couldn't go *in* the coat sleeve. This injury thing was becoming more and more bothersome as the days passed.

However, I anticipated having a good time at choir practice, and I wasn't disappointed. In the beginning, at least. The first person who noticed when Sam and I limped into the sanctuary—we didn't go through the choir room, since I wasn't there to sing—was Lucille Zollinger. Sam and I were heading to the first row of pews when I heard a shriek. Shrieking was uncommon in church, and this one gave me quite a start.

"Daisy!"

After nearly fainting from fright—guess I was a little nervous in those days—I sort of fell onto the hard pew and glanced up to see Lucy barreling down the chancel steps and running over to me.

"Oh, Daisy, how *are* you?" She reached out to hug me, but I fended her off with my cane. I hadn't until that moment realized how useful canes could be, even when you didn't need them for walking.

"I appreciate you wanting to hug me, Lucy, but I'm a little too banged up for that."

"Oh, I know!" She sat beside me and reached for my hand. Since it was my right hand, I allowed this. "I'm so sorry! I heard someone hit you on *purpose*! How terrible for you!"

"It wasn't any fun," I admitted.

She turned to Sam. "But how nice of you to bring Daisy to see us, Detective Rotondo. We were wondering when Daisy would be rejoining us."

"It probably won't be for another couple of weeks," said Sam in his stoical policeman's voice. "She still has a lot of healing to do."

"I should say so!"

By this time, everyone else who'd showed up for choir practice had begun tramping down the chancel steps and over to me. Mr. Hostetter led the bunch, smiling as if he were so pleased, he could hardly stand it.

"Mrs. Majesty! We've missed you terribly! I do hope you'll be able to come back to us soon."

Naturally, his words made me feel guilty. "I'll be back as soon as I can be. Promise," I said to him, smiling and shaking his hand, which he'd held out. I think that's kind of a breach of etiquette—isn't the woman supposed to hold her hand out to the man first? Oh, well, it doesn't matter.

"She has a good deal of healing to do first," Sam told Mr. Hostetter in his most detectival tone. Mr. Hostetter backed up a step. I was impressed with my fiancé. Mr. Hostetter was used to running things and giving orders; he wasn't accustomed to taking them.

"It's *wonderful* to see you, Daisy," said Mrs. Fleming, our organist. "We need you back as soon as you can come, so you and Lucy can sing more duets."

"Thank you, Mrs. Fleming. I need to write about a thousand thank-you notes before I show my face anywhere else, I fear."

"Don't worry about thank-you notes!" said Lucy. "For heaven's sake, it looks as if you can't even use one of your arms!"

"I can't. My left shoulder was dislocated. I kind of wobble when I walk. But Sam gave me this beautiful cane!" I said, lifting and brandishing same. The sanctuary filled with ooohs and aaahs for a second or two.

Lucy, clutching her clasped hands to her meager bosom, said, "Oh, my! Is that a dachshund head on the handle?"

"Yes." I gave Sam a loving look. He'd commenced scowling at nothing in particular. "Sam had it made especially for me."

"How charming." Lucy said, and she sniffled. Even had to lift a finger to her eye to dab away a tear.

"Where in the world did you find a dachshund's-head cane?" Mrs. Fleming wanted to know.

Since Sam was busy scrutinizing the sanctuary and didn't seem inclined to respond, I did it for him. "I don't know where he got the cane part, but he had Arnold's Jewelers craft the dachshund's head."

"It's delightful," said Mrs. Fleming. "And so perfect for you."

I think that was meant as a compliment.

"Very nice," said Mr. Hostetter, daring to inch closer to us.

Sam continued glowering hither and yon, studying the sanctuary as if he suspected ex-Kaiser Wilhelm of hiding out in one of the pews. I'd have kicked him if I'd been in full possession of all my bodily parts. There was no reason for him to have gone all policemanly at church, of all places! The Voodoo juju I always wore steamed up a little. Probably because Sam was being such a pill.

If I hadn't turned my head at that moment in order to give Sam the stink-eye, the knife would have sliced clean through my throat from front to back. Instead, it hit with a sharp *crack* into the back of the pew and stuck there, quivering.

ELEVEN

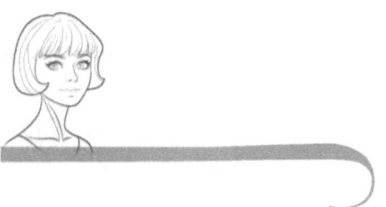

Everyone except Sam screamed. I believe even the men screamed. Well, and I didn't scream, either, but that's because I was in a state of stunned shock. I flattened my right hand over my warm juju, which lay near my heart—and *that* pounded like a drum in a downtown Los Angeles speakeasy.

Sam leaped out of his seat and ran as if the devil pursued him to the door from which the knife must have been thrown. That door led to a small side yard in our church that wasn't used for much except maybe sipping lemonade on warm days after Sunday services, but it was pretty and was home to lots of rosebushes, none of which flowered on this chilly January evening.

I don't think Sam considered his wounded thigh as he tore out the door and into the side yard. He didn't even bother picking up his cane!

Confusion reigned for several seconds. I wanted to jump up and rush to see what Sam was doing outside, but I was unable to jump up or rush anywhere at all just then.

"Good Lord!" Mr. Hostetter said at last. He reached for the knife.

"*Don't touch it!*" I screeched at him. His hand flew away from the knife as if I'd slapped it.

Heart thundering and nerves a-tingle, I said, "It might have fingerprints on it. Don't put yours on it, too, or we may never know who's trying to kill me."

"Fingerprints? Fingerprints! In *our church*? *Kill* you!" Mr. Hostetter exclaimed, as if the mere notion of fingerprints and people being killed in church was sacrilegious. Huh. A couple of years ago, two people had dropped dead—one of them via murder—during two separate communion services. I didn't appreciate Mr. Hostetter's attitude.

"Good heavens!"

"Mercy sakes!"

"My land!"

I can't remember all the expressions people spouted during the aftermath of this latest attempt to put an end to my short life, but those are an example. Somebody—I can't remember who it was—fainted.

And then, as if life weren't awful enough, Miss Betsy Powell, who must have entered the sanctuary right before whoever it was threw the knife at me, started screaming. I swear to God, that woman had the loudest, most piercing scream I've ever heard in my life. I wanted to jump up and holler at her but, as mentioned above, I couldn't jump. Heck, I could barely move.

However, I *could* sort of stand up and, with the help of my charming new cane, and limp to the side door. I heard, over the din inside the sanctuary, a disturbance going on outside.

"Who the devil are *you!*" I heard Sam holler.

"God damned son of a bitch!" a rusty masculine voice hollered back, shocking me. I expect the words shocked the rest of the church-goers, too, although I didn't bother to look. Betsy Powell continued to scream, and I wished somebody would slap her across the face. I'd wanted to do that several times in past years. The rusty voice continued, "Leave go that sumbitch, dammit! He's mine!"

"He's not yours," growled Sam. The voices were coming closer to the door from which he'd exited. "He's my nephew, and he just threw a knife at my fiancé."

"Well, dammit, I got a dodger on 'im! He's mine! The money's mine, anyways."

"Come in here. Let's get this sorted out."

"Is that there a church?" Rusty Voice sounded as if he'd rather not enter a church. "Shit."

"Yes, it is. Get in here."

"Dammit! I claim the bounty on that curly wolf!"

I'm not sure about anyone else, but my own eyes felt as if they were about as wide as they'd ever been. Curly wolf? What in the world was a curly wolf, and what did one have to do with Sam's nephew and that cursed knife?

"Goodness sakes, what's going on out there?" Lucy Zollinger asked. Considerably taller than I, she had one hand on my shoulder, another on the door jamb, and she peered out into the darkness, squinting. Of course, she wasn't wearing her cheaters, so I don't know how much she'd have been able to see, even if a light was on out there.

"I'm not sure," said I.

Betsy Powell screamed again, and my short temper flared. "Will someone please shut that woman *up!*"

I heard a sharp *smack*, and Miss Powell said, "Oh!" Then I heard a thump. I figured she'd probably fainted from the shock of being slapped, but I didn't take time to look. She shut up, and that's what mattered.

"Let me turn on the yard light," said Mr. Hostetter, who went to a bank of switches on the wall next to where the choir sat on the chancel.

And there was light! What's more, it illuminated a most interesting scene.

Sam Rotondo and an old man who looked as if he'd been ridden hard and hung up wet—my father used to say that, and the expression has always tickled me—held an arm each. Both arms belonged to Sam's no-good nephew, Francis Pagano, who was *supposed* to be working in his Uncle Salvatore's Italian restaurant in New York City. Frank's head sagged on his neck, and he kind of hung between the two large men. I think he was unconscious.

"Is that *Frank?*" I asked of my beloved, astonished.

"One and the same," said Sam, growling mightily. His limp was pretty heavy. I guess his left leg wasn't quite up to running yet.

"He's mine, dammit!" said Rusty Voice.

Lucy, frightened by the spectacle before her, backed up, her hand over her mouth. Can't say as I blamed her. Sam is a large man and rather obelisk-like in appearance until one gets to know him. Whoever Rusty Voice was, he was as tall as Sam, but thinner, extremely rugged-looking, and he limped along with the help of one of his own legs and a wooden stump in place of the other. I presume he'd had two func-tioning legs at one time, but one of them had gone missing.

"What's going on here?"

Mr. Hostetter, evidently having got his own fear under control and strutting like a pouter pigeon, his chest bulging out and his face a mask of outrage, marched up to Sam, Rusty Voice and Frank.

I put a soothing hand on his arm. "It's all right, Mr. Hostetter. I think it will be better if we let Sam handle this." I turned my head and bellowed into the sanctuary, "*Don't anybody touch that knife!*" With a smile for Mr. Hostetter, I added, "You'd probably be better off starting choir practice. I'll let you know what this is all about as soon as I know myself."

"Good idea," said Sam, his voice gruff.

"Hell," said Rusty Voice.

"And *you!*" I said, stabbing Rusty Voice in the chest with my forefin-ger, "stop swearing! You're in a church of God."

He jerked, frowned at me, then grumbled, "Aw, hell."

"Why don't you lug Frank to the back of the sanctuary, Sam? Want me to do anything with the knife?"

"Yeah. This fellow and I will take him to the back. Leave the knife be for right now. I'm going to call a couple of uniforms in."

"Tarnation! That's my find, cuss you!" Rusty Voice said. At least he didn't quite swear.

"You know where the minister's office is, right?" asked Sam of me, ignoring RV.

"Yes. Want me to call the station?"

"Yeah. No. Wait. Get someone else to do it. You can't move well enough yet. But have someone see if they can get a couple of uniforms out here, and have them hurry. This is getting complicated."

"Shee-oot," said Rusty Voice.

I turned, balancing on my cane—golly, that thing was useful!—and called, "Lucy, will you come here for a second?"

Mr. Hostetter frowned at me, and I told him, "It'll just be for a minute. We need to call the police station."

"Cripes," said RV.

"Very well," said Mr. Hostetter, willing to do his duty but not liking it much.

Lucy obediently trotted to the back of the sanctuary, where Sam and the other man had deposited Frank, whose head still drooped, and who still seemed to be unaware of his surroundings.

"Yes, Daisy?" she asked shyly, shooting terrified glances at the elderly stranger. As if to prove her trepidation was not without foundation, the man gave her one of the more hideous frowns I'd ever seen. Lucy jumped a little.

"Could you please call the Pasadena Police Department for us? Use Pastor Smith's office, if you will. It has a telephone. Ask for two uniforms to come to the church as soon as they can get here, please."

"Oh. Well, yes, I can do that," Lucy said uncertainly. She kept shooting scared glances at RV. Honestly, I didn't blame her. He looked like something out of a wild-west show or maybe a wanted poster on a post-office wall in 1880 or thereabouts.

And that reminded me of something else I needed to do. Turning to Rusty Voice myself, I said, "Just precisely who are you, sir? My name is Daisy Majesty. This"—I pointed at Sam—"is my fiancé, Detective Sam Rotondo, and this"—I pointed at Lucy—"is Mrs. Albert Zollinger. What is your name?"

"What the hell's it to you?" he snarled.

"I told you to stop swearing in my church," I said, my words spaced far apart so as to make them clearly heard, even to the hardest of hearing, which this guy might have been. He was sure old enough. At least he looked old. And used up. "And I want to know whom to thank for catching the fellow who threw that knife at me." There. If that didn't soften him up, he was un-softenable. Or maybe not, but it couldn't hurt to be nice, could it?

"Name's Lou Prophet," he said as if he didn't want to admit it.

"Thank you, Mr. Prophet," I said. I smiled kindly at him. He curled his lip at me. Giving up on him, I turned back to Lucy. "Will you do that, please, Lucy?"

"Yes. Of course." And, with one last frightened glance back at Mr. Lou Prophet—and why did that name ring a bell?—Lucy loped off.

Something struck me as an afterthought, and I yelled to Lucy, "And please bring us a glass of water!"

"All right!" she didn't yell. Lucy was one-hundred percent lady, unlike some of us.

"Now," I said, turning back to the three men in the pew. "Was it Frank who threw that knife at me?"

"Yeah," said Lou Prophet.

"I didn't see him do it," said Sam, as if he hated admitting it. "But I guess he did. When I got outside, Frank was trying to climb the back fence, and this yahoo was battering him with this empty bottle of hooch." He brandished the bottle.

"*What?*" Mr. Prophet hollered. He yanked the bottle, which was square and quite heavy-looking, from Sam's hands, squinted at it, then turned it upside down. Nothing dripped out. "Well, God damn. That was some good tangleleg."

Deciding to ignore his language—and to ask him what the heck tangleleg was later—I eyed Mr. Prophet with some approval. "Did you really batter Frank? Thank you!"

Sam rolled his eyes. He did that a lot when he was around me.

"The bounty's mine," said Mr. Prophet by way of a you're-welcome. He handed the empty bottle back to Sam, who stowed it on the pew a few feet away from us. Guess he didn't want Mr. Prophet absconding with it. I got the feeling Mr. Prophet didn't know he'd managed to pour the booze on Frank when he went about quelling him, and was disappointed at having learned he had.

"What bounty?" I asked, curious.

"Got me this here dodger," Prophet said, eyeing the empty bottle with the same wrath an Old Testament prophet might have heaped upon a congregation he'd discovered worshiping a golden calf. Contorting his long, lean body, he reached into the back pocket of some kind of coat—I'd never seen its like among my friends in Pasadena—and hauled out a folded paper. He handed it to me, and I opened it.

"Well, for goodness' sake!" I said after reading what turned out to be a "wanted" poster. It looked as if it had been tacked up in a post office somewhere. Quite a long time ago, to judge by its yellowish properties. "Will you look at this, Sam! Seems as though your nephew has graduated to bigger stuff than numbers running."

"Criminy. Why am I not surprised?" Sam took the poster from my hand and squinted at it. Then he reached into his coat's front pocket, pulled out his reading glasses, propped them on his nose and read. "The sorry son of a—"

"You're in church, Sam," I reminded him.

"Shee-oot," he said, just as Mr. Prophet had earlier. "Yeah, I know. Poor Renata."

"Who the hell…Uh, who's Renata? And what kinda name is Roton-do?" asked Mr. Prophet.

"Renata is Sam's sister. Sam's family is Italian. Renata lives in New York City, and this idiot"—I slapped Frank upside the head before Sam could do it for me—"is her son. He's also Sam's nephew."

"Great kin ya got," said Prophet.

"Yeah. I know," said Sam.

"The bounty's mine," Prophet said again, as if it were the refrain from a hymn I didn't know.

Since Sam was no longer reading the poster, I took it and peered at it again. The light wasn't any too good at the back of the sanctuary, but I could make out the words. Under the large word WANTED, printed in capital letters, was a photograph of Frank Pagano, greasy hair slicked back and looking like a hoodlum. Then came the words, "Robbery, Escape." And then there was a big $500 printed at the bottom of the page.

I gazed at the dozing Frank, who had begun to groan a bit and move his legs.

"Five hundred bucks, eh? I don't think you're worth two cents," I told Frank.

"Hey!" said Lou Prophet. "That five hundred is mine."

"Fine with me," I said. I folded the poster up and was about to hand it to Prophet. After a second thought, I asked Sam, "May I give it back to Mr. Prophet, Sam?"

"Sure. We'll have it on file at the department."

So I handed Prophet the poster, he refolded it and stuck it in the same back pocket from whence he'd fetched it.

"I caught 'im," said Prophet, as if to cement the reason for his being the proper recipient of the $500 offered for Frank's capture. At least the poster hadn't added the dread words, "Dead or Alive".

With another eye-roll, Sam said, "Yes, yes. We all agree you caught him. However, we now have to take care of the legal processing of the cook. And we'll have to file new charges. I think attempted murder would be appropriate." His lips curled into a small, deadly looking grin.

"Uncle Sam?" came a croaky voice from the vicinity of Frank Pagano's face.

I frowned at Frank. "What a worthless piece of garbage *you* turned out to be," I told him. I'm not often that brutally honest with people, but that nincompoop *did* just try to kill me!

"Don't 'Uncle Sam' me, Francis Pagano," Sam said, sounding ferocious, even though he didn't raise his voice.

"Did you throw that knife at me, Frank?" I demanded.

"D-Daisy?" Frank stuttered. He blinked his eyes as if he couldn't get them to focus very well.

"It's *Missus Majesty* to you, young man." I wrinkled my nose. "You smell horrible, too," I told him, both because it was the truth and because I wanted him to know how much I loathed him.

"That's 'cause I spilled all that good rye on him," said Lou Prophet. He looked as if he wanted to spit on the floor, but remembered where he was and only growled, "Hell."

Sam chuckled.

I didn't. "I asked you not to swear in my church, Mr. Prophet."

"Yeah, yeah. I wasted good tangleleg on that sumbitch."

I guess he'd just explained what tanglelag was: rye whiskey. "That last word—I mean those last words—count as swearing," I told Prophet in a stern voice. He eyed me with what I could only call disdain.

"Well, he had a head start," said Prophet sulkily.

"What do you mean, he had a head start?" I asked.

"He was already kinda drunk."

"Do you mean to tell me you threw that knife at me while you were *drunk*?" I asked Frank, outraged. At the same time I was kind of impressed. I'd never touched alcohol in my life, but my understanding was that it impaired the body's ability to see, think and walk straight. If Frank had been sober when he'd thrown that knife, I'd probably have been dead for several minutes by then.

And the thought of *that* made me so mad, I wanted to spit railroad spikes and batter Frank Pagano about the head and shoulders. Therefore, and before anyone could stop me, I whacked him with my dachshund-head cane. Right on top of his head. *With* the pointy nose of dachshund. Then I checked to make sure I hadn't dented the dachshund. When I examined it closely, it looked fine.

Frank, on the other hand, covered his head with his hands and said, "*Ow!*"

"Cut it out, Daisy," Sam warned me. "We'll deal with him at the station."

"I'd like to deal with him right here and now," I said, feeling vicious. "I want to break that bottle and stab him with it."

"Hey, girlie, you ain't so bad," said Prophet.

When I looked at him, I saw him grinning and could kind of make out remnants of the handsome man he must once have been. Nevertheless, because I didn't appreciate his nonchalance under the circumstances, I sniffed.

Lucy came back. She gave me the glass of water, which I instantly threw into Frank Pagano's face.

Frank said, "Hey!"

I didn't even hand him my hanky with which to dry his face. Lou Prophet gave a grainy chuckle.

Lucy backed up until she stood in the aisle at the end of our pew. I figured she didn't dare come any closer. She said, "I called the police station as you asked, and two uniformed officers will be here shortly. I told them to come through the side entrance, since the front door is locked."

"Thank you, Lucy."

"You're welcome." She stood there staring at the four of us for a moment before she took off, walking as fast as she could, back to the choir's chairs on the chancel.

The choir, by the way, was practicing "Christ, Whose Glory Fills the

Skies" in honor of Epiphany, which falls on January sixth. I loved the hymn, which owed its words to Charles Wesley, one of our glorious founders—well, if you're a Methodist, anyway—and was sorry I wouldn't be singing it. By the way, I've never been quite sure what Epiphany meant, but I think it was the day Jesus was recognized as the Christ, if that makes any sense. I'm sure it only even kind of makes sense to people who practice Christianity. I can't imagine why, say, a Hindu or a Buddhist would need to know that. Or a Jew or a Muslim, for that matter.

Oh, never mind.

TWELVE

By the time Frank Pagano was fully awake—or as awake as he ever got, which wasn't very—two uniformed policemen from the Pasadena Police Department had shown up. I recognized them both from times past: Officer Doan and Officer Oversloot. Officer Doan was all right in my books. Officer Oversloot had been a bully to me once right after Sam had been shot, and I still held it against him. He didn't know that, so I suppose it didn't matter.

Sam took Oversloot in hand and led him to the front pew, where the knife still stuck. He left Doan to guard Frank. Officer Oversloot carefully pulled out the knife and put it in a paper bag. He used some kind of grippers to get the knife unstuck, and it seemed to be kind of hard to do and required a lot of tugging. In other words, it had struck the pew with great force. I glared at Frank Pagano.

"If you weren't drunk, that knife would probably be in me," I growled.

He gave me a glassy-eyed glare. "Yeah, well, I wish it was."

This time it was Lou Prophet who smacked him upside the head. I smiled at him in appreciation. He grinned back. His teeth resembled a broken picket fence.

"Hey," said Frank.

"What you got against this pretty lady, old son?" Prophet asked Frank.

It seemed to me Frank had a difficult time focusing his eyes. His struggle might have been due to drink or the several head-whacks he'd received since he'd been hauled into the church. I neither knew nor cared.

When he turned those watery orbs Prophet's way, he said, "What's it t'you?"

Pressing his wooden stump on the toe of Frank's right shoe, Prophet said, "Oh, you don't wanna be talkin' to me that way, old son. I'm bigger'n older'n meaner'n and a whole lot smarter'n you."

"Huh," said Frank. Then he said, "Ow!"

"Answer my question, boy," said Prophet.

"What question?" Frank whined. "Ow! Quit it!"

It was I who smacked Frank this time. I hissed, "Keep your voice down, you pig! You're in church."

"Church?" Frank wobbled his head to look around. "This ain't a church. It's got no cruce'fix."

"Eh?" said Prophet.

"Frank calls himself a Roman Catholic," I told Prophet. "He doesn't think a church is a church unless it has a depiction of Jesus nailed to the cross hanging on the wall. We Methodists prefer the risen Christ in our depiction of crosses."

Prophet's nose wrinkled as if my words hadn't made sense to him. Perhaps the distinction between a cross and a crucifix doesn't matter to some people. How odd. Or maybe it isn't. Once more, I'd wager a Buddhist or a Hindu wouldn't care. Or, again, a Jew or a Muslim.

"Anyway, Frank doesn't want Detective Rotondo to marry me because I'm a Methodist and not a Roman Catholic."

"That's one of the stupidest reasons I've ever heard for not marryin' someone," said Prophet. I was beginning to like the guy.

"S'true!" Frank whined. "Uncle Sammy can't marry you," he said to me. "The whole family's against it. You ain't Cath'lic, and you ain't Italian."

"Most people aren't," I told him frostily.

"She's got a point there, old son," said Prophet.

"Why you callin' me son?" asked Frank.

Prophet lifted his wooden peg and slammed it down on Frank's toes once more. Frank said, "Ow!"

"I don't like fellers who're mean to ladies, and this here's a lady," said Prophet.

I think I blushed. I know; how silly of me.

"Lady? Her? She's marryin' my Uncle Sammy, an' she ain't even Italian! Or Cath'lic!" Frank sounded as if he couldn't be more offended if his mother stripped naked before him.

Prophet stole a leaf out of Sam's book and rolled his eyes. "Not the sharpest tack in the box, is he?" he asked of me.

"Far from it," I agreed.

Frank said, "Hey."

"Why'd you try to kill the lady," Prophet persisted. "Just because you don't want your uncle to marry her? That's a damned fool reason if I've ever heard one."

"She's not Italian!" Frank cried.

"Neither am I," said Prophet. "What of it?"

"But...She ain't Catholic, either!"

"Neither am I," said Prophet. "I guess I can't marry your uncle, either. Is that right?"

Gazing in perplexity at Prophet, Frank said, "Huh?"

"Shut up, all of you," said Sam, walking back to us via the middle aisle of the church. "Doan, please take this prisoner down to the station. He just threw a knife at Mrs. Majesty with the intention of killing her. We have a witness." His nose wrinkled a little, as if he weren't quite sure Mr. Lou Prophet was what one might call a proper witness.

"And I get the bounty," added Prophet, returning to the theme of his evening.

"Yes. There's a bounty on this oaf's head." Sam thumped a fist on Frank's head, eliciting a pained, "Hey" from Frank. "And Mr. Prophet, who foiled the criminal and captured him, gets it. Five hundred dollars, according to the wanted poster Mr. Prophet showed Mrs. Majesty and me."

"Five hundred, eh?" said Doan. "Doesn't sound like enough to me."

He eyed Frank with disgust. "We don't cotton to murderers in Pasadena, you."

"Hey," said Frank.

"Shut up," said Sam.

Frank, after one angry look at his uncle, swallowed and held out his hands for the metal cuffs Doan had ready for him. Doan wasn't gentle when he snapped them shut. I think Frank wanted to say "Ow" or something, but didn't dare. He might not have much of a brain, but I guess he could learn lessons if people whacked him often enough. Or stamped on his toes with their wooden limbs.

Thinking about that nearly made me giggle. I think I was merely giddy. The realization that I might well have been a dead Daisy finally struck me with some force, and I sank back onto the pew and sort of sagged there, hurting and exhausted.

"I'm afraid we're all going to have to go to the station, Daisy. Want to drop by your house first for another sip of syrup? I need some aspirin." Sam rubbed his left thigh.

"What's the matter with the two of you?" asked Prophet, his gaze sliding from Sam to me and back again.

"I got shot in the left thigh five or six months ago, and Mrs. Majesty was struck by an automobile on New Year's Day. Her left shoulder was dislocated, and she sustained quite a few scratches and bumps."

"Too bad," said Prophet. "What's all that got to do with the knife kid?"

"Maybe nothing," said Sam. "But I want to find out."

"We can stop by the house for some aspirin," I told Sam. "But I don't want to take any more of that horrible syrup."

"Want to bring the bottle in case you need a nip later? I don't know how long this will take."

"No, thanks. I'll just suffer." I put on a fake anguished expression, and Sam grinned.

Prophet didn't. "What kind of nip you got at your house?" He sounded honestly curious.

"Morphine syrup." I elaborated. "It's to help me with the pain since my accident, but I don't like to take it."

"Ah. Thought maybe you maybe got some hooch in your house someplace." Prophet sighed in disappointment.

"Hooch! We're in Pasadena, California, and Prohibition has been the law of the land for five years!" I was truly shocked, although I'm not sure why. Heck, the man had hit Frank with a bottle that had contained, if I'd managed to figure out Mr. Prophet's speech accurately, rye whiskey.

"Yeah, yeah. Prohibition," said Prophet as if he wished he could batter to death it along with Frank Pagano.

"The three of us can go in my Hudson," Sam said, indicating Lou Prophet and me. "Doan and Oversloot will take Frank to the station."

"I gotta go?" asked Prophet. "I don't like police stations."

"You want your five hundred dollars?" Sam asked him.

"Yeah, yeah," said Prophet, his broad shoulders slumping slightly. "All right. I'll go with you two. Better than with them two suits and that polecat."

Very well, I thought I knew what a polecat was. Wasn't it another term for skunk? If so, Mr. Prophet had pegged Frank Pagano quite well. If it didn't mean skunk…Well, I could always ask Regina Petrie. I still wanted to know what a curly wolf was. But I could ask Prophet at the station. Every time I've ever had to visit the Pasadena Police Department on official business, it had taken *forever*. I guess they have to be careful to dot their I's and cross their T's, and that makes things move sluggishly.

So a sullen Frank Pagano, with a uniformed policeman on either side of him, walked out to the police car parked on Marengo Avenue next to the side entrance to our church. Sam's machine was parked only a little bit farther down the street.

Sam opened the front passenger door for me, and I did my best to achieve a graceful entrance to the automobile. Didn't succeed awfully well. Sam opened the back passenger door for Prophet, who managed, with a couple of grunts and a swear word or three, to get himself and his wooden leg into the car, too.

We drove in silence to my house. I stayed in the Hudson with Mr. Prophet while Sam went inside to get himself some aspirin tablets and water. He wanted me to come inside with him, but I hurt too much.

He eyed Lou Prophet and said, "Don't move. I'll be back in a minute."

"He won't move!" I cried, feeling sorry for Mr. Prophet who, while a rather unusual character, at least for Pasadena, remained a human being with feelings. "Gee, Sam, have some faith."

"In him?" Sam asked hooking a thumb at Prophet.

Prophet growled something I didn't hear. Sam just said, "Oh, hell," and trod up the front walkway to the porch. I heard Spike barking like an insane creature until the door was opened—I couldn't see by whom —and Sam went into the house.

"He don't like me much," grumbled Prophet.

"He doesn't know you," I countered.

"Hellkatoot."

"I beg your pardon?" I said, flummoxed.

"Nothin'."

Very well, then. As long as we were stuck in Sam's Hudson, I decided to ask Mr. Prophet a couple of questions. "How did you know Frank Pagano was at the church? It was lucky for me you were there too."

"I followed him."

"Why?"

"Whattaya mean, why?"

"Why did you follow him?"

"Because I wanted the money they're gonna pay for catchin' him."

"How did you know he needed catching?"

"I keep up with things. Wanted people. Criminals. Stuff like that."

"Goodness, what an odd hobby." I hoped that didn't sound rude.

"Ain't a hobby. Was a living for most of my life."

"Keeping tabs on people who were wanted by the law?"

"Yeah."

"Goodness, I didn't know people could make a living finding people wanted by the law."

"Where you been all your life, girl? People like me been chasing curly wolves like that stupid kid for a hundred years or more."

"Oh. Well, I've lived in Pasadena all my life. We…uh…don't have a whole lot of criminals in Pasadena, I guess."

"Yeah," said Prophet, sounding disgruntled. "I know. That bastard nephew of your copper pal was pure dumb luck. Saw his face in the post office and saw him in the flesh as soon as I stepped out of the post office."

"Why didn't you capture him then?"

"Hell, lady, I didn't have my weapons on me. That kid's fifty years younger'n me. He might be a damned fool, but he's a young one."

"I guess that's a good point."

"Huh."

"Um...Mr. Prophet, what precisely is a curly wolf?"

It was dark in Sam's car, so I couldn't see Mr. Prophet's expression very well, but I could tell my question had astonished him. He sat there silent for a few moments, then said, "Shee-it. I'm too goddamned old for this world, I reckon."

"What does your being old have to do with curly wolves? I've never heard that expression before."

"A curly wolf is a bad man, Miss Majesty," said Lou Prophet, enunciating carefully, as if I were a slow student.

"It's actually Missus Majesty."

"Missus Majesty," growled Prophet, sounding disgusted.

"I see." Although his tone had annoyed me, I decided not to start a fight or anything. "And is a polecat a skunk?"

"What? A polecat? Hell, no. A skunk's a skunk. A polecat's more like a...I dunno. A weasel, I reckon. A polecat's another name for a bad man, in case you wondered about that."

"I see. Thank you. Are those two expressions common where you come from?"

"Georgia? Naw. I picked 'em up when I was workin' around Arizona and Mexico and places like that."

"You captured men who were wanted by the law in Arizona and Mexico? Your work must have been fascinating! And dangerous."

"I guess."

And then I had an Epiphany of my own! I finally figured out where I'd heard the name Lou Prophet before.

"Oh, my word, I know who you are! I've read all about you! You're Lou Prophet, the old-west bounty hunter!"

THIRTEEN

"Cripes," said Lou Prophet, former old-west bounty hunter. Actually, I think he said another word, but I changed it here because the one he used was impolite.

"I read you were hired by a studio in Hollywood to be an advisor on the set of some of the western flickers they're making now. I'm so excited to meet you! And under the circumstances, too! I mean, you saved my life!"

"Hell, I didn't save anyone. I caught the young scamp what flung that knife at you." He added in an undertone, "Wasted a good bottle of rye on the sumbitch while I did it, too."

"Well, I think you're wonderful," I told him.

He said, "Huh."

Very well, I had met some movie stars. It was difficult to avoid them when you worked in a profession like mine in Pasadena, California, where a whole bunch of them had homes. The worst of the lot so far had been a deranged actress named Lola de la Monica, who pretended to be from Spain, but whose east-coast accent slipped out now and then when she wasn't careful.

But *this* man was the real thing! He'd actually *done* the things the flickers tried to depict. Why, he'd been a *bounty hunter*! I was so excited, I could hardly stand it.

I vowed to telephone Harold Kincaid on the morrow to tell him I'd met the famous—well, semi-famous—old-west character, Mr. Lou Prophet!

Harold probably wouldn't care, but I'd bet anything Regina Petrie would. It was through Regina that I'd read about Lou Prophet. Many of her fiancé, Robert Browning's, collection of old yellow-back novels were about Lou Prophet and his like. I'd telephone her, too. Maybe I'd call Flossie Buckingham, as well.

Oh, wait. Flossie, a former gangster's moll, might not appreciate meeting a man who, a generation or so earlier, might have been the one "keeping" her. I hadn't read anything about Mr. Prophet and women, but if I had to guess, I'd bet—

The front door of the Hudson opened, and Sam slid in behind of the steering wheel. I'll bet I jumped a yard in the air, he startled me so badly.

He looked at me funny. "You were expecting someone else?" He didn't sound particularly cheerful, and he shot a killing glance at the back seat.

Prophet held up his hands in an "I give up" gesture. "Warn't me," said he. "I didn't do nothin'."

"He's telling the truth, Sam." I was going to babble on and tell Sam Lou Prophet's story, but I thought it might be more diplomatic to ask about his wounded thigh first. "Did you get some aspirin?"

"Yeah. Thanks. Your father was still up. I told him he might as well go to bed, since this will probably take a long time."

"Did you tell him what happened?"

"Not the knife-throwing part. Just said I'd be late getting you home because of some police business."

"Good. I don't want my parents any more scared than they are already."

"I don't, either. But at least your father knows you'll be late, and he won't worry."

"How late?" asked Prophet from the back seat.

"I have no idea. But you're going to have to tell your story, Daisy's going to have to tell her story, and my idiot nephew is going to have to invent some story he hopes will keep him out of the electric chair."

"For attempted murder? That's harsh, ain't it?"

"I *beg* your pardon?" I cried, glaring at Mr. Prophet, who'd said the words. "If his aim had been true, I'd be dead now!"

"Well, yeah, I know that, but—"

"Hold on!" Sam raised his voice just a little, but it sounded like a fog horn in a barrel. He had one of those voices. Commanding, I guess you'd call it. "It will take as long as it takes, and there's not much I can do about that."

"But I gotta be home by nine," said Prophet, sounding perhaps the least little bit worried.

"Why?" I asked. He seemed a trifle old to be operating under rules set for him by parents.

"Because those bastards lock the door at nine," said he.

"What bas-people are those?"

A corner of Mr. Prophet's mouth turned up, undoubtedly because I'd nearly said the word "bastard." Ornery old cuss, this Mr. Lou Prophet.

"The bastards at the Odd Fellows House of Christian Charity." He chuffed out an aggrieved breath. "*Call* themselves Christians, anyways."

"Oh." Suddenly a rush of compassion flooded me. This poor old fellow, who used to be one of the most dangerous gunmen in history—if Robert Browning's book collection was telling the truth—now lived in an old folks' home. In Pasadena, California, of all places! I glanced at Sam, who didn't look at either Prophet or me. He just kept scowling through the windshield of the Hudson. I deduced it wouldn't be prudent to ask him to intercede with the Odd Fellows on Mr. Prophet's behalf. But if I approached him in a roundabout way, maybe he'd do it.

"Um…Perhaps Detective Rotondo can call the House and explain why you've been detained if we have to stay at the police station past nine."

"That'd be great," said Prophet, sounding surly. I didn't know why until he went on to say, "I can just see them stuffed shirts getting a call from the coppers. They'd never let me through their precious doors again. They already think I'm dirtier'n pig slop and goin' straight to hell. If your pal there called them, they'd think he was a drinking buddy of mine or somethin'."

"Oh." A drinking buddy? Did the USA still contain drinking buddies? Hmm. To judge from the stories in the newspapers telling about people dying after drinking bathtub gin, not to mention gangsters in Chicago and New York murdering each other by the dozens, maybe it did.

"Let's not worry about that for a while," Sam said churlishly. "We can work something out."

"Thanks, Sam. After all, Mr. Prophet saved my life tonight."

"No, he didn't. He let Frank throw the knife and then tackled him."

I glared at Sam, who couldn't see me. "That's not…Well, it's not… Well, *I* think he saved my life, and I think he should be treated with respect and kindness."

"Huh," said Sam.

Mr. Prophet said the word that sounds kind of like "Cripes" again.

I swear. Men could drive a person nuts faster than anything else in the world.

They probably say the same thing about women, but they're wrong. According to me, anyhow.

We arrived at the police station. Sam parked his Hudson in back of the station, which was itself located at the back of Pasadena City Hall, and the three of us limped to the station door. We probably looked like a trio of car-crash survivors. Come to think of it, I *was* one of those, but neither Sam nor Mr. Prophet was.

It took until quite a while past nine p.m. before we were ready to leave the police station. I was taken into an ugly cell-like room where I reported to one policeman my version of what I'd witnessed during choir practice. Another policeman was there working as a stenographer and taking down everyone's words.

After the two officers were through with me, they led Mr. Prophet into the same room. I wanted to be in there with them, but—according to Sam—officers liked to question witnesses individually so they couldn't influence each other's statements. That kind of made sense to me, but I was nosy, darn it, and I wanted to hear what Mr. Prophet had to say. Too bad for Daisy, I reckon.

When Mr. Prophet was led out to the waiting room where I sat—I might have twiddled my thumbs if my hands had been up to the effort —I patted the hard wooden seat next to me. He gave me a look clearly telling me he thought I was strange, but he sat in the chair I offered.

"That wasn't too bad, was it?" I asked him.

"Naw. Better'n some interviews I've survived."

"I'm glad of that," I said, wondering precisely which interviews had been worse than the one he'd just endured. "You'll be getting the five-hundred dollars, won't you?"

"Damned well better be gettin' it," he said.

"Do you have to swear every time you open your mouth, Mr. Prophet?" I asked, sounding prissy to my own ears.

He turned and looked at me up and down and back and forth, making me incredibly uncomfortable, then said, "Reckon I do."

"Oh."

"But I won't get the money until that sumbitch is convicted."

"I'm sorry."

"Not as sorry as I am."

"I suppose not."

We sat in silence for a second or three.

"Um…Mr. Prophet, would you mind if I asked you some questions about your career?"

He turned to stare at me again, only this time he concentrated on my face. "My career?"

"Yes."

"What career?" He gave me a look that should be outlawed, it was so scathing.

Only slightly daunted, I went on, "Your career as a bounty hunter. It must have been terribly exciting."

"Exciting?"

"Yes! Exciting!"

"Exciting," he muttered as if the word tasted bad.

"Exciting." This time the word left my mouth a miniature of its former full-bodied self. Sort of like women's fashions, I decided on the spot. Women's fashions had no shape to them, and neither had that word, "exciting", as I'd just spoken it. If I were to bet, I'd bet Mr. Lou

Prophet preferred women in the olden days, when a harlot wore nothing but one of those short, old-time corset things and maybe some pantaloons. Nowadays, unless a woman was quite chubby—Mrs. Pinkerton springs to mind—you couldn't tell a boy from a girl unless you looked at the person's hair. Even then, now that women were getting their hair bobbed, sometimes you couldn't determine the sex of the person.

"Ain't a whole lot to tell," said Prophet after I'd decided he wasn't going to answer my question.

"I'm sure that's not true. Why, I read in…Well, I can't remember the title of the book, but you were in it, and you were working with Wyatt Earp!" The name Wyatt Earp conjured all sorts of images in my mind.

"That sumbitch? Never worked with him."

"Oh." How disappointing. "You didn't like him?"

With a shrug, Prophet said, "What's to like? He was stiffer'n an iron rod and about as humorous."

"Oh. I thought he was a famous lawman who helped tame the old west."

"Tame the old west?" Prophet gazed at me as if I'd lost what was left of my mind.

It was my turn to shrug. It hurt. "Well…Yes. I mean, you helped round up those bad guys like Jesse James and people like that."

"Never had nothin' to do with the James boys," said Prophet.

"But—" I got no further, because Prophet suddenly stood up. I gaped at him, hoping he wasn't going to walk out and not have anywhere to lay his head for the night. "Where are you going?" I asked, feeling panicky, wanting to leap up and follow him. As we all know by this time, however, I was unfit to leap and follow.

"Just outside. Gonna build a quirley."

"A quirley?" What in heaven's name was a quirley?

"Yeah."

I didn't have time to ask Prophet what a quirley was, because he took off limping to the door. I thought about following him, but I hurt all over, so I didn't. It did occur to me that Johnny Buckingham might be able to put Prophet up for the night. But what about Flossie?

Flossie had turned her life around and was now as firmly committed to the Salvation Army as was her spouse. After all, as a captain in the Salvation Army, Johnny saw people who were worse off than Lou Prophet—and, what's more, helped them—practically every day of his life. And I didn't really think Flossie would mind. After all, she and Mr. Prophet were at least one generation apart in age, and he didn't have to know her history.

And then it occurred to me to wonder if Lou Prophet, who didn't seem to hold a high opinion of churches, would countenance staying at the Salvation Army. But heck, he was coping with the Odd Fellows, and the Salvation Army folks were *much* less odd than they. That's just a joke. I don't know why they called themselves the Odd Fellows, but it seems a strange name to me.

Do I sound crazy? I don't think I am, but you may be right. I can report for a fact that I was worn out and in physical agony by the time Lou Prophet went outside to build his quirley. Whatever that was.

And was Wyatt Earp still living? I know Bat Masterson, another hero of the old west, had died only four years earlier, and several lawmen and outlaws had lived well into the twentieth century. Why, I think Frank James had died only a few years before 1925. I'd have to ask Regina about Earp. And what a name *that* was. I'd always thought Gumm was a stinky name to tag onto a child, but Earp? Egad.

You know, it might be interesting to interview a bunch of people who had actually *lived* in the old west. Not that you could get much more westerly than California unless you wanted to go for a swim in the Pacific Ocean, but California couldn't hold a candle to places like Tombstone, Arizona; Lincoln, New Mexico; Deadwood, South Dakota; Cheyenne, Wyoming and hellholes of a like nature. California was, unfortunately, civilized. Maybe San Francisco in its early days was a trifle wild, but it certainly wasn't any longer, unless you count a Tong war every now and then. Gee, I was missing the good old days, and I hadn't even lived through any!

Maybe I really *was* crazy.

FOURTEEN

My state of lunacy or lack thereof didn't matter, however, because just then Sam walked into the waiting room. I would have risen to greet him, but…Well, you can end that one on your own.

His limp wasn't as heavy coming out of the cells as it had been when he went in. Guess the aspirin tablets he'd downed at the bungalow had worked. I wished I'd thought to have taken some when we'd stopped there. Oh, well.

The first thing he said to me was, "Where's Prophet?"

And how-do-you-do to you, too, darling, I thought. I didn't say it, knowing my peevish mood to be prompted by pain. "He went outside."

"Criminy. He coming in again?"

"Um, I think so."

"Crap." Sam strode to the door as well as he was able—I was pleased to see his stride was getting much stronger as his wound healed —and flung the door open. A cloud of acrid smoke blew inside the building, and he waved it away from his face. "You ready to find a place to stay for the night, Prophet?"

I saw Prophet draw what I presumed to be a cigarette from his mouth, throw it onto the ground, and stomp in it with his peg leg. Littering. Huh.

Sam bent, picked up the squished cigarette, and put it into the receptacle that had been placed outside the police station for just such a purpose. Prophet frowned at him as he did so.

The two men came inside the building, Prophet saying, "Didn't see that thing."

"It's all right," said my beloved upon a deep sigh. "Lots of folks manage not to see it. But we do like to keep Pasadena looking nice."

Prophet's nose wrinkled. But Sam was correct. Pasadena is a beautiful city, and those of us who live in it and love it, *do* want to keep it that way.

On the other hand, I guess I now knew what a quirley was. I decided to make sure. When the men drew close to my chair, I said, "Mr. Prophet, is a quirley the same as a cigarette?"

"Eh?" He scowled down at me for a moment. Merciful heavens. The man might be old, and he might have only one leg, but he had a presence about him that could cow a person in no time flat. At least he managed to cow me with one look and that "Eh." I'm not normally a coward, either. Oh! I wonder if that's how the word, coward, came into being. Cow. Coward.

Never mind.

"Quirley?" he said. "Yeah. A coffin nail. Least that's what some folks call 'em. Don't know why. I ain't ready to be fitted with no wooden overcoat yet."

Coffin nails? Wooden overcoat? Clearly, I had to learn a new language. I asked again, "Um, so a quirley and a coffin nail are both cigarettes?"

He looked at me as if I were as dim a bulb as Frank Pagano. "Ain't that what I just said?"

"Um...not in so many words."

He gave me a *really* you've-gone-'round-the-bend look then. I gave up trying to communicate with him for the nonce.

Then I wanted to know what Frank had told Sam that might justify his trying to murder me with that knife. I didn't believe Frank would go so far as to kill me just because I was neither Italian nor Catholic, although with Frank, who could know? However, I decided to wait until we'd found sleeping quarters for Mr. Prophet before I asked Sam about Frank. "Are you going up to speak with the Odd Fellows, Sam?"

"Figured I might as well."

"Shit, they won't let me in! They already want to kick me out of that place."

"Have you been…unruly or something there?" I asked, pretty sure I shouldn't.

"Unruly? Hell, no! How the hell can a one-legged man with no money get unruly? They just don't like me, is what."

"Oh." What the heck. He might be right. I said to Sam, "Do you think Johnny Buckingham might be a better choice?"

"Why don't we try the Odd Fellows first," said Sam.

"Who's that Buckingham galoot you know?" asked Prophet suspiciously.

Humph. The man must have had some harrowing experiences if he could be suspicious of Johnny Buckingham upon merely hearing his name. Not that he knew Johnny, but for pity's sake!

"He's a very good friend of mine," I told Prophet in as cold a voice as I could achieve. "He's the captain of Pasadena's Salvation Army organization, and he's accustomed to finding sleeping quarters for people who are down on their luck."

"Down on my luck, eh?" muttered Prophet.

"Well, you are, aren't you?" I demanded. Pushy of me, I know, but he was annoying me.

"Yes, dammit!" he said, fury fairly radiating from him. "I was livin' the good life until that broad drove that car off that damned cliff in Santa Monica!"

Puzzled, I said, "I beg your pardon?"

"Goddamn woman drove me, another whore, and a crate of booze off a hill in Santa Monica. I'm the only one who lived to tell the tale, but I lost my damned leg. So, yeah, I reckon I *am* down on my luck, dammit!"

"Oh," I said, hornswoggled (I think that's an old-west word). "I didn't know that's how you lost your leg. It must have happened fairly recently."

"Yeah. Six months ago. Put paid to my working on western flickers.

Dammit. Made good money doin' that. Better'n bounty-hunting. Hell, you oughta go into the pitchers. You're pretty, and if you get in the pitchers, you don't have to do nothin' but look good and swan around."

"Um…" Very well, I didn't know what to say.

I knew some picture folks, and some of them did considerably more than swan around. Some of them didn't. But I *had* learned, both from personal experience and through Harold Kincaid, who had worked as a costumer in the moving pictures since forever, that it didn't matter what you looked like on the street. What mattered was what you looked like on celluloid. It's an unforgiving medium; some people look good on celluloid and some don't. I didn't bother explaining that to Lou Prophet. I doubted he'd have believed me, being somewhat grumpy about his condition, although what he'd been doing in an automobile with two women—whores? Good heavens—and a crate of liquor, I had no idea. I also had no idea why he was so crabby about it. I mean, he'd been breaking the law, hadn't he? He probably didn't look upon his accident in that light. I'd already concluded that the law and Lou Prophet didn't always see eye-to-eye.

"I'll bet it hurt a lot," I said in a small voice.

"What? Losin' the leg? Yeah, it hurt. No worse'n getting shot, I reckon, but it hurt."

"Getting *shot?*" Good Lord!

"We're here," said Sam in a voice meant to carry above Prophet's and mine. Made me jump. Didn't have the same effect on Prophet, which figured. I'd be willing to bet not much startled him.

"They ain't gonna let me in," said Prophet in a dead tone.

"Yes, they will," said Sam in a positive tone.

I believed Sam on this one. Nevertheless, since I couldn't know for sure unless I saw for myself, I said, "May I come with you?"

"Can you move?" asked Sam in a not-very-lover-like voice.

"Probably," I said, having momentarily forgot about my various injuries. Maybe Lou Prophet was good for me! Interesting notion. I'd have to think about it another time.

"Ain't gonna work," said Prophet. Nevertheless, he opened the back door to Sam's Hudson and hobbled out onto the sidewalk.

Greatly daring, I too opened my door. Unlike Prophet, I didn't hobble from the automobile. I sort of plopped. But I landed on my feet! I figured that was good enough, so I shuffled after the two men.

Lou Prophet grumbled non-stop on the way to the front door of the Odd Fellows' charity home. It was a bleak-looking place on South Fair Oaks Avenue. I'd read in the *Pasadena Star News* that the Odd Fellows planned to build a new temple (that's what they called it) on North Los Robles Avenue in the future. How far in the future, I had no idea, but I hoped the new building would appear more welcoming than this one.

Sam got to the front door ahead of Prophet and clanged the bell hanging outside really loudly. I winced but didn't stop walking. Sort-of walking. Shambling, I guess is a better term for my movements at the time.

I heard Lou Prophet say, "Kee-rist." Guess he didn't approve of loud bell-ringing any more than I did.

When the door opened, I could tell the opener thereof was peeved about the bell, too. A small man with a shiny bald head and a miserly frown, he said, "What is the meaning of this?"Then he saw Prophet and said, "*You*," in a voice that told the listener precisely what he thought of Lou Prophet.

"Me," said Prophet.

"I'm Detective Sam Rotondo, with the Pasadena Police Department," Sam said in his official voice, which was quite intimidating to some people.

The little man wasn't one of the some. "If that creature has been in trouble with the law—"

"He hasn't," said Sam, his voice a trifle more deadly now. "In fact, he helped save a woman's life and capture a wanted criminal. He's been of material help to the Pasadena Police Department and he feared, since it's after nine p.m., you wouldn't allow him into his room here." Just in case the little man wanted to argue some more, Sam reached into his pocket and brought out the leather case in which he kept his badge and other police credentials.

The little bald man stared from the leather case to Sam and then to Lou Prophet, and his nose wrinkled. "Well…"

"Mr. Prophet has a room here, has he not?"

"Well…Yes, he has, although—"

"Fine then," said Sam, stomping on Baldy's words as if they were pesky bugs. "See him to his room. I'll want to talk to him again tomorrow, so keep his room available to him."

"Mister Ro—"

"*Detective.* Detective Sam Rotondo, with the Pasadena Police Department, and you will do what I say or be in violation of the law."

"What?" the little man squeaked.

I squinted at the nametag sewn on to his coat. I think it said his name was Elmer J. Crimstone. Funny name. Then again, I'd been saddled with the last name Gumm for seventeen years of my life, so I shouldn't talk.

"You heard me. Now, do you want me to accompany Mr. Prophet to his room, or will you let him in and keep him here until we need him?"

"They gonna *keep* me in this hellhole?" asked Prophet. I wished he hadn't, since I wanted to get home sometime soon.

"What do you mean 'hellhole,' you old reprobate?" squeaked the little bald man.

"They won't *keep* you, in that you won't be allowed out and about," said Sam, this time softening his voice a little for Prophet. "But they'll keep your room available for you." He turned to Baldy. "Won't you, Mister Crimstone?"

Fuming, Mr. Crimstone finally seemed to have to force himself to say, "Very well. But I don't like this!"

"You don't have to like it. All you have to do is keep the man's room available for him. If you don't, I'll be back."

"Thought you was comin' back anyways," said Prophet.

I couldn't see him do it, but I'd bet Sam rolled his eyes. "Yes, yes. I'll be back to talk to you some more. Tomorrow, in fact."

After pursing his lips and looking as if he might erupt and spew all over Sam—and the rest of Pasadena, too—for a few moments, Mr. Crimstone stepped back. "Oh, very well. But I will countenance no disturbances of the peace in this facility. Mr. Prophet has been a source of noise and confusion more than once during his short tenure here."

Sam turned on Prophet. "Stop making a pest of yourself, Prophet.

You've got a bed to sleep in and food to eat. Maybe we can work out a better arrangement for you if you have to stick around for my nephew's trial."

"Stick around?" Prophet spat on the front porch of the Odd Fellows' Home.

"That's so rude!" I told him.

He turned and scowled at me.

"Daisy's right," said Sam.

"Shit," said Prophet.

"Humph!" said Crimstone.

I decided then and there his name should be Brimstone rather than Crimstone.

But Prophet pushed past the little bald beast and stomped into the Odd Fellows' Home. I didn't envy him. If all the staff were like Crimstone, I'd have rebelled, too. On the other hand, it was nice to know people like those belonging to the Odd Fellows and the Salvation Army were available to people who needed help.

The Odd Fellows might take a page from Johnny Buckingham's book and at least be nice about it, though.

Sam held my arm as we made our way back to his Hudson. I was mighty achy just then and wanted my bed more than I wanted about anything else. However, I also wanted to ask Sam some questions, so I did as he drove me home.

"What kind of coat was Mr. Prophet wearing?" I asked Sam. I'd been curious about that long, battered coat of Mr. Prophet's since I first set eyes on him.

"His *coat?*"

"Yes. Gentlemen in Pasadena don't wear coats like that."

"In case it's escaped your attention, Mr. Prophet isn't a gentleman, Daisy," Sam said, not unkindly, but as if Mr. Prophet's rough edges were merely part of his personality.

"I guess you're right about that. But his coat. It looks...I don't know. Old-fashioned or something."

"It is," said Sam. "It's a good, old-fashioned frock coat. I understand all the best villains in the old west wore them."

"Oh! Of course! I've seen pictures of men in frock coats. And you're right. All the men wore them back in the 1880s or thereabouts."

"Some of them still do," said Sam. "Prophet probably can't afford to replace it."

We were silent for a moment or two. I don't know about Sam, but I was feeling a wee bit sorry for poor old Lou Prophet who, according to the reports I'd read, had been a real, true, wild-and-woolly character back in the day. Not sure precisely what day, but I think it had passed long since. Ah, well. I decided to ask Sam more questions, only this time about Frank.

"So, what was Frank's story? Did he decide to kill me by himself, or did somebody pay him to murder me?"

"Not sure yet."

My lips pressed together until I reminded myself of the squinchy-lipped Mr. Crimstone, and I smoothed them out. I was a spiritualist-medium, and I had a certain air of fashion to maintain and protect. Wrinkles from frowning wouldn't go at all well with my established persona.

"Well, what did he *say*?"

"He said he acted of his own volition, but I have a feeling there's more to the story than that. Frank's never been known to think up things for himself before. He said he did it because he doesn't want us to marry, but I suspect someone else at least prodded him to do the deed."

"Why do you think that?"

"He's wanted for robbery back in NYC," said Sam. "And he ran out on his bail. Poor Renata." He shook his head. "That's what the wanted poster was about. But Frank's dumb as a box of rocks. I don't think he'd actually try to kill you unless somebody else suggested doing so might be a good idea, especially if he offered Frank money to do it. Somebody wants you out of the way."

"We've already gone over lists and lists of people who might want me dead," I said, feeling not merely sore and sleepy, but quite dispirited.

"I'm going to cable Renata tomorrow. If I can get moved into the house across the street from you soon, I'll put Renata up there—providing she's willing to visit Pasadena for her son's sake. I know she's as fed up with him as I am. But attempted murder is a *much* more serious crime than any he's been picked up for before now. I wish her husband would come out here. He's about the only one Frank might listen to."

"What's his father's name?"

"Francis. Same as his. Frank's a junior, although the name is the only decent thing he inherited from Frank Senior, who's a good man. Renata and he are lucky to have each other. But he's washed his hands of Frank Junior."

"That's kind of sad, although I'd just as soon wash my hands of him, too. It's not every day somebody tries to murder me. And to think it was your nephew."

"Yeah. Too bad we can't prove he was adopted and give him back to whoever spawned him. I fear it was just bad luck on Frank and Renata's part to have reared a pig like Frank."

"I'd say so." This conversation was downright depressing. "Do they have any other children, or is Frank their only one?"

"They've got another boy and a girl. They're both good kids. Carmine is a couple of years older than Frank, and Pia's a couple of years younger."

"Pia's a pretty name, too."

Sam shrugged.

"Why do you think Frank went so wrong?"

"Honestly? I don't have a clue. He's got great parents, aunts, uncles and grandparents on both sides of his family But Frank? Frank grew up rotten. I don't know how or why."

"Boy, you never know about these things, do you? I'd hate to have a child go wrong like that."

"Renata and Frank Senior aren't too thrilled about it, either."

"I suppose not."

"Wouldn't surprise me if he was the bacon-grease painter, either," said Sam.

"That sounds more like something he'd do than knife-throwing," I said. Then I wondered if I was right. "How the heck did he learn how to throw a knife so well, anyway?"

I saw Sam's head shake, even though the light was dim. "Damned if I know."

"You and Lou Prophet," I said, feeling cranky. "Can't say a single sentence without putting a swear word in it somewhere."

Sam laughed.

It figures.

FIFTEEN

The house was dark when Sam walked me to the front door. Spike stood just inside the door, wagging. I'd taught him not to go into a barking frenzy when a family member came to either the front or the side door, and he generally remembered. Not always, but I was pleased he remembered that night. Nobody ever came to the back door. As soon as Sam pushed the door open, however, Spike was all over the both of us. But he *didn't* bark.

My physical condition didn't take kindly to my well-meaning dachshund, however, and I spoke sternly to my darling hound. "Spike. Sit."

A little hurt—I could tell—Spike sat. And he looked up at me with the most mournful eyes I've ever seen. I wanted to squat down beside him and pet him for an hour or two, but I couldn't squat. I could hardly stand. Therefore, because I was a total mess, I started to cry. Just a little bit, mind you.

"Sam," I said, sniffling pathetically. "Will you please bring me that horrible morphine syrup? I need some. I c-can't even pet my d-dog!" Those words made me cry harder.

"Sure, sweetheart. Spike, come along with me, and we'll get your mommy something that'll make her feel better."

Because Sam hadn't spoken the proper code word to release Spike from his seated position, I did it for him, "Okay, Spike. Go with Sam." And he did. What a brilliant dog I had!

Sam was as good as his word. I'd managed to make my way to the dining-room table and had more or less fallen into a chair when he returned with the morphine syrup, Spike, a spoon and a peppermint drop. I squinted at the latter object. "Where'd you find a peppermint drop?"

"Guess your father left 'em in a bowl on the kitchen counter. I took one because I know the syrup tastes bad."

"Thanks, Sam." I drank the spoonful of syrup he poured out for me, grimaced, and had opened my mouth to receive the peppermint drop, when Sam stopped it on its way to my mouth. "What?" I asked, irked. That syrup was *awful*. I *needed* that peppermint drop, darn it!

He didn't answer me, but lifted the peppermint drop to his nose and sniffed at it. He reminded me of Spike.

"Well?" I demanded.

"This doesn't smell like a peppermint drop to me."

"Let me smell it."

He closed his fist around the little candy tidbit. "Don't put it in your mouth."

"But—"

"No buts. This thing smells like almonds, not peppermint. Maybe it's an almond drop, but unless I know for sure, I'm not giving it to you."

"Why?"

"Because compounds of cyanide smell like almonds. Bitter almonds."

"*Cyanide!*"

"Yes. Cyanide."

"And cyanide smells like almonds?"

"Bitter almonds."

"Bitter almonds? Why bitter? Is a bitter almond different from a regular one?"

"How should I know?"

"I'll never get that taste out of my mouth now," I said, my voice quavering. Shoot, I was a disaster.

"I'll see if there's something else in there for you to eat. Something I know is safe."

"Why is somebody doing these things to me?" I asked. I felt like wailing, but I didn't want to wake up my folks or Aunt Vi. I also didn't want to sound like Mrs. Pinkerton, who was the best and most accomplished wailer I'd ever met in my life.

"I wish I knew," said Sam as he went back in the kitchen. He returned a moment or two later with a piece of bread. He'd buttered it and spread some of Aunt Vi's raspberry preserves on it.

"How do you know the preserves aren't poisoned?" I asked, hesitating to take the bread.

"I sniffed them and tasted them. No almonds."

I took the piece of bread and gobbled it down. If I died, I'd at least die with a pleasant taste in my mouth. "Thanks, Sam. Do you think it was Frank who put the candy dish in the kitchen?"

"Wouldn't surprise me. You don't lock your doors, do you?"

"Not very often," I admitted.

"I don't like this," said he.

"Nor do I."

"I'll interrogate Frank again tomorrow. I can probably get him to tell me who he's been talking to recently. He might have been manipulated into using that knife on you. He's as dim as a fading ember, and he wouldn't know if someone were twisting him to do his will."

"How poetic," I said.

"Yeah. Anyway, I packed the rest of those drops and the bowl in some waxed paper I found in the pantry. Tomorrow morning I'll take them to the station to be tested, so if anyone asks about them, that's where they went. You might ask your father if he left a bowl of candy on the kitchen counter."

Thinking—not awfully hard, because I was sore and tired—I said after a moment or two, "It would be most unlike anyone in the family to leave sweets on the counter."

"Why's that?"

"Ants. They love water and sweet stuff."

"Good point. You might also ask if anyone bothered to lock the door this evening after we left."

"I will, although I doubt anyone did. The front door was unlocked when we came home. As I already told you, we don't generally lock the doors."

"Better start locking them."

"I guess so." What a bleak thing to have to do. *Nobody* locked their doors in Pasadena. Well, not in my neighborhood, anyway. I suppose the rich folks in the San Rafael Hills or on Orange Grove did. But the folks in my neighborhood didn't have a whole lot to steal. I decided to talk about something else. "What did you think of Lou Prophet?"

Sam grinned, surprising me. I'd gained the impression he strongly disapproved of Mr. Prophet. "He's quite a character."

"He sure is. I really have read about him, you know. Robert Browning owns quite a collection of what he calls yellow-back novels, and Mr. Prophet features in several of them. I don't know how much of what's written in them is true."

"Probably not much," said Sam.

"Probably. But even so, he's lived an interesting life."

"I'd say so."

"He fits into Pasadena like Cinderella's stepsisters' feet fitted into that glass slipper."

Sam chuckled. He said, "I'm going to talk to Mrs. Killebrew tomorrow, too. I'd like to move into that house as soon as possible. Maybe…" His words trailed off.

"Maybe what?"

With a huff, Sam said, "This may be one of the biggest mistakes I'll ever make, but maybe Prophet can stay there for a while. He could be a kind of watch-guard or caretaker, although I doubt he's taken care of a whole lot in his life so far."

"According to the dime novels, he had a big dun horse, and he took care of him."

"A horse?" After giving me one of *those* looks, Sam said, "I see."

"Yes. A horse. He was some kind of bay which, I think, is a color. Of a horse. Not just a bay. Some adjective comes before bay. But I don't know anything about horses."

"Me, neither. There were lots of horses in New York in the poorer sections. Kids got paid to pick up the horse poop. Street kids." Sam shook his head as if he didn't like remembering the squalor in some parts of his native city.

"Oh, dear."

"Yeah." Sam sighed heavily.

Because I didn't want to think about poor little children having to scoop horse poop off the streets of New York City, I said. "He named his horse Mean and Ugly, too." Then I giggled, not quite able to imagine anyone naming an animal something like Mean and Ugly.

"Great name," said Sam. His mouth kind of crinkled, as if he wanted to smile but was trying to be stern. He gave that up after a second or three and grinned.

"Mean and Ugly." Glancing down, I saw my faithful hound staring up at me, hope writ large on his features. Spike loved the kitchen and the dining room, because that's where food resided most of the time. He'd learned long ago that food wasn't *always* to be found in the kitchen and dining room, but he lived in hope. "I'd never name you anything so horrid, Spike. Your daddy named you." Instantly, I wished I hadn't thought about Billy. I'd originally got Spike to cheer Billy up. My ploy had worked. For a while. It was my turn to sigh.

Sam reached over and took my hand. "It's all right, Daisy. Billy loved you and Spike."

"Yes. He did. But about Mr. Prophet. Do you really think he might want to stay at Mrs. Killebrew's house? Or at least agree to do it?"

"It'll be our house if he stays there. But I think having him there might be a good idea. I'm sure he'd prefer it to the Odd Fellows' Home of Christian Charity."

I chuffed my scorn. "Christian charity, my foot. Mr. Brimstone is about as full of Christian charity as…as your stinky nephew."

"You're right. And I like the name Brimstone. Fits him. Anyhow, Prophet might keep an eye on things while I'm at work. I hate to think people are coming in and out of your house as easily as they seem to be doing. Or painting the steps with bacon grease. Prophet could…I don't know. Watch the place and keep an eye on this house, until we tie the knot and move in there."

"That would be a kind thing to do, Sam."

"Maybe. Maybe it's stupid, too. I'm not sure I trust him very much."

"I don't know why not. He's…a little strange, but that's only because he's old and…and…well, not from Pasadena."

"Ha! Neither am I."

"No, but you're from a big city. I got the feeling Mr. Prophet hasn't lived in very many big cities."

"He seemed to like Los Angeles until that accident with the two ladies and the liquor."

"He didn't call them ladies."

"No, he didn't." Sam laughed out loud.

I shook my head, extremely glad to have met Mr. Lou Prophet, and that's not even including the gratitude I felt toward him for bashing Frank around.

"As I said, if I can get into the house soon, it would also be a good place for Renata to stay, too, if she comes out here. And if she and Prophet can stand each other. Heck, Prophet could stay in the little back house."

"I kind of liked him. He's certainly not like anyone else I've ever met."

"Nope. I think he's one of a kind."

"There used to be more like him. At least according to the dime novels and the flickers."

"Right." Sam used his palms to push himself to his feet. "Well, I'd better get going. Have to work tomorrow, and I want to talk to the Killebrews and Prophet again. *And* Frank. I'll wring the truth out of that little pipsqueak one way or another."

"After you wring the truth out of him, maybe you can wring his neck," I suggested, only half-joking.

"Good idea." He saw I aimed to get up and walk him to the door and said, "Stay there until the syrup starts to work. Then lock all the doors in the whole house before you go to bed."

"Nobody ever comes in through the back door," I said.

Sam gave me a you've-got-to-be-kidding-me squint. "Somebody might try now, Daisy. Somebody wants you dead. *You* don't want you dead. *I* don't want you dead. Your parents don't want you dead. Spike doesn't want you dead. So just lock the damned doors, will you? Including the back door. Hell, that door leads right into your bedroom, doesn't it?"

"Yes," I admitted, feeling silly to have protested locking the back door. I told myself I had to get a firm grip on what was now the reality of my life—which, apparently, included someone who wanted me out of it.

How depressing.

Spike and I sat in the dining room until the morphine syrup began making me feel giddy, so I got up, balancing myself on the table—I don't know how my Billy could have drunk so much of that stuff and stayed conscious—then slowly made the rounds of the doors, using my new cane to brace me as I walked. I made sure every single door in the house was locked, including the door to the basement. Heck, for all I knew, a murderer might be lurking down there at that very moment, just waiting for me to go to sleep so he could do me in.

I wished I hadn't thought about that.

Oh, well. If a bad guy really *was* down there, he couldn't get out now. Maybe I'd just leave the basement door locked and let him die there. We didn't use the basement much. Heck, if a nasty murderer died down there, we wouldn't even know about it until he began to stink.

It was definitely time to stagger to bed. I'm generally not so ruthless. Or weird.

Spike and I had a peaceful night's sleep. I do believe that, because Sam had me lock all the doors, any last little frizzle of nervousness I might have felt about being murdered left me for a while. Or maybe that was just the morphine syrup working its magic. I could hardly wait until I didn't need to use the stuff any longer.

SIXTEEN

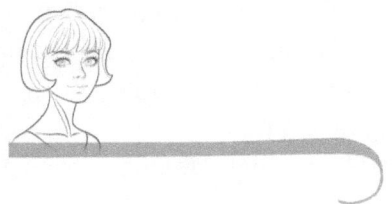

Friday morning I slept later than usual. That's probably because I got to bed later than usual on Thursday night. By the time I crawled out of bed, tested my various limbs to see if they would support me without my having to drink morphine syrup, deciding they would although they'd hurt, I was almost ready to tell my family about last night's choir practice.

Unfortunately, the only family members at home that morning were Pa and Spike. Spike had already figured out my tale of woe from the way Sam and I had spoken to each other Thursday night. Pa was horrified and outraged. He slammed the newspaper he'd been reading onto the kitchen table, crunching it, and stared at me.

"That lousy son of a bitch tried to *knife* you?"

Now, my father *never* swears. I guess I have to amend that to *rarely* swears. I don't think I'd ever heard him utter a bad word until that Friday morning in January.

"Yes, he did. Sam locked him up, and he's going to be charged with attempted murder."

"Why the devil does Sam's nephew want you dead?"

I'd have shrugged, but my shoulders weren't quite up to the effort. "I don't know. I'm neither Italian nor Roman Catholic, and those are two qualities Frank deplores in me."

Pa stared at me as if I'd told him I'd been hiding a second head in my bedroom drawer. "He wants to kill you because you're neither Catholic nor Italian?"

"That's what he said."

"There's got to be more to the story than that."

"I don't know. That's what he said was his reason."

"That's insane." Folding the newspaper neatly, Pa laid it aside, got up from his chair and walked to the stove.

"Yeah, well don't tell him that. He might use it as a defense."

"There is no defense for that boy."

"I agree." I recalled the peppermint drops. "Say, Pa, did you leave a bowl of peppermint drops on the kitchen counter last night?"

"What?" He'd reached the stove and had just opened the door to the warming oven, but he turned and gazed at me in puzzlement. "No. Your Aunt Vi would kill me if I left sweets on the counter. Ants. She hates 'em."

"That's what I figured." Gazing at my darling father, I saw him take a dish out of the warming oven, using the oven mitts I'd made for Vi sometime or other. Can't remember precisely when. "Did Vi leave us something good?"

"She sure did."

My heart wasn't quite up to leaping for joy, but it staggered to attention. "Oh? What is it?"

"Looks like fried mush and bacon to me."

"Oh, yum."

Very well, so I know that if you offered, say, Mrs. Pinkerton some fried cornmeal mush and bacon for breakfast, her aristocratic nose would point right, smack into the air. But if you've never eaten fried mush with butter and maple syrup, you really shouldn't throw stones. Well, you shouldn't throw stones anyway, but...Oh, you know what I mean.

As Pa brought the dish to the table where he set it, steaming, on a trivet, he asked, "Why'd you ask about the peppermint drops? I got a tin of them from Crosbys', and as far as I know they're still in the cupboard. With the lid clamped down tight."

"There were some things that looked like peppermint drops in a bowl on the kitchen counter last night. You guys were all in bed when Sam and I finally got home from the police station. Sam brought me the morphine syrup since I was about to fall down dead, and he thought those candies were the same as the peppermint drops you'd given me earlier. But he didn't let me eat one, because he said they didn't smell like peppermint."

Pa had retrieved the maple syrup—replenished by our kind relations in Massachusetts every year at Christmastime—and set it on the table. He didn't bother to heat it for the two of us. Vi would never serve unheated maple syrup, but Vi was Vi. Pa and I weren't fancy chefs like she was.

His eyes furrowing, Pa said, "What did they smell like?"

"Sam said they smelled like bitter almonds, which means they might have been laced with cyanide."

Pa dropped the knife with which he'd about to cut into the chunk from the butter he'd taken out of the Frigidaire. "Cyanide! *Cyanide?*"

"Sam packed them up, bowl and all, last night and aims to have them tested at the station today."

"Good God, Daisy, who's doing this to you?"

"Wish I knew." I buttered a slice of mush for myself. "I also wish I knew why."

"Could Sam's nephew be behind everything?"

"I kind of doubt it. I can see Frank painting the front steps with bacon grease, but I don't think he's smart enough to steal a rich man's car and run into me with it. And where'd he get cyanide? If the candies contained cyanide, that is, and we don't know that yet."

"But we do know there were no candies left on the kitchen counter last night. At least none left by a member of the family."

After I swallowed—honestly, if you haven't eaten fried cornmeal mush with butter and syrup, you really ought to try it—I sighed heavily. "Yes. I guess we do."

The telephone rang. Since I'd nearly been killed by that car, I never knew for sure who was ringing until somebody answered the silly thing.

Before January first, most of the telephone calls coming to our house were for me, and they generally involved my work. After Pa and I glanced at each other over our breakfasts, Pa got up and went to the 'phone.

"Gumm residence," said he.

Silence ensued. I guess Pa was busy listening. I also hoped whatever he was listening to wasn't incendiary or intimate, because unless he shooed off our party-line neighbors, they'd all be listening with gusto. If you can listen with gusto.

Finally Pa said, "Right. Thanks, Sam. See you soon." He hung the receiver in the cradle and made his way back to the table, where he sat and picked up a piece of bacon—when Pa and I are eating breakfast, we don't cut up our bacon with a knife and fork, either. Before taking a bite, he said, "Sam will be here in a few minutes. I think he's already made a deal about the Killebrew house. Fast worker, your fiancé."

"Goodness, I should say so," I said, impressed. Mind you, now that I knew Sam had money—although I had no idea how much— this quick work on the house didn't surprise me as much as if he'd had to live on his police earnings. Even a Pasadena Police Detective, which position was far above the common herd of police officers, didn't make so much money that he could get things that usually took forever—real-estate deals, for instance—to move quickly. But money talked. And people listened. I guess that wasn't fair, but really, what was?

"Did he mention the peppermint drops?"

"Over the 'phone?" Pa grinned. "Your Sam's too canny for that. He'd never talk in front of Mrs. Barrow."

For the record, Mrs. Barrow was the most officious and nosy of our party-line neighbors. She *loved* listening to my conversations. They were undoubtedly a whole lot more interesting than any she had, but still...

"Will he be here for breakfast?" I asked, having suddenly thought about Sam's stomach.

"He didn't mention breakfast."

"Guess we'll find out when he gets here."

Pa and I finished our breakfast, and Pa took away the dirty dishes. He set them in the sink to soak. After I felt a little better, I'd wash them and dry them and put them away. With only one arm. The notion caused no leap of joy to enter my heart.

The doorbell scritched.

Pa and I looked at each other.

"Sam?" I asked.

"Don't know. I'll find out."

Spike, however, already knew. He raced to the front door as if there were a mountain of chopped beef piled on the other side of it. *Must be Sam*, I concluded. Spike knew his friends.

I guess Pa was a little startled to find the front door locked, because he rattled the doorknob a few times before he figured out why it didn't open when he turned it. I heard Sam's deep bass rumble, Spike rapturous barklets, Pa's friendly voice, and another voice. That of a female. I frowned. Sam had brought a woman to the house in which his fiancée lived? Of all the nerve!

I told myself to calm down and reminded myself how much of a fool I'd made of myself the last time I jumped to a conclusion about Sam and another woman. Therefore, I maintained a demeanor of serenity—I hope—when Pa, Sam and the female walked into the dining room. I glanced up and was overjoyed to observe the woman Sam had brought with him to be a middle-aged person of small stature, plump build and iron-gray hair.

"Daisy," said Sam, smiling at me. "How are you today?"

I smiled back. "Sore, but getting better."

"I'd like to introduce you to Mrs. Rattle. She's going to come here in the mornings for a few weeks to help with chores around the house. Mrs. Rattle? This is my fiancée, Daisy Majesty."

"How kind of you!" I cried, pushing myself to my feet. Not a sound plan on my part, although Sam's thoughtfulness had quite overwhelmed me. Before I even got upright, every muscle in my body yanked on every nerve in my body, and I darned near howled. Suppressing my agony, I said in a thin voice, "It's wonderful to meet you, Mrs. Rattle." I'd have held out my hand for her to shake, but I couldn't.

"You just sit yourself down, young woman. Your Detective Sam here has told me all about what happened to you. You don't have any business getting up to meet an old lady who's the hired help." She gave such merry peel of laughter, I almost laughed myself, although my eyes were watery with tears from the stupid pain of my injuries.

"Better do as she says, Daisy," said Sam, grinning. "She can be quite a tyrant. I have it on good authority."

"Whose?"

"Officer Doan's. Mrs. Rattle is Doan's mother. Mr. Doan passed away, and she married a Mr. Rattle. Doan told me she's a strict disciplinarian."

"Get along with you, Detective!" said Mrs. Rattle, using one of Aunt Vi's favorite expressions. I'm still not sure what it means.

"This is very nice of you, Sam," said Pa. "Poor Daisy keeps trying to do all the things she used to be able to do, but she can't use her left arm and she really needs to rest more."

"That's why I hired Mrs. Rattle," said Sam.

"I love you, Sam," I said with not too much of a sniffle. Maybe a just little, teensy sniffle.

"You haven't taken any syrup this morning, have you?" Sam said, gazing at me as if I were a cow at a fair he was considering buying.

"No. I thought I could tough it out."

"Nuts to that. I'll get the syrup. And, Joe, are those peppermint drops still around, or are they all gone by now?"

"They're in a tin in the cupboard. I'll get them while you get the morphine syrup."

"Sounds good," said Sam.

"Thank you. I love you, too, Pa."

He kissed me on top of my head. I sniffled just a weensy bit more. "And you, too, Mrs. Rattle. I've met your son a few times, and he seems like a good man." Better Officer Doan's mother than Officer Oversloot's, thought I. I still hadn't forgiven Oversloot for being mean to me once a year or so back. Not that I ever hold a grudge or anything.

"Oh, he's a good man, all right." Mrs. Rattle had a cheerful laugh. I was glad to hear it. It made me even gladder Sam had brought her to help me. What a guy my Sam was! I really did love him very much. When I didn't want to kill him. If you know what I mean.

"All right. Here we go," said Sam, pulling a chair closer to mine. He poured out the syrup. Pa set the tin of peppermint drops on the table and pried off the lid. I leaned over a little, nearly upsetting the spoon Sam had poised before my mouth, to see if the candies in the tin really were peppermint.

"They're the real thing," said Pa, understanding my trepidation. "I smelled them and ate one."

"Oh. Good. Thanks, Pa."

"Ready?" asked Sam, slightly exasperated, although I don't know why. Shoot, somebody was trying to kill me, for pity's sake.

I drank the syrup, sucked a peppermint drop to death, and then I sat at the kitchen table for a few minutes longer, trying to get my body ready for the jolt it would receive when I stood up. Stalling, I asked Mrs. Rattle, "Do you want me to tell you where everything goes?" She'd donned an apron and was busily splashing away at the sink, washing the breakfast dishes.

"That's all right, Mrs. Majesty—"

"Oh, please, call me Daisy. Everyone does."

"Very well then. Please call me Elvira."

Elvira Rattle. I don't know why the name tickled me. It was probably the morphine syrup taking effect. "Thank you," I said.

"I'll just look around. I'm sure I'll figure out where things belong."

"And if you can't figure it out, just ask me," said Pa.

"I'll do that," said Elvira.

"Let me help you get to the living room," said Sam, putting a hand under my right elbow. I'd be *extremely* happy when Dr. Benjamin let me used my left arm again. Or I would be if it had healed enough not to hurt like heck.

"Thanks, Sam."

"We've got some things to talk about."

"We do?"

"We do."

So we did.

SEVENTEEN

T he first thing Sam wanted to talk about was me. "You need to take these days while Mrs. Rattle is here to rest."

"Can't do much else," I said, thinking how nice it would be to sleep for a week or two. Spike, who had jumped on the sofa upon which I sat, wagged his tail in accord, I'm sure, with my unspoken wish.

"Good. Don't go out unless I'm with you."

"Not even into the back yard?"

"Why would you want to go into the back yard?"

It was a sensible question. Not sure why I asked it. "Guess I don't. Pa can harvest any stray oranges he finds on the navel-orange tree."

"Yes, he can. He doesn't need you to help him."

I heaved a sigh, beginning to feel like a prisoner in my own home.

"Next, I'm going across the street to sign the final paperwork on the house, and I can begin moving in tomorrow and Sunday, unless I have to work. My schedule is chancy at the best of times."

"Oh, my goodness. That's fast!"

With a grin, Sam said, "Well, it's not quite as fast as it sounds. I'd been looking into buying that place as soon as I heard it would be going on the market. I met Eric Killebrew some time ago, you know."

"Oh, yes. I remember telling us you met him a while back."

"Yup."

"Huh," said I, borrowing from Sam himself. Did I like knowing the man I aimed to marry was so good at keeping secrets? From me? I'd have to think about it.

"I also cabled Renata this morning. There will probably be an answer from her when I get back to the station."

"Poor thing. I'm sorry her son is such a toad."

"Toads are useful," said Sam. "Don't tar them with brush of Frank Pagano."

"True."

"Next, I'm going to pay a call on Mr. Prophet at the Odd Fellows' Home to see if he'd like to move in across the street to keep an eye on things while I'm at work."

"I wish I could work again."

"You do?" Sam sounded surprised.

"Yes. I miss seeing people. Mrs. Pinkerton's a bother, but most of my clients are nice people and awfully good to me. Well, so's Mrs. Pinkerton, in spite of that flowered-dachshund monstrosity." I cast a significant glance around the living room, where traces of my clients' generosity yet flourished.

And I still had ten million thank-you notes to write. Oh, Lord...

"Wait until we lock up whoever's behind the attempts on your life before you start working again." Sam's nose wrinkled. He didn't appreciate how I earned my family's living. Billy hadn't, either, but so far Sam hadn't requested—or demanded—I cease being a spiritualist-medium after we were married. I think he knew I wouldn't comply if he did.

"I will. Can't do much else."

"Good. After I talk to Prophet, I'm going to have a long conversation with my nephew."

The expression on Sam's face told me he was looking forward to this "conversation." I hoped he wouldn't injure Frank too badly. Not that I cared if he hurt Frank, but his job might be in jeopardy if he killed a prisoner.

Not that Sam would ever do anything like that.

The rest of that day and all of Saturday I pretty much spent on the sofa, reading, with Spike on my lap. He was convenient. I could just prop a book on him and read away. It was kind of hard to turn pages with only one useful arm, but if I positioned my left hand in its sling just so, I could manage. Mrs. Rattle brought my lunch about twelve-thirty, and it was quite tasty considering it wasn't made by Aunt Vi.

On Saturday evening after dinner, Sam surprised me by saying he aimed to take the whole family to church the next day. "If you're up to it," he said.

"Oh, sure. All I've done for the past two days is read and sleep. I miss my friends."

"According to your father, the telephone has rung non-stop for the past several days, and Harold Kincaid brought you lunch from the Hotel Castleton today."

"Well, yes, it has and he did. But it's not the same as being able to just go out and about."

"Also according to your father, Miss Petrie has been bringing you new books daily. And Browning has brought you more of his dime-novel collection."

"Well…Yes, they have." I grinned, remembering. "Pa's fascinated with Mr. Prophet. He can't wait to meet him."

"He'll get his chance if things work out the way I hope they will."

"Good."

"Joe said Mr. and Mrs. Buckingham have been here with flowers and knitted items."

"Crocheted," I corrected. "Although Flossie can knit, too. Yes, people have been very kind to me. I guess I just don't like feeling trapped."

"According to Joe, Dr. Benjamin has been visiting you daily."

"Yes, but that's as a physician." I thought of something else. "And he hasn't been here today."

"There's still time. Anyhow, you know he's a friend, too."

"True," I admitted.

"You can't forget Pudge Wilson, either," said Sam, grinning. "I'll bet anything he's over here at least once a day, hoping you'll let him do a good deed for you."

"Yes, yes, yes. I suppose I shouldn't complain." But I did it so well.

Sam, who I swear could read my mind sometimes, said, "But you complain so well."

"Nertz," said I.

With a chuckle, Sam said, "Could be a whole lot worse. You could reside in one of Mr. Prophet's wooden overcoats."

"Oh!" I cried, sudden clarity shining like the sun in my brain. "*That's* what a wooden overcoat is! A coffin!"

"Got it in one."

I giggled. "All right. I'll stop whining."

"Good. Now I have things to get done."

"Thanks, Sam."

"I'll pick you and your family up in plenty of time for church tomorrow."

"Why don't you come to breakfast?"

"You talked me into it," he said with a grin.

"You're *so* hard to persuade."

"One of my few weaknesses."

And off he went. Spike and I meandered to the bedroom. I guess resting all the time was a good cure for what ailed a person, because I noticed my aches and pains were considerably less tender that evening than they'd been even the prior day. This, in spite of the fact I hadn't taken any of that detestable morphine syrup. Things were definitely looking up. If you discounted the fact that someone seemed determined to murder me.

I hoped Dr. Benjamin would unwrap my left side soon. I was tired of being unbalanced, darn it. And I'd *never* speak that sentence aloud in front of Sam or Harold because they'd make a joke out of it, and I'd get mad. Being unable to use my left arm was downright annoying, however.

Crumb.

At that moment, a knock came on our front door. Saturday evening after dinner seemed a peculiar time for someone to be paying a social call, although I hoped a social call was what the knock portended, and not the arrival of yet another villain. Spike zoomed to the door, always elated to greet a visitor. Because I didn't want to open the door in case someone who wanted to murder me stood on the other side, I was pleased when Pa called out, "I'll get it!"

"Thank you!" I called back.

"Just me," came Dr. Benjamin's always-welcome voice. "Want to check on my patient."

"Good evening, Dr. Benjamin," I said. "I'm feeling a whole lot better."

"Happy to hear it. Sorry I couldn't get over here earlier. Two emergencies had me running around all day long."

"I'm sorry."

"One of them was to assist bringing a healthy baby girl into the world, so that was a happy emergency. The other was a little boy's broken leg. Poor kid fell out of a tree."

"In January? What was he doing climbing trees in January?"

"I have no earthly idea. Turned out to be a bad choice on his part, though. But let's go to your room, and I'll check that arm of yours. It's been wrapped up for two weeks. If I think you're healed enough, I'll unbind it."

"Yay!" I cried. "I'm so tired of being unbalanced!"

Doc Benjamin laughed. "Don't know if this will balance you, but you might be able to get around better. *If*," he cautioned, "you're up to it. And I'll be the one who will make that decision."

"That's all right. I trust you. But I sure hope you can unwrap me. I feel like a mummy."

So the doctor and I retired to my bedroom along with Spike, who was an eager participant in most things that went on in our house. Because I had expected Dr. Benjamin to visit me some time that day, I'd worn a loose house dress that could easily be slipped from my shoulders so he could inspect my left arm. He first inspected all my cuts, scrapes and gouges.

"These are healing very well, Daisy. Are your muscles still sore?"

"Yes. They twang a good deal, although not as much as they did at first."

"Good. Good. You might be able to get by on aspirin tablets now. You needed the morphine syrup at first because you were so banged up, but this is the end of your second week of recovery, and aspirin might do just as well."

"I'd like that. I hate morphine syrup. Not only does it taste vile, but...Well, Billy killed himself with it."

"I know, Daisy. You and Billy went through some rough years together. But I think you and Sam make a great couple."

"Thanks, Doc." I think I sniffled a bit. Pathetic. But not *as* pathetic.

"All right, now. Let's look at your left arm."

I lowered my dress and he palpated my arm and shoulder, squinting at my bruises.

"That car really got you, didn't it?"

"It did," I agreed.

He carefully took the pins out of the bandage holding my left arm to my body. "Don't drop your arm suddenly. Move it slowly," he told me.

I complied. "Oh, my! It doesn't hardly hurt at all!"

"Good. Good. Let me move the arm a little bit, just to be sure the shoulder is properly in place."

So he did. The shoulder hurt some, but not too badly. I began to think I'd actually live through this ordeal.

"Don't lift anything heavy for a couple of weeks," he told me. "And don't try to play baseball or anything."

"Baseball?"

"Just a little doctor humor, Daisy."

"I figured as much."

"But you do need to be careful. No lifting of crystal balls. You might be able to use the Ouija board, but I suggest you stay away from your work for another week at least. And yes, I know Mrs. Pinkerton is your best client and she calls you every day, begging you to read the cards or whatever, but you'll have to stand firm, or I'll wrap you up again, and this time I'll tie *both* arms to your torso."

"Golly, what a dreadful threat."

We both laughed.

"Just be careful, Daisy. I know you want to be able to do all the things you used to be able to do, but don't push yourself. I'd even recommend no shuffling of cards at this point."

"What about the piano?"

Dr. Benjamin cocked his head to one side as I repositioned my day dress. Boy, doing things like that was *so* much easier if you could use two arms instead of only one.

"You can try the piano. Maybe a couple of Chopin's etudes to start with. They're delicate. You can begin with them."

"I think I have some Chopin sheet music in the piano bench."

"If you can play an etude without hurting yourself, you can work your way up to…I don't know what young people sing these days."

"I don't know about singing, but I love to play 'The Charleston.'"

"Catchy tune," said Dr. Benjamin as he closed his black doctor's bag. He rolled up the yards and yards of gauze with which he'd wrapped my left arm and handed it to me. "If your arm hurts at night, you can just cut some of this off and tie your arm to your body. You might need someone to help you."

I instantly thought I'd like Sam to help me with that chore, but until we were married, I guess I'd have to call on my mother if I needed help wrapping myself.

Then I blushed. Dr. Benjamin looked at me as if my blush puzzled him. I didn't enlighten him.

I did, however, remove myself to the piano in the living room. There, after the kindly doctor opened the lid for me, I rummaged in the piano bench until I found some easy sheet music.

Playing the piano didn't hurt!

SAM WAS as good as his word. He knocked on the front door at about eight o'clock on Sunday morning. Spike galloped to the door. Pa followed. I didn't, but sat wrapped in my bathrobe at the kitchen table. I hadn't been awake for very long that morning, and I hadn't yet determined the precise soundness of my physical condition. My left arm, having been allowed its freedom all night, was slightly sore that morning. I moved it carefully, hoping I wouldn't have to have it wrapped again.

"Good morning, all," called Sam, hanging his hat and overcoat on the stand beside the front door.

"Good morning," I called back.

"Happy Sunday, Sam," said Vi, who was busily frying bacon in a big cast-iron skillet. She could fling that heavy thing around as if it weighed a mere nothing. Amazing woman, my aunt.

"Morning," said Ma, walking into the kitchen. I was pleased to see she wore the pretty blue suit I'd made for her and given her at Christmas. "How does it look?" she asked me, giving a little twirl in front of those of her family who'd gathered in the kitchen—which was all of us by that time.

"Lovely," said Sam, nodding.

"Looks great," said Pa, smiling.

"Beautiful," said Vi, tonging bacon from the skillet and onto a piece of butcher's paper she'd flattened out as a grease receptacle.

"It really does look good, Ma," I said. "I like that color on you. Goes with your eyes."

"And yours," said Ma, walking over to deposit a kiss on my head.

"I'll be glad when I can sew again, too," I said, wishing time would fly and it were about a month later than it was, my would-be killer was locked up (or dead. I didn't care at that point), and all my wounds had healed. Even though my left arm was sort-of usable, I couldn't lift the lovely White side-pedal sewing machine out of its case yet, because the machine weighed too darned much.

"Soon enough," said Sam. "But I've brought a guest for breakfast."

"You have?"

"Don't fuss at Sam, Daisy," Vi advised. "He called and asked if it was all right."

"I wasn't going to fuss," I said, feeling my cheeks heat. Very well, so I *had* been prepared to tell Sam he was a mighty pushy fellow to spring a guest on Vi and the family on a Sunday morning without warning.

"Ladies and gents," Sam said, smiling at all of us, "please allow me to present Mr. Lou Prophet, who will be residing in the house across the street until we can figure out who's trying to do in my fiancée."

And darned if Lou Prophet didn't shamble into the doorway between the dining room and kitchen! He looked as if he felt out of place in our pretty Pasadena bungalow. He'd probably have been more comfy in an adobe hut or something of that nature.

"Mr. Prophet!" I cried, standing with a little too much precipitation.

"How good to see you again." I didn't wince or anything, even though my sudden getting-to-my-feet maneuver had severely twanged several of my muscles and scabs.

Holding a disreputable-looking bowler hat in his hand, Mr. Prophet scanned the room with a scowl, then said, "Howdy."

"Thank you so much for rescuing my daughter, Mr. Prophet. Daisy's told us so much about you!" said Ma.

Eyeing me without favor, Prophet said, "Probably ain't true."

Puzzled, Ma said, "What isn't true?"

Flipping a hand my way, he said, "What she told you."

"Nonsense," said Pa. He walked to Prophet, grabbed his hand, and shook it vigorously. Prophet looked at my father as if he wished he hadn't done that. "Daisy said you saved her life. Or nearly saved her life, anyway."

"She saved her own life," said Prophet in his smoky, rusty growl. "She turned her head right in time. Otherwise, she'd still be skewered to that bench."

"And on that note," said Sam in a loudish voice, "let me show Mr. Prophet the house across the street. We'll be back in a few minutes."

They left. I gazed after them in some bemusement.

So did Ma. "What a curious character," said she.

"He is," I agreed. "He used to be a bounty hunter in the wild, wild west."

"The wild, wild west?" Ma gazed at me as if I were someone other than her staid Pasadena daughter.

"Yes. Pa and I have read several stories about him." I turned to my father for confirmation. "Haven't we, Pa?"

"We have indeed. Wonder if any of them are true. If they are, he's lived a…colorful life."

Vi laughed and began breaking eggs into a big bowl. "I expect that man's seen a lot in his days on this earth. He certainly doesn't look as though he belongs in Pasadena, though, does he?"

"No," I said. "I guess I already told you he'd been hired by a studio as a consultant on the set of some western flickers. But he…had an accident. Lost his leg."

"Goodness," said Ma, looking as if she might just cry for Mr.

Prophet's lost leg. "That's too bad." She sat on a chair near mine at the kitchen table. "Did you say he used to be a *bounty* hunter?"

"Yep," I told her, keeping the western theme alive in my response.

"My word. The old west seems…so long ago."

"It does, doesn't it?" I agreed. "Maybe it isn't, but it seems odd to have found a relic of it living here in Pasadena."

"True," said Pa.

"He's just a man," said Vi. "Like any other man. Did a job for money, just like most of us do."

Silence filled the kitchen along with the delicious cooking smells residing there. I wondered if Vi was right about Lou Prophet. Somehow, I kind of doubted it.

Mr. Prophet didn't return to the house with Sam for breakfast. This caused Vi no end of upset. "The poor man needs his food!" said she, looking at Sam as if he'd deliberately withheld Lou Prophet from her table for some fell purpose.

"He's kind of a strange man, Vi," I told her. "I don't think he's awfully sociable."

"You should etch that on a plaque and hang it on the wall," muttered Sam. "I'll take him a plate, Vi, if you trust me not to drop it."

"Nonsense! I know you won't drop it," said Vi. "Here, I'll just fix a nice breakfast for him. And don't forget to take silverware, unless you have some over there already."

"Not yet. Mrs. Killebrew left several items of furniture, but she took all her silverware and so forth."

"You can probably get some cheap at Nelson's Five and Dime," I told my beloved.

He turned and looked at me with a squinty-eyed frown. "Or you could come with me to Nash's or another nice store and pick out a pattern you like."

"Oh." I felt silly, although I'm not sure why. Ours would, after all, be a second marriage for both of us. I didn't have any silverware or china left from my marriage to Billy, but that's because we'd never had any. I'd just graduated from high school, and we'd only been married a few weeks before Billy was shipped off to fight in the Great War. Then, when he'd come home again, I'd had to work like the devil to support us, he being unable to do so. He'd hated that.

Anyway, I'd also neglected to remember the salient fact that Sam was, evidently, rich.

"How sweet, Sam," said Ma mistily.

"Yes, that's very nice of you, Sam," said Pa. He didn't sound as if he aimed to burst into tears any time soon.

"Here you go," said Vi, handing Sam a plate piled high with scrambled eggs, bacon, and three (maybe four) of her light-as-air biscuits. She wrapped a fork, spoon and knife in a napkin and jammed them into the breast pocket of Sam's Sunday suit. Then she then added a huge dollop of butter to the plate. "I'd better give you some preserves to go on those biscuits, too," she said.

To give Sam credit, his knees—even his left knee, which was attached to his wounded left thigh—didn't buckle. He did stare with fascination at the huge pile of food before him. I suspect he was wondering how he was going to carry the plate, silverware and whatever kind of preserves Aunt Vi aimed to give him with only two hands. "Um…"

Pa rose from the table. "I'll help you, Sam," he said, grinning.

"Thanks, Joe." Sam sounded relieved.

EIGHTEEN

"Mr. Prophet isn't coming to church with us?" I asked as my family piled in to Sam's Hudson. I had my trusty dachshund-head cane with me to assist with my balance as I maneuvered around the church.

"No," said Sam. "I asked, and he politely declined my invitation." The way his lips twisted into a grin made me doubt the "politely" part of Mr. Prophet's refusal. "Anyway, he's staying there to watch for trouble or people lurking around your home."

"That's nice of him. I'm just kind of sorry we won't get to see more of him."

"I think you'll get your chance."

I hoped so.

That Sunday's church service was uneventful. Of course I didn't sit with the choir because I was still lame, although I was no longer wrapped up like the silverware Vi'd given Sam that morning. The choir sounded good even with me not in it. I kind of resented that.

After church, we walked to Fellowship Hall for tea and cookies. Sam assisted me so I didn't limp too badly. He was so good to me. Most of the time. My cane helped, too.

I sat at one of the tables in the hall while Sam went to the front of the room to get some cookies for himself. I didn't want any cookies, since Aunt Vi had a lovely pork roast cooking away at home, and I wanted to save myself for pork. That doesn't sound right. Never mind.

"Oh, Mrs. Majesty!" came the voice of Miss Betsy Powell. I turned as much as I could and saw her clinging to the arm of a person whom I presumed to be her new gentleman friend, the owner of the car that had nearly killed me, Mr. Bernard Randford.

I smiled and said, "How do you do, Miss Powell?"

"I'm fine, thank you. But please. Let me introduce you to Mr. Randford."

I faced the gent in question. I didn't like his looks. Not that I'm the least little bit judgmental or anything, you understand. He was a little taller than Miss Powell, who was maybe five feet, five inches tall; had brown hair with lots of white hair scattered in it; he was little chunky; and he had one of those stupid tiny mustaches that looked as if somebody'd drawn a line with a pencil above his upper lip. Or maybe he'd glued a black worm there. Anyway, I disliked mustaches of that nature and, for some reason unknown to me, I disliked Mr. Randford upon our first meeting.

"How do you do, Mr. Randford?" I said politely, holding out my right hand for him to shake. I'd propped my cane against the table and hoped nobody would trip over it or knock it down.

He had a damp, limp handshake, which was another thing not to like him for. Not that I wanted anyone to shake my hand so hard he mangled it, but I think a man's handshake should at least be firm. Bet you anything Lou Prophet's hand wouldn't feel like a dead halibut when he shook hands with somebody else. Mr. Bernard Randford, upon first viewing, was about as different from Mr. Lou Prophet as a man could get.

"I'm very sorry my machine was used to do you harm, Mrs. Majesty. I trust you're recovering well?" said Mr. Randford. He had a nasal voice. Yet one more reason not to like him.

Dislike, however, didn't negate the fact that, as a spiritualist-medium with a long client list, I had to be gracious no matter to whom I spoke. Therefore, I said, "Thank you, Mr. Randford. It's been a difficult couple of weeks, but I'm healing nicely according to Dr. Benjamin. I'm sorry your automobile was used for such a nefarious purpose. I hear it didn't escape unscathed."

"No," said he, frowning. "It didn't. But it sustained much less damage than was done to you, and I'm terribly sorry."

"Well, you didn't run it into me, so I don't suppose you should be sorry," I said, not watching my tongue as well as I usually did.

"Oh, Mrs. Majesty!" Miss Betsy Powell giggled. Her giggle wasn't as annoying as her scream, but it wasn't at the top on my list of pleasant things to listen to.

"It's nice you're coming to church with Miss Powell lately," I said politely.

"Isn't it?" Miss Powell squeezed Mr. Randford's arm.

With a thin smile, he said, "Yes. I'm enjoying being a member of the congregation."

"Did you have a church home before you began attending here?" Not that I cared, but I was trying to be polite.

"Not really. I have no family in the Pasadena area except for a cousin. We're really more like brothers than cousins. His health has been poor in recent months."

"I'm sorry to hear it. And I do hope he gets well soon."

Mr. Randford cleared his throat. "I doubt he will. He's been my best friend ever since we were boys, too," he said, shaking his head in, I guess, sadness.

"Oh, dear. I'm so sorry."

"Yes. Well, it's been nice meeting you, Mrs. Majesty."

"Likewise," I told him, although it was a bit of a fib.

Then Mr. Randford turned and more or less dragged Miss Betsy Powell with him to a table across the room. My chest itched, so I surreptitiously scratched it, trying to be as inconspicuous as possible. It's embarrassing to have to scratch an itch in public, especially when it's on your chest. Probably scratching an itchy leg would be more embarrassing. Oh, bother, never mind me.

Sam returned at that moment and sat next to me. He set a teacup at my place. How sweet. "Thanks, Sam." Ma, Pa and Aunt Vi were chatting with friends scattered around the room.

"You're welcome." He gazed after Miss Powell and Mr. Randford. "I see you got to meet Randford."

"Yes. I don't like him."

Sam chuckled. "Why doesn't that surprise me?"

"What do you mean by that?" I demanded of my darling. "Do you think I'm too quick to judge or something?"

"Good Lord, no!"

"You do, too. I can tell."

"Don't worry about it, Daisy. I don't like him much, either, but I don't know anything about him that might be considered criminal."

"Huh. Miss Betsy Powell has a penchant for selecting the worst men available to her."

Sam chuckled again and bit into a sugar cookie. His eyebrows lifted. After he swallowed, he said, "Pretty good."

"Bet it's not as good as one of Aunt Vi's sugar cookies."

"I'm sure you're right." He finished the sugar cookie and then ate an oatmeal cookie, however.

"Are you two ready to leave?" asked Pa as he walked to our table. "Vi wants to get home and make sure the potatoes are mashed and the gravy's gravied."

"Gravied?" I tilted my head to look at my wonderful father.

He shrugged. "Better than gravid, I guess."

"What does gravid mean?" asked Sam as he helped me to stand.

"Full of eggs," I told him.

He looked at me as if I were a strange and unusual creature. "How do you know that?"

I nearly shrugged myself, but remembered not to in time to save my iffy shoulders. "I don't know. I guess I read it in a book and had to look it up once or something. The definition stuck."

"You know the strangest things, Daisy," said my fiancé.

"I don't think knowing what a word means is strange."

"But why would anyone invent a word that means full of eggs?"

"How should *I* know?"

"I'm sure there's a reason," said Pa in an attempt to thwart a verbal spat before it began. Sam and I had been known to bicker from time to time.

Sam only grinned, and I wanted to thump him. Since my mother, father and aunt were with us, I didn't.

An interesting scene awaited us when Sam drove up to the house.

"Oh, my goodness!" cried Ma, staring out the Hudson's window.

"What on earth?" came from Vi.

"Good Lord," Pa muttered.

They had reason to exclaim. Sitting on the stairs leading up to the Gumm-Majesty bungalow's porch—to distinguish it from the Rotondo bungalow across the street—rested Lou Prophet, his wooden leg extended in front of him, smoking one of his quirlies. Next to him, squirming like a caterpillar, lay a man bound with rope. As Sam parked, Prophet heaved himself to his feet. Or his foot and his peg. Sam got out of the car and hurried to the porch. I wanted to do likewise, but couldn't. My folks and Vi beat me to Prophet and the caterpillar, but I heard what everyone said.

"What's going on, Prophet?"

"Caught this toughnut trying to get into your house."

Toughnut? I wondered if that was another word for a curly wolf. I decided then and there I'd compile a dictionary of western terms. Didn't have single clue what I'd use it for, but it might be amusing to read all the odd words and definitions to Harold.

"Really?" Thanks to my trusty cane, I'd managed to make it to the porch. "Which door?"

"Back."

Sam and I exchanged a glance, and I appreciated Sam having bullied me into locking all the doors.

"Do you know why?" I asked.

"Prob'ly had something to do with this." Prophet held up a gun, swinging it by its—well, I don't know what you call it—the thing that encircles the trigger. Don't know what kind of gun it was, either. I knew it wasn't a rifle or a shotgun, but that's about as far as my knowledge of weaponry extended.

Sam got out his handkerchief and took the gun from Prophet. "Have you touched it anywhere except the trigger guard?"

Aha! It was a trigger guard!

"Naw. No need."

147

"Thank you, Mr. Prophet," said Ma, staring hard at the bound man and cringing a little. I couldn't blame her. It's not often someone with a gun tries to get into your house while you're not in it. Or even while you are.

Sam turned to my family. "Why don't you go on inside. Mr. Prophet and I can discuss this matter. I'll let you know if I have to make an arrest and take this fellow"—he touched the caterpillar with his shoe tip—"to the station."

"Good idea," said Pa, herding Ma and Aunt Vi into the house. He had to unlock the front door, which was unusual, and which he'd forgot all about until the knob didn't turn. He fished a key out of his pocket and opened the door. I'd be awfully glad when things got back to normal.

I stayed outside, in spite of Sam and Mr. Prophet frowning at me. "It's *my* life, darn it!" I told them both. "I want to know what's going on and who's trying to end it and why, and I'm not leaving until I hear what this…man, I guess you'd call him, although I think he's probably some other kind of animal…has to say."

"Grmph," said the caterpillar. Guess he didn't like my disparaging comment. Too bad.

With a shrug, Prophet said, "Fair enough."

Sam only heaved a large-sized sigh. "So do you know this fellow's name?"

"Nope."

"How'd you discover him trying to get into the house?" Sam asked.

"Followed him."

A little exasperated at Prophet's terseness, I said, "Why did you follow him? I mean, when did you decide to follow him and why? When did you first see him?"

With a squint for me, Prophet said, "Saw him goin' up your drive. The detective here told me nobody should be doin' that, so I crossed the street and trailed him. Went into the back yard, and I got him when he was trying to jimmy the back door lock."

The door to my bedroom. I think I shuddered.

"How'd you get him?" asked Sam.

"Hit him with a stick."

One of Sam's eyebrows lifted. "Where's the stick?"

"Back there." Prophet gestured with his thumb to the back yard.

Sam and I walked to the back yard. Yes, I hurt, but I was more interested in the stick that had quelled a gunman than I was my aches and pains. Besides, I used my lovely new cane, thus taking some of the weight off the rest of my mangled body. A giant branch lay at the foot of the ramp Pa had built for Billy's wheelchair. I watched closely as Sam walked over and picked it up. It appeared to be heavy. It was certainly thick.

"That's a big branch."

"It is," Sam agreed.

"It doesn't look like a branch from any of our trees," I said as he brought it to me.

"I think it came from one of the trees in the back of the yard across the street."

"Goodness."

"Or something."

"Did he damage the lock as he tried to jimmy it open?"

"I'll take a look." So he did. "Looks fine. Prophet must have cracked him over the head before he had a chance to do much damage, although I'll check it more thoroughly later."

"Thanks, Sam."

We returned to the front porch, Sam dragging the branch. Prophet had sat on the steps again and rolled himself another coffin nail. Which was a quirley. Which was a cigarette. Definitely had to start my dictionary of old-west sayings. Maybe somebody would even publish it.

"Is this the stick you hit him with?" asked Sam, brandishing same.

"That's it."

"Broke it off a tree in the other yard?"

"Hacked it off."

"You brought an axe with you?" I asked.

Prophet glanced at me and squinted as if he considered my question a particularly inane one. Then he said, "Yeah."

"Very well then," I said and moved to the other side of the porch

149

where I had a better view of the caterpillar. "You tied him up with rope?"

"What's it look like?" asked Prophet. Clearly I'd asked another dimwitted question.

"Well, it looks like rope, but…Well, where did you get rope?"

"Silly li'l thing. Any man worth two shots of cheap tangleleg comes prepared."

What was this tangleleg of which Mr. Prophet kept speaking? Rye whiskey? Or did the term include other spirituous liquors? If I ever figured out what it was, I'd be sure to add it to my dictionary. "I see." Then, since I didn't know what else to say, I rested my back against a porch pillar, leaned a bit on my cane, and watched.

Sam dropped the branch issue—and the branch itself—and walked over to the caterpillar. "And you have no idea who this is?" he asked Prophet.

"Nope."

"All right. Let me see here."

He reached down and grabbed the squirming bundle by one of his ropes. Prophet had done a spectacular job tying the man up. I doubt Vi had ever trussed a turkey or a goose so thoroughly. I noticed, when Sam rolled him over far enough to reveal his face, that Prophet had stuffed a gag in his mouth. I guessed it was a handkerchief or bandanna or something of a like nature. My nose wrinkled, thinking I wouldn't want one of Lou Prophet's hankies stuffed in my mouth.

And that is pure prejudice speaking. For all I knew Mr. Lou Prophet laundered his handkerchiefs every single night. Another glance at Prophet, idly smoking and staring at what Sam was doing from his perch on the porch, squelched that thought nearly before it had been born.

Sam pulled the handkerchief, or whatever it was, from the man's mouth. The man spat and cursed. Prophet reached over and whacked him on his ear with the back of his hand.

The man said, "Ow!"

"There's a lady present," said Prophet. "So watch your mouth, you gutless cur."

Oh, my. Was this the famous "Code of the West"? Or did I just make that up? I thought I'd heard the term somewhere but decided not to ask Prophet about it. He didn't seem to care for my questions.

"What's your name?" asked Sam, hauling the trussed fellow into a semi-seated position. He couldn't bend very well because of the ropes binding him from tip to toe.

"Go to hell."

Prophet smacked his ear harder.

"Ow!"

"Answer the man," Prophet told Trussy.

"You go to hell with him," said Trussy.

What the heck. Since I had my lovely dachshund-head cane with me, I bopped the guy on the ear, too.

His "Ow!" was much louder that time.

"Your name," Sam growled in his I'm-going-to-kill-you-and-hide-your-body-in-the-foothills voice.

"Bruce."

"Who Bruce?" Sam.

"Or Bruce who? Or whom?" Me.

"Go to hell."

This time Prophet swung his arm out and clobbered the man across the mouth. The semi-seated, bound man fell over backwards and conked his head on the cement porch.

"Ow!" he hollered.

"Answer my question," said Sam in the same deadly voice. "What's your name?"

The man wriggled and wriggled as if he were trying to sit up. Finally Sam grabbed one of his rope ties and jerked him up. "Answer... My...Question."

The man's eyes were as round as pie plates by this time. "Bruce. Bruce Petrie."

"Another Petrie!" I said. Well, I kind of shrieked it. But really, the Petrie family—except for Regina, who was a pearl among women—had been doing bad things to me and to people I loved for about three or four years by then. "Why doesn't your clan stay the heck in Oklahoma where it belongs and leave us peaceful Pasadenans alone?"

Mr. Bruce Petrie didn't answer me, although I don't think he was being obstinate. I got the feeling that he was more or less petrified with fright.

Good.

NINETEEN

I stayed on the porch while Sam interrogated Bruce Petrie. Prophet sat there, too, looking on with faint interest and smoking one coffin nail after another. I thought about asking him if he thought all that smoke was good for him but decided not to. I got the feeling Mr. Lou Prophet didn't worry a whole lot about his health.

After several long minutes of questioning, I learned Mr. Bruce Petrie had been hired by someone—he claimed not to know whom—to sneak into my bedroom and shoot me dead when I returned from church that day. It was a distressing thought, being killed by a total stranger who'd been hired by another stranger. Why would anyone want to do that? To me, of all people? I'd never done any harm in the world, darn it!

Then again, perhaps a few Petries might retain villainous thoughts about me. After all, it had been a Petrie who'd seduced Stacy Kincaid away from the Salvation Army and into a vile child-trafficking scheme. And Stacy's precious Percival Petrie had died after tripping over my prone body—prone because Stacy Kincaid had bashed me over the head with a chair—fallen down some basement stairs and killed himself. But I was the good guy in all my dealings with the dread Petrie clan! *They* were the bad guys. Or curly wolves, if you were Lou Prophet.

However, I'm pretty sure neither Stacy Kincaid nor the rest of the evil branch of the Petrie clan saw matters in the same light as I.

"Bet Stacy's behind all of it, Sam," I said to him as he was winding up his chat with Bruce Petrie.

"Wouldn't surprise me. If we can tie this to her, she's ruined her chance at turning states' evidence and getting off easy."

"Oh, I hope we can!" I said.

Lou Prophet grinned up at me. "You're not so bad, Miss Daisy."

"Neither are you, Mr. Prophet."

The front door opened. Ma stepped outside, looked at us all, and said, "Vi has dinner on the table. Will you be joining us?" Her head turned Prophet's way. "You're invited, too, Mr. Prophet."

"He should be," I said enthusiastically. "He saved my life again!"

"He did?" Ma appeared more appalled than gratified, but I understood.

"Whatcha got cookin'?" asked Prophet.

"I don't cook," said Ma candidly. "Neither does Daisy. Fortunately for the family, Daisy's Aunt Viola cooks for us. Today we have roasted pork, mashed potatoes, gravy, peas, carrots, and I think she made a pie for dessert, although I'm not sure what kind."

"Do join us, Mr. Prophet. Vi is the best cook in the world, and you deserve a good meal."

"Just had one," said Prophet. "She cook that breakfast I ate?"

"She did," I said with pride.

Glancing from Sam to Bruce Petrie and then back to Sam, Prophet said, "What do you say, Detective? I could use a good meal, but what do we do with this hardtail?"

Hardtail. Yet another word for which I didn't have a definition. I hoped Mr. Prophet would warm up to me enough to tell me what all those words of his meant.

Sam stood back, staring down at the still-bound Bruce Petrie, then shrugged and said, "Why not? We can store this pig somewhere while we dine on another pig, and then you and I can go to the station. I'll take your statement there, and we'll lock up this bimbo."

Prophet pushed himself to his foot and peg once more. He took off his disreputable hat and bowed to my mother. "Thank you kindly, ma'am. I'd like that just fine."

"You really will," I told him. "Vi's pork roast is wonderful."

"It is," Sam agreed.

"I'm sure you'll enjoy it, Mr. Prophet," said Ma.

"What are you going to do with this piece of Petrie scum while we eat?" I asked Sam.

Sam pursed his mouth, squinted, and said, "Why don't I just take him inside. I'll stuff him under the piano bench, and he can wait there until we've finished eating dinner."

"You got a piano in there?" asked Prophet?

"Yes. I play it a little," I told him with becoming modesty. "Guess you didn't see it when you came in the house this morning. It's in the living room, but it's not immediately apparent." I told myself not to yammer at Mr. Prophet. He didn't need a detailed explanation of our home's floor plan.

"I like me a piano tune from time to time," said he. Turning to Sam, he said, "Want me to help you drag that vermin into the house?"

"I think I can do it," said Sam, who was a big man.

And he did do it. Dragged Bruce Petrie into the house by his ropes and, true to his word, hauled him over to the piano in the northwest corner of the living room and shoved him underneath the piano bench. He made sure to cover the man's mouth with the gag before he left him there because nobody wanted to hear him whine and curse as we feasted. The rest of us retired to the dining room.

Naturally, discussion around the table centered on the scoundrel who'd try to break into our bungalow and murder me and who might have hired him. I reiterated my belief that Stacy Kincaid remained the ultimate source of this latest incursion into my peace of mind and body. "I think I'll telephone Harold. He might know something, even if he doesn't know he knows it."

Everybody looked at me. Lou Prophet seemed to be savoring his meal. In our brief acquaintance, I hadn't seen him appear so placid and serene as he did then. He actually smiled at me—a little.

"That's a good idea," said Sam. "Maybe even his mother knows something she doesn't know she knows."

"She doesn't know a whole lot," I muttered. Unkind, I know.

"Daisy," said Ma. She always does that when I'm rude or catty. I was used to it.

I heard Lou Prophet chuckle under his breath and decided I really *did* like him.

We finished our meal in a leisurely manner, not rushing ourselves in spite of the occasional thumps and groans from the living room. Bruce Petrie could just stay there and suffer, as far as I was concerned. In fact, if I had my way, I'd stick him in the basement with the other killer I'd locked in there and let him die and rot, too.

Sometimes I'm not very nice, but please don't tell my clients.

I was well enough by that time to help clear away the dishes, so I did, with Ma's help. Then I bought out the pie—apple, by golly—and set it at Vi's place at the table. She cut big wedges of pie and handed them around on the plates Ma had set at her place for the purpose. Vi deposited a thick chunk of cheese on each plate, too.

As he always did when we had apple pie and cheese, Pa recited, "'Apple pie without some cheese is like a kiss without the squeeze.'"

"Joe," said Ma. "That one's so old, it's growing whiskers."

"Still true, though," said Pa, grinning at her.

"Sure is," said Lou Prophet.

I studied him surreptitiously and decided he'd probably been quite the lad—I think the British use that expression to describe womanizers—in his day. Which had been about thirty or forty years prior to that day. I could tell he'd been handsome once. Actually, he still had an earthy, if rugged and well-worn, appeal about him. Not that I wasn't totally devoted to Sam, but heck, a girl can still look, can't she? Men do. All the time, curse them.

After we finished dining, Sam and Lou Prophet hauled Bruce Petrie out from under the piano bench, dragged him to Sam's Hudson and stuffed him in the back seat. I was sorry to see them go. Not Petrie. The other two.

"Come back later," I called after them. "We can have roasted pork sandwiches for supper, and then I can play the piano."

"You up to playing already?" asked Sam.

How nice of him to ask. "Dr. Benjamin unwrapped my left side last evening, and I've practiced a bit. I can play without injuring myself." I hoped.

"I like me a good piano tune," said Mr. Prophet again.

So Sam shrugged and said, "Sure. We can tell you if we find out anything more from this source after we question him at the station."

"Source," muttered Prophet. "I'd call him a sumbitch."

"We try not to use language like that in front of the ladies," said Sam, clearly trying not to laugh.

Oddly enough, although I scolded Sam about his swearing from time to time, Prophet's didn't bother me. I think that was because he looked so much like a man to whom curses came naturally, they just seemed part of him. That doesn't make any sense. Oh, well.

Spike and I took a nap after Ma, Pa and I cleaned up the dinner dishes. I was so full of good food, I nearly swooned even before I fell onto my bed. Then I was sorry I hadn't taken more care about positioning myself, because falling had aggravated a lot of my aches and pains and twanged my left shoulder. Therefore, because it helped and because I didn't need as much of it as I had a couple of weeks earlier, I got back up, went to the kitchen, pried the lid off the peppermint drops, took a sip of morphine syrup, popped a peppermint drop into my mouth and returned to bed. I swore I'd take no more morphine syrup after this. It would be aspirin for me.

We napped for about two hours! Boy, I never knew naps could feel so good. When I arose again, I took off my church clothes—bad me for not doing so before my nap—put on a fairly respectable house dress— blue, like my eyes—and went to the kitchen. There I hauled a chair to the telephone and sat myself on it before dialing Harold Kincaid's number. Spike sat beside my chair, gazing longingly up at me, hoping for food. Poor Spike. "In a little bit," I promised him. He didn't appear appeased.

For the record, Harold lives in a community called San Marino a little south of Pasadena. Nobody but extremely wealthy people lived in San Marino. I don't think they even allowed middle-class folks like the Gumms and the one remaining Majesty to purchase property in their hallowed grounds. The Castleton estate was there, and Harold lived not far from it. Mr. Castleton, after making a fortune on the backs of the Chinamen and Irishmen who'd built the railroad, had retired there on his estate and built a hospital, which also carried his name.

I knew his daughter, Emmaline. In fact, Emmaline Castleton was an actual friend of mine. Every time I talked to her, I felt as though I were speaking with royalty, although she never acted snooty or above-it-all. Very nice person, and one with whom I had something unlucky in common. My Billy had been injured during the late war and had then taken his own life. Emmaline's fiancé had been killed outright—sort of outright. He'd been shot and suffered for a week or so before succumbing to his wounds. Odd as it may sound, a young German soldier helped him through the days during which he'd suffered. In effect, the war had slain both Emmaline's man and mine, but at different times. Gloomy thought.

Anyway, as soon as I ascertained none of our party-line neighbors were on the 'phone, I called Harold's home. His houseboy, Roy Castillo, a very nice young man who had been kidnapped from his home in Tortuga and brought to the United States to serve perverted men, answered the telephone.

"Good afternoon, Roy. This is Daisy Majesty."

"How do you do, Mrs. Majesty?"

"Oh, call me Daisy, please. We don't need formalities anymore."

With a little laugh, Roy said, "Very well, Miss Daisy."

"Is Harold home today, Roy? If he is and he's not doing anything important, I'd like to speak to him."

"I'll fetch him for you," said Roy. He had the loveliest accent. Lilting and musical. I guess people from Tortuga all sound like that. Roy's the only Tortugan I've ever met.

After a few moments, Harold's somewhat high-pitched voice came over the telephone wires. "What is it now, Daisy? Somebody run you over with a freight train this time?"

"What a delightful mental image *that* conjures up, Harold."

"Always happy to do my part," he said. "What's up, Daisy? To what do I owe this delightful interruption of my peaceful Sunday afternoon?"

"Another Petrie has slithered out from under his rock. He tried to break into the house and shoot me today."

Silence on the other end of the line lasted until Harold burst out, "*What?*"

"You heard me. Bruce Petrie. I'd never heard of this one before, but he tried to jimmy the lock on our back door. Good thing Sam forced me to lock all the doors. We usually don't bother."

"How'd you find out about him before he did the dastardly deed? Clearly, you're not dead."

Had I told Harold about Mr. Lou Prophet? By golly, I don't think I had! How could I have not told my best friend about such a colorful, old-timey character? Silly me. I guess I'd confined most of my conversations about the old bounty hunter to the family, Sam, Regina Petrie and Robert Browning.

So I told Harold about Mr. Lou Prophet.

"He was a what?" Harold sounded slightly stunned.

"A bounty hunter. In the old west. He used to go out and capture criminals, bring 'em in dead or alive and collect the reward money for them. People used to write dime novels about him."

"Good Lord. And he's here in Pasadena? How old is this guy, anyway, if he was chasing crooks in the 1880s and '90s? He's got to be a hundred years old!"

"Not quite. I'd guess in his mid- to late-seventies. He was hired as a consultant on some picture sets where they film all the westerns they show nowadays, only he can't do that anymore. He has a wooden leg because he was with two ladies of the night and a crate of bootleg liquor in an automobile that drove off a cliff in Santa Monica. He was the only survivor. Well, most of him survived anyhow. His leg didn't."

"Good Lord. And Sam's awful nephew threw a knife at you? In your *church?*"

"Yes."

"Good Lord."

That was Harold's third "good Lord." I considered the good Lord and Lou Prophet for a second or two and couldn't help but laugh. After I stopped—actually, Harold told me to shut up—I said, "I have a feeling the good Lord and Lou Prophet don't have a lot to do with each other on a regular basis."

"I've got to meet this man."

"Sure! Come on over any old time. He's staying in Sam's house across the street."

Another spate of silence ensued. Crumb, I guess I hadn't told Harold about Sam having bought the Killebrew house, either. I'd been a total failure in the gossip department these past couple of weeks.

So I told Harold about Sam buying the Killebrew house.

Harold came out with his fourth, "Good Lord."

TWENTY

After Harold recovered from his state of shock, I asked him if he thought his sister might be the person behind all the recent attempts on my life.

"Wouldn't put it past her, although I don't know how to find out."

"Hmm. Do you visit her in jail?"

"Why would I do something like that?"

"Valid question. Does your mother visit her?"

"Mother? Visit anyone in jail? Get a grip on your senses, Daisy Gumm Majesty. Do you honestly think my mother would be caught dead walking into a police station and asking to speak with a prisoner?"

"Not even her own daughter?"

"Mother doesn't seem to be as fond of my darling sister as she once was."

"Really? I'm astonished!" I meant it, too.

"Really. In fact, Mother is totally disgusted that Stacy, *her* daughter, did something that disgraced the family so thoroughly."

"I don't know about the thoroughly part. Anyone who knows about your father probably blames him for Stacy's behavior and acquits your mother of any negligence or wrong-doing. Heck, *he's* the one who disgraced the family, although I do know your mother's not the firmest of disciplinarians—"

"Ha!"

"But she's not an evil person. She's just been too rich and pampered all her life. Sort of like Stacy, actually, only your mother didn't use her wealth for evil. She used it for...well, supporting me, for instance." For a couple of years my income from catering to Mrs. Kincaid as a spiritual-ist-medium had pretty much supported my entire family, in fact.

"I guess you might be considered a good cause."

"Thanks, Harold."

"But let me think about how we can get Stacy to spill her guts—"

"Ew."

"Don't interrupt. I'm trying to think of someone Stacy might talk to. Someone not of her ilk, I mean."

"What about Johnny Buckingham?"

"The Salvation Army fellow?"

"Yes."

"I...don't know. I think Stacy's through with the Salvation Army at this time in her nefarious career."

"They aren't through with her," I said, thinking about how Johnny and his Army didn't ever seem to give up on people. Even people like Stacy. Johnny had rescued her a couple of times before. Why not now?

"I don't suppose it would hurt if you asked him to talk to her," Harold admitted.

"Sam says if he finds out she's the one who hired Bruce Petrie to kill me, she won't be able to turn states' evidence."

"Really?" Harold sounded pleased.

"Really."

"Then that makes it even more important to pin it on her."

"If she did it," I cautioned.

"Oh, hell, who cares at this point? My sister is a disgrace to human-ity. She's done enough evil deeds in her short life to send her straight to hell."

"I thought you didn't believe in heaven and hell." My voice was teasing, but Harold's attitude about religion had at first shocked me. Then it didn't anymore. I don't know why, except that most people who consider themselves Christians don't countenance Harold and his ilk, and I don't think people like Harold are in any way sinful. Harold himself told me he was born the way he was, and choice had nothing to do with it. Heck, Del Farrington, Harold's all-but-spouse, was a firm believer. He even went to Saint Andrews every Sunday of his life and believed wholeheartedly in his Roman Catholic Church. Harold called Saint Andrews "Our Lady of Perpetual Malice," but not in front of Del.

Catholicism didn't go over very well in my family, either, but not for the same reason. Both Ma and Aunt Vi considered Roman Catholics little better than idol worshipers. But how did I get on this subject? I beg your pardon.

"I only hope there's a hell waiting for Stacy. I don't care about anyone else. Except my father. He can go to hell, too," said Harold, sounding as if he considered himself magnanimous. "But let me think about this. I might be able to come up with an idea about tricking Stacy into confessing she hired someone to wipe you out."

"Thanks, Harold."

"So when can I meet this old-west character of yours?"

"Um...I don't know. Why don't you come to dinner tomorrow evening? We dine at the unfashionable hour of six p.m., but maybe you can force yourself. I'm sure Vi won't mind, and I'll see if I can get Mr. Prophet to dine with us, too. He's an interesting bloke."

"I doubt he calls himself a bloke, sweetie."

"No, I'm sure he doesn't." I chuckled as Harold and I disconnected our call.

Then I called the Buckinghams. I kind of expected they wouldn't be home as it was still Sunday, and their Sundays were filled to the brim with services and stuff like that. I was right. Hmm. I wracked my brain to think of someone else who might be able to help me. And couldn't. Fudge.

"What are you doing, Daisy?" asked Ma as she walked into the kitchen rubbing her eyes. Guess she'd napped, too.

"Trying to think of someone who can make Stacy Kincaid confess she's hired people to kill me."

Ma gasped. "Oh, my! Do you really think it's the Kincaid girl who's behind this?"

I got up, slowly so I wouldn't twang all over, and said, "I don't know, Ma. I just hope we can find out who's doing it before they succeed."

"Oh, Daisy! Don't say that!" Ma threw her arms around me. Because she did it out of love, I didn't scream, although it hurt a good deal to be squeezed at that particular time in my life.

"I'm sorry, Ma. Didn't mean to upset you, but...Well, somebody *is* trying to kill me, you know?"

"Good Lord." Now my mother was saying it.

I hoped Sam and Mr. Prophet would come home soon.

Vi walked into the kitchen. She, too, was rubbing her eyes. I guess Sundays are big nap-days for folks who are lucky enough not to have to work on Sundays.

"What's going on?" she asked, peering at my unhappy mother.

"We were just talking about who might be trying to kill me," I told Vi. "Oh, and can Harold come to dinner tomorrow night? He wants to meet Mr. Prophet." That didn't sound diplomatic, but I'm not sure what precisely was wrong with it. I added, "And also because you're the best cook in the universe. Even Mr. Prophet knows it now." Not sure if that made it any better, but I was stuck for something to say next. Luckily for me, it didn't matter.

"Get along with you, Daisy," said Vi, giggling.

"It will be nice to see Harold again," said Ma, who didn't know about Harold's one eccentricity. In fact, I suspect she'd once hoped I'd marry Harold after Billy's demise, but she was happy with Sam.

"He's one of my very best friends," I said.

"What time is it?" asked my father as he, too, walked into the kitchen. He didn't rub his eyes, but he looked a little heavy-lidded and I'd bet anything he'd napped, too.

I glanced at the clock on the kitchen wall. "Five-thirty."

"Hmm. Are Sam and Mr. Prophet back yet?"

"Not yet, Pa. I hope they get here soon so they can tell us what happened at the station."

By gum, the moment I finished that sentence, Spike took off like a rocket for the front door. We all knew what that meant. At least I hoped it meant what Spike thought it meant.

"I'll get the door," said Pa. "You just stay here, Daisy." What a nice man my father was. Always considering other people's feelings. And their aches and pains.

"Will you be making sandwiches, Vi?" Ma asked.

"As soon as I know how many to make, I will. Let's see if that really is Sam and Mr. Prophet first."

"Good idea." Ma walked from the kitchen into the dining room, which led into the living room.

I hauled the chair I'd sat in back to the kitchen table. "I don't suppose we have to set a fancy table for sandwiches, do we?" I asked my aunt, hoping her answer would be no.

She obliged me. "Oh, no. We can just use those cunning placemats you got in Chinatown last year. They'll be fine." Then she, too, walked to the living room.

Good. I'd removed the formal tablecloth after dinner at noontime because it was stained in spots. Of course, that meant I'd have to wash it. Which would hurt—

But wait! Sam's gift, Mrs. Rattle, would be doing laundry for the family, at least for another week or so. Bless Sam's heart. And that of Mrs. Rattle, too, of course. The mere notion of hauling baskets of laundry up and down stairs and hanging sheets and tablecloths on the lines out back made my arm and leg muscles ache in anticipation. Feeling left out, I joined everyone in the living room.

Sure enough, Sam and Lou Prophet stood just inside the house, removing their coats and hats. Mr. Prophet's frock coat looked as if might be as old as he was. It was a curious, old-fashioned garment, long and with lots of pockets. I guess frock coats could be handy, even if Mr. Prophet's looked out of place in so modern and civilized a city as Pasadena, California. Didn't people used to call those coats Prince Alberts? I think so. It's because Queen Victoria's husband, Albert, wore them. Of course, so did thousands of other men, but Albert was famous. I think they should be called Lou Prophets, by golly!

"How'd it go at the station?" I asked Sam as I walked over to him, got on my tiptoes and kissed him on the cheek. That hurt a little. Not the kiss; the stretch. This blasted pain, while much diminished from what it had been, was getting tiresome. In fact, if they ever *did* find out who'd ordered my slaughter, I just might take matters into my own hands.

That's mere braggadocio. Sam would never allow me to skin Stacy Kincaid with a dull butter knife. But it was a pleasant thought.

"We learned some things," said Sam. "And we didn't learn some other things."

"How helpful," said I, a little irked.

"But I think we're closing in," Sam said, trying for a conciliatory tone.

"Goody gumdrops."

"Daisy!" said Ma.

Lou Prophet laughed. "We'll get 'em, Miss Daisy. Don't you worry."

"Thank you, Mr. Prophet. I hope you're right."

"I am," said he, sounding as if he believed himself. Good for him. Wished I believed him.

"Anyone want a roasted pork sandwich?" asked Vi, pitching her voice a little louder than usual, probably to forestall an unpleasant exchange between Sam and me.

"Sounds good to me," said Prophet.

"Thanks, Vi. I can tell you what happened at the station as we eat," said Sam. He'd hung his nice-looking black overcoat next to Lou Prophet's old beat-up one. I wondered if Mr. Prophet would dislike it if I made him a new coat. I expect he would. He'd probably think it was charity. Some folks are touchy about taking anything from anyone. Then there are the Stacy Kincaids of the world who think everything should be theirs for no reason at all.

Life confuses me a lot sometimes.

"Can I set the table or anything?" asked Sam, probably trying to make up for annoying me when he first arrived. He needn't have. I was at fault for finding fault, I guess. Still and all, it was my life on the line, and I felt rather sensitive about it.

"Nonsense. You and Mr. Prophet and Joe stay in the living room and chat. I'll set the table," said Ma.

"I'll help," I said, willing, if not eager, to do my duty.

"You just stay in the living room, too, dear. You still have a good deal of healing to do."

"Thanks, Ma."

"Maybe you could play us a tune on your fine piano there," suggested Prophet, tilting his head piano-wards.

Why not? I usually played after we ate supper, but there was no law prohibiting me from playing before supper, was there? No. There was not.

"Will you please open the bench for me, Sam?" I asked politely. "I got some new sheet music recently."

"Sure." He did as I asked. Boy, if he were only that obedient all the time, I'd be *so* happy. Unfortunately, I doubted he'd appreciate it if I offered to take him to one of Mrs. Pansy Hanratty's obedience-training classes for dogs at Brookside Park.

So I rummaged a while and came out with "California, Here I Come," by Mr. Al Jolson; "Rhapsody in Blue," by Mr. George Gershwin; and "The Charleston," by Mr. James P. Johnson. I loved the latter, a catchy tune from Mr. Johnson's Broadway show, *Runnin' Wild*. I also loved "Rhapsody in Blue," but hadn't mastered it as well as I'd have liked. I only removed the music from the bench in case I managed to feel up to it in a bit.

A couple of Chopin's etudes remained on the piano stand from my earlier practice, but I expected both Sam and Mr. Prophet would prefer livelier music. "Tea for Two," a happy song from the musical stage play *No, No, Nanette*, also sat on the piano stand, so I started with that one. After I'd played a few notes, I was absolutely flabbergasted when a rusty bass voice started singing: "Just you for me, and me for you." I didn't stop playing, although I wanted to whirl around and actually *see* the wild and woolly Lou Prophet singing the lyrics to that song. I didn't even play a false note, by golly.

And then, as if to add icing on the cake, Sam Rotondo joined his superb bass voice with Lou Prophet's scratchier one: "Picture you upon my knee, just tea for two and two for tea."

I didn't realize Ma was standing in the archway between the living room and the dining room until I'd played the last chord. Then she clapped. Almost scared me off the piano bench.

"You men sound wonderful together," raved Ma.

"Don't they?" I agreed, pretty much. I'd known for a long time by then that Sam had a great voice. Mr. Prophet's, while a bit rough around the edges, at least didn't veer off-key and go sharp or flat. If he hung around, maybe I could get *both* men to join the Methodist choir. Slowly turning on the piano bench and taking a gander at Prophet, I decided I'd fight that battle if it came to me. Sam would be trouble enough for one poor Methodist alto to entice into joining the choir.

"Vi's got sandwiches and a lovely apple salad ready for supper," said Ma.

"Sounds great," I said, sliding carefully off the piano bench.

Sam gently took one of my arms and Lou Prophet took the other. I thought that was sweet of both of them. They led me into the dining room, and everyone took seats at the table. Sure enough, either Ma or Vi had rummaged through the drawer in the dining room hutch and hauled out the beautiful Chinese place mats I'd bought the prior year. Suddenly I wanted to visit Chinatown again.

"When I'm well again and this is all over, will you take me to China-town, Sam?" I asked wistfully.

"Sure," he said, looking at me strangely.

"Been there. Interesting place," said Mr. Prophet.

Pa said a short grace before we started our supper, then Vi began handing out plates filled with pork sandwiches. The bowl full of apple salad—which also contained celery and walnuts, and which was deli-cious—got passed around, and we each took some.

"This is a mighty tasty meal, Mrs. Gumm," Prophet said to Vi.

"Delicious," said Sam as he always did.

"It surely is," I agreed.

"We're so lucky to have you, Vi," said Ma.

For the next few minutes silence prevailed except for the quiet munching and swallowing that always happened during meals. Lou Prophet, I noticed, ate tidily. That kind of surprised me, although I don't know why, since he'd been perfectly gentlemanly at dinner that day. This serves to point out that most of us have notions about people based on nothing more than surmise and chancy reports. All the dime novels I'd read about the fellows who populated the old west painted them as wild and fierce and unmannerly. Which only goes to prove yet again that you can't judge a book by its cover. Or at least that you can't trust the subject matter of a book to behave the way it's written when it comes to real life.

Did that make any sense? I decided my capacity for thought hadn't returned to normal yet, so I introduced another topic having nothing to do with pretty much anything, although it did involve me going somewhere I couldn't visit at the moment.

"You know another place I'd like to visit?"

"No. What?" asked Sam.

"A dude ranch."

"A dude ranch?" asked Prophet, staring at me from across the table.

"Yes. I think it would be fun."

Mr. Prophet's eyebrows lifted, but he didn't make another comment.

"If you think I'm going to get on a horse," said Sam, "you're out of your mind."

"Not even for me?" I wheedled.

"Not even for you."

Lou Prophet said, "I had me a great horse way back when."

"Mean and Ugly?" I asked, grinning.

"Daisy!" said Ma.

"No, no, Ma. That was the name of his horse. Right, Mr. Prophet?"

"Right as rain, Miss Daisy. Big guy. Line-back dun. Ol' Mean and Ugly and me, we had ourselves some good times." His face held a reminiscent expression.

"Why did you name him Mean and Ugly?" asked Ma, clearly confused.

With a shrug, Mr. Prophet said, "Seemed to fit him." He grinned, and I figured we'd be better off not asking any more questions about his late horse.

"Well, phooey. You're a spoilsport, Sam," I told him.

"Big one," agreed Sam. "I used to want to ride a horse when I was a kid, but I'm over it now."

"I always wanted to ride a horse. We had a horse, Brownie, but he went to the great pasture in the sky about three years ago."

"Probably up there rompin' with Mean and Ugly," said Prophet.

"Probably." I sighed a little. "Well, I guess I can go to a dude ranch by myself someday." I then thought of somewhere else I'd always wanted to visit. "But I'll bet you'd to like to go to the next place I want to see, Sam."

"Oh?" Sam sounded skeptical. "And what's that?"

"Gay's Lion Farm in Westlake Park."

"There's a lion farm around here?" asked Prophet. He appeared startled. Could hardly blame the man. After all, lions didn't grace Southern California's landscape a whole lot. Well, except for mountain lions, but they lived, as their name implies, in the mountains.

"It's not precisely around here, but it's in a park—Westlake Park—in Los Angeles. They train lions for the flickers there."

"I'll be da…darned," said Prophet.

I smiled at his almost-profanity.

"Harold Kincaid, who's one of my best friends, told me all about it. Harold works as a costumer at a motion-picture studio. I guess when the studios film jungle pictures, they get their lions from Gay's."

"You've got a best friend who's a man?" asked Prophet, his brows lowering a trifle, as if he didn't approve of my having male friends.

"I do indeed," said I, willing to fight for Harold. "Harold Kincaid. When my husband died, Harold took me to Egypt and Turkey to help me with my grief."

"Yeah?" said Prophet.

"Yes. And it even worked. In a way."

"Sort of," said Sam in a grim voice.

"Sam doesn't like Harold," I told Prophet.

"I wouldn't like my gal going on trips with other men, either," said he. "I thought the two of you were engaged to be married." He glanced at Sam as if he thought Sam should have put a stop to such goings-on.

"We weren't back then," I told him.

"Even if we had been engaged at the time, there's nothing to fear in that regard when it comes to Harold Kincaid," Sam said drily.

"Oh?"

"Yes." I spoke firmly, too. "Harold is a great friend of mine. While we were in Turkey and some horrible men kidnapped Sam, he even shot one of them. Harold did, I mean."

"He shot a man in Turkey?" Prophet was dumbfounded. I could tell.

"Yes. In Constantinople. Only these days, people are beginning to call it Istanbul." And I'd never tell Lou Prophet that, after shooting the villain, Harold had fainted. He'd done a masterful job of helping rescue Sam, and that's all that counts.

"Huh," said Prophet. "You got kidnapped in a foreign country?" He turned his head to eye Sam.

"Yes," said Sam, growling. "They wanted Daisy, but they got me first. And I'll admit Kincaid helped get me out of the mess I was in. Surprised the he...heck out of me. He's not..." Sam's words trailed off as he tried to think of some way to say what he wanted to say. I commenced scowling at him to let him know I'd brook no criticism of Harold. "Um, that is to say he's not the most masculine of fellows."

"Ah," said Prophet as if he'd just figured out what Sam and I weren't saying. He nodded sagely. "One of them lavender cowboys, is he?"

Sam chuckled and nodded.

I did neither of those things. "He's no kind of cowboy," I said, turning my scowl on Prophet. "He's my *friend*, and a good one. Oh, and he'll be coming to dinner tomorrow night, so you'll get to meet him." Since that thought made me happy, I ceased scowling.

"Harold is a very nice person," said Vi. "His mother is my employer, Mrs. Pinkerton, who used to be Mrs. Kincaid."

"Who are all these Kincaids?" asked Prophet. "Your best friend is a Kincaid, and isn't Kincaid the name of the girl who wants you dead?"

"Yes, although I'm not sure Stacy is behind all the incidents. I wouldn't put them past her. She's Mrs. Pinkerton's daughter and Harold's sister. Harold and Stacy Kincaid are Mrs. Pinkerton's children, only Harold is nice and Stacy is..." I eyed my mother and decided not to use the word that had instantly popped into my mind to describe Stacy, which was "evil."

"Stacy isn't." There. Insufficient, but true.

"Oh."

"It's kind of confusing," I admitted. "Mrs. Pinkerton is my best client and her two children are Harold and Stacy, only their last name is Kincaid. Mrs. Pinkerton divorced Mr. Kincaid after he stole a lot of bearer bonds and almost ruined the bank he managed."

Prophet held up a hand as if to question me about something.

I said, "Yes?"

"What kind of work do you do that you have clients for?"

"I'm a spiritualist-medium," I told him proudly. I'd be darned if I'd allow another man to disapprove of what I did for a living.

"Yeah?" Prophet slowly grinned. "Ain't that something? Good for you, Miss Daisy."

Sam commenced frowning. I ignored him.

"Thank you," I said modestly. "Anyhow, Harold is a gem among men. Stacy is a glass bauble." As soon as the words left my lips, I glanced again at my mother, waiting for a stern "Daisy" to issue from her lips. But it didn't! Maybe Ma was becoming more accepting of me disliking people for trying to kill me. Although, to be fair, Sam hadn't pinned the crimes on Stacy. Yet.

"I like Harold a lot," said Pa, who didn't suffer any prejudices at all that I'd ever detected. "And he's done Daisy a world of good several times."

"Yes, he has," I confirmed.

"Good," said Prophet, nodding his head. Then he took another bite of the delectable sandwich Vi had made for him.

"Yes," said Sam with something like a longsuffering sigh. "Harold Kincaid is all right."

"Well, glory be! I never thought you'd admit it, Sam!"

"Daisy," said Ma.

Bother.

TWENTY-ONE

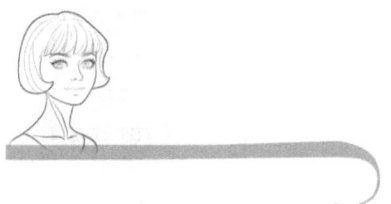

The following morning, Monday, Pudge Wilson had to return to school after Christmas vacation. Therefore, he didn't come over early to help Pa walk Spike. Pa and Spike had to walk by themselves. I don't think either of them minded. I did, however, wonder what kind of good deed Pudge aimed to spring on me when school was out for the day. I'd have had him give Spike a bath, but it was too cold for that. Oh, well, I'd think of something.

And I did! I'd have Pudge open up my sewing machine case and haul out the sewing machine. Oh, boy, I loved to sew, and I could do it now that my wounds and arm were healing so well, even though I couldn't yet lift the heavy machine out of its case.

Mrs. Rattle arrived at our front door at eight o'clock, bless her heart. Pa answered the door when she knocked, because nobody in the family wanted me answering the door until my tormenter was found and locked away.

Pending Pudge's return from school, and thanks to Mrs. Rattle, there wasn't much for me to do. Therefore, I picked up one of the books Regina had brought me, hied myself to the living room, and plopped on the sofa. Spike joined me, so I laid a cushion on top of him on my lap and propped the book on the cushion. That way I didn't have to hold the book using only my arm muscles. Boy, I remembered the days when Billy was alive and I had shoulders like a football player from assisting him in and out of his wheelchair, helping him walk and so forth. Not pleasant memories, so I decided not to think about them.

By that time I'd graduated from Kipling's *Just So Stories*, but still wasn't up to trying anything I couldn't be sure of enjoying. Regina knew this, so she'd brought me some of my favorites from the library. Therefore, I picked up *The Case of Jennie Brice*, by Mrs. Mary Roberts Rinehart. I loved pretty much anything written by Mrs. Rinehart. Except *The Amazing Interlude*, which she'd written during the war and which had made me cry.

Along about ten-thirty, Spike raced to the front door, singing his happy song. He was followed by Pa, who opened the door.

"Sam! Good morning to you," said Pa.

"It *is* a good morning. I have great news for all of you."

I rose from the sofa and met Sam as he turned from the hat rack. "What's the good news? Do you know who's trying to kill me?"

Golly, I just this second realized a person's notion of what constitutes good news depends a whole lot on one's circumstances, doesn't it?

"We're narrowing it down."

Crumb. I'd hoped he'd found the would-be murderer and shot him dead. "Oh?"

"Yes. Come on in and sit down, and I'll tell you. You, too, Joe," Sam said to Pa.

"Thanks, Sam," said Pa.

So we all sat in the living room; Sam, Spike and me on the sofa, and Pa in one of our two pretty wing chairs.

"Frank spilled the beans," said Sam, smiling hugely.

"What beans did he spill?" I asked, thinking Sam's words were all well and good, but what did they *mean*?

"Bruce Petrie hired him to knife you."

"*Bruce* Petrie?" said Pa.

"Bruce Petrie," Sam confirmed.

"The fiend!" I cried.

"Yeah. They're both fiends. But the most interesting bit of news popped up when I interviewed Bruce Petrie."

"Oh?" This, from Pa.

"Yes. Do you remember the woman who shot me?"

"Eloise Frances Petrie Gaulding. I'll never forget that name as long as I live." I shuddered. That had been a truly horrifying time. I thought for sure Sam would bleed to death before help came.

"I won't, either," said Sam. "But she's the one."

"The one what? Or who?"

"The one who's behind the attacks on you."

"You mean *she* wants me dead?"

"According to Bruce, she's never forgiven you for spoiling the profitable endeavor she, her nephew, and Leo Bannister were engaged in. She also hates me, but figures it would hurt me more if she kills you before she kills me."

Outraged, I blurted out, "That so-called profitable endeavor was kidnapping children to act as sex slaves for disgusting men!"

"True, but it made a lot of money for the ringleaders."

"Those poor children," said Pa, who had been revolted and horrified when told about the market for children financed by depraved men. I think it was hard for my father to understand there were people that evil in the world. And not merely in the world, but in *Pasadena*. I understood his reaction, because mine had been the same.

"Those people are..." I couldn't think of bad-enough words to describe them, actually.

"Depraved perverts and rapists," Sam supplied.

"Yes. And evil," I added.

"Pure evil," said Pa.

"Is Mrs. Gaulding in prison now?" I asked.

"She's been out on bond for several months. Her trial is coming up soon. This will get her locked up with no bail, I suspect. Officers are on their way to her house right this minute."

"Do you mean I won't have to remain a prisoner in my own home any longer?"

"You're going to remain a prisoner until we're sure we've got all the bad guys locked up," said Sam. "Don't push your luck, Daisy. We need to be sure there aren't any more of Mrs. Gaulding's hirelings running around before you go anywhere by yourself."

"Right. You stay put, Daisy," said Pa. "Don't take any chances until Sam is sure the danger is over."

"I know you're right," I said, although I didn't much want to. Well, except that I *did* want to stay alive. I wasn't going to be stupid and wander off by myself unless and until I knew all the Petrie vermin and all the Petries' venomous employees, friends and sidekicks were locked up tight and couldn't get out.

Sam left to go back to the office soon after delivering his news. I was excited and almost happy for the first time since that blasted Cole Sportster had smashed me against that poor pepper tree on New Year's Day.

Speaking of that motorcar, I couldn't help but wonder if Mr. Bernard Randford was as innocent of evil-doing as everyone wanted to believe him to be. Miss Betsy Powell had the worst taste in men of any woman I'd ever met in my life. She'd already been madly in love with two perfectly ghastly men, one of whom had tried to kill me with a syringe full of insulin. The other one was the founder of the Underhill Chemical Company, and he was a total rotter, although I don't know if he actively did any harm to anyone except Miss Powell and his own wife and children. Well, and a whole lot of his employees. Fortunately for everyone, Miss Powell's at-that-time current love had murdered him. During a communion service at our church, as I believe I've already mentioned.

You know, when I'm living my life from day to day, it feels pretty boring, but when I write it down, it almost has an element of excitement to it. Strange, that.

Anyhow, I got bored after Mrs. Rattle fixed lunch for Pa and me, and I wasn't sure what to do with myself. What I wanted to do was go for a walk with Pa and Spike. I didn't think my arms were well enough to hold Spike's leash, but I could walk along side them and at least get out of doors for a few minutes. It wasn't terribly cold that late-January day.

I decided to step outside and stand on the back deck for a few minutes. That couldn't hurt, could it? I'd stay near my bedroom door and take Spike with me. He'd bark or growl if anyone with bad intentions lurked anywhere within sniffing range. Spike was, after all, a mighty hunting dog. According to Mrs. Bissel, the woman who'd given him to me in return for ridding her basement of a ghost, dachshunds had been bred to hunt badgers. Badgers were ferocious beasts, so Spike was a tough cookie. Or he would be if the occasion called for it...At least I was pretty sure he would be.

Maybe Pa would join us. That idea made me feel better about my adventure.

Adventure.

Standing on the back deck.

My life was pitiful. Nertz.

"Pa!" I called after I'd decided on my daring plan.

"Yes, sweetie?" Pa had been chatting with Mrs. Rattle in the kitchen.

"Would you be willing to join Spike and me on the back deck for a few minutes? Just so I can get out of the house for a little bit? I promise I won't go anywhere. I only want to breathe fresh air for a second or two."

Pa and Mrs. Rattle turned to look at me. Both frowned.

After a moment of strained silence, Pa said, "Sam wants you to stay in the house until he has all the bad guys rounded up and in jail, Daisy."

"I know that, but...Just a minute on the back deck? With you and Spike? Would that be so bad?"

"Detective Rotondo would probably think so," said Mrs. Rattle, sounding matter-of-fact and practical.

Bother.

Another several seconds of silence bloated with fear and uncertainty passed. Pa finally got up from the kitchen table and said, "I'll look around before you take a single step outside, young lady."

"Thanks, Pa. Do you really think I'm being...I don't know. Silly? Rebellious? I don't mean to be."

"I think you're going stir-crazy," said Mrs. Rattle with a sweet smile. "Trapped in the house for so long."

"Right," said Pa. "Especially now that you're starting to feel better. At first, you couldn't do anything but lie in bed or on the couch, but now that you're healing, you're getting antsy."

"I think you're both right." I didn't mind admitting it since it was true.

"I'll check first," said Pa, heading to my bedroom, which was right off the kitchen.

That room would be great for Vi, but Billy and I had taken it because by the time Billy came home from the war, he couldn't climb stairs. Therefore, although there were two nice rooms upstairs, Vi used them, and I had the room off the kitchen. Now, since Sam and I aimed to be married soon, we'd probably just keep things the way they were. After that, Vi might decide to move downstairs.

I heard the back door open. Spike sped to join Pa. He loved sniffing in the back yard. Every now and then he'd scare up an opossum or Samson, the Wilsons' cat, but there wasn't a whole lot of wildlife extant in Pasadena. Maybe a lizard or a spider here and there.

"Looks all right to me," Pa called after he'd scanned the yard and the surroundings. We'd planted several trees and bushes back there along with a bunch of rose bushes in a special bed reserved just for them. I loved to garden when I could, always wearing gloves to protect my spiritualist-medium's silky hands.

I heaved a gratified sigh and walked through my room to the back door. Spike was already outside and had descended the short flight of stairs from the deck to the yard, where he was sniffing happily. I swear, that dog did everything happily. Wish I could do that. As I approached the back door, I felt something warm against my chest and stopped in my tracks.

Was that my Voodoo juju heating up?

Sam's juju, made for him by the same Voodoo mambo who'd made mine—Mrs. Jackson, whose beignets the family had recently devoured —had become so hot every time he was near a murderer, he'd had to take it off.

Nonsense. I was a phony spiritualist-medium and, while I wore the Voodoo juju Mrs. Jackson had made for me because I appreciated her for having made it, I didn't believe in any of that stuff. Therefore, I ignored my juju and boldly walked the rest of the way to the door. Pa stood outside, his hands on the deck railing, surveying things. Spike continued to roam in the yard until he suddenly stood stock still, lifted his long nose into the air, and then took off like a bat out of a hot place toward the hibiscus bushes in back of the rose bed.

A loud noise made me jump.

Pa hollered, "Daisy! Get inside!"

Another noise—good grief, those were gunshots!—turned me around like a top, and I all but fell into my bedroom.

I heard a scream.

"God damned sumbitch!" roared Lou Prophet.

Whimpers sounded as if they came from the hibiscus bushes. I didn't know what to do, but I had definitely lost my taste for standing on the back deck. Kneeling hurt my still-tender muscles, but I knelt in front of my back window and peered through the glass. There were Pa and Lou Prophet, Pa running, Prophet hobbling as fast as he could, in the direction of the hibiscus bushes. Prophet carried the longest gun I'd ever seen in my entire life—not that I'd seen very many guns—next to his body as he thudded across the grass, making holes where his stump landed.

Well…That would prevent mushrooms from forming fairy circles in the springtime. The holes, I mean. I doubt Mr. Prophet knew that, or would have cared had I told him. And why was my mind running around in circles?

Lord, Lord, Lord, what did this mean? Did someone just try to kill me? Again? I couldn't take much more of this!

I watched as the two men approached the rose bed. Pa'd just pruned the rose bushes, because that's what we folks in Pasadena did in January. I hadn't been able to help him with the chore this year. Prophet held his gun out horizontally in front of my father to stop him. I couldn't hear what he told Pa, but Pa stayed where he was as Prophet slowly limped through the rose bushes and reached down to grab something lying between a couple of hibiscus bushes. I loved those bushes. One of them had pink blossoms and one had yellow blossoms, only not in January. In January, everything looked dead.

With a jerk, Prophet pulled a body out of the bushes. Waving to my father, Prophet beckoned him forward. Pa joined Prophet and the prone man. Was he dead? Did I care?

Not a whole lot, no, although I'd like to know who he was and who'd hired him.

As Pa stood beside the man who, I noticed, bled copiously from a thigh wound not unlike the one Sam had sustained months earlier, Prophet went a little farther into the hibiscus trees, bent over, and picked up a gun. The gun he picked us was short; I guess it was a revolver or a pistol, unlike the weapon Prophet carried, which was…well, long. A rifle? If I could ever leave the house again, I told myself I was going to go to the library and look up the makes and models of firearms.

Then it occurred to me I probably should be doing something more useful than kneeling before my window, so I pushed myself to my feet—which hurt again, dad gum it—and went to the telephone on the kitchen wall. When I picked up the receiver, I heard Mrs. Longnecker, who lived down the street from us, screaming into the receiver on her end of the wire.

"I don't *know!*" she shrieked. She shrieked almost as well as Mrs. Pinkerton; I suspect she practiced on her husband, a mild-mannered little fellow who liked to putter in his yard. "All I know is that I heard two gunshots! *I* don't know what kind of gun they came from!"

A voice proceeding from, I deduced, the police station asked her if she knew what she'd heard were really gunshots, and could they possibly have been firecrackers?

"*Firecrackers?* No! No one in this neighborhood is stupid enough to shoot off firecrackers in January! Get over here! I don't know which house they came from, but I suspect it was the Gumms' place. If there's any trouble in the neighborhood, it'll be at their house!"

I cleared my throat. Mrs. Longnecker screamed again. Guess I'd startled her.

"I'm sorry to interrupt, Mrs. Longnecker, but you're correct. Two gunshots issued from our back yard a few minutes ago."

"Daisy Gumm Majesty, what in the world is going on at your house? First you get hit by a car, and now someone's shooting at you?"

Clearly, Mrs. Longnecker disapproved. Well, so did I. "I'm sorry, Mrs. Longnecker, but none of this is my fault."

"Humph," said she. I heard her receiver clunk into the telephone cradle at her house.

I cleared my throat again. "Officer?"

"Yes?" Whoever he was, he sounded peeved. Too bad. "Who is this?"

"This is Mrs. Majesty. Will you please connect me with Detective Rotondo?"

"Hold on a minute. Did you say there was a shooting at your house?"

"Not a shooting, no—" I remembered the body Pa and Mr. Prophet had hauled from the hibiscus bushes. "I mean, yes, there was a shooting. Oh, please connect me with Detective Rotondo! He'll know what to do!" I'd begun to sound rather shrill.

"Excuse me, dear." Mrs. Rattle gently took the receiver from my hand and spoke into it. "Officer, this is Mrs. Rattle, Stephen Doan's mother. There's been a shooting at Detective Rotondo's fiancée's house, and we need a couple of officers. Perhaps an ambulance." She gave our address.

Because I no longer held the telephone, I don't have a clue what the policeman on the other end of the wire said to her, but she said, "Yes. That's right. Two officers and an ambulance, please. And please notify Detective Rotondo as soon as possible. Yes." Another moment of quiet, and then she said, "Yes. Thank you. And be sure to alert Detective Rotondo." She hung the receiver on the hook.

"Thank you, Mrs. Rattle. I didn't know your son's name was Stephen."

"Yes, dear." Mrs. Rattle had the sweetest smile. "He was named after his grandfather, my father, who was a wonderful man."

"How nice."

All of a sudden I felt as though I was going to collapse. I grabbed a kitchen chair and pretty much fell onto it. Then I commenced shaking.

"There, there, dear." Mrs. Rattle put her hands on my shoulders and gently massaged them for a couple of seconds. "I know this is terribly unsettling for you. But it will be cleared up soon. I know it will be. Detective Rotondo is the finest man on the force, except for my Stephen, and he'll fix it all up. Just you wait and see."

Guess I'd have to, wouldn't I?

TWENTY-TWO

Once I stopped shaking, Mrs. Rattle began heating a saucepan full of milk on the stove top. "I'll just make us all some hot cocoa. That will be good for your nerves. And your father's."

"And Mr. Prophet's."

"Oh. Yes. He was responsible for the second gunshot, I imagine. Right?" She sounded so calm and self-assured, so...well, everything I wasn't just then.

"Yes. He was."

"Good thing, too." She shook her head as she stirred sugar and cocoa powder into the saucepan. Mrs. Rattle was very good at her job, and I appreciated her immensely just then.

I heard thudding on the back steps and then a thump, as if perhaps my father and Mr. Prophet had yanked a body up the stairs and deposited it on the deck. I aimed to hose off the deck as soon as I possibly could so as not to leave a bloodstain thereon. Maybe, once I got myself all healed again, I'd paint the damned thing, too.

Oh, dear. I'm sorry about that word. My predicament and Lou Prophet seemed to be telling on me more than I wanted to admit.

Pa walked into the kitchen from my bedroom. "You all right, sweetheart?" he asked, coming over and giving me a hug as I huddled in my chair.

"Yes. Thank you, Pa. Um…Do you know what happened? I mean, I think someone shot at me, and then Mr. Prophet shot whoever it was who did it. Is that correct?"

"Correct," said Pa. "Don't know who the shooter is yet. But I have to get a sheet and some tape or rope or something like that. Lou shot him in the thigh——"

"Just like Sam," I said in a tinny, tiny voice.

"Um…Yes, I suppose so. But I'd better get some gauze or tape to wrap around the leg above the wound, or the man might bleed to death."

"I want him to bleed to death," I said, thereby appalling myself.

Pa only chuckled. "I don't blame you, but we probably should at least try to keep him alive until he can tell us who hired him or if he was operating on his own."

"Oh. Yes. I forgot about that. Good idea."

So Pa, who plainly wasn't in a rush, went to get a sheet—I guess he aimed to roll the bleeding man onto the sheet in order to help protect the deck's finish—and something with which to bind the man's leg.

Lou Prophet called, "Knock, knock," from the back door. "Joe?"

"He went to get some bandages," Mrs. Rattle said.

"Don't need 'em," said Prophet. "I tied his leg with my ketch rope. But we'd best get a sheet or something under him, or he'll ruin that nice porch y'all got out here."

His ketch rope?

I'd ask later. And, if he told me what it was, I'd add it to my old-west dictionary.

"Just get sheets, Pa!" I called to my father. "Mr. Prophet bound the leg with his…Um, he bound the leg."

"Ah, good." Pa walked into the kitchen carrying one of our oldest sheets; one with holes in it. He must have dug hard to find it. I suspect he'd retrieved it from the pile of old linen and clothes we aimed to donate to the Salvation Army. I was glad. Didn't want to waste a good sheet on a man who'd just made an attempt on my life.

Spike, who had evidently become bored roaming the back yard, trotted into the kitchen and then raced, barking like mad, to the front door. I wondered why he wasn't still on the deck lapping up blood until I heard a pounding at the door. Aha. Probably the police. I glanced at Mrs. Rattle, who turned down the fire under her cocoa pot and headed to the door.

Sure enough. Sam, followed closely by Stephen Doan and Officer Oversloot, ran into the kitchen. Sam stopped at my chair, but the two officers, at Sam's instructions, continued through my bedroom to the back deck.

"Are you all right?" Sam asked, sounding a wee bit panicky.

"The bullet missed me, if that's what you want to know," I said, not unkindly, but thinking Sam shouldn't be panicking. To me, panic on his part bespoke something terribly wrong.

"Thank God for that," said he, and went to join the rest of the police contingent, my father and Lou Prophet on the back deck. I decided what the heck, got up from my chair and joined them. Six people and a grown man mewling inside a bed sheet made the deck fairly crowded, but we managed.

"Do you know who this is?" Sam asked of Prophet.

"Never saw the owlhoot before in my life. Saw him goin' up the drive, though, and followed him. He ran to the bushes in back of that rose bed. I didn't see him draw, but I saw the flash. I shot him then."

Owlhoot? I hoped I'd remember all these words.

"Thank you," said Sam. Kneeling next to the prone man, he said, "Who are you?"

"Hurt," whimpered the man.

"Yeah. I know. You tried to kill my fiancée. Who the devil are you, and who hired you?"

More whimpers.

Lou Prophet nudged the man's thigh with his peg. The man howled. "Tell the detective what he wants to know, old son," advised Prophet. "Or I'll open that wound up consider'ble with my peg here. You think it hurts now!"

"*Petrie!*" squealed the man. "Clifford Petrie."

"*Another* one? How many of you *are* there?" I demanded of Clifford Petrie. "And do you *all* want me dead?"

"Don't know," said Petrie. "Big family we got."

"Yes," I said, wanting them all to die. Except Regina, of course. "You have an excessively big family. Entirely too big."

"Is your Chevrolet in the driveway, Joe?" asked Sam, standing again. I thought it a strange and irrelevant question until my father answered it.

"Ah, yes. I'd better move the machine so the ambulance can get back here."

Very well, so Sam and my father and Lou Prophet were all thinking more clearly than I. No surprise, under the circumstances.

"Who hired you to kill me?" I asked Clifford Petrie.

"M'mother. Didn't pay me," said Petrie. "Did her a favor."

"Some favor," I growled. Sam put his hand on my shoulder, probably to keep me from kicking Mr. Petrie to death.

"Who's your mother?" asked Sam.

"Mrs. Petrie," sobbed Petrie.

"*Which* Mrs. Petrie?" I asked, still growling.

"Myrtle. Myrtle Petrie."

Sam and I exchanged a glance of incomprehension. I'd heard of all sorts of Petries since they'd crawled out of the pig sty in which they lived in Tulsa, Oklahoma, but I'd never before heard of a Myrtle Petrie.

"Who's she?" I snarled.

"M'mother," Petrie said, still whimpering.

"What does she have to do with Bruce Petrie or Eloise Petrie Gaulding or Percival Petrie or any of the other accursed Petries who've been darkening my life for the past three or four years?"

"I should probably do the questioning," suggested Sam gently.

"She's doin' all right," said Prophet, grinning at me. "Let her take the devil by the tail." Whatever the expression meant, I appreciated him for it.

Sam shrugged. He probably figured it didn't matter who asked the questions as long as this particular putrid Petrie answered them.

"Aunt Eloise is m'mother's sister."

"Oh." That figured. "Are you Bruce's brother?"

"Yeah."

"I swear to goodness, you people ought to have stayed in Oklahoma.

185

We don't want you here in Pasadena. You bring down the tone of the place."

"Daisy," said Sam. He was trying not to laugh, curse him. "Leave the man alone. He's hurt."

"If he'd had his way, I'd be dead."

"True." After saying that, Sam kicked Clifford Petrie, too.

Petrie shrieked. Lou Prophet laughed. I felt somehow vindicated.

Just then we heard the siren of an ambulance approaching from the south. I expect it had originated at the Castleton Hospital, which sat on the corner of Orange Grove and Pasadena Avenue. I stepped back so the ambulance attendants would be able to get up the steps and retrieve Clifford Petrie's lousy carcass. Well, he was still alive, so technically he wasn't a carcass. Yet.

And then *everyone* except Clifford Petrie, walked into my bedroom. I didn't want them there. Well, Sam could stay...

"Come on into the kitchen, fellows," said Mrs. Rattle chirpily. "I've made some hot cocoa to warm you up, and Mrs. Gumm has some wonderful Scotch shortbread in the cookie jar."

"Doan, you and Oversloot go in the ambulance with Petrie. Be sure he's booked as soon as a doctor patches him up. Attempted murder."

Doan saluted. I didn't know people actually did that, although Sam could sound awfully authoritative when he wanted. So Doan and Over-sloot didn't get any of Mrs. Rattle's hot cocoa or any of Aunt Vi's Scotch shortbread. Poor fellows.

"Save that rope," said Prophet to the two policemen. "That's a good rope."

Doan and Oversloot glanced at Sam, who nodded and said, "Just keep it. I'll pick it up at the station."

"Right," said Doan.

"Come on in here, fellows," said Mrs. Rattle. "Cocoa's all ready."

"Thank you, Mrs. Rattle," Sam said as he walked into the kitchen, followed by Lou Prophet, still holding his gun.

Pa blinked at the firearm. "I haven't seen one of those in decades," said he.

Prophet lifted his rifle. "This here purty lady? It's my Winchester

'73. Haven't used her much lately, I'm sorry to say. She gets lonely, this lady does."

"Did you use it when you were bounty hunting?" I asked, wishing he'd prop the thing against a wall somewhere other than the kitchen. It looked deadly. Which, all things considered, I guess it was.

He patted the weapon lovingly. "'Bout brings tears to my eyes, remembering all the curly wolves me an' my lady here turned toe-down." Tears of fondness, I gathered. From a different place in time, Mr. Prophet...

Shaking his head, Pa said, "My father had one of those Winchesters. Used to hunt with it."

"So'd I," said Prophet, grinning.

"But you hunted men," I said, deciding a grin wouldn't do me any harm either. "I think my paternal grandfather hunted deer and rabbits and stuff like that."

"I've bagged a few of those in my day, too," said Prophet. "Men pay better, though."

Grim thought. Mr. Prophet took his gun to the service porch, for which I was grateful, and came back to the kitchen where he took a seat.

"Guess you're going to have to arrest a Myrtle Petrie now, Sam," I said. "Do you think you'll ever be able to clean up the squad of Pasadena Petries? I swear they're like ants! They just keep coming back."

"More like rats," said Prophet. "Or cockroaches."

"I guess so. But Spike could do away with any rat or cockroach having the poor judgment to enter our house."

"Yeah?" Prophet squinted down at Spike, who smiled up at him. "Never saw a dog looked like that one before. What kind is it?"

"Dachshund."

"Bless you."

I laughed. "No, no. I didn't sneeze. That's the breed of the dog he is. Dachshund. They were bred in Germany to hunt badgers." I sniffed. "They're the only thing from Germany that's worth a rap, if you ask me."

"Badgers?" Prophet repeated, round-eyed. "Them things are bad bas—I mean, cusses."

"Yes, they are. But Spike is a mighty hunter."

"He is, is he?" Prophet seemed doubtful.

"He really is," I said in hot defense of my wonderful dog. "In fact, he's brought us more than one opossum during his tenure at our house."

"'Possums make for good eating," said Prophet.

Ew. I didn't pursue the opossum subject.

"Where did you live that you ate 'possums?" asked Pa, sounding interested.

"Georgia. When I was a tyke. 'Possums, squirrels, rabbits, all of 'em. They're all good in a stew."

"Oh, you're from Georgia? I didn't know that." Again I wondered how old Lou Prophet was. I didn't ask, believing it would be impolite. I did, however, ask, "I suppose you were too young to fight in the Civil War."

Prophet pinned me with a squinty, flinty glare. "The War of Northern Aggression? I was a tadpole, but I got my licks in."

"You fought for the Confederacy?"

"Oh, yes. I'm a Georgia boy! It was hell. The war, I mean. Not Georgia. Georgia was heaven on earth. Leastways, long as your skin was white." He winked at me.

"So I've heard," I said tartly. "My grandfather fought for the Union Army."

"I'm sorry."

"Nertz."

"You won't hold it against me?" Prophet grinned some more.

"Of course not. After all, our side won." I gave him a genteel smile.

Mr. Prophet's grin faded some.

"Daisy," said Pa.

"I'm sorry, Mr. Prophet," I felt obliged to say.

But he only laughed. "You're something else, Miss Daisy. But hell, neither the war nor the curly wolves got me. I'm still on this side of the sod, stompin' with my tail up."

Whatever that meant.

TWENTY-THREE

S am left shortly after we'd each eaten several pieces of Vi's Scotch shortbread and drunk a cup or two of cocoa. I felt considerably less anxious after Sam said he'd be sure the Pasadena Police Department found and locked up Mrs. Myrtle Petrie.

I called the library and asked to speak to Miss Regina Petrie. She didn't generally take telephone calls when she was at work, but I wanted her to know about this latest attack on my life by one of her awful kin.

"Oh, Daisy, I'm so sorry!" she cried. Well, she whispered because she was in the library, but you know what I mean.

"Not your fault. But I'd kind of like to know how many more members of the rotten side of your family live in Pasadena at the moment."

"I have no idea," she said sorrowfully. "I wish I did. I'll call an exterminator."

I chuckled at that. "I'll help pay for one. I'd never even heard of Bruce or Clifford or Myrtle Petrie until the past week or so."

"I think Myrtle is an aunt of mine or something. My family has nothing to do with those people. I've told you about what some of them have done. I used to think Percival was the worst of the lot, but now I'm not so sure."

"Do you think either Bruce or Clifford killed girls and fed their bodies to pigs?"

That question isn't as irrelevant as it probably looks, because Percival Petrie *had* killed girls and fed them to his parents' pigs.

"I think that was only Percival, although don't know for sure. Given the rest of that rotten limb on the family tree, they all might have been in cahoots with each other. I wish none of them had moved to Pasadena."

"Me, too."

"They were *personae non grata* in Tulsa, but I wish they'd moved to… well, anywhere but here."

"Did Myrtle's family have trouble with the law, too?"

"Oh, my, yes. It was difficult for my parents and me to hold our heads up with that gang of monsters living in the same town."

"I'm sorry. You'll be marrying Robert soon, and your last name will be Browning. That will probably make you feel better."

"It will *definitely* make me feel better. I'm almost afraid to tell Robert about these latest crimes. I wouldn't blame him for not wanting to marry into my family."

"Nonsense. He knows all sorts of things about me, and he still speaks to me. He loves you, Regina! He won't hold the bad side of your family against you. In fact, from what I've learned about Robert Browning in the past few years, he's a wonderfully tolerant and kind-hearted man. And he can keep a secret like nobody's business." That aspect of Robert's character had peeved me at the time, but I honored him for it now.

"Yes." Regina sounded wistful. "He's a wonderful man."

"I'm so happy for you."

"Me, too."

"And I'm getting better by the day, so I'll definitely be able to make your bridal gown and bridesmaids' dresses soon."

"Don't worry about those things," said Regina. "Just get well. Do you need any new books?"

How sweet she was! "Not at the moment, but thank you for asking. Everyone's been so nice to me."

"We thought we'd lost you, Daisy. We were all frightened for you."

"Yes. Thanks. I was kind of worried, too." I hesitated for a second, then blurted out, "Actually, I'm still scared. All sorts of people I've never even heard of seem to want me dead. I don't know why, and I hope Sam gets them all locked up soon."

"There can't be an endless supply of bad Petries in Pasadena," said Regina, although she didn't sound too awfully sure of herself.

"I suppose not."

We said our good-byes, and I went out to the deck to see if Clifford Petrie had made a mess on the paint. Mrs. Rattle was already there with a bucket of soapy water and a mop, scrubbing away like mad.

"Is there a big stain?" I asked.

"Not very. And I got at it with the soap and water before the blood dried."

"That's good." I sounded feeble. Truth to tell, I felt feeble. Getting shot at isn't any fun. In fact, it's downright terrifying.

Spike and I retired to the living room sofa, where I curled up next to my hound and took a nap. I felt a little better when I woke up about an hour later.

HAROLD KINCAID and Lou Prophet liked each other. I could tell. Harold brought Vi home from Mrs. Pinkerton's house at about four o'clock, and he and Mr. Prophet exchanged pleasantries in the living room. Pa joined them as Vi worked in the kitchen. I made sure to be there with them, just in case either man got out of hand. I'm talking Harold and Lou here, because my father never got out of hand.

And what an odd expression that is. Never thought about it before I wrote it down, but what does "out of hand" mean, anyway? Oh, never mind.

"So you work in the flickers?"

"Yes." Harold heaved a sigh.

"I was hired to consult on a couple of what they call westerns," said Mr. Prophet. "Didn't look like any west I've ever been in, but the money was good." He squinted at Harold. "You're not an actor, are you? Don't recall seeing you in any of the pictures I've been to."

"No. I make costumes for the folks who act in them," said Harold.

"I wouldn't mind dressing some of them women," said Prophet.

"Actually, you probably would. Most of them are nitwits."

"Yeah?" Prophet shrugged.

"They are. If they ever figure out how to make talkies, most of the so-called stars will be out of jobs, because they'll have to be able to read and remember lines."

"That's a little harsh, isn't it?"

"No." Harold sounded definite.

"I worked on a picture set once, Mr. Prophet. Lola de la Monica hired me to be her spiritual advisor."

Harold chuffed out a large-sized guffaw. "Spiritual advisor, my foot."

"Well, that's what she hired me for," I said, because it was the truth.

"Now that woman's got fire in her," said Prophet. "Gorgeous female. I would've liked to've met her forty years or so ago."

"She wouldn't have been alive then," I reminded him.

"Yeah, but *I* would'a been. If we were the same age, I guess is what I'm saying."

"I understood. Just thought I'd give you a hard time."

"Miss Daisy, you ain't got the stuff in you to give me a hard time. I've been worked over by experts."

"She *is* a little too nice," said Harold in a musing sort of voice, eyeing me sideways.

"I am?" I didn't think people could be too nice.

"Yeah," said Prophet. "She is. She's had some problems lately, though."

"Yes. I heard about today's dust-up," said Harold.

"Dust-up," I repeated. "I guess that's one word for it."

"Two words," said Prophet.

Harold laughed.

I said, "Picky, picky. I didn't know you were so persnickety, Mr. Prophet."

"Damned right I am. Anyhow, I said the wrong thing. What I meant was, I wouldn't mind *un*dressing some of them women."

Harold snickered.

I frowned at Prophet and he rolled his eyes. I swear, he and Sam might as well have been twins. Only Mr. Prophet was older than Sam.

Speaking of Sam, he arrived not long after Harold brought Vi home. Harold went to the door to let him in, since I wasn't allowed near any door in the house any longer. Of those that led outdoors, I mean. I did, however, rise and walk over to greet him. He surprised me with a hug and a great big kiss. Right in front of Harold, Lou Prophet, Pa and Vi!

After I recovered, I said, "What was that for?"

"Because I love you, and because we've got all of them locked up at last!" He hung his hat on the rack, shrugged out of his coat and hung that up, too.

"*All* of them?" I said, my voice faint. I pressed a hand over my heart, hardly daring to believe Sam's news. "Are you sure?"

"As sure as I can be," said he.

"That doesn't sound like you're absolutely, positively sure," I said. I grabbed his hand and walked him into the living room, where Harold, Pa and Lou Prophet stood, Pa and Harold smiling broadly, Prophet with a calm expression on his weathered face.

"Is that so, Sam?" asked Pa. "You really have all the bad guys—"

"And girls," I said, interrupting. Impolite, I know.

"And girls," said Sam, squeezing my hand gently. "Yes. As far as I know, they're all locked up and, from what we've been able to gather by questioning them all, there are no more people who want to kill you out and about in Pasadena."

I pressed a hand over my heart. "I can hardly believe it."

"You're still going to have to be careful," warned Sam. "Just because I think we have all the culprits stowed away, we can't be sure until we've thoroughly questioned all the ones we have."

"Need any help?" Prophet asked. "I'm purty good at getting folks to spill the beans."

I could imagine how he did it, too.

With a grin, Sam said, "No, thanks. We'll handle the questioning at the station."

"Suit yourself," Prophet said and shrugged.

"Joe and Sam, will you please come here and help set the table?" Vi called from the kitchen. "It's just about dinnertime, and I don't want Daisy lifting heavy plates and so forth for a while."

193

"But Ma's not home yet," I called back.

"Yes, I am," said my mother, surprising me.

"Where'd you come from?" I asked her.

"Through the side door," she said with a laugh. "That door's easier to unlock than the front door, which is heavy."

"Oh, dear. I'm sorry, Ma. I wish we didn't have to keep all the doors locked. But Sam thinks they have all the bad guys locked up now."

"Really? How wonderful! Joe and Sam, get back in the living room and talk to Harold and Mr. Prophet. I'll set the table."

"I'll get the silverware out," I said. "That's not heavy."

"Very well. If you're sure," said Ma.

So my father and my fiancé—men don't have to do any work around the house, which I don't think is fair, but nobody asked me—loafed on into the living room to talk to Harold and Lou Prophet. I got out a neatly folded tablecloth from a drawer in the dining room's built-in hutch, flapped it open—gently, so as not to jar my left arm too much—and smoothed it over the dining room table. Then I set seven places at the table and put folded napkins under each knife and spoon. Gee, there usually weren't so many people dining at our place, except on holidays and times like that.

Sniffing the air, I called to Vi, "What are you fixing us, Vi? Whatever it is, it smells wonderful."

"Hungarian goulash," she answered. "I just have to put it in a serving bowl. I've got some buttered carrots to go with the goulash."

"Have you ever made Hungarian goulash for us before? I don't remember it."

"Nope. Got the recipe from Evelyn McCracken."

"Boy, she gives you lots of recipes, doesn't she? And they all seem to be from other countries. First it was chorizo, then it was Swedish chicken, and now it's Hungarian goulash."

With a laugh, Vi said, "Mrs. Bannister's late husband liked to travel."

Yes. He had liked to travel. He went to foreign countries to kidnap children and bring them to the United States. If he hadn't beaten his wife nearly to death, and had she not then been rescued by Flossie Buckingham, hidden by Harold and me, and treated by Dr. Fred Greenlaw, Mr. Bannister would probably still be doing his evil work. But Mr. Bannister had been murdered by another ghastly Petrie person. Every now and then, I reckon a Petrie will kill someone who needs killing. But I wasn't one of those people. And I was glad Bannister was dead and the rest of his gang locked up—and that Mrs. Bannister didn't have to live in terror any longer.

Ma brought out plates and set them at Vi's place. She put the bowl of buttered carrots in the center of the table, stuck a serving spoon in the bowl, stood back and surveyed our work. "Did I forget anything?" she asked me.

"I don't think so." Thinking of other meals Vi had fixed for us, I called, "Do you have a basket of rolls or biscuits, Vi?"

"Nope. There are dumplings in the goulash."

"Dumplings. My goodness," said Ma, a worried frown on her face. Ma wasn't an adventurous diner.

"It will be great, Ma," I assured. "Everything Vi cooks is great."

"That's true," said Ma, her frown lines smoothing out.

"Here we go!" said my marvelous aunt, toting a gigantic serving bowl to the table and setting it carefully at her place. "See? Everything's in there: meat, potatoes, onions, and we have carrots on the side."

"It looks…interesting," said Ma, never one to take chances on things until she was sure of them.

"It's delicious," said Vi. "It's become one of Mr. Pinkerton's favorites, and I got Mr. Larkin to cut the beef into chunks for me, so I didn't have to do it."

"It sounds as though you're getting mighty chummy with Mr. Larkin, Vi," I said, a little worried myself, but not about dinner. I didn't want Vi to marry Mr. Larkin and desert us for him.

"Daisy!" said Ma, shocked.

Vi only laughed. "Mrs. Larkin would probably have something to say to me if I ran off with her husband, Daisy Gumm Majesty."

"Oh, he's married? Thank God!" Relief flooded through me.

"Daisy," said my mother again. I didn't mind.

"It's all right, Peggy. Mrs. Pinkerton is one of Mr. Larkin's best customers, and he's very nice about doing little favors for me now and then. You know what he said to me about cutting up a beef round?"

"No. What?" Maybe I should write down cooking tips from Vi. If I could create an old-west dictionary, why not a recipe booklet? Except that every time I try to do anything in the kitchen, havoc ensues.

"He said that if you freeze the beef first, and then partially thaw it, it's *much* easier to cut!"

"Oh," I said. "How does he freeze the beef?"

"He has a freezer in the butcher's shop at Jorgensen's, Daisy! How else do you think they keep meat fresh?"

"Um…I guess I never much thought about it."

"That doesn't surprise me," said Vi, not sounding mean about it. "But for this goulash, you need to slice a hunk of about two or three pounds off the lower part of the beef round and then cut the hunk into approximately one-inch cubes. You need a sharp knife, and Mr. Larkin said the beef cuts more easily when it's slightly frozen. That way, the meat's harder and isn't squishy when you cut it."

Squishy meat. Oh, dear. If Vi ever died, I'd have to hire a cook, I reckon. The mere notion of squishy beef made my stomach feel funny. "Want me to call the men in to dinner?"

Vi and Ma and I took another long look at the table, and Vi said, "Looks like everything's ready. Go fetch the men. I have some lemonade all made up. Your father can bring in the pitcher. There's some ice in the ice box, too."

"Thanks, Vi!" The one thing I *could* do at mealtimes without incurring disaster was call folks to the table. So I did.

For the record, Vi's Hungarian goulash was delicious. We didn't even leave enough in the bowl for lunch the next day.

TWENTY-FOUR

The rest of that week passed peacefully. Nobody would allow me out of the house by myself, but I was able to build up my strength slightly by taking short walks with Pa and Spike in the mornings.

Lou Prophet pretty much settled in to the cottage behind Sam's bungalow across the street from us where, Sam said, he'd still be able to keep an eye on things. Just in case.

I didn't want there to *be* a just in case, but I didn't argue. My poor battered body was healing nicely, but it still wasn't one-hundred percent better, especially my left arm, which ached when I used it too much. I found that out on Thursday evening at choir practice.

Sam and Lou Prophet sat like a couple of carved statues in the front pew as we choir members sang. Every now and then, Sam would turn his head and survey the sanctuary. Mr. Prophet just crossed his arms over his chest and stared at us. Their presence was slightly—only slightly, mind you—disconcerting. I tried not to glance at them very often.

Our anthem for the coming Sunday was "Ye Servants of God," yet another hymn written by one of Methodism's founding fathers, Charles Wesley. It was an all-right hymn. Not my favorite, but nice.

"Mrs. Majesty, are you up to singing a duet with Mrs. Zollinger on

Sunday?" asked Mr. Floy Hostetter, our choir director. "The third verse would work nicely as a duet."

"Um…" The truth of the matter was: I wasn't sure. Mr. Hostetter, who didn't cotton to equivocation, stared at me critically.

"Um…I can try. My left arm is still a little weak."

"Humph." Mr. Hostetter didn't cotton to weakness either.

"Perhaps we should allow Mrs. Majesty another week or two to mend," said Lucy, surprising me. Lucy wasn't known for stating her opinions out loud in front of people.

"Let me try," I said, smiling at Lucy, appreciating her support.

"Very well," said Mr. Hostetter, tapping his music stand with his baton. "The both of you please step up to the front here, and we'll see how it goes." He expected it to go well; I could tell.

So Lucy and I stepped up to the front of the chancel, and lifted our hymnals. My left hand gave out and I instantly dropped mine. It landed with a thump. It landed pages-down, what's more, and I gazed at it in horror. One doesn't damage hymnals in our church, especially if one is standing smack, dab in front of Mr. Floy Hostetter.

He scowled at me.

"I'm sorry," I said, bending to retrieve my hymnal.

"I'll get it," came Sam's thunderous bass voice. He stomped up the chancel steps, retrieved my hymnal from the floor and turned to stare down at Mr. Hostetter, who backed away a step. Sam wasn't enormously tall; maybe six feet. However, he was formidable, especially when compared to the pallid, soft, musical Mr. Floy Hostetter.

"Um…" said Mr. Hostetter.

"Use a music stand," came from the first pew in a rusty voice.

Glancing pew-wards, I saw Lou Prophet grinning at the group of us.

"Great idea!" I said, aiming for a perkiness I didn't quite feel.

"Very good idea," said Sam, still glowering at Mr. Hostetter.

Lucy gave me a big smile. "Brilliant!" said she. I don't think she quite dared look at Mr. Prophet. She also avoided eye contact with Sam.

"Um…Yes," said Mr. H at last, fluttering a trifle. It didn't take a whole lot to make him nervous. I suspected Lou Prophet and/or Sam Rotondo could do it any old time one of them took it into his head to do so. "Using a music stand is an excellent idea. That way you won't need to hold the book, Mrs. Majesty, and the two of you may share a hymnal." He spoke the last words to Lucy and me. "I'll set it up before the third verse."

"Good," said Sam. He unbent enough to return to his pew next to Lou Prophet.

"Sounds like a great plan to me," I told him.

"Me, too," said Lucy.

So he did.

As for me, I couldn't remember the last time the choir had sung this particular hymn, but since I could read music, I didn't have any trouble following the alto part. Lucy and I sounded good together. We always did. That's not an unseemly boast. It's the truth. Believe me, if Mr. Hostetter didn't agree with me, we'd never be asked to sing duets.

After Lucy and I had sung the third verse of the hymn and seated ourselves next to each other in the first row of the choir, I turned a little and whispered, "Would you like to come over and practice one day before next Sunday, Lucy?"

"Good idea," she said. "How about...Well, what's a good day for you?"

"It really doesn't matter. I'm not going to be able to work for a while longer, so any old time is fine with me."

"Albert is taking me to Gay's Lion Farm on Saturday, so perhaps Friday evening? Tomorrow?"

"Oh! I've always wanted to go there!" I said, irking Mr. Hostetter, who whacked his baton on his music stand a little harder. "Whoops. Tomorrow evening it is. Want to come to dinner?"

"What a lovely offer!"

Another whack from Mr. Hostetter, and Lucy and I shut our traps.

After choir practice ended, however, Lucy and I set a date. Sam and Mr. Prophet joined us in the choir room, where we members of the choir stored our coats, handbags, hats, robes, books and hymnals. "We dine at six, Lucy. Not fashionable, but who cares?"

"I certainly don't," she said, laughing. "Will your aunt mind another two people coming to dinner on such short notice?"

"Naw. Vi loves feeding people, and she also loves company."

"Thank you so much. Albert and I will be at your home tomorrow a little before six." She glanced around the choir room and leaned over to whisper in my ear. "Um, will Mr. Prophet join us?"

"Yes. He's living in the cottage behind the house that used to be Mrs. Killebrew's, but which Sam bought for us to live in after we get married."

"He did?" Lucy's eyes went huge. "And Mr. Prophet is?"

"Mr. Prophet is what?" asked the gent in question. Guess he heard Lucy's whisper.

"You're living in the little house behind Sam's bungalow," I told him. "So you can keep an eye on things for us."

"Oh, my," said Lucy, her enthusiasm suddenly less intense. "I thought you said all the villains had been locked away."

"They have been," I said firmly. "Only...Well, we want to make sure."

"I see."

"It's not fun to know somebody wants to murder you, Lucy. I can attest to that from first-hand knowledge."

"Oh, my goodness. I'm so sorry, Daisy."

"We *think* the bad guys are all locked up now, though," I said, perhaps a little too brightly. I hoped like heck all the bad guys were locked up, was what I meant. Since nothing had happened to me, the house, or anyone or anything near me for several days, I believed they were. I hoped.

You know, I'm not being wishy-washy here. Unless you've been targeted for death by a person or persons unknown, you can't possibly imagine the anxiety and terror the situation wreaks on one.

"Ready to go?" asked Sam, looking impatient.

"Yes, dear," I said in a mock-loving tone. "Don't get out the hickory stick yet."

He rolled his eyes at me. Figured.

Lou Prophet grinned.

When Sam, Mr. Prophet and I got home that evening, Vi was still up and about, so I asked her if she'd mind having another couple of people dining with us on the morrow.

"Mind? I love feeding people!" she said, thus confirming the statements I'd made to Lucy. "Who's coming?"

"Lucy and Albert Zollinger. Lucy and I are singing a duet on Sunday, but I can't quite hold my hymnal steady yet, so Mr. Hostetter's going to put a hymnal on a music stand for us. Lucy and I can practice tomorrow after dinner."

"What's the hymn?" asked Pa.

"'Ye Servants of God'," I told him.

Wrinkling his brow, Pa said, "Never heard of it."

"That's why we need to practice," I said.

Shortly thereafter, Sam and Mr. Prophet walked across the street to Sam's new home, and the rest of us went to bed at our house. Because my left arm ached, I took a couple of aspirin tablets, but I swore I'd never touch that bottle of morphine syrup again. Well, unless somebody else ran a car into me.

Dismal thought.

At any rate, Lucy and her precious Albert arrived at our home at about five-thirty on Friday evening. Vi was already home, having been delivered by Harold Kincaid an hour or so earlier. The entire house smelled heavenly. That's because Vi aimed to serve us Italian-style spaghetti and meatballs. Sam had given Vi the recipe a couple of years previously, and a tastier dish would be difficult to find anywhere. Vi said she had to simmer the sauce for some time in order to bring out its full flavor, but I think she only wanted us to suffer torments of drool as we waited for our dinners.

"I've never smelled anything so wonderful," said Lucy in an awed whisper.

"That's Vi for you," I said, grinning, and showing her where to hang her coat and hat. Well, Lucy already knew, because she'd been to our house before. Albert caught on quickly. He was a nice man, although I thought he was a little old for Lucy. However, after the Great War, eligible young men were thin on the ground, and one had to take what one could find.

Golly, that sounds really awful, doesn't it? However they'd ended up together, Lucy and Albert seemed quite fond of one another, and that made me happy.

Right after Lucy and Albert arrived on our front porch, Sam and Lou Prophet showed up. As soon as he stepped foot—or perhaps it was his peg—inside, Mr. Prophet stopped in his tracks, lifted his head and he sniffed the air. Didn't blame him. The air in our house was most definitely worth sniffing that evening.

"That smells real good," said he, an understatement if I'd ever heard one.

"It is," I said. "It's Italian."

"Yeah?"

"My recipe," said Sam.

Prophet looked at him as if he'd lost his mind. "You cook?"

"Sure. I'm a bachelor. That is to say I'm a widower. If I didn't cook, I wouldn't eat."

"Until you met us," I reminded him.

With a grin, Sam said, "Yeah. Until I met you." He turned to Prophet and said confidingly, "That's the only reason I'm marrying her, you know."

"Sounds like a good-enough reason to me."

I whapped Sam softly on the arm. "Don't listen to him, Mr. Prophet. He adores me."

Both men laughed. I led them into the living room and introduced Mr. Prophet to Lucy and Albert. Prophet had more or less met Lucy before. The two men shook hands, Mr. Z giving the impression he wasn't sure he should be touching anyone who looked like Prophet. To be fair, Prophet looked at Mr. Z the same way. Not cut of the same cloth, those two, although they seemed to get along all right after they were introduced.

The men chatted in the living room whilst we ladies set the table and got the foodstuffs settled thereon. How come women do all the work in the world? Not that being a bounty hunter or a policeman or whatever Mr. Zollinger was didn't count as working, but really. Lots of women had to work away from their homes, too, and then they had to come home and do all the household chores, as well. Seemed unfair to me, but nobody'd ever asked me. Nor would they care if they *did* ask and I answered. I swear...

"Mr. and Mrs. Zollinger are going to Gay's Lion Farm tomorrow," I told everyone after we'd been seated at the table and Pa had said the blessing.

"I remember you saying something about that place," said Prophet. "I'd kinda like to see it, too."

"You can come with us!" I said happily. "Harold said he'd take me. We can all three go together!"

"What about me?" asked Sam in a grumble.

"You may come with us, too," I said magnanimously.

"Thanks. I'll probably have to work."

"That's what I figured," I told him. "Anyway, on Sunday Lucy can tell me all about it, and I can then let you know if it's worth the trip to downtown Los Angeles."

"Never saw a lion outside of a zoo before," said Prophet.

"Me, neither." Sam.

In fact, the sentiment was unanimous.

"I've wanted to see Gay's for a long time now," said Lucy. "I can't imagine being a lion-tamer."

After a short, but piercing glance at Sam, I said, "I can."

I do believe Sam would have thrown a piece of garlic bread at me if we hadn't been seated at my parents' dining-room table. Everyone laughed.

"I understand they're going to move the lion farm to El Monte pretty soon," I said after downing an awe-inspiring bite of meatball.

"Yeah? That'd be closer to here, wouldn't it?" asked Prophet.

"Yes, but I don't like El Monte much."

Mr. Prophet lifted an eyebrow. "Why's that, Miss Daisy?"

Sam and I exchanged a glance, and I decided the rest of our dining companions didn't need to know I'd been kidnapped by a couple of murdering anarchists, driven over a police-planted tire-flattener I didn't know was there, and ended up in a ditch in El Monte. I just shrugged. "Not sure, really. There are dairies in El Monte, and you can see cows on the hills there, but you probably don't much care about cows, do you?"

"I like eating them," said Prophet.

Again a round of laughter filled the room.

Then Mr. Z asked Mr. Prophet what he did for a living, and it seems as if the air in the room had suddenly been sucked into several lungs. Prophet, however, remained unfazed.

"Retired now. Used to do me a bit of law-dogging."

"Law-dogging?"

"He was a lawman," I said. "Kind of."

"Oh! You mean a sheriff or a policeman or something like that?"

"Something like that," said Prophet, his voice as dry as the dust on an Arizona desert.

"My goodness. Where was this?" asked Lucy, naively sweet.

"He worked all over the west," I said, hoping the subject would die a natural death.

"The west?" asked Mr. Z. "We're the west, aren't we?" He appeared honestly confused.

"Yes, but this was in the olden days."

Prophet gave me an unfriendly squint.

"Well, I don't mean the olden days, exactly. I mean, he used to work in some of those rough western towns in, you know, Arizona, Texas, New Mexico, those places. Before they were states, I mean. Well, Texas was a state, but when he worked in them, Arizona and New Mexico were territories. He saw a lot of what we think of as the old west," I said, mentally telling myself to stop babbling.

"Oh, my. Fascinating," said Mr. Z. I think he meant it.

"It had its moments," said Prophet acidly.

"More spaghetti?" asked Vi, beaming at us.

"Yeah. Thanks. This stuff is really good. Never had it before," said Prophet.

"You had to cook for yourself, though, didn't you?" I asked. "When you were on the trail of some of those bad guys, you had to cook over a camp fire, right?" The two or three times I'd ever sat at a campfire was when I'd gone to the camp our church held for kids during the summer months in the San Gabriel Mountains. The only things I ever cooked over the fire were frankfurters and marshmallows on sticks.

"Yeah," said Prophet. "Sometimes we could catch a fish if there was a stream nearby. Mostly, though, it was bacon and beans. And hard biscuits. Gets a mite tiresome after a few weeks." He grinned as if in fond remembrance of times past.

If all I got to eat were bacon and beans and hard biscuits for weeks on end, I think I'd have perished from sheer boredom. And, perhaps, flatulence. I probably shouldn't have said that, but it did occur to me.

"Goodness," said Lucy. "I can't imagine having to track bad men in the old west."

"It was a living," said Prophet.

Sam mentioned something about Italian cornmeal, which he called *polenta*, and the conversation ranged away from Mr. Prophet's employment in the old west.

I got the feeling Mr. Prophet was glad of it. Truth be told, so was I.

TWENTY-FIVE

As soon as I walked into the choir room the Sunday after Lucy and Albert's visit to our house on Friday, Lucy attacked me. Well, she didn't precisely attack, but she was on me like a duck on a June bug. That's another saying I got from Mr. Prophet.

"Oh, Daisy!" cried she. "It was so much fun!"

I blinked at her. "What was so much fun?"

"The *lion* farm! It was wonderful! A fellow put on an exhibition and showed visitors how he trained the lions and everything."

"Oh, that's right! I'm so glad. I was hoping it would be worth the ride to downtown."

"It's not really all that far," said Lucy. "It was a fine day for a drive, and the park is lovely."

"That's nice. Harold Kincaid told me he'd take me there, so now I'm looking forward to it even more."

Our duet went swimmingly. Mr. Hostetter was as good as his word, setting a hymnal on a music stand for us so I didn't have to hold the heavy book in my weak left hand.

After the church service was over, my family gravitated to Fellowship Hall. I was moving around *much* better by then, and was able to fetch a cookie all on my own. I didn't even need my cane. Not that I much wanted a cookie, but Dr. Benjamin told me it would help me recover fully if I exercised my arms and legs after having been sedentary for three weeks. What the heck. Fetching a cookie was exercise, wasn't it?

I took it to a table and sat next to Sam, who'd sat next to Lou Prophet. Mr. Prophet had shed his shabby frock coat for the occasion. I don't know if Sam had bought him a new suit or what, but he looked almost respectable. Lou Prophet, I mean. Sam always looked respectable. Harold even said he looked like an Italian count now and then. Anyhow, both men had snagged three cookies each. Vi had a chicken stew bubbling on the stove at home, so we didn't want to overdo the cookies.

"You and your lady friend sounded mighty fine up there today, Miss Daisy," said Mr. Prophet.

"Thank you!" His compliment sounded heartfelt, and it touched me. Not sure why.

"They always sound good together," said Sam.

"Yeah? You two sing together a lot?"

Modestly, I told Mr. Prophet, "Mr. Hostetter has us sing duets from time to time. Lucy has a lovely soprano voice." I didn't say that in the next life, should there be one, I wanted to come back as a soprano because they always got the melody, thinking that might be inserting sour grapes into an otherwise friendly conversation. It did, however, occasionally irk me that we altos always had to learn the harmony while the sopranos warbled away on the melody as if they'd done something interesting when, in truth, it was the altos who had to work hard in order to make a duet work well. All the sopranos ever had to do was not go off-key.

"That's nice. He knows a good thing when he hears one, I reckon." Mr. Prophet went back to munching cookies.

I was surprised when Miss Betsy Powell sat across from us at our table. She smiled at me.

"It's so good to see you up and about again, Mrs. Majesty," she said.

"Thank you," I said, smiling politely. Miss Powell and I weren't enemies, but we'd never been bosom pals, either, so I thought her arrival at our table a trifle odd. It probably wasn't. I'd received a host of good wishes from lots of congregation members that day, and I hardly knew several of them. I guess that's what happens when you sing in the choir; you meet all the choir members, but unless you socialize a lot at church functions, you don't necessarily meet the rest of the congregants.

"Your duet with Mrs. Zollinger was lovely," she said.

"Thank you."

"Mrs. Majesty! You're looking ever so much better today than you did when we last saw you." This came from Mr. Bernard Randford, who pulled out a chair next to Miss Powell's. He smiled at me, too. "Are you feeling better?"

"Much better, thank you. How's your poor motorcar."

With a thin smile, Mr. Randford said, "It's fine again. I had to replace the seats." He shook his head. "Creatures in the wild don't understand the purpose of automobiles, I guess."

"I guess," said I.

"Are you coming any closer to finding who stole it?" Mr. Randford asked of Sam, who'd been quietly nibbling away at his cookies.

Lifting his head, Sam said, "Not really. It's annoying, too. We pretty much have the whole gang who wanted Daisy dead locked up, but we still haven't pinned the vehicle theft on anyone."

Mr. Randford frowned slightly and shook his head. "I hope you do it soon. Whoever stole my car—and then used it for such a fell purpose—should be locked up."

I got the feeling he added on the "fell purpose" comment because he didn't want us to think he was merely interested in who'd stolen his car. Well, that was all right. I suppose that might be my main interest, too, if the only thing I'd had to worry about was a stolen vehicle. As it was, I considered the theft of Mr. Randford's Cole Sportster the least of the problems we'd faced during the past three weeks. Except that it had been used in an attempt to kill me.

Lucy sat in the chair next to me and smiled across the table at Miss Powell and Mr. Randford. "Did Daisy tell you where Albert and I went yesterday?"

Looking puzzled, Miss Powell said, "Why, no, she didn't. Where did you go yesterday?"

"Gay's Lion Farm in Westlake Park! It was so much fun!"

"Goodness, I didn't know there was a lion farm nearby," said Miss

Powell. She turned to gaze upon Mr. Randford. "Oh, Bernard, wouldn't it be fun to see a lion farm?"

After giving the matter some thought, Mr. Randford said cautiously, "Might be interesting."

"Oh, it was," raved Lucy. "They put on an exhibition to show visitors how they train the lions, and they had posters from the various moving pictures their lions were used in hanging in a hall, and…Well, it was an enjoyable adventure."

Smiling besottedly (is that a word?) at his wife, Albert Zollinger said, "It was most entertaining."

All of a sudden, Sam spoke. I jumped a little, having forgot he was even there. "I might be able to get Wednesday off."

"Oh, Sam, really?"

He glared at me. "No. I'm lying."

A soft guffaw from Lou Prophet smote the air. Everyone else at the table chuckled to one degree or another.

"Would you mind if Harold went with us?"

With a shrug, Sam said, "No. That's fine."

"I want to see this place, too," said Mr. Prophet.

"I'll call Harold as soon as we get home, and we'll make arrangements to go to Gay's Lion Farm on Wednesday."

"If Kincaid can get the day off," said Sam.

"Of course," I said. "His schedule seems quite flexible, but he might not be able to take an odd Wednesday off any time he chooses."

"We should go as a church group someday," said Miss Powell and giggled.

Her giggle annoyed me for some reason. I think, by that time in my life, and after hearing Miss Betsy Powell scream on numerous occasions, pretty much everything she did annoyed me. I'm not very nice sometimes.

The rest of my family gathered around our table then, so we all got up to traipse home again. My chest itched a bit, and I scratched it as I got into Sam's Hudson, feeling happy. It seemed a long time since I'd been happy. The day was glorious, and I was starting to get used to being out of danger. It had been almost a week since anyone had tried to kill me and, while it was true I jumped approximately three feet in the air any time a motorcar in my vicinity backfired, my nerves were ever so much calmer than they'd been during those first perilous weeks in January.

As soon as I'd set the table for Sunday dinner, I telephoned Harold Kincaid's home. Naturally, Roy Castillo answered same. He told me Harold was away from the house, but that he'd have him call me as soon as he got home. Pronouns. So annoying. I meant he (Roy) would have him (Harold) telephone me (Daisy) as soon as Harold returned to Harold's house. Nertz.

"He didn't go to church with Del, did he?" I asked of Roy. It was really a joke question. I knew Harold better than to think he'd go to church with Del.

As I might have expected he would, Roy laughed. "No, Miss Daisy. I don't think Harold would go near that place. I think he's afraid of it."

"He might well be." And perhaps for good reason. If anybody called *me* Our Lady of Perpetual Malice, I'd probably be annoyed, too. I'd been to see St. Andrews, where Del worshiped. Its sanctuary was lined on each side by columns made of marble in different colors. I could visualize one of those marble columns crumbling right on top of Harold should he dare enter St. Andrews's hallowed halls.

For the record, the reason I'd gone to St. Andrews was in order to see its innards because they were so widely praised for their beauty. Honestly? I thought the sanctuary would be prettier if the columns were all the same color marble. Once again, nobody'd asked me what I thought about St. Andrews' columns, and I probably wouldn't have answered if they had, because obviously I was wrong. Only I still didn't like all the different colored marble columns. Guess I'm just a Philistine.

I'm sure I don't need to tell everyone how delicious Aunt Vi's chicken stew was. Or how delicate and toothsome her dinner rolls were. Or how much we all enjoyed dining thereon.

Lou Prophet, who had only recently begun to savor Vi's cooking, said it all for us. Shaking his head in rapture, he said upon a sigh, "I swear, Mrs. Gumm, I've never eaten so well in my life. You're the best cook I've ever met."

"Thank you." Vi tittered. She didn't do that often, but Mr. Prophet had that effect on women of a certain age.

Truth to tell, I could get a little giddy around him myself sometimes, but please don't tell Sam. Heck, Lou Prophet must have been nigh onto eighty years old by then and, while remnants of his handsome youth remained—in spots—he was an old man. Not a little old man, but an old man. With a peg leg, for pity's sake.

Trying not to stare as I assessed him, I acknowledged he was undoubtedly telling the truth with regard to Vi being the best cook he'd ever met. He didn't look like a man who lied often. He also didn't look as though he'd dined on top-notch foodstuffs during most of his adventurous life. Beans and bacon and hard biscuits. I hoped he'd at least found the occasional onion to chop up and dump into his beans and bacon to give them some oomph.

The family and Mr. Prophet had just polished off a baked Roman beauty apple (prepared with butter, brown sugar and cinnamon and served with thick cream) for dessert when the telephone rang. I instantly rose from my chair at the dining table. I didn't hurt! Well, I didn't hurt much, anyway.

Feeling quite chipper, I went to the telephone in the kitchen, pretty sure I knew who was on the other end of the wire.

I was right.

"What do you want from me *now*, Daisy?" Harold asked in a simulated-aggrieved tone.

"I want you to take Mr. Prophet and Sam and me to Gay's Lion Farm on Wednesday."

A slight hesitation preceded Harold's, "Oh. Well, hell, why not? Only I don't think we can all fit in the Bearcat." Harold owned a gorgeous, bright red, snazzy, low-slung Stutz Bearcat.

"Hmm. You're probably right. You ought to drive Mr. Prophet there. Bet he's never been in such a fancy car."

"You want me to ride in a moving vehicle alone with that man?"

"Sure! Why not?"

"Because he's a dangerous lunatic?"

"He is not! He's a hero of the old west. Anyway, he has a wooden leg, for the sweet Lord's sake. What the heck can he do to you?"

"I'm not sure, but he looks like a dodgy customer to me."

"Fiddlesticks! He's a nice man, he's saved my own personal hide several times in the last few weeks, and he wants to see the lion farm, too."

A huge, heavy sigh gusted its way through the telephone wires. "Very well. But I swear to God, Daisy Majesty, if that man ropes and ties me or shoots me or anything, I'll make sure you catch hell for it."

I heard a gasp from a party-line neighbor and did a little sighing of my own. "He didn't mean it, Mrs. Barrow," I said, figuring the snooping party was she.

"It's Mrs. Longnecker," said that lady.

"He didn't mean it, Mrs. Longnecker."

"I should hope not." And *wham* went the receiver on her end of the line.

"You really have to get a private line, Daisy."

"I know. I know. One of these days."

"When can you start working again? My mother's already had three nervous breakdowns, a stroke, and several major spasms without you being able to cater to her during the endless days of your recovery."

"Tell you what, Harold. If you agree to take us to the lion farm on Wednesday—*and* let Mr. Prophet sit in your Bearcat while you drive it there—I'll visit with your mother on Thursday. Tell her that, please. Just to prevent her from dying before Stacy does." I hesitated before adding, "Even though Sam hasn't been able to pin any of the attacks on me to her, I still don't trust her."

"You're a wise woman, Daisy Gumm Majesty. Say, are you going to change your last name to Rotondo when you marry the detective?"

His question confounded me for a second or two. I hadn't actually thought about changing my name. I kind of liked Majesty. I mean, really, how many people do you know named Majesty? Now that Billy and his mother and father were deceased, I was the only Majesty I knew. Mind you, Sam was the only Rotondo I knew, too, but Majesty was...I don't know. Such a splendid name for a spiritualist-medium, if you know what I mean. "Um...I guess."

"You guess?" Harold sounded as if he disapproved.

"Well, Rotondo doesn't sound very spiritualist-mediumistic, does it? Majesty does."

"Hmmm. So you're going to continue working after your marriage, eh?"

"Um…I guess so. I don't know! Harold, why are you asking me all these hard questions?"

He laughed. "Don't get upset, Daisy. Just wondered, was all. Take your time."

"Thanks heaps."

"You're welcome. You know, you can always keep Majesty as your working name and use Rotondo for everything else. Actresses do that sort of thing all the time. Which is good, since so many of them change husbands as often as most of us change our bed linens."

"And upon that note…"

"Yes, dear. I'll be in touch about Wednesday."

"Thanks, Harold. You're a true pal."

"Don't I know it."

We disconnected, and I turned around to see that Ma had finished putting all the dishes away. She gave me an understanding look.

"Mrs. Pinkerton?" she asked.

"Well, it was Harold, but we spoke about Mrs. Pinkerton," I confirmed. "I told Harold to tell her I'd visit her on Thursday."

"At least you're well enough to go back to work," Ma said in a weakish voice.

"Yes. And the income will be handy."

"But Mrs. Pinkerton gave you all that money when you were injured. That was extremely generous of her."

"Yes," I said. "It was."

Having thus been reminded of the kindness of friends and relations, I took myself to the sewing room, where I also kept note paper and so forth. I retrieved a box of pretty note paper Aunt Vi had given me for Christmas, a bottle of ink, my fountain pen and Spike—he'd trotted along with me to the sewing room—and retired to the dining room. The men continued playing gin rummy in the living room, and I began writing approximately ten thousand thank-you notes.

My hand wore out before it was time for bed, but I'd made quite a dent in the number of notes I had to write. And really, I was pleased to thank people for their many kindnesses to me when I'd been laid up. People were so nice, sometimes they made my eyes drip a little.

"What the matter with you?" came a gruff question from Sam as I sat at the dining-room table, getting sentimental about the kindness of friends and neighbors.

"Yeah," said Mr. Prophet. "What's the matter? C'mon, girl, don't cloud up and rain all over us. What happened now?"

Peering up to see both men looming over me, I stopped feeling sentimental and became irritated instead. "I'm not raining on you! I'm writing thank-you notes, and it's quite moving to know how many genuinely kind people there are in the world. They almost make up for the snake pit of Petries."

"Guess that makes sense," said Prophet. He'd fetched his new—I guess it was new—suit coat from the coat tree beside the front door and shrugged it on.

Sam bent over to give me a kiss on the cheek. "I'm glad I don't have to write all those notes."

"You probably wouldn't write them even if you were the one people had given gifts to."

"You're wrong there. If I didn't do my duty of politeness, my mother would fly out here on her broomstick and then beat me to death with it."

"Sam!" I said, shocked before I burst out laughing. "Your mother isn't a witch!"

"She can come damned close to it when one of her children misbehaves."

"'Leastways you got a mother. Mine's been gone for a million years."

"Both of you men have a habit of exaggerating the tiniest little bit, you know," I said, pushing myself up from the table. "Anyhow, you should sic your mother on Frank. Maybe she could straighten him out."

"I think both my mother and my father have given up on Frank."

"I don't much blame them."

"Me, neither," said Prophet. "Kid needs a bullet to the brain-pan."

"That's kind of drastic, isn't it?" I asked, a little startled.

214

With a shrug, Prophet said, "He wanted to stick a knife into you. I figure turn-about's fair play."

"Guess I can't argue with you there," I said, still disturbed, although I'd never tell Lou Prophet so.

Pa had joined us in the dining room and was looking upon us with a benevolent smile. He approved of Sam, Lou Prophet and me together. I could tell.

Which gave me pause.

Sam, Lou Prophet and me? Were we, like, a team or something? Oddly enough, the notion held some appeal. And if we added Spike, we'd be an unbeatable quartet of by-gum heroes. Well, three heroes and one heroine. And one of the heroes would be a canine, but dachshunds are mighty hunters. Heck, they'd probably be great at bounty hunting.

That idea made me smile as I walked the men in my life to the front door. Two of them, Sam and Prophet, went across the porch, down the steps, and headed for our—*our*—bungalow across the street.

It was a happy Daisy Gumm Majesty who hit the sack with her faithful dachshund that night.

TWENTY-SIX

The only exciting thing that happened before Wednesday, when we were scheduled to go to Gay's Lion Farm, was news that the largest house on the block had been sold. I hadn't even known it was for sale, but neighborhood telephone wires buzzed non-stop on Monday and Tuesday.

I managed to get a vague idea who'd bought the large house from picking up the telephone at odd times, intending to call a friend, only to hear someone else speaking over the wire.

"…widow woman."

"…Mrs. Evangeline Mainwaring!"

"…private investigator."

"…heard of her."

"…bought that huge old house?"

"…owns a lot of orange groves."

"…name's Bowman, I think."

Merciful heavens. What was this? On Tuesday morning, as I'd been about to call Flossie Buckingham to see if she'd like to take lunch with me at Mijares Mexican Restaurant in downtown Pasadena, I heard that last bit of gossip. I didn't like it when people listened in on my own private conversations, and I tried not to listen to other people's, but golly, you can't avoid learning *some* things by accident. I quietly replaced the receiver on its hook and turned to see Pa gazing at me from the kitchen table.

"Gossip mill running at full-speed, I presume," he said.

"You betcha. Somebody named Mrs. Mainwaring or Mrs. Bowman —or maybe Mrs. Widow Woman—bought that big old house down the street. You know the one. Been empty for a few years? Gigantic? I didn't even know it was for sale."

"I know the one. Looks like it belongs on Orange Grove instead of Marengo? That's the one, right?"

Taking a seat across from Pa at the table and reaching for a part of the morning newspaper, I said, "Right. I think that's the one everyone's talking about. I heard something about an orange grove and a private detective, too, so I'm not sure precisely what's going on, but it sounds interesting."

"I think that was the first house constructed in this part of Pasadena. The other houses grew up around it when the original owner sold off bits of property."

"That sounds logical. Kind of like when Mr. Woodbury sold pieces of his land. He planted that whole row of deodar trees to create a grand entrance to the castle he never built."

"Right. I think someone used to live in the house down the street, though, unlike Mr. Woodbury's un-built castle. Can't remember the name, if I ever knew it."

"I can't remember when it was last occupied."

Pa flapped his section of the newspaper and said, "When the new folks move in there, we should host a welcome-to-the-neighborhood party for them. Your mother and Vi will love that."

"Great idea, Pa! You come up with some doozies."

With a chuckle, Pa said, "It's not exactly an original idea. Folks did it for us when we moved in, if you remember."

"Oh." I rooted around in the junk drawer of memories in my brain for a second or two. "I remember. Yes. That was nice. Mr. Killebrew was alive then, and Mrs. Killebrew baked a chocolate cake, and someone brought a ham and some potato salad, and it was quite a do. I think that's when we got to know the Wilsons, too. Pudge was only about a year old then, and I swear he's been sweet on me ever since."

"You're good with children, Daisy. I hope you and Sam have some of your own one day."

That gave me pause. "Let's get us married first before saddling us with children, all right?"

"Oh, very well." Pa tried to sound pained, but he couldn't carry it off. He chuckled as he resumed reading the paper.

I opened my section of the newspaper, searching for the crossword puzzle. The *Pasadena Star News* had begun running a crossword puzzle every day, bless its inky heart, and I loved solving them.

The telephone rang. I listened for a second to be sure the ring was meant for our house. It was, so I rose and went to the 'phone. "Gumm-Majesty—"

"For God's sake," said Harold Kincaid. "I *know* who you are. But do you know who just bought that house on your street?"

"Hey, Harold. I'm fine, thank you. And how are you today?"

"Cut it out. Do you *know*?"

"Who bought the house down the street? Not really. I've managed to pick up the 'phone and hear party-line neighbors talking to each other, but I haven't gathered much about the owner except, I think, she's a widow, and her name is either Mainwaring or Bowman."

"Mrs. Evangeline Mainwaring! She owns the largest orange grove in Pasadena! She moved here in ninety-six, and I heard she lived a *very* interesting life before she moved to staid old Pasadena."

"What do you mean by a *very* interesting life?"

"Like the kind of life Pasadena matrons would deplore if they knew about it. In rugged towns in the west."

"We're in the west."

"For God's sake, stop being so literal. She's another refugee from the Tombstone and Deadwood era."

"Good Lord. You mean she's the female equivalent of Lou Prophet?"

Harold roared out a laugh. "I didn't think of it that way," said he once he could speak again, "but you may well be right."

"Hmmm. You'll have to come to the neighborhood party we throw for her once she's all settled in."

"Wouldn't miss it for the world. You ready for tomorrow?"

"Yup. I'm even ready to see your mother on Thursday."

"You're a better man than I am, Gunga Din."

"Yeah, yeah. Pretty much anyone's a better man than you are, Harold Kincaid."

"That's not nice, Daisy Gumm Majesty."

"I know. I'm sorry."

"That's all right. It's the truth. So I'll be at your house at ten a.m. We'll go to the lion farm and then stop at Philippe's for a French dip sandwich."

"Whatever a French dip sandwich is, I'm game."

"Daisy, Daisy, Daisy, where have you been all your life."

"Right here in stuffy old Pasadena."

"Ah, right. That explains it."

Harold and I disconnected, and I returned to the table to tell Pa who was moving in down the street. Not that I knew much more than I had minutes earlier, but at least I had a name. And a tidy piece of gossip I decided I'd keep to myself. I personally didn't know a single, solitary thing about Mrs. Evangeline Mainwaring—hadn't even known her name until Harold confirmed it—and I wasn't going to blacken it before the rest of the neighborhood even learned what it was.

"Owns an orange grove, eh? Profitable business, oranges."

"I guess so," said I, and I went back to my crossword puzzle.

A little after I finished the crossword, I tried again to get in touch with Flossie, and this time I succeeded. She said she'd be delighted to go to luncheon with me at Mijares, but she wouldn't hear of me picking her up.

"That's so far for you to drive," she said. She was such a lovely person. Always thinking of others, by golly.

"Nertz. I have to drive to downtown anyway, in order to get to Mijares. Besides, you've not only knitted and crocheted approximately three thousand afghans, robes and bed jackets for me, but you're one of my best friends, and I owe you a whole lot for seeing me through my recent ordeal. Also, I want you to bring Billy." Billy was Flossie and

Johnny's son, named after my late husband, but I think I already mentioned that. "Anyway, Mijares is close to where you live, so I won't be driving much farther than I would be anyway."

"Nonsense. Are you even fit to be driving yet? You were in *such* bad shape for a while after your accident."

"It wasn't an accident."

Flossie sighed. "Yes, I know. Johnny talked to your Sam about it."

"He did?" That surprised me.

"You bet he did. Johnny and I don't want anything else bad to happen to you. When Detective Rotondo came by, he asked us to be alert for anyone who looked the least bit suspicious."

"He came by?" Now I was more than merely surprised.

"Of course, he did!" said Flossie, as if I were an idiot for even asking the question. "He adores you, Daisy! He doesn't want anything to happen to you. And neither do Johnny nor I."

Wow, Flossie Buckingham had said "nor" after "neither." I was impressed. I doubt she'd had any education at all after she hit her teen years. Not that she wasn't a smart cookie; but she'd come from miserable circumstances and hadn't had many chances in this old life until Johnny had taken her under his wing.

Oh, very well. I'd kind of thrust her at him, if you want the bare truth. What's more—this makes me cringe every time I think about it—I'd been trying to get rid of her at the time. But really. She'd showed up at our door, escorted by Pudge Wilson—doing his good deed for that day—beaten to a pulp, and I couldn't *not* help her. At the time, I also had a crippled, cranky husband; a full-time job as a spiritualist-medium, and…Oh, all right. The complete truth is that Sam had more or less blackmailed me into helping him round up a gang of bootleggers. Flossie had been entangled with the gang. However, all things considered, matters had worked out just fine.

Which just goes to show that, even when you aren't happy about it, doing a good deed can sometimes be worthwhile. Flossie and I were now great friends, and I adored both Flossie and Johnny. And, of course, little Billy.

"I'll pick you up," I said in a voice against which no one could argue.

"Nonsense." No one except Flossie. Darn it.

"It's not nonsense. I'll pick you up at eleven-thirty. Does that adorable little sailor suit you made for Billy still fit him?"

"No, but I made another one for him."

"Have him wear that. Everyone dining at Mijares will fall in love with him." He was a good-looking little boy even when he wasn't wearing his sailor suit, but the sailor suit was…well, precious.

"Very well, Daisy, but I don't like it."

"Fiddlesticks. I've about gone stir-crazy during these last few weeks when I wasn't even allowed to go out on the back deck." I shuddered as I remembered the one time I'd dared venture onto the back deck.

"Are you sure it's safe for you to go out now?" asked Flossie, sounding worried.

"Sam has assured me—pretty much—that all the bad guys are locked up," I told her.

After a noticeable hesitation, Flossie said, "All right. But you bring that fellow with you. The one who's living in back of your new house."

Astounded, I nearly bellowed, "Lou Prophet? How the heck do you know about *him*?"

"He was with Sam when he came to visit us. He's an interesting fellow. Sam told us all about him when he warned us to watch out for Petries. And we found a great suit for him in our thrift shop. That old frock coat of his was a little worn out."

"Yes. It was."

"But the suit was almost new, and it fit him perfectly," said Flossie, explaining the suit Mr. Prophet had worn in church on Sunday.

Interesting. "Did either one of them tell you Mr. Prophet used to be a bounty hunter in the old west?"

"The old west?" Flossie laughed. "Not in so many words, but I gathered he's lived a pretty rough-and-tumble life. So many of us have, you know."

I sighed. "Yes. I know. You lived a rough life in New York City, and Mr. Prophet lived a rough life in some of those old towns in the wild, wild west. I think he even went to Mexico."

"Yes, but we're both in Pasadena now."

"Yes," I said, feeling a little awed as I said it. "You are."

"So you get him to come with you, and we'll have a fun time at Mijares. I hope Billy will behave."

"I'm sure he will."

"He's two years old, Daisy. Two-year-olds aren't known for behaving themselves."

"Aw, I bet he'll act like a little angel. If he doesn't, Mr. Prophet will just throttle him with his ketch rope."

"His what?"

"Never mind. I'll tell you later."

"Just be sure he comes with you," said Flossie, sounding incredibly firm for her. I guess motherhood toughened a woman. Not that she hadn't been tough before, but she'd been tough in a gangster-ish way, not a mother-ish one. I preferred her present toughness, because it had been born of love.

Merciful heavens, I can get soupily sentimental at the drop of a hat, can't I?

"I'll do that. In fact, I'll walk across the street right now and ask him to join us."

But I didn't have to. Evidently, as soon as Pa heard me talking about taking Flossie to lunch, he'd gone across the street for me. Before I'd hung up the receiver, he'd returned, bearing Lou Prophet with him.

"Mornin', Miss Daisy," said he when I'd hung the receiver on its cradle and turned to espy him in the kitchen with Pa.

His sudden appearance startled me. "Mr. Prophet! I was just going to see if you'd like to go to lunch with Mrs. Buckingham and me."

"Happy to. Your pa said you were going to go to a Mexican place. Haven't had my trough filled with some Mescin-spiced *frijoles* an' *carne de vaca* since Jehosophat's cat was on his first life."

Wasn't there some guy named Jehoshaphat in the Bible? Given Lou Prophet's earlier years, I decided I'd be better off not asking. "Do you like it? Mexican food, I mean?"

"Oh, yes. Like me some tarantula juice, too, but I reckon you can't get any of that here, what with Prohibition and all." His face took on a forlorn expression.

I almost asked him what tarantula juice was, too, but again decided against doing so. "Why don't you and Pa wait in the living room while I get dressed to go? I'd like to visit the library after we eat, if you're up to it."

"The library? That where the good Petrie friend of yours works? I heard from Sam there's at least one good Petrie in town."

Smiling at the thought of Regina and Robert—and of Robert's collection of yellow-back novels—I said, "Yes. Regina Petrie. She's a great friend of mine, and she works as a librarian there."

"It'll be nice to meet a good Petrie," said Prophet, and he and Pa turned around and walked to the living room.

Spike followed them, deserting me. Oh, well. I couldn't really fault the dog. Lou Prophet was ever so much more interesting a fellow than were most of the guests at our house. Or me.

As this would be my first real outing since New Year's Day—I didn't count choir rehearsals and going to church—and as the early February day was brisk, if not downright chilly, I decided I'd wear a new creation I'd sewn for myself in December. It was a straight, two-piece suit I'd made of green wool jersey, bought from a bolt-end at Maxime's Fabrics. I wore it with a low belt I'd bought at Nash's Department Store when they had a huge sale. The top had a V-neck and a lacy, pointed white collar. I'd added a green velvet bow at the neckline, and it hung nearly to where my waist would have been if women had been allowed to have waists back then.

Hmm. Does that sound strange? It shouldn't. A woman was supposed to be shapeless in 1925. I even had to wear a bust-flattener, thanks to the generosity of Mother Nature. I'd be glad when women could look like women again. Being a female in 1925 could be down-right painful if you had any curves at all.

When I walked into the living room to fetch Mr. Prophet, I had a feeling he felt the same way about women's shapes, although probably not for the same reason. In fact, several times since I'd met him, I'd seen him eyeing a woman as if he wished she weren't wearing all the curve-flattening things women had to wear in order to be fashionable.

Ah, well. With luck, both Mr. Prophet and I would live long enough to see women look like women again. I never wanted us to go back to the tightly corseted waistline and bustle days, though. I'd seen pictures of how some women's rib cages had been deformed by those cursed corsets. Fashion could be a cruel mistress, darn it.

"You look mighty fetching this morning, Miss Daisy," said Prophet.

"Thank you."

"Yes, Daisy, you do. Is that new?" asked Pa.

"I made it in December, just after Christmas. Haven't had a chance to wear it until today."

"You got a coat?" asked Prophet. "It's crisp outside."

"Yes. It's the black one on the coat rack. I'll get it."

"I'll fetch it for you," said he. And he did. Gentlemanly fellow, Mr. Lou Prophet. Occasionally. He even held it out for me as I put my arms in its sleeves. My left arm still hurt a bit when I lifted it, but I felt so much better than those first few days after the car hit me, I wasn't about to grouse about a slightly achy arm.

"And would you mind carrying these for me, Mr. Prophet?" I asked scooping the few books on the table reserved for books the family had read and were ready to be returned to the library.

"Happy to help," said he, and he took the books from me. At my instruction, he laid the books on the back seat of the motorcar.

After I backed the Chevrolet out of the driveway—which took all my concentration, since I'm not a very good backer-upper—I said, "I understand Sam took you to meet the Buckinghams when I was laid up."

"Yes, he did. Nice folks. Miss Flossie's a right pretty gal."

I smiled in remembrance. "Yes, she is." She was a heck of a lot prettier now than she used to be, when she'd slathered makeup all over her face and dyed her hair silvery blond. At least I thought she was.

"She says you saved her life."

I darned near ran up over the curb and onto the sidewalk, Mr. Prophet's words so surprised me. "She said *what?*"

"Take it easy, Miss Daisy," said Prophet, clutching his seat back. "Miss Flossie said you saved her life. Sam said you did, too."

"He did? Gee, Sam doesn't usually give me credit for much of anything. Especially…Well, especially given the way Flossie and I met."

"You mean in the speakeasy?" When I glanced his way, I noticed Mr. Prophet grinning not unlike Mr. Carroll's Cheshire Cat.

"He told you that?"

"He did."

"Oh. Well, I wouldn't go so far as to say I saved her life. I think Johnny Buckingham did that. I just sort of introduced them."

"I see."

"I get the feeling you don't believe me."

"Oh, I believe you, all right, but I'll wager there's more to the story than that."

"If Flossie wants to tell you her story, she can do it. I'm not going to tell tales about my friends." Boy, I sounded snooty, didn't I?

It didn't matter. Mr. Prophet only chuckled.

TWENTY-SEVEN

Flossie and her adorable little Billy were waiting for us in front of the Salvation Army Church. Almost before I'd come to a full stop, Mr. Prophet had the front passenger door open and was holding it for Flossie and Billy. He bowed politely at Flossie. "Cute kid you got there, Mrs. Buckingham," he said, smiling at Billy, who stared at him and clung to his mother. I guess Billy and Mr. Prophet hadn't met when Sam had taken Prophet to meet Flossie and Johnny.

"Thank you, Mr. Prophet. It's so good to see you again." She sounded as though she meant it.

"You, too." So did he.

Little Billy, still clinging to his mother, stared as Mr. Prophet got into the back seat. Billy seemed kind of scared. I considered this understandable, as there were so few people who looked like Mr. Prophet in Pasadena. In fact, I do believe he was the only one. Very rugged-looking individual, Mr. Lou Prophet.

"As a friend of both Daisy and Sam," said Flossie, "I'd also like to thank you for taking such good care of Daisy. Sam told us how you rescued her several times during her imprisonment at home."

"Golly, Sam sure is a blabbermouth, isn't he?" I said. Unkind of me. But for pity's sake, had Sam spread tales of my travails all over town?

And why hadn't he told me he'd done so? I didn't like the idea of marrying a man who held secrets so close to his vest, darn it.

Laughing, Flossie said, "No, he isn't really. But he wanted everyone who loves you to know your life was in danger. You have to admit it was, Daisy. And you also have to admit Mr. Prophet was of material assistance to you several times."

"Aw, it wasn't nothin'," said Prophet, grinning like a Chinese imp I'd seen in a Chinatown shop once. "We have to take good care of this pretty little gal. The detective needs her." With a wink I witnessed in the rearview mirror, he added, "She needs him, too."

Because I didn't like being talked about as if I weren't there, I changed the subject. "Mr. Prophet said he hasn't eaten Mexican food for a long time, and that he likes it."

"Mijares is a wonderful place to eat," said Flossie. "I'm from New York City, and I'd never even heard of Mexican food until I moved to California."

"I been all over the southwest and down into Mexico," said Prophet. "Don't seem like folks living in a place like this'd be big fans of Mexican food. Mexican food is…well, kinda folksy."

"And we citizens of Pasadena aren't," I said, smiling. He was right, by golly.

After chuckling, Prophet said, "Depending on where you are in Mexico, the food'll taste different. It'll be interesting to find out what variety crawled up into Pasadena."

"I didn't know that," I told him, keeping my eye on the road because I decided peering into the rearview window was probably not good for anyone's health and safety. "But it makes sense. We here in California don't eat all the codfish and lobsters and so forth my relations in Auburn, Massachusetts, dine on."

"We can get really good fish, though," said Flossie. "So near the ocean as we are. But you're right about regional food. I haven't had clam chowder since I moved here."

"That's all right with me," I told her. "I don't like clam chowder. Fried clams are another matter altogether. The one time the family visited our relations in Massachusetts, I loved fried clams and boiled lobster. And crab. Crab is delicious."

With a sigh, Flossie said, "Yes. There's not a lot I miss about New York, but the seafood was wonderful. I haven't seen a lobster for ten years or more."

"I never saw a lobster," said Mr. Prophet.

"They're delicious," said Flossie. "Although I don't like the idea of dropping them into boiling water while they're still alive."

Ew. I wished she hadn't said that.

"And I also," said Flossie, "never saw a tortilla in New York."

"I do like me some tortillas," said Mr. Prophet. "Filled with *carnitas* and *frijoles*, you can't beat 'em."

I dared another glance into the rearview mirror. "What's a *carnita*?"

"Not sure how they make 'em, but they're cooked pork. They fix 'em with onions and chilies, wrap a tortilla around 'em, and you can't beat 'em."

"I don't think Mijares has *carnitas*," I said, feeling a little sorry about our lack of such a flavorful food.

"They'll probably get here eventually," said Prophet philosophically. "Never saw me a *sopaipilla* outside of Mexico or New Mexico, either."

"Goodness. I've never heard of either *carnitas* or *sopaipillas*," said Flossie.

"Me, neither," I said. "What's a *sopaipilla*?"

"Fried bread. When they fry the stuff, the dough puffs up, so they're hollow inside. You can eat 'em like bread, fill 'em with beans and meat, or rip 'em open and pour honey inside of 'em. Delicious. Louisa and I used to eat 'em whenever we hooked up."

"Louisa?" I said. "Um…is Louisa a friend of yours, Mr. Prophet."

"Love of my life," he said succinctly. "Six feet under now."

"I'm sorry," I said.

"Yeah. Me, too."

Prophet turned his head to stare out the window, and I decided to allow the subject of Louisa to drop. I vaguely recalled someone called the Vengeance Queen in one or two of the dime novels I read. I think her name was really Louisa Something-or-other. What an odd nickname to acquire: the Vengeance Queen. How did a woman come by such a sobriquet, anyway? Probably not by nursing sickly individuals back to health or anything like that. Mr. Prophet had lived an *extremely* interesting life. I hoped I'd be able to find out more about him in person, since I don't think the yellow-back novels did him justice. Maybe he'd even tell me about Louisa if I continued being nice to him. And, shoot, there was no reason *not* to be nice to him. Flossie had been absolutely correct about Mr. Prophet having saved my life several times.

We'd arrived at Mijares's tiny parking lot by that time, so I nudged the Chevrolet into a free space, and we all got out of the car. Billy still stared worriedly at Lou Prophet.

As for Prophet, I guess the mention of Louisa had dampened his spirits. I hoped we could lift them, Flossie, Billy and me. I didn't care for the notion of Mr. Lou Prophet being sad.

He played the gentleman again once the Chevrolet had stopped puttering. He climbed from the back seat as agilely as if he had two sound legs, first opened the passenger door for Flossie and Billy, and then almost made it to my side of the car to open my door, but I beat him to it.

"Thanks, Mr. Prophet, but you don't need to cater to me."

"No trouble at all, Miss Daisy. I like catering to pretty women."

I know I blushed, because I felt the heat creep up my neck and into my cheeks. How could an elderly man have such a devastating effect on a female my age? I suspect the man had lots and lots of practice wooing and winning women, Louisa or no Louisa.

If he weren't so nice and old and one-legged, I might even call him a cad. The word made me grin, but my grin faded as soon as Mr. Prophet opened the restaurant's door for Flossie, Billy and me. Flossie held Billy's hand, and he marched like an adorable little sailor into the place. I loved that sailor suit!

Wouldn't you know it? The first people we saw when we entered the restaurant were Miss Betsy Powell and Mr. Bernard Randford. Were they following us?

No. That was silly. They'd arrived before us, so they couldn't have followed us. And why was I so suspicious of Mr. Randford? Just because he was walking out with Miss Betsy Powell and worked at the Underhill Chemical Company? Those were two really stupid reasons.

Therefore, because I don't like stupid reasons, I smiled at the pair. They were seated at a table close to the entrance of the restaurant. Mr.

Randford rose from his seat and smiled back at me. Taking in the rest of our company, his smile faded slightly. I think Mr. Prophet had something to do with his change of mood. When I glanced at Prophet, I noticed his eyes had narrowed, had gone kind of flinty, and his face was set into austere lines.

Billy wrapped his arms around his mother's leg. He'd begun to relax in Mr. Prophet's company in the motorcar, but I guess Prophet's latest expression of sternness—if not outright hostility—had him worried again. Flossie bent to pick him up, and he nearly strangled her as he hugged her around the neck.

"Good day to you, Mrs. Majesty," said Randford. "I don't believe I've met your friends."

"No, you haven't," I said, not sounding any too friendly to my own ears. I tried to warm my tone up when I introduced my allies. "Miss Betsy Powell and Mr. Bernard Randford, please let me introduce you to Mrs. Johnny Buckingham, her son Billy, and Mr. Lou Prophet. They're very good friends of mine."

Flossie stuck her hand out to be shaken first. Then Mr. Prophet did likewise. I saw Mr. Randford wince a bit when the two men shook hands, but Miss Powell tittered like a love-struck schoolgirl. I swear to goodness, I don't think I'll *ever* understand the effect Mr. Prophet had on vulnerable women!

"I've been trying to talk Bernard into visiting that lion place you told us about, Mrs. Majesty," said a still-twittering Miss Betsy Powell.

"Gay's Lion Farm? Yes, we're going to go there tomorrow. I'm looking forward to it. Should be interesting to see how people train lions to do tricks and so forth."

"Tomorrow, eh?" said Randford. "Don't get eaten by a lion." He smiled, probably thinking he was being funny.

I didn't. I said, "I'll try not to," in a voice about as arid as the Mojave Desert.

Fortunately—I didn't like either Miss Powell or Mr. Randford, which probably bespeaks some character flaw on my part—a waiter came and escorted us to a table in the back of the restaurant. He pulled out chairs for Flossie and me and asked Flossie if she'd like a highchair for Billy. She said yes. I scratched my chest surreptitiously as I sat, wondering why it was suddenly itchy. It wouldn't surprise me if proximity to Miss Betsy Powell had given me some kind of allergic reaction.

"I didn't know they provided highchairs for little kids," I said, surprised at the sophistication of Mijares's customer service.

"I'm glad they do," said Flossie. "It's hard to feed Billy when he's on my lap."

"I think he's scared of me," said Prophet, tilting his head and peering at Billy.

Billy instantly covered his eyes with his hands and hid his head on Flossie's shoulder.

"I think he is, too," I said. "I wonder why."

"Oh, I'm a hard case, you know," said Prophet, grinning. "Kids know stuff grown-ups have forgot all about."

"You're not, either, a hard case," I said. "You're a wonderful man who's saved my life more than once."

"If you say so, Miss Daisy, I reckon I'll just have to agree with you. I'm not a man to argue with the ladies."

"Good thing, too," I said with a grin of my own.

The waiter came back with the highchair and three menus. Billy wasn't too pleased to vacate his mother's arms and reside in the high-chair, but Mr. Prophet then did something that fairly astounded me.

As Billy peered at him askance, looking as if he aimed to leap out of his highchair and into his mother's arms any minute, Mr. Prophet reached into his coat pocket and said, "Want to see some pretty things, young Billy?"

Frowning in suspicion, Billy repeated, "Pwetty?"

"Got me some rocks here that're real pretty. Don't eat 'em. They're only to look at. And pick up and play with. Just don't stick 'em in your mouth."

"Wocks?" said Billy, a little less frightened and more interested. I think.

"Yes. Pretty rocks. Got me these here rocks in different places years ago. I still collect a rock every now and then. This one's called a Pecos Valley Diamond. These are only found on the banks of the Pecos River there in New Mexico. New Mexico's a state now," He confided in Billy, who had begun gazing at him with rapt attention.

Mr. Prophet continued showing Billy the contents of his coat pocket, narrating as he did so. "And this here one is a black fire opal I picked up in Nevada. Here's some turquoise from Arizona. Here's some freshwater pearls and a few agates from Tennessee. Have you ever heard of New Mexico, Nevada, Arizona or Tennessee, Billy?"

His attention firmly fixed on the colorful display on his highchair tray, Billy shook his head.

"Here's the last of the lot. These here are a couple of gold nuggets I found right here in California. Not on this trip."

"Pwetty," Billy said in a reverential tone.

"How nice of Mr. Prophet to let you see them, Billy. What do you say when someone does something nice for you?" Flossie-the-Mother to the fore, by golly.

"Tank'oo," said Billy, his wide blue eyes now turned upon Mr. Prophet. He didn't seem scared any longer.

Nearly sniffling from emotion, I said, "That's so nice of you, Mr. Prophet."

"Didn't want a bawling kid to disrupt a good Mescin lunch," said he, an impish expression on his own lined face.

"You're very kind, Mr. Prophet. It might be difficult to wrest those rocks away from Billy when we're finished eating, though," said Flossie, smiling wistfully at her son.

"Oh, I got plenty more. I'll give him a couple to keep."

"That's so nice!" I darned near started sniffling *again*.

Prophet eyed me askance. "Don't get your under-frillies in a twist, Miss Daisy. They're only a few rocks."

Under-frillies? Another entry for my dictionary, I reckon.

The waiter returned, and we each perused the menu. Mr. Prophet wanted some tamales. I couldn't recall if I'd ever eaten a tamale, so I ordered the tamale plate, too. Flossie, concerned about her son's tender tongue, asked the waiter what the least-spicy dish on the menu was. He recommended a soft taco filled with shredded chicken for Billy.

"You, *señora*, can get the same thing, only with some flavor to it." He smiled at Flossie.

"Do your lunch meals come with *frijoles* and *arroz*?" asked Prophet.

"*Si, señor. Todas nuestros almuersos veinen con arroz y frijoles.*"

"Good enough," said Prophet with a happy smile. "Then I'll take the tamale plate."

"Me, too," I said, wondering what I'd just ordered.

"And I'll take the soft chicken thing you told me about for my son, and the other one—the one with flavor to it—for me," said Flossie, smiling at the waiter with what looked like hope. Guess she wasn't entirely sure of herself, either, when it came to Mexican food.

As the waiter walked away, headed for the kitchen, I asked Mr. Prophet, "What did you and the waiter just say to each other? I took Spanish in high school, but I don't remember much of it. Nobody to practice on, I guess."

"I just asked if the lunch plates here come with rice and beans, and he said they did." Prophet smiled at me. "I got to talkin' Spanish pretty good when I was in Arizona, New Mexico and Mexico. Did a lot of work in those parts."

"Oh," I said, thinking hard. "Maybe you can help me brush up on my Spanish skills."

"Could," said Prophet. "I reckon I know some words you won't want to know, though."

"You can leave those words out," I told him.

"What would be the fun in that?" he asked, trying to sound ingenuous.

Flossie giggled. "Probably because his mother did it, Billy giggled, too.

I didn't know precisely what "a twinkle" in a person's eyes meant until I looked into Mr. Lou Prophet's not-so-guileless light blue orbs that lunchtime at Mijares.

TWENTY-EIGHT

Lunch was delicious. I was intrigued with my tamales. "What do you call this stuff?" I asked Mr. Prophet, forking the thick, soft dough encasing a delicious combination of…Well, I don't know what it was. It was Mexican, and it tasted good.

"*Masa*," said Prophet, sounding as though he knew what he was talking about.

"Hmm. Looks a lot like cornmeal to me," I said, digging a little deeper.

"It is," he said.

"You mean we call this stuff cornmeal, Mexicans call it *masa* and Italians call it *polenta*?"

"Reckon so. Different languages for the same stuff, I expect."

"Fascinating."

Good mother that she was, Flossie had thought to bring a bib for Billy. She also collected all of Mr. Prophet's rocks from the highchair tray before the waiter set Billy's soft tortilla filled what looked like shredded chicken on it. Billy seemed to enjoy his meal, although it seemed to me he pasted more of it on his face, his bib and the tray's surface than he managed to get into his mouth. I guess kids are all like that.

When I asked Flossie for confirmation of my supposition, she laughed and said, "Oh, my, yes. That's why I brought the bib. I'll still have to wash him from stem to stern before I pick him up again."

Children are a lot of work. I'm not sure why my parents decided to have three of them, although I'm glad they did. If they'd quit after two, I wouldn't be here. That might not be a big deal to anyone else, but it was to me.

Out of curiosity, I asked, "Do you have any children, Mr. Prophet?"

He stopped chewing for a second, swallowed, and said, "Not that I'm aware of."

Flossie and I exchanged a speaking glance across the table. Not entirely sure what each of us meant our glances to mean, but we understood each other.

This points out yet another *huge* difference between men and women. A man might dally with any number of females, as I suspect Mr. Prophet had done, and then he could waltz off—or ride into the sunset on his horse—neither knowing nor caring if his seed had taken root. A woman doesn't enjoy such a carefree prospect. If a woman gets "with child," she knows it. In fact, the whole world around her knows it, too, and if she's unmarried, she's generally scorned and vilified.

How come men aren't looked down upon for doing the same darned thing? But they aren't. They're called "ladies' men" or "roués" and strut and swagger and think they're the bee's knees. The *women*, on the other hand, are called sluts and whores, and a whole lot of other derogatory terms and often shunned outright. I've said it before, and I'll say it again: life is unfair, confound it! I didn't approve. Which makes as much difference now as it ever did, which is none.

Life annoys me a whole lot sometimes.

Anyhow, after spreading approximately half of his lunch on himself, the highchair tray, his bib and the floor, Billy began to flag and get fussy. That was all right, as the rest of us were finished with our lunches, too. Flossie asked for and received from the waiter a wet towel and a dry one. She more or less hosed her son down with the wet towel, and then dried him off. Billy was crying by the end of his ordeal.

Therefore, even though I'd had hard thoughts about him only a few moments earlier, I applauded Mr. Prophet's attempt to soothe the little boy by again handing him some rocks. I think Billy ended up with a gold nugget, a pretty piece of agate and one of the freshwater pearls. I can't even remember where they came from, and Mr. Prophet had told us not an hour earlier. Shows how much attention I pay to things.

"Thank you very much, Mr. Prophet. We don't want to take your treasures, though," said Flossie, smiling sweetly at him.

It was evident to all of us that Billy had a different opinion on the matter. He clutched the three treasures to his chest, his fist tight around them, and looked mulish. I got the impression he aimed to fight his mommy for the possession of his new toys.

"Naw. I've got tons of 'em. Let little Billy enjoy something new."

"That's extremely kind of you, Mr. Prophet." Flossie turned to her son. "What do you say to Mr. Prophet, Billy?"

For a second there, I thought Billy aimed to say nothing—or start screaming—but after thinking the matter over, he decided to be a good boy. "Tank'oo, Mistew Pwophet."

"You're welcome, Billy." Prophet gazed affectionately at the child. I guess he meant it. The affection, I mean.

Huh. It wouldn't surprise me if Mr. Lou Prophet could have looked fondly upon some of his own children if he'd stuck around long enough to discover he'd sired any.

Never mind me. I just get grumpy about the inequities of life some-times. Oh, very well. All the time, curse it.

Then I had to fight Mr. Prophet for the bill, but he eventually relin-quished it after I told him I'd hit him with my cane if he didn't. I think I was kidding, but I'm not sure.

Flossie asked that I drop her at home before Mr. Prophet and I continued to the Pasadena Public Library, so I did.

"Thanks so much, Daisy. This was a fun treat for Billy and me. Good to see you again, Mr. Prophet."

"Good seeing you, too, Mrs. Buckingham. You have a fine, hand-some son there."

The fine son, Billy Buckingham, lay sound asleep in his mother's arms by that time. Mr. Prophet opened the front passenger door for the two of them and took Flossie's arm to steady her on her way out of the motorcar.

After waving at Flossie, and after Prophet had re-entered the Chevrolet on the front passenger side, I drove us to the library. I don't know about Prophet, but I was having disagreeable thoughts about men and life's inequities.

We were about halfway there when Mr. Prophet said, "I do something to annoy you, Miss Daisy? I didn't mean to, and I'm sorry if I did."

I heaved a gigantic sigh. "It's not you, Mr. Prophet. It's life. Things are just so unfair."

"Yeah? How?"

Hmm. It might be embarrassing to tell him. But what the heck. He was a grownup. He could take it. Or maybe he couldn't. Only one way to find out. I felt heat begin to rise from my chest to my cheeks, but I forged onward anyway. "Well, for one thing, when I asked if you had children, you said you didn't know if you had any."

"Yeah?"

I was probably red as a beet by then, but I didn't much care. "Well, if you were a woman, do you think you'd be allowed to be so cavalier about having children? I mean, for all you know—and I'm only assuming you've bedded your share of women—any number of those same women might have had children sired by you, and you wouldn't even know it! But if you *did* sire any children, the women would sure as heck know it. And they'd probably be paying for what they'd consider to be their so-called *sin* to this day. But the men get away scot-free."

After a second or two, he said with a single, slow wag of his head, "Yeah, go figure that one out."

"What?" I asked in surprise.

"It ain't right. Not one damn bit right, but there you go. Most of us fellas needed the, uh...the *stuffing*...kicked out of both ends, but there was no one around to do it, so—here we are in our black-hearted nastiness." He rolled one of his infamous (to me) quirlies. "Havin' to live with our fool selves at the end." Prophet took a deep drag off his quirley and blew the smoke out the window.

"So you agree with me?" I asked, more than a little astonished.

"Sure, I do, darlin'. Women don't deserve half of what men shove at 'em. Includin' what I've shoveled at 'em." He puffed the quirley again and stared pensively, maybe a little sadly, through the windshield. "I'll tell you somethin'. I guess you can call it a confession, really."

"Oh?"

"A long time ago, when I was still wet behind the ears—we talked about this once before—I survived the War of Northern Aggression."

"I remember you telling us about it." The War of Northern Aggression, my left hind leg! But don't mind me.

"You Yankees call it the Civil War." Lou Prophet had a masterful sneer.

He was right. We did. Because it was a civil war. Again, don't mind me.

"But don't get me started on that nasty topic, or I'll likely go on a three-day—oh, never mind. Back to my point. I was so damned relieved to have made it through that horrible bloody mess not only alive but intact, when so many of my friends and family—most of 'em, in fact—got blown to smithereens by minie balls and mortar shells or cut to pieces by…Well, you get the drift. I was so damned relieved to have survived that nastiness, I made me a pact with Ole Scratch."

"With whom?"

"You know—Beelzebub. Old Nick. *El diablo.* The devil. The fork-tailed, green-fanged demon his own nasty self!"

"Oh, Satan! You made a pact with the *devil?*"

"Him an' me made an agreement. I'd shovel all the coal he wanted me to shovel down beyond the smoking gates to keep his furnace stoked and the butane burnin', so the evil sinners could keep on swimmin' them flamin' rivers throughout eternity…swimmin' an' wailin' away… as long as he gave me one hell of a real good time on this side of the sod for all the time I got left."

"Oh…oh, uh…Mercy sakes." I'd never heard of such a thing.

"Sure enough, we shook on it, Ole Scratch and me. In a matter of speakin', ya understand. And you can say what you want about Ole Scratch, darlin', but the ugly cuss does keep his promises. I had me a real good time for a lot of years. Until…" He punched his wooden leg. "Yessir, a real good time. But it not only cost me an eternity of coal-shovelin', it cost me somethin' else."

"What's that?"

238

He turned to me with those big, round, sad eyes of his, set in their sun-wizened sockets. "The love of a good woman."

"You mean Louisa, Mr. Prophet?"

"Louisa. I loved her. And she loved me. But she knew me too damned well. I never could settle down. I had to drink and run around with them women you were just talkin' about, spillin' my seed here and there and everywhere, with no consideration of the consequences. I reckon I was tryin' to drown out the war memories, but that was no excuse. I was just bad. Rotten. Most men are. Except Sam. You did well there. Believe me, you dodged a bullet, Miss Daisy. Anyway, I now consider the consequences of my nasty ways aplenty. In spades. I coulda settled down with Louisa, but she knew me too damn well and wouldn't have me, though I knew she wanted me somethin' fierce. Just like I wanted her somethin' fierce. My heart burned every time we were together. We were two peas in the same damned pod, and she knew it, and I knew it, but—" He punched his wooden leg again, hardening his jaws and gritting his teeth. "But I couldn't tame the raging demon in my own heart, and neither could she."

I swear his eyes were glazed with tears.

He didn't say anything for a long time, and neither did I. I guess we both just sat there, digesting what he'd said.

He heaved a ragged breath, took another drag off his quirley and said as he blew the smoke out his mouth and nose at the same time, "So we get away with a lot, we fellas do. Guilty as charged." Mr. Prophet turned to me again, and his eyes were grave and shiny with emotion. "But we don't get away scot-free. I know it seems like it, but we don't."

We'd reached the library, and I parked the Chevrolet at the curb as near to the front entrance as I could get. His confession had given me pause to think, and I didn't want Mr. Prophet to have to climb or walk more than necessary.

I still think men get away with too darned much in this life, but then again, women don't have to fight wars. On the other hand, it's the men who usually *start* the stupid things, so it's only fair that they fight them. Then again, it's usually *old* men who start the wars. Then the *young* men get to die in them. Or become hopelessly wounded and crippled, as my Billy had been.

Nertz. Life was just too complicated for one phony spiritualist-medium to figure out.

"I'm sorry you'll have to climb so many stairs, Mr. Prophet."

He'd been staring out the window at the library building. "You mean that there's the *library*?" he asked, visibly surprised.

"Yes. That's the Pasadena Public Library where my friend, Miss Petrie, works."

"Holy shee-oot, it looks like a castle."

I, too, peered at the building. "It does kind of look like a castle, doesn't it?"

"*Kind* of? With all them turrets and arched windows and so forth, it looks more like a castle than most of the castles I've seen."

"Oh. Have you seen many castles?"

"Naw. Only in books. Some of the churches in Mexico look sort of like castles. Them Catholics, you know? They like to spend money on their buildings, even if most of the people who pray in their churches are poorer than dirt."

"Oh, my. Maybe that's one of the reasons Sam has rejected his Catholic roots."

With a chuckle and a perceptibly lightened mood, Prophet said, "Yeah. Sam was a Catholic once, wasn't he?"

"Sure. I think all Italians are. He goes to the Methodist Church with us now, though."

"Huh."

"When he was married to his first wife—I aim to be his second and last—he began attending Unitarian services with her. She'd been born into a Roman Catholic family, too, but I guess she wanted out."

"Don't blame either one of 'em. Not much of a church-goer myself."

"You know something?"

"No. What?"

"That doesn't surprise me one little bit."

Mr. Prophet laughed outright, then said, "You stay right there, Miss Daisy. I'm going to get out of this here motorcar, walk around to your side, and open up your door for you."

"You don't need to do that."

"I know I don't need to do it. But I've got a lot of making-up to do, and I'd appreciate it if you'd let me act like a gent, even if I'm not one. Just this once, all right?"

I laughed, too. "Oh, all right."

So he did. He even carried the books I aimed to return for me.

TWENTY-NINE

Regina Petrie was overjoyed to meet Lou Prophet.

"Oh, I've read *so* much about your daring exploits over the years, Mr. Prophet!" she whispered when I introduced them.

"Probably not much of the stuff you read is true," said Prophet, putting a slight damper on Regina's enthusiasm.

"Perhaps not much of what's in those dime novels is true," I said, "but you've had a life filled with danger and adventure anyway. Not only that, but you've saved my own personal life quite frequently in recent weeks. I think you should be celebrated for that alone."

Prophet peered at me slanty-eyed, clearly skeptical.

"It's true!" I insisted. In a whisper, of course, since we were in the library.

Her hands clasped to what would have been her bosom if she had one, Regina said, "Daisy told me! I'm so sorry so many of my family members are such ghastly people. It's embarrassing, actually."

"The bad eggs aren't your fault," said Prophet.

"It's embarrassing, all the same. Oh, I do wish Robert were here. He'd love to meet you."

"That the gent you aim to marry? Miss Daisy told me about him. Some."

"Yes. He's a wonderful man," Regina said in a voice so sweet, it nearly gave me a toothache. Then again, I'd been married before. Regina would have to learn about marriage before she could be cynical about it. Anyhow, I thought Regina and Robert would be extremely happy together, as they wouldn't have to face the obstacles to a happy union Billy and I had not quite overcome.

"Is he the one with the collection of yellow-back novels?" asked Prophet. From his tone of voice, I got the impression he wasn't a huge fan of that particular brand of literature.

"He's the one, all right," I answered for Regina. If Prophet was going to grumble at someone, I wanted it to be me, because Regina didn't deserve any grumbles. "He's a great fellow, Mr. Prophet. He, Sam and my father fixed my radio so I could listen to it without having to put on those clumsy headphones."

"Yeah? What's a radio?"

"You've never listened to a radio-signal receiving set?"

"Is that one of those things you turn on and music comes out of it? Like a piano, only smaller and without the keys?"

"That's it all right." Dear me. Guess I'd have to entertain Mr. Prophet with my radio. Not that I used it a whole lot. Heck, maybe I'd *give* it to him.

But no. That wouldn't be fair to Pa, who liked to listen to sporting games on it. As for me, I wasn't a big sports fanatic. I'd be happy if people began producing more radio dramas, though. Now that would be fun listening while I plied my—actually, my mother's—side-pedal White sewing machine. Hmm. The noise of the sewing machine might drown out the radio. Well, I'd figure something out. Providing the radio people ever *did* begin producing more radio plays.

Why am I talking about radio plays?

Regina brought me back to the here and now by reaching under her desk and withdrawing three books from the shelf there. "But look what I have for you, Daisy!"

"They look like books to me," Prophet observed.

"They are books," I said, smiling at his naïve pronouncement. Naivety and Lou Prophet didn't seem to go together, at least in my—

ahem—book. Sorry about that. "Regina saves all the best ones for me when they first get catalogued."

"That's right nice of you, Miss Petrie."

"I'll be *so* glad when I don't have that name anymore," said Regina with a small shudder. "Anyhow, I think you'll like this one. It's *The Green Bay Tree*, by Louis Bromfield. It's not a detective story, but I found it fascinating. This is Mr. Bromfield's very first novel, and he's *such* a good story-teller."She picked up the second book and held it to her already-mentioned non-bosom. I knew, because I'd helped modernize her, that Regina actually possessed a bosom, but I've already deplored what women were supposed to look like in 1925. In an almost reverential whisper, she said, "It's by Baroness Orczy."

"Oh, my!" I'd have shouted hallelujah, only we were in the library and everyone would have looked at me funny. Might even have kicked me out.

"It's *The Pimpernel and Rosemary*." Regina handed the book to me as if it were a fragile ornament.

I clutched it to my own bosom. "Oh, thank you, thank you, *thank* you! I wish the baroness would write faster."

"As do I," said Regina. She sighed. "But I suppose we should be happy for what we're given."

"You're much more philosophical on the subject than I am," I said with a small, veritably soundless, laugh.

"And you're going to *love* this last one," said Regina, smiling hugely. And darned if she didn't place *Atavar, the Dream Dancer*, by Mr. Arthur B. Reeve on her desk.

I snatched the book up as if I expected it to run away before I could get my mitts on it. "Oh, *thank* you! Is this a Craig Kennedy novel?"

"It is indeed."

"Who's Craig Kennedy?" asked Mr. Prophet, befuddled.

"He's a detective," I told him. "A *scientific* detective. Sort of like Sherlock Holmes, if you know who he is. Fictionally speaking, I mean. The Craig Kennedy books are written by a fellow named Mr. Arthur B. Reeve."

"Oh, yeah. I read a couple of Sherlock Holmes stories. I liked *The*

Hound of the Baskervilles. Wouldn't mind goin' to England one day. Not that I have that many days left."

His comment jarred me. I glanced at him, noticing the many creases in his weathered face which, I have no doubt, were etched there by time and the sun and the rugged circumstances of his life. "I have a feeling you're going to outlast all of us," I told him, not really meaning it, but thinking he needed a boost to his morale. What with his talk about surviving the Civil War and losing the love of his life, his mood had drooped some.

"Not likely," he said, but he grinned at me, so I'm glad I fibbed.

"But thanks, Regina. I'd better be getting home now. I do *so* appreciate the books."

"And I appreciate you introducing me to Mr. Prophet." She leaned over her desk, her own hazel eyes shining through her spectacles. "It was such a pleasure to meet you, Mr. Prophet. I still want you to meet Robert."

"Maybe you two can come to dinner with us again one of these days," I told her. "Mr. Prophet is taking care of the house Sam bought. It's right across the street from ours."

With a lovely smile—Regina Petrie was an extremely pretty woman when she did a little work on herself—she said, "We'd both love that. And I heard about your new house. That's so exciting! Robert and I are going to be looking for houses soon."

"Oh, my. Life does seem to fly by, doesn't it?" I shook my head and glanced at Mr. Prophet, wondering if his life had seemed to fly by.

"Doesn't seem like it while you're living it," said he, answering my unspoken question. "But when you get old and look back, you tend to wonder how you got so old so fast."

Regina and I both laughed, although I don't think he was kidding. Guess I'd learn for myself, providing I lived to be his age, whatever it was. He *had* to be in his seventies, at least.

"And your friends start dying, too," he said, causing both Regina and me to stop laughing. "Until it feels like you're left all alone in the world." He shook his head. "Never wanted to die alone, but hell, nobody else I used to know is still around to be with me at the end."

I might have scolded him for that "hell," but his words so stunned me, I didn't. What a melancholy way to look at one's life. "You're not alone any longer, Mr. Prophet," I said as I carried my books to the check-out desk. "You have Sam, and you have me. In fact, you have my whole family."

"Yeah?"

"Yeah. I mean, yes, you do. Heck, Sam and I have a whole house for you to live in. It's small, but it's there, and you can use it for as long as you want." Or for as long as he lived, but I didn't want to say that.

"Yeah? You talk to Sam about this?"

"Um…Not yet, but I know he wants you there."

"Why? I'm not good for anything."

We'd reached the check-out desk, so I set my books before the library clerk manning—well, womanning—the desk. As she wrote down my library-card number on the book tickets and wrote the date I needed to return the books on the lined paper pasted inside the covers, I said, "That's not true!" The clerk looked at me in alarm.

"Sorry," I said. "Not you."

She shrugged and went back to doing her job.

"Well, I ain't," said Prophet. "Old, feeble, one-legged fellow who doesn't belong in this world we got today."

"Oh, piffle! Stop feeling sorry for yourself. You have not merely my entire family on your side, but you have the Buckinghams and the whole Pasadena Police Department!"

"Now there's a scary thought." Prophet scratched a stubbly cheek.

"Anyway, stop telling me you're worthless and worn out. You might *feel* worn out, but you've done yeoman's service these past few weeks, and I'm not going to let you go. So there."

"Guess that's tellin' me, huh?"

"Yes. It is." I turned and smiled sweetly at him. "Will you please carry my books to the motorcar?"

With a shrug, Prophet picked up my three books.

Then I had another thought. "But wait!" I was still whispering, by the way.

"Fer what?"

"I want to look up pictures of firearms. When you and Pa were

246

talking about guns the other day, I realized I don't know a single, solitary thing about them. I want to look at some pictures."

"Yeah? Where you going to find pictures of firearms?"

"This," I said sternly, "is a library. Libraries have *everything*."

"Do they now?" He didn't sound convinced.

"Yes."

"You aiming to shoot one or just look at 'em?"

"Just look. I wouldn't want to handle one. They're far too dangerous."

I didn't precisely see him do it, but I know he rolled his eyes. Just like Sam, Lou Prophet. Well, not *just* like him, but close enough.

Regina was surprised to see the two of us show up at her desk again. When I asked her about books with pictures of firearms in them, she led us to the reference room and to the shelf holding books classified in the 600s.

"I think they're in six twenty-three," said she, running a manicured fingernail along the row of books. "Ah, yes. Here you go. This one has photographs of various firearms in it. It's a reference book, so you can't check it out, but you may look at it all you want."

"Thank you!"

Mr. Prophet, still acting like a gentleman, took the heavy tome from the shelf and lugged it over to a table, where he set it down gently. No plopping of books for Mr. Lou Prophet. I approved.

We sat in chairs next to each other, and he opened the book. "What are you lookin' for? Or do you know?"

"I don't really know, I guess. I just kind of wondered what kinds of guns you old-west-type fellows used to use."

"*Used* to use?"

"Use, I mean."

I heard him chuckle under his breath, and he opened the book.

Holy cow, until that moment I didn't have a single, solitary clue how many different kinds of firearms existed in the world. And to think Mr. Prophet used to use several of the lethal weapons depicted on the pages of that book gave me a tiny—an almost non-existent—shiver of uneasiness. The man next to whom I sat that day in the staid and conservative

Pasadena Public Library used to…well, kill men for a living. Sobering thought.

Mr. Prophet, however, was far from a sober-sides as he turned the pages of that book and pointed out all the firearms he'd used in his colorful career. He was nearly gleeful when he indicated a couple of those deadly monsters.

"This here's a Winchester '73. That's the one I used on that sumbitch in the rosebushes. This here one," he said, pointing at another picture, "was my favorite for a long time, though. My coach gun."

"Coach gun?" I said in a feeble voice.

"Yeah. Shotgun messengers on stagecoaches used 'em. Sawed-off, twelve-gauge Richards shotgun. Loved that gut-shredder."

"Gut-shredder?" My voice had become feebler.

"Tears up a man real good. Wore it on a leather lanyard around my neck. Best barn-blaster I ever used."

I didn't even ask what a barn-blaster was, figuring the name to be self-explanatory, as had been the gut-shredder. I'd have to remember those for my dictionary of the old west, though.

Mr. Prophet and I went through the whole book, Prophet explaining darned near every one of the guns depicted therein. I guess I already knew the firearms industry was big, given the way human beings had always been unable to get along, but I didn't know it was *that* big. Almost made me afraid to walk to the Chevrolet.

But no. I had Mr. Lou Prophet to protect me. He might be old, and he might have only one leg remaining to him, but he'd proved himself over and over since I'd met him. It seemed like longer than three or four weeks. It seemed almost like a lifetime.

He was definitely part of the family now, whether he wanted to be or not. Daisy Gumm Majesty—or Daisy Gumm Rotondo—wouldn't allow this rough, elderly man to die alone, darn it.

I hoped I could convince Sam and my family to look upon the matter as I did. Being persuasive by nature—some people might call me pushy, but I'm really only determined—I was sure I'd win them all over.

Heck, for all I knew, they were already won. Wouldn't surprise me.

THIRTY

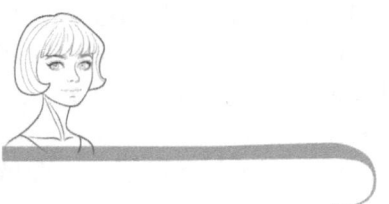

On Wednesday morning, Sam and Lou Prophet showed up at our door in time for breakfast. Vi had left some of her spectacularly delicious cinnamon rolls and some cooked sausage patties in the warming oven. She didn't trust me to cook the sausage patties. For good reason, although I'd bet Pa could have cooked them without burning down the house.

I was *so* glad Sam had bought the house across the street. If he hadn't, the two of us might have starved to death. Or been burned up in a tragic house fire.

"Your aunt sure is a good cook," said Prophet as he dug into his cinnamon roll.

He'd taken my suggestion to spread butter on it. I know, I know. Butter makes people fat. It would take a whole lot more than a couple of buttered cinnamon rolls to fatten up Mr. Lou Prophet.

After Sam had swallowed a bite of sausage, he said, "Vi is the best cook in Pasadena. I have it on good authority."

"Your own taste buds," I said, grinning at him.

"And other people's, too," he said, smiling back.

"Including mine," said Pa, who was extremely happy to have Vi living with us for reasons already specified.

"It's a grand thing to have a good cook in the family," said Prophet. "Can I have another one of those rolls, Miss Daisy? Haven't had anything so tasty in...well, hours. Dinner last night was damned...I mean darned good, too."

It kind of tickled me that he tried not to swear around me.

Sam helped me clean up the breakfast dishes, while Pa and Mr. Prophet retired to the living room. After putting the last dish away, Sam and I joined the other two men there, and I sat on the piano bench. "Do you fellows mind if I practice Sunday's anthem?"

"Not at all," said Pa.

"What's an anthem, when it comes to church?" asked Prophet, sounding genuinely interested.

"Beats me," said Sam. Big help.

"It's a hymn that highlights what the sermon will be about. At Christmas, we sing Christmas carols. Same with Lent, although most Lenten hymns are slow and sad. I prefer the Easter hymns, which celebrate the resurrection."

After a moment of silence, Prophet said, "You'll have to tell me more about this stuff sometime. I still don't understand it much."

"Nobody does," said Sam.

Pa said nothing, but his smile was wide.

Men.

I tried again. "What I meant was that there are different holidays—or events—every year and the church...acknowledges them in music. If you see what I mean. Like, Christmas is the birth of Jesus, so we sing Christmas carols. Good Friday is when he died on the cross, so we sing sad hymns. Easter is when he arose from the dead, so we sing joyful songs."

"Never saw nobody do that," Prophet observed. "Rise from the dead, I mean. I've seen a fair share of dead people, too."

With a smile of my own, I said, "I haven't, either. But I'm a good Methodist girl, so I go along with what my church says I should do."

"What's coming up on Sunday," asked Pa.

"We're getting close to Abraham Lincoln's birthday, so we're going to sing 'The Battle Hymn of the Republic' this coming Sunday."

Prophet grunted. "Think I'll stay home for that one."

Sam laughed. "Don't blame you. Lincoln's not one of your favorite presidents, I gather."

"Nope."

"Well, *I* think he was wonderful," I told my audience. "Really, Mr. Prophet, the south's way of life depended on slavery, and I think slavery is wrong."

"Does it say that in the Bible?" asked Prophet.

He would. "Actually, no, it doesn't, but let's not get in to that at the moment."

"Right," said Prophet in a voice that, if captured, would have scattered little, sharp splinters all over the place.

I still disapproved of slavery, no matter what the Bible doesn't say about it. However, deciding not to argue, I said, "It's more exciting if there's a drum opening, but I can't play the drums, so it'll be the piano for me."

Instantly Sam started whapping the coffee table in an amazingly battle-hymnish rhythm. Pa joined him. Mr. Prophet sat still with his arms folded across his chest.

When the time was right, I hit the opening chords of "The Battle Hymn of the Republic," which even Lou Prophet would probably admit, if asked, was quite a stirring song.

When I began singing, Pa and Sam joined. With a sidelong glance at Prophet, I saw him sitting on the sofa, Spike on his lap, his arms still crossed, frowning hideously. Well, what could you expect from a former Confederate soldier? I asked myself. If I'd been born in Georgia, I probably wouldn't have liked Lincoln much, either. Although nobody can ever convince me slavery is a good idea. I'd had a hand in rescuing several children who'd been kidnapped and were about to be sold into slavery. They wouldn't be working in fields, though. Those poor kids would have been working in evil men's bedrooms. The mere thought made me sick.

Be that as it may, I got through four of the verses—the ones we generally sang in church, which left out the third verse—and came to a thundering end at the final "His truth is marching on."

All three men applauded, so I rose from the piano bench and bowed, as if I were on stage.

"What did you think of that?" I asked Prophet.

"Still don't like Lincoln, but that's a pretty lively song," said he.

It was better than nothing.

Suddenly Spike leaped from Prophet's lap and barreled joyfully to the front door.

"Bet that's Harold," I said, and dared walk to the door all by myself. Nobody tried to stop me, so I guess Sam truly *did* believe all the people who wanted me dead were confined.

I flung the door open and Harold, who had been to our house many times, instantly knelt to pet Spike. He was a good man, Harold Kincaid. Heck, he was taking us all to Gay's Lion Farm that very day!

"Was that you playing the piano?" he asked as he rose to his feet with something of a grunt. Have I mentioned Harold was a trifle plump? Well, he was.

"Yes, t'was I."

"Sounded good."

"Thanks, Harold."

The three men who had been sitting in the living room all walked over to greet Harold.

"Hear you're going to drive me to this shindig in your fancy car," said Prophet, holding out his hand for Harold to shake.

"Absolutely," said Harold.

"Mind if I take a look at it before I get in? Not that I'm backing out or anything, but I want to see this motorcar Miss Daisy's so keen on."

"I'm going to get a new one soon," said Harold. "But come on outside, and I'll show you everything."

So he did. We all joined Harold and Prophet. Even Spike, who gamboled merrily about as if he were a spring lamb. The February day wasn't as chilly as most of the days in January had been. Not that I know this from first-hand experience, of course, since I'd been restricted to the house for what seemed like forever. I sucked in a huge breath of Pasadena winter air and was happy. It was *so* good to feel safe in my world again.

As Harold showed Mr. Prophet the wonders of his Stutz Bearcat, I said, "Why are you getting a new car, Harold?"

"Because I want one."

Lou Prophet laughed. Sam grinned. So did Pa.

"Will it be another Bearcat?"

"Haven't decided yet. Del wants me to buy a more sober-looking motorcar. He says I'm too flamboyant already, and I need to tone down."

"You're kidding!"

"Nope. You know how serious he is about everything, Daisy."

"Yes, I do. And that's a good thing, too, or your father's bank would never have survived when your father took it on the lam with the loot."

"I know, I know. But I'm not going to buy a damned Ford because it's black."

I eyed my friend closely for a moment and then said, "You're right. Black doesn't suit you. Get another bright red motorcar."

"I appreciate your approval," said Harold. He turned to Lou Prophet. "Are you ready to go? Hop on in, and we'll zoom to Gay's Lion Farm."

"Fear my hoppin' days are over." Mr. Prophet had been staring at the Bearcat for some moments by then. He glanced skeptically at Harold and then at me. "I don't know about this. I'm used to riding horses, not critters that hug the ground."

"You were in a motorcar when you had that accident," I reminded him.

"Yeah. That was sure a load of fun." He sounded rather sour. Not that I blamed him. It must be difficult for anyone to lose a leg.

"This really *will* be fun," I told him, patting him on the back and hoping I wasn't lying.

"Yeah? First I have to figure out how to get into the thing. I got a wooden leg, you know, and I ain't a small guy."

"That's true. I didn't think about that. Well, try it. Honestly, it's fun to tootle around town in that machine. I've had plenty of experience going places with Harold."

"Yeah. So you and Sam have told me."

"Aren't you at least going to try it?" I asked in a small voice, disappointed.

"Aw, what the hell," Prophet said after another several seconds. "If I

253

can get into the damned thing, I guess I'll give it a whirl. Gotta take the horns with the hide."

And there was yet another expression I'd never heard before and which I didn't understand. I'd ask later. What I did then was hold the passenger door open for him. He kind of folded himself up and stuffed his left leg into the car first, then lifted his peg leg and maneuvered it inside, too.

"Tight fit," I said, a trifle concerned.

"It'll be all right," said Prophet, and he shrugged philosophically.

"I hope you don't get a cramp or anything." Now I was concerned about his poor body being so squashed in the Stutz. As he'd mentioned, he was a tall man and, while he was considerably skinnier than Sam, who wasn't fat but who was well-muscled and just larger overall than Lou Prophet, he might find riding all the way to Westlake Park somewhat uncomfortable in Harold's car.

Oh, well. We could all come back in Sam's Hudson. Except, of course, for Harold, who'd have to drive his Stutz back home.

Pa said he didn't really want to go to the lion farm and would prefer to stay home with Spike and read the latest issue of *National Geographic*. I was disappointed, but didn't press him to come with us. Evidently visiting lion farms wasn't at the top of everyone's "things I want to do" list.

So it was just Sam and I who followed Harold's Stutz Bearcat down Marengo, right on San Pasqual, left on Pasadena Avenue, and then left again. The drive to Westlake Park took us through a lot of twisty streets, and I enjoyed it.

"Boy, there's sure a lot to see around here, isn't there? I get so used to being in Pasadena, I never think about how many unpopulated miles there are around it."

"I guess. Not fond of the stench of the ostrich farm, but the landscape's nice."

"Trust you," I said to my beloved. "I'm really looking forward to this, Sam. It feels as though I've been confined forever, not just three or four weeks."

"I know, sweetheart. We'll have a great time today. I've always kind of wanted to see how people train those big cats to act in pictures."

"I read somewhere that the people who opened the lion farm are French. Their last name is Gay. Hence, Gay's Lion Farm."

"Makes sense. Maybe we can open a farm featuring dachshunds. We can call it Rotondo's Weenie Ranch or something along those lines."

I laughed. "You'd really let me get more dogs?"

Sam eyed me askance. "I was joking, Daisy. Not that I don't love Spike, you understand."

"I understand."

He reached over and patted my knee.

It took about forty-five minutes to get to Gay's. When we followed Harold's Bearcat into the parking lot, I gazed around with interest.

But first things first. As soon as Sam and I exited the Hudson, we hurried over to Harold's car, where Lou Prophet seemed to be struggling a bit. Sam offered him a hand, Prophet took it, and Sam pretty much hauled him out of the little car.

"Are you all right, Mr. Prophet?" I asked, concerned. I hadn't meant to damage the poor old guy.

After stretching experimentally a couple of times, he said, "I'm just fine, Miss Daisy. Thank you for your concern."

"He was a hero," said Harold, grinning at Mr. Prophet, who grinned back.

"I don't think real heroes use so many cuss words," Prophet said. "Some of those roads were bumpy as hell, though. You expect to bounce some when you're on the back of a horse, but a motorcar…Not so much."

"At least you can drive back to Pasadena with Sam and me," I told him, wishing now that I hadn't made such a big deal out of having him ride in Harold's car. Oh, well, it wasn't the first mistake I'd ever made—by far—and I was sure it wouldn't be the last. Curse it.

"Don't get the fantods, Miss Daisy. I've survived worse than riding in that…" He stared at Harold's car for a moment. "That little thing."

We all laughed, and I decided not to feel guilty any longer.

As we approached the entrance to the lion farm, I was pleased to observe all the buildings were evidently inspired by African villages, with thatched roofs and African masks hanging here and there. Harold kindly paid admission for the whole group of us, for which we all thanked him. I glanced around and noticed the parking lot was almost empty except for the two machines we'd driven there. Oh, well. It was a Wednesday. I expect the place did a booming business on weekends, when people had more time for visiting interesting places like zoos and lion farms and so forth.

"So what do you know about this place?" asked Prophet as we walked through a turnstile and entered the grounds.

The farm was big, and we were greeted by the roar of a lion, which was not unexpected, given where we were, but which did send a shiver up my spine. "It was begun by some French circus performers, whose last name is Gay. They decided to open a breeding and training farm for lions here in Los Angeles. They rent the cats to studios when they make pictures set in jungles and so forth. Like the *Tarzan* flickers. I think one of the studios uses one of the Gays' lions at the beginning of all its pictures." I glanced at Harold. "Which studio uses the lion, Harold?"

"Metro-Goldwyn-Mayer," said he. He knew pretty much everything about moving pictures, having worked in the industry for so long.

I continued. "I read this place uses an entire *ton* of horsemeat every single day to keep the lions fed."

"Good. Better horsemeat than man-meat," muttered Prophet, glancing around suspiciously. Guess he didn't trust the safety of the cages in which the lions were kept. "Hope they already fed the cats before we got here."

"I do, too," I said with a laugh.

What an interesting place! Not only were there thatched cages everywhere, but there were lots of vines and straw huts scattered about. Weeping willow trees added to the jungle-y feel, and so did the ivy crawling up the sides of the chain-link fences holding lions inside. I gazed about, glad we'd come, and taking interest in everything I saw.

Then I stopped dead-still and slapped a hand over my suddenly burning chest. Was that my juju? It was! "Oh, my Lord! Something's wrong!"

"Huh?" Harold looked at me as if I'd lost my mind.

"Shit," said Prophet.

"Get down, Daisy," said Sam, shoving me earthwards. I landed on my hands and knees and was about to bellow wrathfully at Sam.

But I didn't. All at once, Sam toppled over beside me, and I saw Bernard Randford, a huge board in his hand, aiming a blow at Lou Prophet.

Sam hollered, "Run!" at me as he rubbed the back of his head and reached into his coat pocket.

If I weren't so busy fumbling myself off the ground and running (actually, it was more like stumbling), I'd have marveled that Sam had carried a gun with him to Gay's. I heard him shoot the gun, however.

I didn't see what happened next. I did, however, hear the unmistakable, hideous, outlandish, and incredibly loud sound of Miss Betsy Powell. Screaming. Curse the woman!

And then I was grabbed from behind and upended into a lion's den.

THIRTY-ONE

Another gunshot rang out and a man shrieked.

I'm not sure what happened next, because I was staring, petrified, at an enormous lion with an enormous mane, who tilted his head and peered at me in some surprise. I expect he wasn't accustomed to people being plopped into his enclosure.

Oh, Lord. Oh, Lord. I hoped I didn't look like food to the beast.

Miss Betsy Powell continued to scream until, I guess, someone gagged her. I didn't look to see what had happened, although I was glad the screams had died. Then I wished I hadn't thought that word, mainly because I expected myself to die next. I'd landed on my bottom, and started to push myself along backwards, hoping to find a fence or something I could climb.

"Hold on, Miss Daisy!" came Lou Prophet's unmistakable, rusty voice. "Sam's got the sumbitch!"

"I'll hold him!" Sam hollered. "Get Daisy!"

"I'm tryin' to!"

"Good God, that's a *lion* in there with her!" came Harold's terrified treble.

I was aghast when the lion rose in a leisurely fashion from where he'd been lying, relaxing in the grass. He stood still for a moment, peering at me. I glanced behind me to see if I was near a fence. Whoever'd dumped me in here *must* have hurled me over a fence, right? But I couldn't see one. Searching frantically around me, all I saw were vines, willow trees and straw things woven into the fencing. Then there was that lion…

Scared nearly out of my wits, I said in a shaky voice, "Good kitty. Nice kitty."

Stupid, stupid, stupid, Daisy Gumm Majesty. But honestly, what would you do in that situation?

The lion must have thought I was stupid, too, because it tilted its head the other way and kept staring at me with slitted amber eyes. Frightening eyes. The eyes of a predator, for heaven's sake! Then it started ambling, very slowly, toward me.

Oh, Lord. I didn't dare scream for fear I'd annoy the lion into attacking me. Anyhow, my mouth was so dry, I doubt I'd have been able to scream if I'd tried. Not made of the same stuff as Miss Betsy Powell, I.

"Hold on, Miss Daisy!" Lou Prophet bellowed again.

I didn't say so—again, for fear of startling the lion—but there wasn't much else I *could* do, was there?

I heard a new voice holler, "Slats! Slats!"

Then I heard the unmistakable sound of foot falls heading, fast, toward the lion's den. Why the heck was somebody talk about slats? At the top of his voice? I didn't approve, especially since the lion was coming closer and closer to my own personal self.

Whoever it was did it again. "Slats! *Slats*! Good boy!"

Good boy? I didn't know what was happening, except I finally bumped up against the fence I'd been seeking—sort of—and slowly pushed myself to my feet. My legs were shaking like aspic, but I wanted the lion to think I was tall and scary.

I think the lion laughed when he heard my unspoken wish.

"Slats!" came the unknown voice again.

"Hold on there, Miss Daisy!" Lou Prophet shouted. I heard his uneven foot-and-peg steps as he tried to run to the lion's den.

Suddenly a rope flew over the fence holding the lion and me in its enclosure. The rope's loop barely missed the lion's neck, although the lion did turn his head and look at it oddly. After it was finished examining the rope, it continued sauntering toward me. I shoved myself harder against the fence and felt behind me for maybe...maybe *slats*! Perhaps that's why the fellow was yelling "Slats," because there were some I could climb. I didn't feel any. Slats, I mean.

Oh, Lord.

By this time, the lion had reached me. It lifted one of its huge paws, and I knew I was doomed.

"Slats!" came the shout again.

I wanted to ask what slats and where they were, but my mouth was too dry.

The lion's paw came down on my head, and I knew I was dead. It would open its huge mouth next, and Daisy Gumm Majesty would become but a faint memory in the history of Pasadena, California. I squeezed my shut eyes and began praying. I probably should have started praying earlier, huh? Well, it was an unusually terrifying situation, and I'd like to know how much praying *you'd* do in similar circumstances. I tried to pretend I was elsewhere.

And then I smelled an almighty stench, and darned if I didn't feel a huge cat's scratchy tongue against my cheek.

"Slats!" the fellow who'd been shouting shouted again.

I dared open my eyes.

Darned if the lion wasn't licking me!

"Don't panic, miss," came the "slats" voice. It had a French accent.

"Want me to rope the beast?" Lou Prophet asked of someone whom I presumed to be Mr. Charles Gay or a member of his circus family.

"No. He likes the young lady. I'll get her out."

The lion liked me? I almost fainted with relief. Then the stupid cat licked my face again, and I nearly fainted from the reek of its breath. A diet of nothing but horsemeat does that to a cat, I reckon.

THINGS GOT CONFUSING AFTER THAT. Mr. Gay—it *was* he who'd yelled at the lion in a French accent—got me out of there through a handy gate I hadn't noticed before. Even if I'd seen it, it was locked. The reason he'd been hollering "Slats" was because Slats was the name of the lion into whose enclosure Mr. Bernard Randford had dumped me.

"That's the MGM lion, Daisy," Harold told me.

Sam hugged me tightly and murmured, "It's all right, Daisy. You're safe now. Everything's all right." He had to tell me those things several times, because I was shivering and crying onto Sam's lapel for quite a while, and I didn't understand language for the first few minutes after my escape.

Not escape. Whatever you call it when someone rescues you from what you perceived as a dire threat to your life. Not to mention your limbs. For weeks after that, I'd awaken from nightmares featuring one of my arms or legs hanging out of that stupid lion's mouth.

Aw, heck. Escape's as good a word as any other.

Anyway, when I finally managed to haul myself away from Sam and stop quaking and sobbing, I learned that Mr. Randford and Miss Betsy Powell had arrived at the lion farm a half-hour or so before we did. Mr. Randford had sent Miss Powell into the gift store the Gays operated on their property, and in which they sold souvenirs consisting of lion pictures, posters from flickers in which their lions had been featured, decorative ashtrays, statues, boxes, toys and so forth.

As Miss Powell had toddled around in the gift shop, Mr. Randford had subdued two of Gays' trainers, using rags soaked in chloroform and then tying them up. The poor trainers were taken by ambulance to a local hospital, but were expected to recover. Chloroform, however its use is depicted in the moving pictures, isn't an innocent gas, and people have died from being exposed to it.

After Sam had pushed me to the ground, Randford had walloped Sam over the head. Then Randford had picked me up, staggered to Slats's quarters, and flipped me in. Although Sam's first bullet had missed its target, his second shot got Randford in the side. Unfortunately, it didn't penetrate his black heart, but it did make him fall down. Lou Prophet then used his famous ketch rope to tie up the despicable fellow.

Then it was that Miss Betsy Powell hurried out of the gift shop and began screaming. Lou Prophet had silenced her with a sock to the jaw and a handkerchief stuffed into her mouth. She was awake again by this time but not, thank God, screaming. Pressing a hand to her swollen cheek, she was shaking darned near as much as I was, however. She was the lousiest picker-of-men I'd ever met in my life.

Anyhow, after he'd silenced Miss Powell, Mr. Prophet had hobbled to the lion's den and tried to rope Slats. I'm kind of glad he missed, because, although it didn't feel like it at the time, a rope around his neck might have angered old Slats, and he might have done something other than merely lick my cheek.

Mr. Gay, who had been working in his office, heard Sam's gunshots and had come a'runnin'—as Mr. Prophet might have said—fearing some idiot was shooting his lions. When he saw what was up, he didn't pause to think, but raced to Slats's enclosure, unlocked the gate, and hauled me out, praising Slats the entire time.

As we sat in his office, he explained, "My cats are all accustomed to people, so they wouldn't harm you. Anyhow, as a rule, you really don't need to fear a male lion, Mrs. Majesty. It's the females who stalk and capture prey for the most part. They're the ones who feed their family."

I'll be darned! Even in the *animal* kingdom, women did all the work! Nertz.

We were still huddled in Mr. Gay's office when the police showed up. A detective named Bigelow and a couple of uniformed members of the Los Angeles Police Department wrote down all the information we had to give them and hauled Mr. Randford away.

Sam had tried to staunch the flow of blood from Randford's wound, but Randford was still sore, both mentally and physically. And I was glad to hear it. The man who had tried to kill me with a lion—a terrible way to go, as far as I'm concerned—kept whining about his tiny little bullet wound until Mr. Prophet said, "Shut up, old son, or I'll shut you up."

Everyone except Mr. Randford and Miss Powell smiled. Even the coppers. Mr. Randford shut up.

Mr. Gay closed his lion farm for the rest of that day. A very nice fellow, he offered us free passes should we ever want to visit Gay's Lion Farm again. I'd have to think about that for a while. A long while.

We didn't dine at Philippe's that day. Rather, Sam, Lou Prophet, Harold and I had to visit the Los Angeles Police Station. We all signed our official statements and, by the time we were through doing that, I only wanted to go home.

"Good idea," said Sam.

"Why did he want to kill me?" I asked plaintively. Very well, maybe it was more of a whine.

"Don't know yet, but I'll find out," said Sam.

"Bastard got what he deserved," observed Lou Prophet. "Only your aim was off. You should've got him in the heart."

"I agree," said I.

Harold shuddered.

Lou Prophet handed me a stuffed lion. I looked from it to him, and he winked. "Thought you might like a souvenir from your adventure, Miss Daisy."

I'm pretty sure I thanked him, but when we got home again, I aimed to stuff that stuffed lion into one of the drawers of my bird's-eye maple bureau. I might take it out again one day. One day a long, long time from *that* day.

So. I still lived as of the first week in February, 1925. Here's the skinny.

Mr. Bernard Randford, who wasn't a Petrie but who was just as awful as the rotten apples on the Petrie tree, turned out to be the cousin and best friend of Eloise Frances Petrie Gaulding's husband. I didn't know until Sam told me, but evidently Mr. Gaulding became so upset after his wife's evil deeds came to light, he suffered an apoplectic stroke and had yet to recover from same. Mr. Randford blamed me for his cousin's problems. *Me!*

"Darn it! It's not *my* fault his cousin's wife turned out to be a wicked witch!" I growled when Sam told me this.

"No, it isn't. Mr. Randford, however, sees things differently."

"Bother Mr. Randford. As if it wasn't bad enough to have a whole clan of putrid Petries after me. Not to mention your disgusting nephew."

My mother said, "Daisy," but not forcefully.

Good thing, too, if you were me. *She* hadn't had to hide out in the house for three solid weeks after having been deliberately smashed against a pepper tree by a fiend driving Mr. Randford's motorcar. *Which*, by the way, Mr. Randford had lent him specifically to do me in. I think it was Bruce Petrie who'd driven the motorcar that slammed me into the pepper tree, although there were so darned many Petries loose in the city, I might be mistaken about which one had done what.

Mr. Lou Prophet, who sat with us in the living room of our bungalow—that is to say the bungalow belonging to my parents... Hmm. This might become confusing if Sam and I ever had the chance to get married—chuckled.

"Speaking of my disgusting nephew," Sam said before anyone else could butt in, "Renata will be arriving on the two-thirty train tomorrow."

"Oh, my! I'll be so happy to meet one of your sisters, Sam!" I said.

"Yes, well, I'm not altogether sure your sentiment will be recip-rocated."

I stared at him. "But *why*? Frank's the one who tried to kill *me*! I never did anything to him!"

"You ain't Italian or a Catholic," said Lou Prophet, still smiling.

Sam grinned back at him. "That's it, all right."

"Good Lord. I don't think I'll ever understand human beings if I live to be a hundred," I said, torn between frustration and fury.

"You're not alone there," said Prophet.

"Sometimes I don't think there's anything in the world as divisive as religion."

My mother said, "Daisy," again.

"Nertz to that, Ma. The truth is the truth."

My mother merely sighed. Pa tried not to smile.

As for Sam, he only laughed and said, "I think you're right."

Lou Prophet chuckled again. "Never had much use for sky pilots myself," said he.

And there was yet another expression I'd have to include in my dictionary of old-west sayings. I decided to ask him what it meant later. At the moment, I was still under the influence of terror and the recovery therefrom.

"Oh, Mr. Prophet, please continue coming to our church with us," said Ma.

I think she was attempting to save the old reprobate from hell. I didn't think he needed saving. I liked him just fine the way he was.

Before I could say so and start an all-out war in the family, Vi called us in for dinner.

Dinner was good. Now that all the people who wanted me dead were locked up, even *life* was good. I hoped it would remain that way for a long, long time.

I did, however, decide not to hold my breath.

The End

Don't miss Aunt Vi's recipe for HUNGARIAN GOULASH right after the excerpt from *Scarlet Spirits*. It's all waiting, just ahead!

SCARLET SPIRITS

A DAISY GUMM MAJESTY MYSTERY, BOOK 15

After taking a gulp of lemonade and fanning herself for a second or two, Angie looked at me, almost accusingly. "You didn't tell me you knew *Lou Prophet!*"

"Uh…No, I didn't. Why would I?" Because her voice held an edge of panic, I didn't get angry.

She put her glass down and covered her face with both hands. "No. You're not at fault. I'm sorry, Daisy. But those cards and that Ouija board were absolutely right, although I didn't expect things to happen so quickly. Talk about someone from my *past*! Oh, Lord." I was pleased to note she wasn't a weeper, unlike some of us.

"You know that peg-legged fellow, Angie?" asked Mr. Bowman, a frown creasing his magnificent brow. Well, magnificent in that he was a terribly handsome man. Too old for me, of course.

Smiling at my fiancé, I said, "Thanks for thinking of the lemonade, Sam."

"Sure thing," he said, squinting at me and knowing *precisely* what I'd been thinking. Sometimes I think he knows me too well. But, golly, Sam was a terribly handsome man, too, if not *quite* as decorative as Mr. Bowman.

The four of us straightened in our chairs when we heard the thud-

267

plop-thud-plop of Lou Prophet's leg and peg as he walked past the orange trees lining the gravel pathway leading from his cottage to our porch. He looked mad enough to spit railroad spikes. I don't think that's an Old-West saying. I think I got it from my father.

Hoping to avert a duel, or something equally catastrophic, on the porch, I got up and walked to the porch steps. Standing on the top step, I barred Mr. Prophet's entry.

"Mr. Prophet," I said sweetly. "I get the feeling you and Mrs. Mainwaring have met before."

"Mrs. *Who?*" Prophet growled. "That there's no *Missus Mainwaring.* That there's Angie Smith, and she fleeced me of a whole lot of money in Tombstone some years back."

"Now, Lou, don't be like that," said Angie, attempting a sweetness equal to my own and missing by a mile.

"The hell you say!"

"Exactly who *is* this person, Angie?" asked Mr. Bowman, still frowning fiercely. On him fierce looked good.

I probably shouldn't have noticed that, should I? Oh, dear. Sorry.

"For that matter," growled Prophet, "who the hell are *you?*"

"All right, let's all settle down," Sam said, rising from his chair, putting on his Italian-Count-Police-Detective mien, and using his I'm-going-to-kill-you-and-dump-you-in-the-ocean-in-cement-overshoes voice. "Mrs. Evangeline Mainwaring, this is Mr. Lou Prophet. I take it you two have…met before, only perhaps you had a different name then, Mrs. Mainwaring?"

"Different name, my ass. That's Angela Smith, and she ran the biggest whorehouse in Tombstone! Evangeline Mainwaring, shit."

Nearly shocked out of my pretty blue pumps, I still managed to said, "Mr. Prophet, please!" in an attempt to curtail his profanities, although I already knew the task to be impossible.

"Daisy," said Sam in the same deadly voice. "Sit down."

So I sat. Didn't dare do anything else. When Sam got into one of *those* moods, it was better to do as he said.

He continued, "Lou, come up here onto the porch and sit down. Let's sort this out. There's no need for violence. Or profanity," he added, shooting me a glance.

"Hell," said Prophet. But I moved out of his way and he continued up the stairs and sat on a chair as far from Angie as he could get.

But merciful heavens! Had Lou Prophet spoken the truth? Was Evangeline Mainwaring or whatever her real name *truly* a former scarlet woman?

Oh, boy, I sure hoped so!

"Now," said Sam remaining on his feet, probably so he could catch anyone should he or she try to leap up and attempt some type of brutality on another one of us, "please explain these allegations." He turned to Angie. "Ladies first." He didn't even sound cynical

"Lady!" spat Prophet. "Hell." He, on the other hand, raised cynicism to a level surpassing any I'd heard before.

"Quiet, Lou. Ladies first." Sam sounded even deadlier that time, a feat of which I hadn't believed him capable until that moment.

Grasping Mr. Bowman's hand and squeezing it hard, Angie whispered, "Yes. Yes, he's telling the truth. I ran a parlor house—"

"Parlor house, my ass," Lou interrupted.

Turning his man-eating gaze upon him, Sam said, "Shut up."

Lou lifted his hands and said, "Shit," but shut up. Probably for the best, all things considered.

SCARLET SPIRITS
Available in eBook and Print From Your Favorite Online Retailer or Bookstore

Aunt Vi's Hungarian Goulash

Ingredients:

1 pound potatoes
2 pounds cubed beef
2 garlic cloves
salt
pepper
24 pearl onions
3T Butter
3T Flour

Preparation:

Wipe two pounds beef cut from lower parts of round with a
piece of cheesecloth, wrung out of cold water, and cut in one
and one-half inch cubes. Put in saucepan, add one quart boiling
water to which has been added two cloves of garlic and let boil
five minutes. Cover and let simmer until meat is tender.
Pare potatoes and cut in three-quarter inch slices, then cut slices
in cubes; there should be one and one-half cups. Cover with
boiling salted water and let boil five minutes; drain and add to
meat fifteen minutes before serving-time to finish the cooking.
Peel twenty-four tiny onions and cook in boiling salted water to
cover; drain and add to goulash.
Cream three tablespoons butter, add three tablespoons flour and
work until smooth; then add by small pieces to stock in stewpan
(of which there should be two cups), stirring constantly. Season
with salt and pepper and turn on a hot plate.

ABOUT THE AUTHOR

Award-winning author Alice Duncan lives with a herd of wild dachshunds (enriched from time to time with fosterees from New Mexico Dachshund Rescue) in Roswell, New Mexico. She's not a UFO enthusiast; she's in Roswell because her mother's family settled there fifty years before the aliens crashed (and living in Roswell, NM, is cheaper than living in Pasadena, CA, unfortunately). Alice would love to hear from you at alice@aliceduncan.net

www.aliceduncan.net

 facebook.com/alice.duncan.925

www.ingramcontent.com/pod-product-compliance
Lightning Source LLC
Chambersburg PA
CBHW020545020726
47494CB00006B/1926